SISTERS

IN

SORROW

FIRST EDITION
Sisters in Sorrow © 2018 by Rachael Robie
Cover art © 2018 by Erik Mohr (Made By Emblem)
Cover design © 2018 by Alyssa Cooper
Interior design © 2018 by Alyssa Cooper

Distributed in Canada by
Fitzhenry & Whiteside Limited
195 Allstate Parkway
Markham, Ontario L3R 4T8
Phone: (905) 477-9700
e-mail: bookinfo@fitzhenry.ca

Distributed in the U.S. by
Consortium Book Sales & Distribution
34 Thirteenth Avenue, NE, Suite 101
Minneapolis, MN 55413
Phone: (612) 746-2600
e-mail: sales.orders@cbsd.com

Library and Archives Canada Cataloguing in Publication
Library and Archives Canada Cataloguing in Publication

Robie, Rachael, 1986-, author
        Sisters in sorrow / Rachael Robie.

Issued in print and electronic formats.
ISBN 978-1-77148-454-1 (softcover).--ISBN 978-1-77148-455-8 (PDF)

        I. Title.

PZ7.1.R59Sis 2018   j813'.6   C2018-904660-0
                                                    C2018-904661-9

CHIZINE PUBLICATIONS
Peterborough, Canada
www.chizinepub.com
info@chizinepub.com

Edited by Halli Villegas
Copyedited and proofread by Leigh Teetzel

Canada Council   Conseil des arts
for the Arts   du Canada

We acknowledge the support of the Canada Council for the Arts which last year invested $20.1 million in writing and publishing throughout Canada.

ONTARIO ARTS COUNCIL
CONSEIL DES ARTS DE L'ONTARIO
an Ontario government agency
un organisme du gouvernement de l'Ontario

Published with the generous assistance of the Ontario Arts Council.

Printed in Canada

To my husband,
for his unwavering support in our adventure together.

SISTERS IN SORROW

RACHAEL ROBIE

ONE

On her first night at the Genoquip facility Raima dreamed about her mother. She saw faceless men, pounding her mother with their fists, kicking her with booted feet. She heard her mother's cries, a mixture of English and Hindi. Raima rushed forward to stop the assault, but an invisible barrier stood in her way, trapping her. She beat on it, crying hysterically. *I can stop this. I have to stop it.*

Then a hand touched her shoulder and gave her a firm shake. "Wake up."

Raima lifted her head and blinked. She tensed under the stranger's grip, anticipating pain, but there was none. The hand withdrew. In the cold dark room, she recognized the scent of industrial cleaners that she'd smelled during her time in Elysia City Hospital. Yet she wasn't in the hospital. She wasn't even under the dome of Elysia City. Genoquip—GC as the agents at the Martian International Humanitarian Organization called it—was her new home, and there were no cities or settlements attached to it. Outside, only Martian desert sprawled in every direction.

"Bad sleep?" asked a girl from the cot across the room. Her thick accent made her difficult to understand. In the short time since Raima had met her, the girl often lapsed into her native Mandarin Chinese.

Qi was Raima's new roommate. They'd met the previous day, but Raima found the Chinese girl overwhelming. Qi's friendly nature baffled her and Raima resisted her roommate's efforts to socialize.

Raima said nothing. She rolled over and pulled her thin covers up to shield herself from the endless cold of the Martian night. They were deep underground in this facility and all the walls were insulated, but it hardly mattered. The chill of Mars always managed to find its way in. Raima didn't care. She'd been numb and cold for years.

"You said *Ma*," Qi said. "Dream of your Ma?"

The shadowy shapes of the men from her dream came to mind again, violent and fast, swinging their fists, pumping their arms. Raima's mother cried out as she had in the dream, but now it transformed, becoming the pathetic, breathy moans of agony that were the last sounds Raima ever heard her mother make.

She closed her eyes, focusing on her present need for sleep. Behind her in the dark Qi sighed and shifted, giving up.

In the morning a wakeup alarm blared. The sudden sound from the speaker in the low ceiling set Raima's heart hammering. She sat up and flung her covers off, ready to cower before the first blows fell on her head.

Qi woke with a loud yawn that brought Raima back to the present. When she realized the danger was only in her mind, she closed her eyes and cradled her head in her hands, waiting for her heartbeat to slow.

"Wakeup alarm. Loud. Annoying, right?" Qi asked.

"Yeah," Raima said, her tone flat, deflecting Qi's concern.

Qi clapped her hands together—another noise that made Raima tense with automatic fear—and said, "Time get ready. Breakfast. Eggs today."

Time to *get ready*. Raima corrected Qi silently, finding some small satisfaction in knowing that she had a better mastery of English than her Chinese roommate.

A nurse came for Raima, leaving Qi to go to breakfast alone. Doors lined the halls of the facility, each one marked by a coded card resting in a plastic pocket in the middle of the door. Raima assumed the numbers and letters identified the occupants. Some doors had only one code, but most had two, one atop the other. Raima saw only girls in the facility, excepting a few nurses and security guards. The nurse escorting her wore pale blue scrubs that wrinkled with each movement. She walked a few steps behind him, examining the thickness of his arms and legs for a time before she risked speaking.

"Where are the boys?" she asked.

He craned his neck and peered at her over his shoulder. "In another wing," he replied. "Why? Did you come in with someone you know?"

"No," she said and left it at that. She wondered what he knew about her past. The nurses and doctors at Elysia City's hospital had known. Sometimes they tried getting her to talk about it with open-ended questions or sympathetic words. Raima had nothing to share with any of them. She hoped this nurse at Genoquip didn't know anything about her. That way he wouldn't feel obligated to cheer her up or express concern.

They entered a small room outfitted with medical equipment and a chair where Raima sat while he took her blood pressure, heart rate, and other vital signs. Then he prepared a syringe and prepped Raima's bicep for the injection by rubbing it with an alcohol wipe. The acrid smell burned Raima's nose. She turned away when he inserted the needle.

"There you go," he said to soothe her as he worked. "All done." He capped the needle and placed the empty syringe in a biohazard collection box mounted on the wall. "How have you been feeling? Any unusual symptoms? Headaches? Nausea? Lucid dreams?"

Raima shook her head. "I'm fine." She'd been queasy after her first shot the previous day and her head had throbbed, but she'd tolerated the discomfort easily.

"Excellent," the nurse said and smiled. "You don't have to be afraid to tell me if something's wrong, though. You understand?"

Raima learned a long time ago that complaining never brought about good things. It drew unnecessary attention—and punishment. "Yes," she said.

"Well then," the nurse said. His nametag read *Terry*. "I'll bring you to the cafeteria for breakfast. I'll see you tomorrow for your next shot."

Terry led her to an enormous rectangular room with off-white walls and a low ceiling. Raima struggled to keep her heart steady and breathing calm when she walked into it. Something about the cafeteria's ceiling and lighting reminded her that she was deep below ground, beneath tons of rock. When she saw the boys standing in line for breakfast she stopped halfway across the room, forgetting all about the ceiling's oppressive nearness.

Qi had told her that all subjects shared the cafeteria, meaning the boys emerged from their separate wing during mealtimes and waited in line for food. On her first day Raima was surrounded by other girls, including her roommate, but today she'd have to stand in line with the boys. They self-segregated by sex when they sat at the tables to eat but stood together in line. In her panic Raima had stopped in the boys' half of the cafeteria. Now she felt their curious stares like needle pricks on her skin.

Nothing was worse than standing out. She made herself start walking again, heading toward the end of the line. Her legs were stiff, her heartbeat thundering in her ears. She stared at the floor as she took up a position in line, inhaling and exhaling in a slow, deliberate rhythm. She kept her arms crossed with her hands tucked under each elbow and pretended to ignore the boys around her.

She chose an unoccupied table on the girls' side of the room, but by then her tray of scrambled eggs and milk lost its appeal. Nausea stole her appetite. She stared at her breakfast, willing herself to eat it and not vomit. Movement caught her eye and she lifted her head in time to see Qi approaching. Raima sighed and picked up her fork, determined to avoid speaking to Qi by eating instead.

Qi sat opposite her and asked, "Feel sick?"

Raima nodded, reluctant to admit the obvious.

"Too bad," Qi said and gestured at the scrambled eggs. "Real eggs today." She leaned forward and raised her eyebrows. *"Real."*

"Do you want them?" Raima asked.

"No," Qi said and made a face. "Full. No hungry. If I eat more, I explode! I am not greedy. Father is greedy, I not."

Raima forced herself to shove some of the scrambled eggs into her mouth, refusing to speak more than necessary. They tasted rich enough that she could almost believe Qi was right about the eggs. They *were* real. That meant Genoquip pampered its subjects— the orphans, debtors, and juvenile delinquents that made up its population of indentured lab rats. Any perishable product that was difficult to preserve for extended periods of time, such as eggs, milk, yogurt, fruits, and vegetables, were extremely expensive on Mars. Most of it could be faked, like Raima's glass of tasteless milk, made from powder, but much of the flavor was lost. Raima thought the high-quality food must be a bribe, a reward Genoquip gave its subjects to keep morale up. She had seen the practice before. Recognizing it here made her stomach roil. In Raima's experience such rewards always came with a price.

"You want to know why I here?" Qi asked. "Because of my father."

The excitement coloring Qi's face and conveyed in her voice made Raima cringe. She didn't want to know Qi's history, didn't care how her father was involved, and couldn't fathom the other girl's reaction. Saying no would be rude though, so Raima speared another bit of cheesy egg and forced it past her unwilling lips.

Qi didn't wait for Raima to show interest. The story poured out in a way that sounded rehearsed, as if Qi had told it over and over. "I am here because Father liked to drink and gamble. He went to jail, gave me to MIHO," she said, using the acronym for the Martian International Humanitarian Organization that cared for all of Mars' orphans, debtors, and poverty-stricken. "MIHO gave me to Genoquip. I pay Father's debts. For rest of my life, probably." She shrugged, as if this abandonment meant nothing.

"Sorry," Raima replied. Then, feeling the pressure to further interact, she said, "My father died on Earth. I was just a little girl."

The Chinese girl clucked her tongue and looked genuinely sad. Raima thought she'd say something comforting, but instead she asked, "Where are you from?"

"Elysia City," Raima said.

"No, no, no," Qi murmured and frowned with frustration. Her brow knitted with effort and she said, "On Earth. Back there. Where from?"

"India," Raima answered. Nausea fluttered again in her stomach, changing from discomfort to longing as she recalled the fuzzy, comforting images of greenery, the warmth of the huge, hot sun overhead. On Mars the sun was a shrunken disk, weak and puny.

Qi grinned, showing her bright white teeth. "I wish I could see, but I was born here." She pointed one finger upward and spun it around in a circle, indicating Mars. "Can never go back now. You and me, both here forever. Stuck."

A sudden tightness formed in Raima's throat. Her eyes burned, but no tears came. She wanted to make Qi shut up, to stop feeling and remembering. She looked down at her food and said, "I don't remember it." She shoveled more of the eggs into her mouth, burying the sickness along with the emotions.

Raima had lost everything to Mars, but even that didn't satisfy the Red Planet. The cruelest fact about Mars was that it ensnared people with its low gravity. Raima and Qi were both tall and lanky with the Martian physique, a body shape that made their bones too brittle to return to Earth's crushing gravity. It happened because they'd spent their growing years in Martian gravity, which was only a third of Earth's. Terry, the nurse, was clearly raised on Earth because he was almost a foot shorter than Raima. If Qi and Raima stood beside Terry, he would appear to be the child compared to their elongated, graceful bodies.

"I know!" Qi exclaimed, startling Raima. "They have Wishes program. Every week we get to make one wish. I wished for music. You can wish for pictures of India."

"No," Raima said. "I don't need anything like that." She blinked away the memories that rose unbidden from her other life, of a time before Mars.

"You sure?" Qi asked, jerking back with surprise. "Wishes keep up hope. Make you smile." She put her fingers to her lips and pushed at the corners of her mouth, revealing the pretty teeth inside.

Raima gave Qi what she wanted—a feigned half-smile—and the Chinese girl laughed with triumph. "See! I make you smile. Good for us both."

Days passed, each beginning with another injection, always administered by Terry. The illness accompanying the shots progressed to the point that it became impossible to hide or ignore. Raima vomited often and barely managed to eat. Her arms were bruised from the continuous needle pricks and she dreaded each new injection but faced them without comment or complaint.

Qi doted on her like a mother. She encouraged Raima to eat, brought her snacks, tried to get her to laugh or talk, and even cleaned up after Raima when she couldn't make it to the toilet to puke. The nurse-like care from her roommate embarrassed Raima and made her uncomfortable. She tried to reject the other girl's help, pushing her away when Qi offered, but the illness grew too severe for such stubbornness.

Eventually Raima's physical weakness left her bedridden. Her head pounded, and her skin prickled and tingled. She refused food, unable to tolerate the sight or smell of it. Fevers made her delirious and left her joints and muscles in constant pain. Soon she was too weak to haul herself the distance from her bed to the bathroom so she could throw up, shower, or use the toilet. She couldn't even find respite in sleep.

Raima tossed and turned, lost in a nightmare that was as much memory as dream. It was the same one she experienced most nights. She was in her cell in the brothel, surrounded again by the bare rock walls deep below ground in Elysia City. Dankness and mold hung heavy in the stale air. Her body ached from endless hours of abuse at the hands of her captors, and her skin still crawled with revulsion at every touch from the johns. But the promise of food at shift's end made her smile and flirt despite pain and disgust.

Then she heard Kati's screams in the hall outside her cell. Raima found the girl there, her thick-limbed Earther frame riddled with bruises and streaked in blood, her eyes wild and frenzied.

"Please," Kati begged lunging for Raima. She clutched at Raima's clothes in a clumsy embrace. Raima grabbed the girl's elbows, trying to keep them both upright. "I hurt him," Kati cried. "He's going to kill me." Raima stared into Kati's broken face, cold disgust the only feeling she could muster.

"He wanted me to—to—" Kati's voice was thick and unclear with her panicked breathing and hysterical crying. "He put his—" She broke off, making a gagging sound.

"Stupid girl," Raima snapped.

"Please," Kati said, panting. "Help me. Help me get out of here!"

"There is no way out," Raima said, trying to pull herself free of the other girl's grip.

"Please," Kati cried. "I just want to go home!"

Ferde would come after Kati and if he found Raima with her he'd punish them both. Raima pushed Kati away, knocking her to the floor. "Get away from me," she said.

Then the door to the upper level opened and Ferde's thick body charged through. As his fists clenched and his face twisted with rage, Raima knew it was too late. He'd seen them together. Her bones ached in anticipation of the coming pain.

"Raima!" Kati shouted, but her voice changed, warping into a Mandarin accent.

Raima opened her eyes to see a tall scrawny girl outlined by the dim gray light of CF-Gen's fluorescents and recognized her as Qi.

"What do you want?" Raima muttered into her pillow as the rawness of Kati's plea faded back into her memory. Her body ached as though Ferde had just finished beating her. Every movement brought on sharp pain. Even the small muscles in her face hurt when she opened her eyes.

"You get up," Qi said. "Fight. Feel better."

Thinking was hard enough but getting out of bed would've been impossible even if Raima wanted to do it. She said nothing, wishing Qi would just leave. But she didn't. When Raima didn't move, Qi stooped to pick her up. As Qi's hands closed over Raima's arm she flinched at the unexpected touch. Her delirious brain leapt between reality and nightmare, but she was too weak to fight. Raima held on, biting her tongue to keep from whimpering. Qi took her to the bathroom and began to undress her. "Shower," she explained. "Will make you feel better."

"No," Raima said. She tried to resist Qi's actions, but her roommate overpowered her with ease, which only increased Raima's anxiety. Nakedness and vulnerability always led to helplessness and more pain. She shuddered convulsively as Qi stripped away her gray scrubs and tossed them aside.

"Cold?" Qi asked. She pulled a towel from the small cabinet under their bathroom's sink and covered Raima with it. "Shower is warm," she said. "I promise—will make you better."

Raima clutched the towel with one fist. She was grateful for it, but her body continued to betray her, trembling with abject fear. She watched Qi undress, seeing her golden-yellow skin, colored like the inside of a roasted potato—but darker too, perhaps closer to honey. She was lean and healthy, with small breasts and wide hips. She showed no self-consciousness, no hesitation as she knelt, taking away the towel, and pulling Raima upright. Qi's touch was firm but gentle as she took Raima's weight, supporting her with her shoulder. Too many men had handled Raima with such casual authority. Those memories made Raima squirm, knocking them both off balance for a moment, but Qi's strength and determination won out. Together they stepped into the spray of water.

The stall was narrow and painted blue-gray to evoke the feeling of water and cleanliness. After thousands of showers by uncountable subjects—lab rats like Qi and Raima—most of the paint had worn off. The stall wasn't designed for two people, but Qi squeezed them both inside while the hot water worked its magic over Raima's aching head, bones, and joints. The pressure of Qi's fingers, hands, and arms over Raima's body faded from her awareness. The hot water caressed her body until the trembling subsided, transforming into relief.

"It's fever," Qi explained. "So much pain."

Raima's mind skipped over memories from Mars, going beyond that misery to recall a hot, humid night when she'd laid with her head in her mother's lap, lulled to sleep by her touch. It felt dreamlike, unreal and imagined, but she knew it had to be true because the water took her to that same tranquil mindset. She held tighter to Qi, noticing how smooth and hairless the other girl's skin was, the same as her mother's.

She closed her eyes and leaned the back of her head against the shower stall, the water pummeling her neck and chest. She let out a long, deep breath.

Qi chuckled. "I told you. Shower helps."

After several minutes in the heat and humidity Qi guided Raima out of the shower stall and helped dry her off. She kept the bathroom door shut, trapping the warmth inside the tiny space. She used two towels on Raima, one for her body and the other for her hair and didn't bother drying herself until she'd gotten the scrubs back on Raima's emaciated form.

Raima watched her work, drifting in and out of consciousness. "Why?" she asked, her voice rasping. "Why are you helping me?"

Qi's smiling face warped, blurred in Raima's vision. "You need it," she said. "Now you go sleep." She took hold of Raima's arms and pulled her up. They walked together out of the bathroom to Raima's cot where Qi stooped and helped her lay down. Raima fell headlong into a deep, dreamless sleep.

TWO

The next day, for the first time in weeks Raima had the energy to walk with Terry to the little exam room for her next shot. Before she left for breakfast Terry stopped her and held out a yellow medicine bottle with a child-safety lid.

"What are these?" she asked, afraid to accept the bottle. What if it was some kind of trap? Or a test?

"It's a painkiller," Terry explained. "It has a narcotic in it to control your headaches. It works very well for most of the subjects here. Just don't take more than the recommended dose," he warned, then hesitated as a new thought occurred to him. "How well do you read English?"

"I read it very well," Raima said. When she looked at him she noticed the security camera mounted over the door. With a quick jerk of her head she turned away, pretending not to have seen it. She examined the bottle and shook her head. *This is a test.* The camera's lidless gaze pressed on her, a disembodied representative of Genoquip's power. The amount of money this facility required to operate must be astronomical. What hidden price did the pills carry?

She offered it back to Terry. "I can't take this," she said. "Thank you, but I don't need it."

Terry tilted his head to one side, perplexed by her refusal. "Raima—is it okay if I call you that?" She nodded, wondering what else he'd call her. "Your roommate found me when she went to breakfast this morning and asked me to give you these. She said you're in a lot of pain." There was a note of accusation in his tone. "Why haven't you told me how bad your symptoms have become? I can't help you if you don't tell me."

Raima stared down into her lap at the yellow bottle still clasped in her hands. "I'm sorry," she said. "I didn't mean to cause any trouble."

"It's not trouble to ask for help," he reassured her. "Please, take the painkillers."

Glancing at the camera, Raima weighed her options. Would she be punished for refusing the pills? Maybe Genoquip wanted to add to her debts so they could keep her longer. Or was Terry bribing her in a way that'd somehow get them both in trouble? There was no way to know, but she sensed Terry's desire that she take them, so she did. "Thank you."

"You're welcome," Terry said. "But there's no reason to thank me, really. I'm just doing my job."

As far as she could tell, Terry's job was to inflict disease on her. Genoquip was a huge company that made pharmaceutical drugs, devices, and medical equipment. During her stay at the Elysia City Hospital, Raima took numerous pills with the letters GQ imprinted on them. The name was written on her IV bags in big bold letters, making it easy for Raima to read even when she was only half-awake or crying with the excruciating pain of her treatments. For the first time she wondered what this facility planned to do with all its subjects. What was it testing? Had anyone died from the illness the shots caused?

In her room that evening, Raima decided to find out what Qi knew. After swallowing the first of her painkillers, Raima crawled into bed and watched as Qi flipped through a Chinese magazine whose crinkled pages hinted at the countless times it had been read. Occasionally Qi muttered in Chinese and the strange rise and fall of her voice reminded Raima of music.

Raima rarely initiated a conversation. In her experience speaking only ever led to trouble, so she'd learned to be silent and invisible. Though Qi hadn't done anything to harm her, Raima couldn't trust her. If Raima complained about Genoquip, or even said something that could be construed as negative regarding the company, Qi could betray her. Raima had seen girls make up lies to get someone else in trouble—she'd even done it herself a few times.

She'd just decided that the conversation was too risky when Qi looked up and found Raima staring at her. She shut the magazine and tossed it on the floor. "What is it?"

"You got the shots too, right?" Raima asked after a pause. She suspected that everyone in the facility received the same shots at one time or another as part of the test, but she'd never asked until now. When Qi nodded, Raima expanded the question, careful to keep it neutral. "What are the shots? What are they doing to us?"

Qi grunted and blew out a long breath through her lips. She wrapped her arms around herself. "The shots make you sick, like bad food. Give you fevers and bad dreams. In the end they . . . *change* people," she answered with a frown. She gestured, struggling with language. "I don't know the word in English."

"How will it change me?" Raima asked, glad at the stolid strength in the words despite the pressure of fear gripping her throat. She leaned forward on her bed, her hands clasped together tightly. The moisture coating her palms made them sticky.

Qi scanned the room, seeking something. Finally, she snatched the magazine up and waved it, as if that was the answer. "Makes people *read* things," she said and shook the magazine in one hand while tapping her pillow with the other. "The pillow makes words in my head. It talks to you, says what it does for you."

The description was amazing, but also familiar. When she'd been a child on Earth, Raima's mother had explained to her a strange new discovery that shocked scientists around the world. A very rare number of people were found to possess the ability to read objects and manipulate them with willpower. It was touted as humanity's biological future.

The term for those rare people was as bizarre as their talents: *Intuiters*. Raima understood that the name came from their inexplicable ability to *intuit* impossible information from objects. Raima's mother had said they could touch a subway handrail and know who held onto it last, what that person's name was, where he or she lived, worked, and what they'd been doing.

"Are you talking about Intuiters?" Raima asked.

Qi jabbed the magazine at Raima, using it to point excitedly at her. "Yes!"

"Do you know why?" she asked. She wanted to ask what Genoquip would *do* with the Intuiters it created, but she doubted Qi knew anything about it. And Raima didn't want to sound as if she questioned the company's motives or morality. Her shoulders tensed, starting to ache with anxiety.

"Why make Intuiters?" Qi shrugged. "Why not?"

"Are you an Intuiter now? What's it like?" That was friendlier, a much safer question. The light lilt of curiosity coloring Raima's voice took her by surprise. Was that how she really felt? She assessed her body language, the way she'd leaned forward and fidgeted, repositioning to disguise her heightened interest.

Qi's gaze dropped to her lap. The magazine tapped against her thigh. "Yes," she said, frowning. "Hearing things talk all time—annoying. Make your head go crazy." She wobbled her head from side to side and rolled her eyes, demonstrating her meaning.

A small smile tugged at the corners of Raima's lips, but she stopped it and asked, "Why can't I hear anything from objects yet?"

"Too soon," Qi said. "Takes time. Have to be done with shots. Done with sickness."

Cold tingles passed through Raima. Her heartbeat echoed in her ears as she struggled with whether she should ask her next question. There were no cameras in their cell, no obvious way that Genoquip could spy on them. Could she trust Qi not to betray her? The facility had different rules, both visible and hidden. In the brothel girls betrayed each other without a second thought just to survive. They didn't carry girls who were too weak to walk into the shower to comfort them.

She made up her mind and whispered, "Does anyone ever die here? From the sickness?"

Qi's jubilant expression fell immediately. Her head drooped as she looked at the magazine that she'd curled into a tube with one hand. "Many times," she said. "I am—how you say it? I am surprised you not see it happen yet."

Raima had suspected as much, judging from her own symptoms, but having it confirmed gave her an odd satisfaction. Genoquip was just like the brothel, the only difference was that this facility hid its true nature and didn't display its dead to intimidate the living. All Raima's concerns and caution were correct. Her instincts would keep her safe.

I won't die here. Death had stalked her many times, but her body was too strong to succumb, her will too stubborn to let go.

"My first roommate," Qi went on. "She not well. One night, she shake so much—I try to help . . ." She shivered, bouncing on her bed in what Raima realized was a demonstration of a seizure. "I try to stop her, but no work." Qi let out a little whimper and sniffled, quickly wiping her nose. "I called for help. They took her out." She shook her head with a despondent expression creasing her face. "I never saw her again. No more."

"I'm sorry," Raima said. The words sounded hollow. She closed her eyes and saw Kati, the blonde Earth girl, tiny and frail, sobbing. She imagined Qi's first roommate as Kati, quivering with a seizure, and her breath hitched in her throat. Raima swallowed, banishing the image.

An alarm beeped, warning them that lights-out was only five minutes away. Qi wiped her face and her shoulders sagged. "Time go sleep. See you in the morning, Raima."

"Goodnight." Raima rolled over, facing the wall. *Why didn't I die?* she thought, perplexed by her own luck. She'd arrived at the Genoquip facility already weakened by a lengthy hospital stay and a legal battle that had found her innocent in the brutal murder of Ferdinand Gomez, an Elysia City businessman.

That was what the trial lawyers called him—*Ferdinand Gomez, businessman*—but that was a lie. She would always think of him as Ferde, a heartless bastard who owned a significant share in a successful Elysia City brothel. Raima spent four years in that hellish place before a combination of ruthlessness and luck allowed her to escape. Luck brought her the knife—which she'd stolen from a john and hidden beneath a mattress. Ruthlessness came the next time Ferde forced himself on her, giving Raima the chance to stab him to death.

Of course, she'd never thought about what she'd do afterward. She'd fled the room, covered in Ferde's blood, and bolted from the brothel before anyone could stop her. But she quickly found herself locked away, charged with Ferde's murder. Yet Elysia

City's pleasure district had no interest in prosecuting a sixteen-year-old ex-prostitute. No one in the largely male-dominated city wanted to face the truth behind its booming sex trade—that its sex workers were girls, not grown women, and they'd been enslaved. A trial risked public outcry and a crackdown from Earth. The court wasted no time determining that Raima killed Ferde in self-defense. She was a victim, not a criminal. They agreed she needed rehabilitation, both medically and socially, not incarceration. The court turned Raima over to MIHO's care. From there she underwent countless tests: psych exams, blood screenings, and checkups.

One of their first tests, considering Raima's past, was to check for HIV. When a doctor informed her that she was positive she hadn't been able to muster the energy to care about the diagnosis, or anything else. For the very first time she had the luxury to feel the depths of her losses. Nothing physical could compare to the anguish already inside her. The doctor and Raima's MIHO agent warned her that the treatment for HIV was harrowing and could kill her, but Raima gave her consent anyway. She was already dead inside. What difference did it make if the procedure killed her?

Somehow her stubborn body managed to survive the treatment—a complete bone-marrow transplant from a donor who was genetically immune to the virus—and she emerged cured. The doctors, nurses, and even her MIHO agent, they all called her *lucky*. Raima often thought about that. *Lucky?* How could anyone call her *lucky* after everything that had happened to her?

She let out a sigh in the dark, waiting for sleep to take her, but it stayed just out of reach. Across the room Qi mumbled something incomprehensible in Mandarin and shifted in bed, rustling her covers. The breech in the silence made Raima's muscles go rigid, but she stretched, forcing the irrational fear away. Her mind continued churning, preoccupied with the past.

So, what kept her alive? Why, if she didn't even care if she lived, did her body cling to life? Was it her promise to her mother?

She usually avoided thinking of her mother. Grief was an enemy, a weakness that dulled the mind and never earned any sympathy from her captors in the brothel. At CF-Gen she sensed she could explore the loss, but she feared the pain. She squeezed her eyes shut tighter, anticipating it. Heartache was like quicksand, dragging her down, far worse than any physical pain she'd ever suffered. Maybe probing the place in her mind where all that grief was buried wasn't such a good idea. She held her breath just thinking about it. Would the grief suffocate her if she let it out? But remembering the promise to her mother meant remembering her mother's death.

Ferde killed her mother, beating her and then neglecting her until infection set in. She'd died sometime after that. Raima wasn't allowed to see her, but Ferde delighted in telling her that he'd broken her jaw, her nose, even blinded her. Raima touched her own face in the dark, tracing the curve of her eyes and the hard bridge of her nose. Some days she couldn't recall what her mother looked like anymore, but she was glad that she never saw the damage Ferde had done. One thing she could remember with intense clarity was Ferde's expression when she killed him.

She opened her eyes and could still see his blood on her hands, his lifeless eyes staring up at her. Clenching one hand in a fist, she imagined holding the handle of the knife she'd used to stab him. The triumph of that moment hit her again, but it was mixed with despair. After killing Ferde she had nothing to live for—he and his brothel had taken everything. She might've plunged the knife she used on Ferde into her own throat if not for the promise she'd made her mother during their first days of torture inside the brothel. *You must survive. You must escape, with or without me.*

That promise kept her stubbornly alive, but she never would have escaped the brothel or killed Ferde without Kati. She saw the pretty Earther's face again, red and swollen with tears, on her knees and pleading with Raima. It was Raima's guilt for Kati's death, the certainty that she'd caused it, which finally impelled her to kill Ferde.

Go away. There wasn't any reason to think about Kati, Ferde, or the brothel. The first heavy tendrils of fatigue wrapped around the edges of her mind. She pushed the nightmares of her past away, burying them deep inside, and embraced the numbness of sleep.

At breakfast the following morning, Raima saw a girl collapse. It was the first time she saw one of the other subjects suffer an extreme reaction to Genoquip's experiment. One moment Raima was sliding her tray along the food line, scooping lumpy oatmeal into a bowl, and the next moment someone shouted with alarm.

There were dozens of girls standing in the line, all nameless, gray with illness. One near the back stumbled, losing control. She fell flat on the cafeteria floor. The tray she'd been pushing along the counter clattered down alongside her frightening Raima like a gunshot. A glass of milk splattered, slipping from someone's hands. Nurses scrambled forward, shouting in medical jargon. A security guard carrying a folded stretcher loped over to the fallen girl.

The girl behind Raima nudged her impatiently. "Go," she said.

Raima turned back to the food, forcing herself to continue. She kept her eyes downcast, afraid to look at the stricken girl.

The cafeteria buzzed with whispers. Faces stared, filled with raw interest. They were like vultures eyeing a weakened animal, waiting for it to die. Others seemed bored, as if they'd witnessed similar incidents many times before. The cafeteria's capacity was over a hundred, and Raima suspected there were upwards of three hundred subjects at the facility. Each day—*sol* as the educated nurses, technicians, and security guards called it—brought another chance for subjects to see such grim spectacles.

She found the table where Qi waited for her and chased lumps of oatmeal around with her spoon, too troubled to eat. The vulture-like stares of the other subjects reminded Raima of the brothel, the way far too many people turned away and ignored suffering that was happening right before their eyes. She'd been one of them, letting daily cruelties go unnoticed. She was as powerless now as she had been in the brothel, unable to stop the misery. But in the end, what could she do? She was just one person. It wasn't her responsibility. All she had to do was survive.

The gloomy mood stuck with her throughout the afternoon as Raima and Qi took turns showering in their room and then waited for the nurses to take them to group activities and testing.

Qi always disappeared for a few hours with a woman who, unlike Terry, didn't have a nametag, but her white scrubs identified her as a technician. All Genoquip's staff wore color-coded scrubs that announced their position and rank within the medical hierarchy. Even though Raima had picked up the knowledge during her stay in Elysia City's hospital, she listened when Qi tried to explain the meaning of the scrubs anyway, letting the Chinese girl's voice fill their small room with the welcome distraction of sound.

Technicians wear white, but they aren't doctors. Nurses wear blue. Security guards wear black uniforms. Subjects wear gray. . . .

Since the end of her second week of shots most of Raima's strength had returned, so once the technician took Qi away, Terry led Raima to the recreation area of the facility. It looked a lot like the girls' wing at first—a long hallway lined with doors. But each room was filled with paper books, e-readers, and tablets. There were desks in the corners with ancient computers that lacked touchscreen function, requiring a mouse and keyboard instead. Subjects bickered over the computer terminals and tablets while nurses and security guards lingered nearby, imposing a strict ten-minute rule on every device.

At the end of the hall was a gym with a basketball court. The subjects using the gym and court were fully recovered, no longer pale with illness. Typically, they were boys, impossibly tall, long-legged and oozing testosterone. Raima stayed clear of both areas, disturbed by the young men's rapid movements as they played basketball. Her mind fluttered with panic whenever she heard their grunts of effort while they lifted weights. The sounds sent her back to the brothel, to the rooms where she lay motionless beneath johns, trying not to cry as they used her body.

She retreated to the media rooms and found the one with the fewest boys inside. She rotated through the different devices and the computer terminals just like everyone else, but when it was her turn with the e-reader or the old PC she only pretended to read news articles or books. Instead she spent her time watching the other people around her. As soon as she got the tablet she sat alone in one corner and devoted her full attention to scrolling through images from Earth. Only with the tablet could she hide her screen from the others. When she stared at pictures of plants, animals, and insects, of all of Earth's brilliant colors, her mind emptied, and her heart slowed.

When Qi arrived, calling her name, Raima gasped and flinched. She glared up at Qi, feeling the blood rush to her face. "What do you want?"

"Sorry," Qi said, recognizing that she'd startled her. "You got tablet! Best one! Can I share?"

Raima scanned the room, checking for unclaimed devices. Seeing none, she held back a frown. Saying no could make Qi into an enemy, but sharing the tablet defeated the purpose of having it at all. She closed the image program and stood up, using the wall for support. She extended the tablet out to Qi. "You can have it for the rest of my time."

Qi's lips pressed together in a tight line. She gave a quick shake of her head. "Not fair. We share. More fun, I promise."

After a moment of hesitation Raima gave in. "Okay."

Qi joined her in the corner, sitting so close that her arms and legs pressed against Raima's. The warm sensation from her roommate's skin felt pleasant, though Raima remained stiff. If Qi moved too suddenly Raima's heart leapt, pounding with alarm. But when Qi opened the image-viewing application and pulled up the same pictures from Earth that Raima was just looking at, some of the tension left her. Qi said very little as they gazed at the tablet's screen together and seemed as enthralled as Raima had been.

When they rotated away from the tablet and onto the e-reader and then the old PC terminal Qi stayed with her. Qi found bits of music in Chinese and sang along to them under her breath while Raima listened, then she searched for news from India. Minutes passed with surprising swiftness and gradually Raima's stress faded. Boys walked in and out of the room, but she didn't care. Raima's mind focused on Qi's words and actions, her overwhelming fears and nightmares pushed away.

When they rotated back to the e-reader Qi took control of it and pulled up an information page from an encyclopedia program. "Now we learn about this place," she said, then struggled to say its name. "Mars."

Raima didn't resist though she would've preferred any topic except that one. She was determined to feign interest to keep

Qi happy. Elysia City would be included in the encyclopedia somewhere and Raima didn't want to know anything about that wretched place. Qi changed the language settings, switching to Mandarin, and typed something into the encyclopedia's search bar. Articles and images popped up of a large domed city. For a second Raima's chest constricted and she almost turned away, but then she saw the landscape around the dome was flat. It couldn't be Elysia City then.

"Zui-Chu," Qi said. "Where I born." She looked at Raima checking that she understood. Raima sensed a deeper significance and waited. "Zui-Chu. First city on Mars. My home. Never go back now."

Qi's pinched expression was difficult for Raima to read. Seeing it made something inside her throat tighten—so she looked away and stared at the screen instead. "I'm sorry," she said.

With a little huff Qi switched the language settings again on the e-reader and passed it to Raima. "You read. Learn?"

Raima nodded, but her hands were slow and clumsy as she took the e-reader. She had no interest in Martian history or in the fact that Qi's home city was the first permanent settlement on Mars. The encyclopedia's article on Zui-Chu included multiple images of the city's architecture and the design of its protective dome, but the hard lines and rust-red dust elicited dark memories.

Their time ran out with the e-reader and they rotated to the tablet. Raima hoped that Qi would select more images of Earth, but she carried on with the same topic, sticking to Mars. Now Qi focused on Martian geography, not human settlements. She found aerial photos of chasms and craters, enormous sand dunes and gently sloping volcanoes. Eventually she picked a bland map of the entire Martian surface and used her fingers to zoom in on a white lump in the western hemisphere. Cracks cut through the ground to the south of the feature like wrinkles in an old, weary face. The tablet showed a floating nametag over the white lump, calling it *Alba Mons*. It was a volcano.

Qi tapped the cracks that ran north to south on the bottom, bringing up a name. *Ceraunius Fossae.*

"Here," Qi said, breaking her long silence. "This is us. Where we are. CF-Gen."

Qi touched the tablet's screen and dragged her finger, hauling

27

the map over to the left, panning east. A new set of smaller lumps appeared on the red-brown surface, much smaller than Alba Mons. Qi tapped on more cracks around the little volcanoes. These were larger and more distinct, but there were fewer of them. A new name popped up: *Tractus Catena*.

"This is where they send me," she said. "Soon."

Raima sat silent for a moment, trying to understand what Qi was saying. "Genoquip is sending you away?"

"Yes," Qi agreed, nodding. She let out a little sigh. "They tell me today. *Sending you away. Better place for you.*" She blew a raspberry over her lips, long and loud. Raima flinched at the unpleasant sound.

"I'm sorry," Raima murmured, not sure what else she should say. The thought of sleeping in their room alone, of sitting at mealtimes by herself, and of never hearing Qi's voice again left her frozen with shock. Qi had been with her for the last four weeks, from her first day onward, a constant presence. Somewhere along the way Raima began to let herself rely on the other girl, to accept her.

It was a foolish mistake.

Qi shrugged and muttered in Chinese. With a swift, irritated motion, she closed the image and passed the tablet to Raima. "You look. Bathroom for me." She got up and left the room, trudging past the security guard at the room's entrance.

Raima watched her go. She'd wanted to say something else but sitting back and saying nothing was easier and safer. She'd wait until Qi was gone, vanished like all traces of water on Mars. Qi was kind to Raima, but that was the exception in life, never the rule. A cold, unsatisfying pride rose within as she realized she'd always known Qi's presence would be fleeting, and her compassion and care were unreliable because they were transitory.

Raima always knew that she'd end up alone.

THREE

Raima stared into the one-way mirror as lab technicians strapped sensors to her forehead, neck, and the back of her head. They shaved some of her hair, exposing the skin of her scalp for easy placement of the sticky sensors. The shaved areas were small, hidden by the rest of her hair when Raima wore it down.

One of the lab technicians offered her a friendly smile, but Raima didn't return it. She focused on her reflection in the one-way mirror. Her cheeks were plumper than she'd seen them in years and the dark circles under her eyes were fading now that the treatments were finished.

Still her eyes, dark brown and too round for her thin face, held the same hopeless stare that she saw in mirrors while she was one of Ferde's prisoners. Her body was healed despite the traumas it endured, but her mind was different. Transformed by cruelty, Raima saw a corpse's eyes peering out of her living body and felt nothing.

"All right, Raima," the male technician said and cleared his throat. He sat in a seat to Raima's right. He was careful not to obscure the view of those mysterious watchers behind the one-way mirror. "We're ready to start."

Raima turned her gaze on the man. Though she'd seen the technicians once a day for several weeks now, Raima never learned their names. The technician held a lumpy black bag. Raima had undergone this test several times already and knew what to expect. She waited as he fished through it and pulled out a red-brown rock. He wore gloves as he handed it to her.

Raima accepted the rock and stared down at it, turning it in her small, pale hands. It left fine but gritty red-brown dust on her palms and fingers. It stank of iron. Raima knew it was a Martian rock—not hard to come by considering they were on Mars. This was the first time the technician gave her a natural object. Usually the things he pulled from the black bag were human items—a hairbrush, a pair of chopsticks, even an empty water bottle.

The procedure with every object was the same. Raima examined each for about a minute in silence before the technician began asking her questions about it. Where did the object come from? Where was it last used? How did it make her feel? What did it *say* to her?

The tests hadn't always been this way. For nearly a week after Qi left, Raima continued receiving injections, but for some unknown reason the final series of shots were in her neck. Raima still had nightmares about those shots. She felt the biting sting of the needle as it plunged into her skin. After those shots ended, the technicians began testing her to see if she was now an Intuiter.

The very first tests were puzzles using math and words, riddles and jokes. Except for the sensors the technicians put on her head they were hardly tests at all. No one cared when she failed a math question or when she spent hours trying to find the right pieces of a puzzle and fit them together.

Then the tests changed, becoming what Qi warned Raima about—the "black bag" test. At first Raima blundered and failed. She asked the technician for clues. What was he looking for her to say and do? The man and woman who administered the test never gave her any hints. In fear of failure Raima faked her answers, guessing. By the end of the first week she could see disappointment in both technicians' eyes.

Then came the object that transformed her perception of the world. It was a small, gnarled hunk of hard plastic, broken and melted on one end. Yet when Raima held it she felt her hands burning. She yelped and dropped it into her lap, then realized just as fast that the plastic wasn't hot at all. When she looked up at the technician he was smiling—not with amusement, but with triumph. At last she realized what being an Inuiter *felt* like.

The plastic was the first item that triggered the sixth sense inside Raima, but it was far from the last. Each day her ability grew and changed. She didn't need the technicians to prompt her anymore.

The rock was still in her hand. It gave off a sensation of deep cold and airlessness. Raima heard metal striking rock. She could feel the impact, a ghostly pressure sent through her hand and wrist. The rock contained a memory of when it was harvested, and it projected the climate that had held it for eons.

"It's Martian," Raima said. "Harvested by a pickax, probably." She shrugged, not impressed with the scant information the rock gave her. "It's silent. It doesn't have anything to say." Manmade objects always *spoke* inside her mind. A hairbrush would say, *I will keep your hair neat.* A fork might say, *Use me on your food.* The rock wasn't man made so it contained no authorial intent.

"Are you sure?" the technician asked, raising an eyebrow speculatively.

The technician had never second-guessed her before. Even when she made up answers for his prompts before her talent awakened the technicians didn't question her answers.

Raima paused for only a moment. "Yes."

The technician reached back into the bag and pulled out another rock. Like the first one it was red-brown, but this one was smaller. He handed it to Raima but didn't take back the first rock. "Tell me about this one. Is it also from Mars?"

The smaller stone felt hot and heavy in Raima's hand. She clutched it, exploring the surface. It lacked the gritty dust of the first rock and Raima felt nothing else from it. The rock could have been from a different location on Mars, perhaps further underground where it could form the memory of heat instead of cold. Still she hesitated, staring at the rock, focusing.

Slowly, Raima caught a deeper sensation from the stone. There was pressure and then heat, and finally lightness and open air. Images flashed through her mind—a blue sky and green trees. Birdsong filled Raima's ears momentarily. She closed her eyes, savoring the sound.

It was almost seven years since her arrival on Mars. Trees, flowing rivers, blue skies, fluffy white clouds, and *green* were all dreamlike and unreal. Sometimes, interspersed throughout her usual nightmares, Raima saw trees, birds, and grass inside her pleasant dreams. She breathed real air from the wind blowing on her face, not the stale recycled atmosphere of all the underground Martian cities.

She blinked, trying to hide her unexpected emotion from the technician. She held up the smaller second rock. "Earth. This one is from Earth."

The technician took the smaller rock from her and examined it himself for a moment before asking, "And the other? Do you still think it's from Mars?"

She nodded and passed the Martian stone back to him.

"Very good," he told her, smiling. "You have some very strong reactions to natural objects." He dug into the black bag again and produced something furry and white. He handed it to Raima.

At first Raima thought it was faux animal fur and that the technician would want her to intuit the details of how it was made and where. But as she stroked the soft fur Raima's fingertips registered phantom heat and the ghostly bumps of a spine. She realized with a jolt that this was the pelt of an animal.

The fur spoke inside her mind with a small, rasping voice, a hiss that Raima shouldn't have understood but nevertheless did. She knew the skin belonged to a weasel of some kind, born and bred inside a small wire cage. She saw flashes of other creatures inside similar cages, pacing incessantly, yearning for escape or release from boredom. She knew the fluorescent lights over the animal's cage were the only illumination it ever saw. It had never seen real sunbeams, yet the animal dreamt of open spaces where it ran endlessly on its short legs. It craved the fresh air and freedom it had never known. Then came the last moments of its life, imprinted powerfully on the pelt beneath the layers of boredom and monotony. Human hands closed around it, restraining it, filling the little animal with a deep frustration at its own helplessness. The shadow of a hand with a needle came toward its neck, the prick of pain from it was barely noticeable through its terror. And then— weightlessness and light. Sunlight and trees. Cold, refreshing air. Relief and peace swamped Raima for a fraction of a second and then her mind emptied as nothingness closed over.

She flinched, pulling both hands away from the pelt and letting it fall into her lap. The female technician behind her wrote feverishly—tapping on a tablet with a stylus as she recorded the results from the sensors strapped to Raima's scalp and forehead. The man beside Raima stared at her with interest. "What can you tell me about this?" he asked.

"It was a weasel," she muttered, swallowing hard. "It lived in a cage all its life."

"It was a mink actually," the technician supplied.

Raima imagined herself behind the wire bars of the mink's prison and a cold numbness spread through her like a stain over white linen. She'd suffered like the mink, but her prison had walls instead of wire, and her tormentors hadn't been content to leave her in boredom. Their demands were for her living body, their hands always grabbing, squeezing, hitting, and punching. Their mouths leering, their throats and bodies slick with sweat and quivering with pleasure gained from her pain and anguish.

She didn't take the animal pelt back into her hands. The technician, perhaps sensing her distress, cautiously reached for the pelt. Raima watched his gloved hands, her body stiff and her throat dry.

"Would you like a break?" he asked.

She shook her head. "I'm fine. What's next?"

The technician produced a small pen. He held it on the palms of his cupped hands, laid out like a gift. Raima took it and tapped it against her other hand and then forearm. She heard a voice from the pen at once, garbled and faint. Raima stopped shaking it and gripped the pen, using all ten fingertips along its length and then moving it to rest against one palm as well. She made as much physical contact as possible.

I am a tool, the pen whispered inside her mind. *Use me and I will share your words.*

All pens repeated this basic message, since they were manmade objects. Raima was unsurprised—but there was another, deeper layer to this seemingly unimportant, generic pen. She closed her eyes, focusing her inner, incorporeal ears on the pen.

I will only write in your left hand, the pen said.

"What can you tell me about it?" the technician prompted.

Raima didn't open her eyes yet. "It says it will share my words—but it won't work unless I use my left hand."

"You're right-handed, aren't you?" the man asked and then clucked his tongue. "It's a shame you can't change that message."

This was a challenge, a test. Raima opened her eyes and looked at the pen. It was black with opaque plastic. It lacked a cap, but otherwise showed no signs of wear or use. There were no bite marks on the end. Raima brought it to her own lips and closed her eyes again. She tried to ignore the tension she sensed from both technicians. She didn't need to look at them—or into the one-way mirror for that matter—to know that they were all riveted by her every movement, no matter how small. That intensity directed at her would have made her heart rate soar, starting it drumming in her ears, drowning the pen's message if she let herself feel it.

Qi warned her about this test too. The object changed each time, but Qi had gone through the test and knew the goal. Qi took this test weeks ago, just before leaving, and passed easily.

The technician cleared his throat, prompting her into action. Raima forced her attention back to the test once more. Against her lips the pen whispered, *I will speak your words wherever I can. But you must write them with your left hand.*

"What are you going to do with it?" the technician asked.

Raima frowned. Answering him broke her concentration but she did it anyway.

"I'm . . ." She thought for a moment, unsure. Qi's reaction to this test had been different because for her the object was a metallic fingernail clipper that refused to open without jamming or breaking outright. Qi was especially frustrated with the test because the researchers knew from a request she'd made to the Wishing Program that she wanted a fingernail clipper. She complained constantly of hangnails and broken nails. During the test she broke the clipper several times, forcing it open, and then realized finesse was required.

"I speak to it. I say, easy. I say, go slow, go smooth. And it listened!"

As far as Raima knew, objects never *listened* to her. They only whispered while *she* listened. Even so, she'd heard the other subjects say similar things. The tests all headed in this direction. It was object manipulation, not just object reading.

Thinking of Qi, Raima said, "I'm going to make it listen."

"Ah," the technician murmured.

Listen, she thought, concentrating on the touch of the pen, cool and solid on her lips. *Listen to me.*

The pen made no response, unless she took its silence as obedience. Raima imagined that its touch was lighter, as her hands relaxed their grip on the tool, pressing it into her lips with less force.

You shouldn't care what hand I use to hold you. My hands are the same. Do you feel them? Do you understand? Can you answer me?

Surprisingly, the pen replied, *I am a tool. I am obedient.*

Raima concentrated harder, certain that she couldn't have succeeded this easily. *Will you allow me to write using my right hand?*

Again, the pen said, *I am a tool. I am obedient.* Raima hesitated, uncertain. Then the pen added: *I will share your words. All hands are left. All hands are the same.*

Satisfied, Raima pulled the pen from her lips and motioned at the technician. "I need a piece of paper."

He provided it, passing Raima a clipboard with a blank sheet of paper on it. Raima cradled it close and then lifted the pen with confidence. She scrawled meaningless shapes and then lapsed into Indic script, recalling distant lessons from childhood. After a moment she stopped, disturbed by the oppressive sadness the shapes stirred inside her.

"Excellent!" The technician twisted around, looking first to the one-way mirror and then to the other technician behind him. "This was one of the fastest I've seen." He reached for Raima's clipboard and asked, "Can I look?"

He could already see her writing from where he sat, but Raima knew what he really wanted. She let go of the clipboard and relaxed in her seat, fidgeting. The sensor straps and nodes attached to her head itched. The technician lifted the board high and turned it to the one-way mirror.

While the researchers rejoiced over Raima's success, the teenager wrapped her arms around herself and avoided looking at her reflection. One cage for another, she thought. Even if Genoquip set her free tomorrow she would still be a prisoner inside her own wounded body, heart, and mind. She could never take back her past and she knew that she couldn't go back to Earth. She'd been on the planet too long, arrived too soon, and grown too tall.

The female technician escorted Raima back to her room once the test was done. The air was chilled but comfortable. The hallway, lined with paneling, was meant to give its occupants the feeling they were merely indoors without windows, not underground. It never fooled Raima. From the moment she entered this subterranean world she felt the difference. She longed for real, true air—but she knew that if she ever really experienced the brush of a Martian wind on her bare skin, it would be just before she died with her blood boiling.

When they had almost reached Raima's room the technician turned and smiled at Raima. "You did very well today."

Though technicians commanded authority with their doctor-like white scrubs, Raima suspected they weren't the true masters at this research center. Raima didn't know how much longer she'd be Genoquip's guinea pig before her debt was paid in full. She knew better than to ask the technicians because Qi warned her not to waste her time questioning them.

"They not know," Qi had told her. "They not care. Not tell if they do know."

"Thank you," Raima replied to the technician, knowing that was the expected response. She'd done nothing extraordinary in any of her tests and knew the technician's praise was for her obedience rather than her actual performance. Captors approved of obedience.

They turned left and walked a few more feet before stopping at Raima's cell, room 152. For the first time Raima noticed that the code on her door was changed again. Originally Raima the door had two codes, one for herself and one for Qi. Since Qi left, Raima's code was the only one on the door, but now there was a second one once again. For a moment Raima stared, wondering how long the second code had been on the door without her noticing.

The technician used a keycard to open the door, showing no interest and no reaction to the changed code. "There we are," she said. "Home sweet home."

Raima had to ask, "I have a new roommate?"

The technician blinked and shrugged. "I suppose you must. You'll take good care of her, won't you?"

Raima could see most of her tiny, cell-like room through the open door. It was enough to know that there was no roommate inside yet. "She hasn't come yet."

The technician gave another shrug. "I'm sure she'll be here soon enough." She smiled with false cheer and motioned for Raima to enter. Raima stepped into the empty room with its two plain cots and the small collection of her own personal belongings cluttering one corner near the bookshelf. The space still felt cold without Qi's presence.

"Have a nice sol," the technician said. The door hissed as it closed and locked. Raima would spend the next few hours inside this room alone until lunchtime. After lunch would come all the other rituals of the day. Socialization, exercise, chores, and sometimes a lesson on her choice of a subject—not from a real, living teacher, but from a computer program.

After a moment Raima moved to her cot and lay down on it, staring at the opposite bed and thinking of Qi. Faint whispers flowed up from her mattress: *I am safe. Use me for sleep.* She ignored them.

At first Raima tried convincing herself that Qi's absence was better for her, that further unexpected kindness would weaken her. Yet, as more time passed, Raima found her empty room to be a curse. When Qi was there Raima had to bite her tongue, to hide her inner demons. Better still, Qi provided a distraction, a new focus for Raima's troubled mind. Without Qi there was nothing besides the monsters inside Raima's mind. They refused to stay inside the cages she'd made for them.

She missed Qi, but she didn't want to admit it to herself. She had been certain that forgetting her would be the easiest and most practical thing to do, but a few days after Qi left, Raima received a gift from CF-Gen's Wishing Program. It was a thick book with pictures of India—monkeys, temples, city streets, Asian elephants, and all the luxuriant greenery of the land. She realized that Qi requested the book in her name, deliberately leaving it as a last present for her.

She didn't want to sleep, but the numb heaviness inside her pulled her easily toward it. Soon she closed her eyes, letting Qi drift from her mind.

FOUR

aima awakened when the door to her room opened. Three security guards paraded in, taking no notice of Raima. Between them they carried a small-bodied young woman. The girl was red-faced and breathing in erratic gasps, her body hanging limp in the guards' hold.

Raima stared, wide-eyed and motionless as they put the girl on the cot opposite her—Qi's old bed. The guards' dark blue uniforms reminded her of the policemen who questioned her after Ferde's murder, needling her with threats when she told them she'd been enslaved for years. They hadn't shown her any sympathy and didn't hide the fact that they thought she was lying. They hoped to bully her into admitting she worked at the brothel willingly, that Ferde paid her, and that she was born on Mars, not smuggled there with her mother as a child. These guards moved in the same brusque way, spoke in the same clipped tones. Raima's breathing quickened the longer they remained.

The guards talked amongst themselves in quiet voices, wondering if the girl needed restraints or if they should summon a nurse. They ignored Raima the same way they ignored dust beneath the cots. Raima clutched her covers, watching their hands, resisting the impulse to cover herself. She knew sheets did nothing to soften blows and movement would turn their attention to her.

"Put a call in," one of the guards finally said. "Let's have someone look at her."

They left, closing and locking the door behind them. Raima heard them fumble with the small computer next to the door. She knew they were using it to summon a nurse. As soon as she heard the steady thump of the guards' boots departing, she rose from her bed and moved a few steps closer to the other cot. The girl's breathless sobbing made the fine hairs on Raima's arms and the back of her neck stand up. Crying was useless and only drew a captor's ire. The sound grated on Raima's ears, making her tremble.

"Hey—*shhhh*," she called, raising her unsteady voice over the girl's sobbing. "Shut up! Stop crying."

Raima was close enough to see that her new roommate was Earth-born and raised there until recently. The girl's small, squat frame revealed the influence of Earth's gravity on her bones and muscles, making her arms and legs shorter and thicker. Though the Martian physique was considered glamorous on Earth, those who possessed the frame despised it for its weakness. The Martian physique trapped them in the lower gravity, closing off the possibility of returning to Earth forever.

Besides her build, Raima's new roommate appeared lucky in other ways as well. She still wore civilian clothing—thick cargo khaki pants and a long-sleeved blue-gray shirt. Whoever this girl was, she had been outside of Genoquip's facility. Raima envied her.

"Stop crying, it can't be that bad," she said.

Raima watched the hysterical girl's fists clench the thin bed sheets, wrinkling them. Raima recognized the anguish in that movement. Raima herself often woke in the middle of the night finding sheets wadded in her fists. When it wasn't sheets, Raima's nails bit into her palms, creating little pink-red crescent moons.

The door opened. Raima hopped up, scurrying back to her bed as fast as she could. She sat there and remained motionless with her knees brought up to her chest. Two nurses in blue scrubs spilled through the door. They surrounded the girl's bed and turned her over, calling her by name.

"Kim? Kim, honey, I need you to calm down for me or I'm going to have to sedate you."

Raima heard a scuffing noise, the sound of a guard's boots dragging on the floor outside the door. She knew that a guard stood watch, but this was more security than they usually bothered with. Perhaps they expected the girl to bolt or lash out. Raima stayed silent, eager for the commotion to end and the guards to leave.

The nurses didn't have the patience to gradually bring the girl—Kim—under their control. They held her still while they injected her with a sedative, then lingered long enough to be certain she succumbed to the drug's effects. They looked over at Raima before they left, surprising her with their sudden attention. She cringed when the male nurse looked at her and then extended his hand. The sudden motion made Raima scramble out of his reach. He stood patiently, his hand opened to reveal a small square tile with a button in the center.

"Press this if she needs medical help," he said.

When the door closed behind the nurses, Kim rolled over and squinted at Raima through red, puffy eyes that were the same shade as Kati's. Seeing Kim's face for the first time robbed Raima of words. She stared, unable even to blink at the incredible resemblance between this living girl and the dead one that haunted her nightmares. The straight corn-silk hair, the refined, narrow little nose, and the smooth line of her jaw, all of it matched Raima's memory of Kati.

But her voice was different, deeper in pitch. The sound of Kim groaning, hiccupping as her diaphragm convulsed with the remnants of her sobbing, jolted Raima out of her shock.

With one final spate of tears, Kim's eyelids drifted shut. "Kaiden," she said, whimpering.

Raima shifted on her cot, palming the button the nurse had given her. The girl's emotional display troubled her. It was a disquieting reflection of Raima's own devastation early after her arrival on Mars. The first few times she was raped tore her apart, physically and emotionally, gutting her and leaving the empty shell that remained. Raima had been certain no pain could match that experience, but then her mother died. Raima descended into deeper levels of agony. She was able to endure the first weeks of torment because of her mother's presence, but as an orphan enslaved in the brothel the weight of loneliness finally crushed her. Raima wanted only to die, to be nothing. She survived in that cocoon of emptiness for another two years before—

She grabbed her pillow and held it over her lap, taking a deep, unsteady breath as she looked at her new roommate. Kim, not Kati, Kim. She allowed herself to scowl at the other girl, realizing that Kim was unconscious and breathing slowly, relaxed by the sedative injection.

"You're not her," she said. "You're not Kati."

Raima had wanted a new roommate to force herself to stay out of her memories, to keep her past away. Yet that silent wish backfired with Kim's close resemblance to Kati.

Karma, Raima thought as Kim whimpered in her sedative-induced sleep. Kim's resemblance was Raima's punishment for letting Kati die, a reminder of her crimes, her selfishness. The cold, pragmatic part of her mind dismissed the idea as foolishness. Her mother always told her all of Earth's religions were made by men to benefit other men. Western and Eastern religions alike, all of them justified a patriarchal system where women were treated like chattel. Despite her mother's attempts to shelter her daughter from religion, Raima managed to pick up some of the ideas anyway. It was difficult not to see *karma* now. She'd brought it to Ferde by killing him, and now Kim was sent to punish Raima in return.

She'd vowed to help Kati in the brothel, to keep her alive. It was a mistake. In hindsight Raima knew she should've done nothing. By helping Kati, Raima set off the chain of events that ultimately killed her. She wouldn't make the same mistake again. This girl would live or die, regardless of what Raima did, so why tangle herself up in Kim's fate? The cold survivalist inside her calmed the panicky thoughts of *karma* and punishment that made her chest ache and her eyes burn. With each passing second the pain lessened and the invisible fist squeezing her heart loosened its grip.

Soon fatigue pulled her mind back into sleep. More nightmares likely awaited, but Raima thought of pleasant topics—her stomach full of CF-Gen's good food, her memories of Earth. She thought about Qi and hoped she was happy and healthy wherever she'd gone. Finally, she drifted back into a mercifully dreamless sleep.

A week after Kim's arrival, invading Qi's space, Raima still struggled to reconcile her confused emotions. Kim's illness began as her body succumbed to the effects of the shots. She refused food and quickly deteriorated, becoming bedridden. She had no interest in interacting with Raima. When not sleeping or throwing up, she spent most of her time crying. It was unnerving, because Kati had spent most of her time crying as well. At about sixteen, Kim was just the age Kati would have been if she'd survived and escaped from the brothel alongside Raima.

On the morning of Sol Lunae—Monday, to stubborn Earthlings like Raima who refused to use the Martian terminology for days and months—Raima attended her usual test with the technicians in the afternoon. Afterward she visited the recreation center, listening and watching the other subjects with wary intensity. She took an e-reader and sat in a corner, searching through entries related to Zui-Chu, Qi's home city and wondering what it'd be like to live free beneath the dome with no memories of Earth at all. Would she be as happy as Qi, or would she still long for the sight of greenery and hot, nourishing sunlight?

Soon she switched devices, taking a tablet instead. As she sat down again in her corner she overheard two girls chatting in lowered voices, debating the legality of Genoquip's genetic studies. Raima could barely see the girls where they stood together outside the room, murmuring in the hall.

"Do you think MIHO knows what goes on here?" one of them asked. She was gangly and tall, clearly a longtime Martian native. Her companion was shorter, but still had the narrower build of someone who'd spent her growing years in the low gravity. The shorter girl was dark-skinned, and her English was accented with a British lilt.

Raima liked the shorter girl's accent and strained to hear them from her position. She flicked through images of Earth and Martian celebrities trying to appear occupied while she eavesdropped.

"How could they not?" the British girl asked.

"Companies lie or underplay shit," the other replied. "GQ might be able to hide it."

"People *die* here. . . ."

"People die in prison too. Some of the people MIHO handle are juvie killers. GQ could tell MIHO that some juvie went berserk and killed someone else."

"Get real," the British girl shot back. "MIHO knows what's happening here. They *sell* us to GQ."

Raima didn't waste her time pondering this idea, but she heard many other subjects questioning MIHO's involvement in Genoquip's experiments. How could a humanitarian aid group endorse genetic experiments on orphans, debtors, and juvenile criminals? Most of the people they sent to Genoquip were simply unlucky and poor. How could MIHO be selling its orphans and debtors off to the likes of Genoquip without gaining a reputation as liars who exploited the very people they claimed to help? It boggled the mind and seemed unlikely to many of the subjects. Most chose to believe outlandish explanations rather than accept MIHO's crookedness, but Raima knew and accepted the cruel reality because the agent handling her case at MIHO had confirmed the truth.

"Your debts are astronomical. You'd never pay them off even if you were an adult. As a minor and an orphan there's nothing but a life of crime and violence waiting for you once you leave the hospital."

By signing away her rights and debts to MIHO, Raima allowed them to auction her off to the highest bidder. Her agent, a woman who pitied Raima, divulged too much information, as if that would provide comfort or erase the suffering of Raima's past. One of the tests MIHO ran on Raima found that her immune system was compatible with some of Genoquip's experiments. MIHO rented her out to the facility, drawing regular lump sums of money from the company as long as Raima proved useful.

"This way, if you're not doing well at GQ," Raima's agent explained, *"you'll come back to us and we'll place you somewhere else. You know, a portion of that payment goes to you."* But in Raima's cynical mind the truth was obvious: MIHO made more money this way and avoided the accusation that it created *slaves*.

Unlike most of the other subjects at the facility, Raima wouldn't be released on her eighteenth birthday. The two girls in the hallway might leave the system with a little bit of money in their pockets in just a few more years, but Raima was paying off an enormous debt to society. As quasi-legal as MIHO was, Raima was grateful to them. MIHO funded the hospital that restored Raima's health, yet the cost was unimaginable for a penniless orphan like Raima.

That debt would keep her with MIHO long after her eighteenth birthday.

"All right," a voice called out from down the hall. "Rooms 100 through 200 of the girls' wing—time's up. Retire to your rooms."

Raima put away the tablet she'd been using and shuffled out of the recreation center with dozens of other girls. They filed past a security guard who scanned their fingerprints to perform a roll call, ensuring that all the girls really had left. As Raima approached she steeled herself for his touch as she always did, but when his enormous hand snatched hers she couldn't stop herself from pulling away slightly. The man didn't seem to notice and in a second, he released her again. Raima walked on with the other girls, feeling gloomy at the prospect of another night listening to Kim's endless tears.

She reached the door and found it unlocked as it always was at this time of day. The door opened with a hiss and a brief flutter of air—Raima gasped at what she saw inside.

Kim lay sprawled on the floor, motionless and pale. A small puddle of bile was pooled less than a foot from her head. The room reeked of vomit. Raima recoiled with disgust even as she hurried forward to help Kim get up.

"Kim? Do you need a nurse? Are you all right?"

She stopped beside Kim and knelt, but hesitated, unwilling to make a physical connection. Since Raima had become an Intuiter she'd begun sensing emotions and information from objects without trying. A tablet in the recreation center would suddenly give off vibes of joy and excitement, or waves of melancholy and sadness from a previous user. The talent grew almost daily. Raima knew that some subjects could read details off other people when they touched bare skin or even clothing. She'd overheard them complaining that touch overwhelmed them, filling their minds with unwanted information and thoughts.

Kim's eyes opened, and she blinked. After muttering a few incoherent words, she groaned and lifted her hand, grabbing at Raima's socked foot. Raima resisted the desire to pull her foot out of Kim's reach.

"Kim?" she asked again.

The girl's pale hand wormed around her foot, feeling the fabric

45

of Raima's sock, and then her fingers slid higher, grazing the skin of Raima's ankle.

A rush of deep misery crashed into Raima, flowing from Kim's fingers where they contacted the bare flesh. She felt Kim's weakness and nausea, much the same as what she'd experienced during her first weeks at the facility, but beyond it was Kim's crushing loss, grief, and loneliness. In only seconds Raima learned Kim came to MIHO with her brother, a boy of thirteen by the name of Kaiden. They were raised by two loving parents who worked as geologists. They weren't poor, and they weren't mistreated. It was a blissful existence that set Raima burning with envy.

But all that luck ended when Kim's parents died in a landslide while surveying the steep walls of Ganges Chasma. Kim's concerns about her parents' deaths were imprinted on her skin. Had the rocks crushed them, or had their blood boiled in the low pressure of the Martian atmosphere once their suits cracked? Would Kim and Kaiden live long enough to get out of Genoquip and MIHO's clutches?

Kim was given a choice after her parents died. She could return to Earth because her body structure and bones were formed under that planet's heavier gravity. There were relatives who would claim her on Earth—she didn't need to sign away her rights to MIHO. Her brother wasn't as lucky. He was tall and gangly, shaped by the Martian gravity. His bones would snap if he returned to Earth. Kim could stay on Mars, or she could abandon him and save herself. She chose Kaiden and let MIHO take her away, selling her to Genoquip as fodder in their experiment.

Raima jerked her foot out of Kim's grasp. She felt the bizarre, confused rush of emotions settling within her, competing with her own. Clenching her hands into tight fists, she closed her eyes and drew in a deep breath, searching for the familiar cool numbness. Rage boiled up instead, filling her with the desire to strike Kim, to shout at her with an exasperated jealousy. Kim's life had been perfect but now it wasn't, and she couldn't muster any self-control or courage to face it—and her situation wasn't even that terrible. No one beat her here, she had plenty of food, and there were even nurses and doctors ready to dote on her. Kim was never raped, never had to let strange men violate her just so she could have the privilege of eating a meal.

On the heels of her anger, Raima also experienced the strange desire to sympathize with Kim. She'd lost her parents and her whole life, just as Raima had when she'd been trapped alone in the brothel after her mother died. The difference between them was that Raima hadn't been allowed to express her grief, at least not while her captors were watching or when she seduced the johns. Kim could wallow in her misery, languish in her loss until she forgot why she was at Genoquip in the first place—to protect her brother, Kaiden. She was squandering her luck, her life, her family.

That smoldering rage propelled Raima into action. She grabbed Kim around the waist and hauled her up. The little Earther weighed less than Raima imagined. Taking Kim's entire weight was easy.

Moaning, Kim tried to speak. "Put me down."

"You're filthy. You haven't showered in days. You're lying on the floor next to your own puke. It's time for you to take a shower." Controlling the resentment in her voice was hard, but fortunately Kim wasn't in any condition to care.

They were in the bathroom a moment later. Raima switched on a light and Kim moaned, cringing against the unexpected brightness. Gently, Raima set Kim down, leaning her against the wall near the toilet. Lifting the toilet seat, she gestured to Kim to be sure the other girl saw it. "If you're going to puke again, do it in there," she said.

Kim turned her head, resting her temple against the cold tiling on the wall. "Stop this," she said. "I don't want to . . ."

Raima turned back to Kim, glaring at her. "What? What are you going to say next? Are you going to say you don't want to live? You'd rather die?" Her hands balled into fists again, outraged that this pampered girl was so ready to give up after one major loss. Raima wouldn't tolerate it.

Kim swallowed with a thick gulping sound and closed her eyes. Her head rolled to the other side, away from Raima. It was as if Kim thought that if she ignored Raima long enough she'd just disappear.

"Hey," Raima snapped and took a small step away from the shower to kneel to Kim's level. She grabbed Kim by the chin, gripping her hard enough that Kim opened her eyes and moaned, trying to pull away. "*Listen* to me. You want to die? You think your life is so bad? You think *this* is as bad as it can get?"

"Stop—let go." The words were garbled, mangled by Raima's strong hold on Kim's jaw.

"You're an idiot," Raima growled. "You don't know what bad is. So what if you end up the last one in your family? Do you think they'd want you to sit around feeling sorry for yourself while you wither and die? But you're not the last one. Kaiden's here somewhere. What would he think if he saw you now? What would your parents think? And even if you do end up alone, you can leave here. You can go back *home*. You can go to *Earth*."

For the first time Kim's eyes seemed more alert and focused. She stared at Raima, her eyes so similar to Kati's—blue and misty with illness, and red from crying.

Kati always cried when she should have fought to survive, no matter how painful it was, no matter how hopeless. *Stupid Kati*, Raima thought. *Not this time. You're not going to die this time.*

"Are you listening to me?" Raima demanded. "You're going to live, Kati."

The blue-eyed girl frowned and Raima realized that she was talking to *Kim*, not *Kati*. She corrected herself immediately. "Kim. *Kim*. Do you understand?"

"Yes," Kim replied.

"It's going to be hard," Raima went on. "But you can do it. I'll—" She jerked her head away from Kim, desperate to hide her face as emotions hit her from somewhere deep and hidden within. She frowned, unsure whether it was her feelings or Kim's invasive influence. Tears burned in her eyes, flowing as she blinked. She wiped her face, flicking away the signs of her emotion as she forced herself to finish. "I can help you. I thought you would be stronger than this."

This isn't Kati, she reminded herself again and sighed as the intensity drained out of her, flowing invisibly like air currents. Each repetition further calmed her, numbing her heart. She twisted around to look at Kim and feigned a smile as she asked, "Can you stand, or do I need to help shower you?"

"I don't need a shower," Kim insisted.

Raima cocked her head. "Yes, you do. You stink. Even if you can't smell it, I can. So, if you can't stand, I'll help you."

Kim protested, trying to ward off Raima's strong hands as

they moved for her scrubs, pulling at the fabric. Raima ignored Kim's feeble efforts and after several minutes of fighting with the garments, both girls were naked. Kim relied almost entirely on Raima for support as they squeezed into the shower stall. With one arm around Kim's waist, holding her tightly and taking her weight to keep Kim's legs from buckling, Raima turned on the water.

"No soap, no shampoo," Raima said. "Just water. Is it warm enough?"

Kim's head slumped forward as the water ran through her blonde hair. "Yes."

"Good," Raima said, struggling to keep a good hold on Kim. "A hot shower was the only thing that ever made me feel better when I was sick. My first roommate helped me shower like this when I was too weak to do it," Raima explained. "I think they put us together like that on purpose, hoping we'll help each other. It's always one girl who's gone through it and another who's got to go through it still."

Vivid memories played in Raima's mind, recalling Qi's care when she was sick during her first week with the shots. Kim's emotions continued flowing into Raima from wherever their bodies touched, but she was able to ignore it by focusing on her own sensations and emotions. A small horror built in Raima as she realized that Qi must have felt the same things during their shower together when so much of their bare skin touched. What had Qi seen? How much of Raima's past did she feel? And yet Qi's behavior didn't change. She never said anything about the experience, but it seemed impossible that Qi didn't feel something.

Considering Qi in this new way left Raima with an unfamiliar, confusing sensation. She'd known that Qi's kindness was extreme, a rarity in her experience, but knowing about Raima's past should've repulsed her or filled her with pity. At the very least there should have been some sign that she knew. Raima had already used what she'd learned from Kim to manipulate the other girl. Qi hadn't done that. Why? *How?*

Though the water from the showerhead was warm, Raima shuddered as if it was icy cold. What was she doing with Kim, emulating Qi's compassion when she was incapable of understanding it? How could she expect to comfort Kim? She'd screw it up—just like when she tried to help Kati. She buried the thoughts, closing her eyes and leaning into the water, letting it invade her mouth and drown her fears.

Kim seemed to have halfway lost consciousness, slipping into a deep sleep. Raima turned off the shower. She carried Kim out of the bathroom, dried her off with a towel, and then laid her in bed. After dressing she used a washcloth to clean up the little pile of puke Kim had left on the floor and tried to ignore her disgust as she did it, convinced that Qi had done the same. When that was finished Raima sat on her own cot with her knees tucked up against her chest, waiting for the lights-out warning to blare overhead, and watching Kim's slow, regular breaths.

You don't know what bad is, she thought.

FIVE

ood afternoon," the technician said with false cheer. He sat down on his rolling stool beside the elevated seat that all subjects occupied while taking Genoquip's tests. He held a touchpad, something he normally left to the female technician. "This sol we're going to do a test along with a sort of interview. Is that all right?"

Raima nodded. As if she really had a choice. A woman moved behind her and began strapping electrodes and other sensors onto Raima's head. She stared at the one-way mirror in front of her, watching her reflection and that of the female technician until the man at her side cleared his throat and began to speak again.

"Your name is Raima Kothari, correct?"

"Yes," Raima replied.

"And you were born on Earth?"

"Yes."

"Your birth place was Chandigarh, India?" the technician asked.

Raima took in a quick, deep breath. "Yes." The admission forced memories to surface: green fields, lush trees, and the sharp, exhilarating scent of rain.

"You are here at Genoquip to pay off your debts, correct?"

"Yes," Raima replied, ignoring the niggling voice that insisted such a bland description of her situation was an understatement.

The technician glanced up at her briefly and then back toward the woman behind Raima. In the mirror Raima saw the two technicians exchange a look with some hidden meaning. Then the man beside her said, "Okay, now that we have a truth baseline we're going to begin the actual test and the real interview. Are you ready?"

Raima didn't make eye contact with him as she nodded.

He fumbled inside the pocket of his white lab coat and produced a shiny, metallic object that, for a moment, Raima didn't recognize at all. The technician passed it to her, dropping it into her lap where Raima finally saw the glass screen and digital readouts inside. It was a watch. She squinted at it, turning the watch in her lap as her mind grasped what she was reading. The watch had complex readouts and was set to Martian time. It was *Sol Lunae*.

Monday, Raima thought, translating between the Earth terminology and the Martian. A week now since she'd helped Kim, trying to kick-start her roommate's will to live.

"What does the watch say to you?" the technician asked. The man tapped his forehead. "Here. What does it say to you here?"

Without looking back at the watch Raima already heard its message. *I will keep you on time. I will tell you what time it is. I will always be accurate.*

"It says it will tell me the time."

The technician nodded and then cocked his head, offering her a slight frown. "And does it say anything else?"

She turned her attention and concentration back to the watch, closing her small fists over the cold metal and willing her mind to spill into the object, absorbing something deeper than its surface message. For a moment the watch was silent and then, slowly, Raima heard whispered words. She stared ahead at the mirror without seeing it, faintly aware of the female technician behind her recording information and checking her instrumentation.

"The owner was a man named Chuck," she said. "He gave it away at a pawnshop because it was a gift from someone who hurt him."

The technician nodded, glancing over Raima's head in to the one-way mirror, as if checking that everyone, both seen and unseen, caught the explanation. "Can you tell me anything else about him, or about the reasons why he gave up the watch?"

"His last name was McCloud." She slipped the watch over her own wrist, fingering it and tapping at the display. The watch passed its messages to her, layers of memories ingrained into it by its owner.

Small, mundane things and the most common events stood out the strongest: transactions of money, handshakes, keyboards, tablets, mugs of coffee, and pints of beer. Raima could hear the man's voice repeating as he introduced himself over and over, thrusting a hand forward to shake each time, jangling the wristwatch.

"Hi, I'm Chuck McCloud. It's great to meet you."

Underlying the most frequent and commonplace experiences were larger ones, moments etched into the watch by their impact or uniqueness. The memory of Chuck opening the box that contained the watch and exclaiming over it with joy. The first few times he slipped it back on after nearly forgetting it somewhere. Then there was the time Chuck touched it while placing it back inside its box, determined to sell it.

The last one stood out to Raima because it was the final event imprinted onto the watch. Because the owner had been thinking about selling the watch and *why* he intended to do it, Raima was able to pick out the story. Chuck discovered that his fiancée was cheating on him and the watch had been a gift from her. It reminded him of her. In his pain and fury, Chuck decided to pawn the valuable watch to rid himself of her influence.

That wasn't the only thing Chuck thought while placing the watch back into its original box. Along with the resentment towards his fiancée, Raima felt Chuck's intention to seek out a brothel, to lose himself mindlessly in the body of another woman. It was a violent desire, a dark craving. Raima knew it well. He thought that because he was paying for sex he could do whatever he wished to the woman—or girl—he bought. He would be rough with her, possess and punish her in a way he never could with his cheating fiancée.

Raima took off the watch as if it burned. She handed it back to the technician while she explained, "It was a gift from his fiancée, who cheated on him. So, he got rid of it."

"Is that so?" the technician asked with mock surprise.

"Yes," Raima snapped. "It is so." At the man's flicker of surprise, Raima went on. "He was an asshole."

The technician looked perplexed. "Why would you say that?"

Angry and disturbed, Raima didn't give the technician the honest, open explanation he wanted and expected of her. She

53

couldn't be certain, but Raima suspected the technicians and their bosses, the people watching her from the other side of the mirror, designed their tests with the backgrounds of their subjects in mind. Surely, they knew Raima's past, understood her debts, and when it was advantageous to them, they used objects that triggered an emotional response. Of course, they normally didn't see much of a reaction from Raima. She assumed that was why they often called her an *ideal* subject for the tests.

Feeling uncooperative, Raima said, "I just know."

The technician frowned and was silent for a moment before changing the subject. "You should know, Raima, that you've been such an enormous success—and so helpful and obedient—that we'd like to enroll you in a different program at a nearby facility. This one is much better paying. Your debts will be paid off twice as fast."

Against her will a glimmer of interest sprang to life even as she fought down the bitterness that surfaced inside her at the technician's comment: *so helpful and obedient.*

All captors are the same, she thought, seeing Qi in her mind's eye, then Kim beside Kati, both slumped and weak. At Genoquip the slaves were tamed through debilitating illness. At the brothel it was beatings, starvation, and rape. At Genoquip the punishments for disobedience were restrictions on food, entertainment privileges, and solitary confinement. In the brothel it was a fist to the face, hands strangling your throat, mealtimes denied, and more rape.

She took a deep breath, drawing a sick comfort by comparing the two types of slavery side by side. Genoquip was a pleasure cruise, a day spa, an amusement park compared to the brothel. The anger and bitterness left Raima, ebbing out of her and into the cold, sterile whiteness of the room.

She looked to the technician, keeping her expression neutral. "How long would it take me to pay off my debt in the other program?"

"Five to ten years," he answered and as her face fell he added, "I know it sounds like a long time to you, but you're only sixteen—"

"I'm seventeen," Raima said, daring to interrupt him. At the brothel mouthing off like that would earn her a quick slap to the face, but she'd learned by now that Genoquip's nurses and technicians had a lot more patience than the brothel's men and johns.

"Seventeen," he corrected himself. "At your age five years might seem like a long time, but really, it's actually the blink of an eye. Even if it took closer to ten years, you wouldn't even be thirty and your debts would all be gone." He smiled. "Most college graduates can't even say that on Earth! You're really very lucky."

"Yes," Raima repeated. Inwardly she fought both rage and despair, holding onto a logic she wasn't sure made any sense. Genoquip *was* better than the brothel. It was almost like being free. He was right. She *was* lucky.

The technician seemed to sense her lingering doubt. He sighed with what Raima assumed was a mixture of mock sympathy and sadness. "I know it hardly seems fair. You've been through a lot, haven't you?"

Raima said nothing and turned her head to stare at a corner on the one-way mirror.

"You'll get the best medical care and education with us, and you won't incur any other debts. That's not something you can get anywhere else."

This was all true and Raima relaxed a little, her shoulders sinking and her heart slowing. *You're really very lucky.* Raima had never been lucky before, though many adults apparently wanted her to believe she was. She cleared her throat and asked, "What would I do at the other facility?"

"It's a much smaller group," the man said, leaning forward. The motion made Raima tense. The technician ignored her reaction—if he even noticed it at all—and continued his explanation. "You would stay with an all-girls group. There are only ten or twenty girls in the program. Your first roommate, Qi, moved to that program."

Raima jerked her head sharply and stared at the technician. "Qi is already there?"

The technician nodded. "And doing quite well. We only send subjects with the highest scores and best test-taking skills to that program. You've shown a remarkable ability to read secrets and emotions from the objects we bring in, not just the physical facts. We value that trait, and it makes you an ideal candidate for the program at our other, smaller facility." He stopped and smiled encouragingly.

Some dark instinct stirred in the back of Raima's mind. The technician was *selling* this to her, pushing her toward the other, mysterious program without describing any other options except her endless debt, neglecting to mention any downside. Raima was no longer naïve enough to believe that something existed without a negative side. Anyone claiming otherwise, or avoiding talking about those negative aspects, was a manipulative liar with an agenda that wouldn't be in Raima's best interests. Raima and her mother were abducted and brought to Mars by just such a sales pitch.

"What do they do at the other facility? What would *I* do?" Raima asked again.

The technician's gaze flew briefly to the woman behind Raima who continued monitoring the machines, as if deaf and blind to everything else. "The other facility is doing a *social* experiment. Instead of reading objects you and the other girls in the group will be trained until you're able to read people the way you read these things." He held the watch aloft, letting its shiny metal hinges tinkle, like chimes.

There was a strange pause, an incongruous inflection of his voice that Raima hadn't missed. She looked at her hands in her lap and asked, "What about my roommate now? She's so weak. . . ."

The technician lowered the watch and pursed his lips. "She'll be better soon, but we can postpone your transfer for a short time if you'd like. We do value the help that more experienced roommates offer the newcomers. You . . . *improve* their lives immeasurably."

Raima restrained the urge to snort with derision as she translated his careful language in her head: *We do value the help that healthy roommates give to the dying. You save their lives.* No one ever acknowledged that subjects *died* in the experiment. In fact, they were very careful to avoid the topic.

"I'll stay with her for a little while—if that would help," Raima said. Anger nearly escaped through a glare or a snide comment, but Raima's training in the brothel remained and it prevented such outbursts. She knew the technician wouldn't beat or rape her, something she was grateful for every day, but she didn't want to break some unseen rule and receive a horrible, unexpected punishment. The rumor among many of the subjects was that

Genoquip killed uncooperative boys and girls, or orphans who were about to come into a sizeable inheritance at the age of eighteen.

The technician raised his eyebrows, as if she was foolish for not pouncing on the opportunity at once. "But you do want to be enrolled in the program?"

Invisible pressure closed in around Raima. *We've given you so much. We pay down your debts, we feed you, we house you, and protect you from pimps and thugs who would only hurt you and sell your body* . . .

But Genoquip profited from her body too, just in a different way.

"Yes," she agreed quietly. "I'll go to the other facility."

The technician withdrew from her, clapping his hands together in a loud noise that made Raima flinch. "Excellent! I'll arrange for you to have some cake in celebration at your evening meal. What's your favorite kind?"

Raima remembered the brothel, the way the men used gifts and miniscule acts of kindness that created frenzies of jealousy and love in the girls. Cheap plastic necklaces and other jewelry, chocolate snacks, ice cream, new shoes—that was how they bought the undeserved love and adoration of their enslaved girls. Genoquip's method was cake at Raima's dinner meal and real eggs once a week.

Caution made Raima's answer come out in a quiet, shy tone. "I'd like carrot cake."

"Then carrot cake it will be," he said and smiled.

Raima read a thin but real warmth in his smile, in his eyes, but it was tainted with a darker emotion. In a john's gaze Raima would have seen lust and violence, but in the technician's, it was something else.

As the female technician led Raima back to her room, through the cold, sterile maze of hallways Raima considered that smile, troubled by it. Just as the technician brought Raima to her cell door, she realized what she'd seen in his eyes.

Pity.

Though Raima tried to help and comfort Kim through the first two weeks of her injections, which produced the worst of her illness, she couldn't relate to her. Kim's only concern was for her brother,

Kaiden. Her questions about him were endless. Where was he? Why hadn't she seen him? Had he already died? The few times Kim was strong enough to join Raima in the cafeteria she spent more time searching the faces of the boys than eating, but Kaiden was never among them. Though Raima suggested that Kaiden may be too sick to come to the cafeteria, or perhaps his mealtimes were offset from theirs, she knew those answers didn't satisfy Kim.

Before the technician took Raima for testing on Sol Martius, Tuesday afternoon, Kim came down with an incapacitating headache that kept her bedridden for the rest of the day. She was in the final week of her injections, when each shot went into the tender skin of the neck. Now, just after lights-out, Kim recovered from the headache, but new symptoms appeared. She lay in her cot, shifting uncomfortably, unable to sleep.

Raima stared across the dark space of their little room at Kim's fidgeting form. "Is it really that bad?" she asked.

"I can't scratch any of my itches," Kim replied, groaning with frustration. "It's like they're inside of me. I'm ready to rip off my skin and scratch my bones."

Raima sighed. "It wasn't that bad for me."

"Yeah?" Kim muttered. "Well, they like you. They don't like me. They probably gave me the kill shot and I'll be dead tomorrow morning."

The resentment in Kim's voice made Raima bristle. She recalled her own illness with the shots, the physical pain and uncertainty of what was happening to her and tried to summon sympathy for Kim's suffering. But she knew she hadn't complained as much, and she'd never vocalized her distrust of another person or Genoquip. With an effort Raima kept her reply dispassionate. "I'm no different from anyone else here. The tests, the shots, they're all the same."

Kim hauled herself up to a near sitting position, supporting her head with one hand. Raima almost felt her roommate's irritable gaze. "If they cared about us at all they wouldn't put us in a place like this," she said.

Kim lived in a world where this was the worst misery she could imagine, a prison that stripped her of all rights, but Raima couldn't stop appreciating the luxury of a full belly, and of captors who touched her gently. "This isn't a bad place," she said, biting back a harsher rebuke.

RACHAEL ROBIE

Kim moved again on her cot, making the bedframe squeak. "Do you know the nurse guy? Terry? Was he the one who gave you your shots too?" Kim asked.

"Yes," Raima murmured. "Of course. Terry covers a quarter of the girls' wing."

"Yeah, well, he told me they kill people who don't work with them."

A thick silence descended over the girls. Raima resisted the desire to say, *"You're lying."* She tried something subtler. "Terry told you that?" she asked.

"Yeah, when I got mad and asked about my brother, I mean, if he—if they . . ."

"Listen to me," Raima said with an authority and power that startled them both with its unexpectedness. She sat up and faced Kim, letting her resentment and irritation show in her face, certain that the gloom of their room hid it. "There's nothing you can do for your brother." She paused for a second and then asked, "Do you want to survive? Are you willing to do it by doing nothing? By smiling at the people who hurt you?"

Kim reacted with the stubborn, righteous, moral outrage that Raima expected. "Of course, I want to survive! But what they're doing to us is criminal. It's against the law! Someone has to know, to find out and stop it."

"None of that matters," Raima said, her breath hissing. "You said they like me, but—"

"Yeah, they like you! You got cake the other sol with your dinner. No one else got cake!"

Rage exploded in Raima as she leaned forward to see Kim's eyes glittering through the dark.

"I didn't ask for *cake*," she said, spitting the last word with disgust. "It was given to me because I'm obedient. It was a reward. A stupid, meaningless little treat to make me feel like I'm better than you, and to make *you* and everyone else who saw that cake jealous of me. It's to make foolish girls like you try to earn your own cake."

Kim said nothing for several seconds. Finally, she said, "All right, since you know so damn much about this place, how do I survive and get out of here with Kaiden when I turn eighteen?"

"Be obedient," Raima replied. "Do everything they ask and more if you can. Don't talk back. Don't complain. Then things will start to happen for you. They'll grant your wishes in the Wishing Program. They gave me picture books of Earth and India. I've heard others say they got music or movies sometimes. I'm sure they'd give you time with your brother. It's a cheap bribe."

Kim scoffed. "You have a funny way of seeing things. Just go along with whatever they want, right? Just grin and bear it."

Raima snapped, "If you want to survive this place, that's what you have to do." She stopped and sighed. "Soon you're not going to have me here to help you."

"What do you mean?" Kim asked, sitting up.

"I'm being transferred to a different Genoquip facility," Raima said.

"Why are you going?" Kim asked, her voice taking on a sharp note of distress.

The concern made Raima's hostility cool. Even a smidgen of gratitude for her effort defused the negative emotions inside Raima. "It's another program, a different facility called TC-Gen. I don't know anything beyond that. I'm going there because it pays better, and I have huge debts. I don't know if I'll do well there, but I didn't have much choice in it. In five years I might be free and, like you said, they like me."

"I'm sorry I said that," Kim murmured. The apology sounded genuine.

Driving her point home even further, Raima said, "But it's true. They like anyone who's obedient. You'll do well if you remember that."

"I don't want you to go," Kim blurted. "You're the only person I know here."

Raima let out a small, dry laugh. "You don't know me," she said. "You're better off not knowing. It would just make you feel bad."

"What's that supposed to mean?" Kim asked.

Raima let out a long, quiet breath. Just the idea of sharing the secrets of her past left her exhausted. "If I see you again maybe I'll tell you, but don't worry about it now, just go to sleep."

Raima settled back into her bed, ignoring Kim's protest. She fell asleep quickly, managing to ignore Kim's constant scratching long enough that unconsciousness closed over her.

In the morning Raima awoke before the alarm. She left Kim sleeping in her cot and tiptoed to the bathroom to wash up, careful not to wake her. As Raima left the bathroom, wiping the last bit of toothpaste foam from her mouth, she pulled up, surprised to see Kim awake. Kim smiled at her. Raima felt like their strange chat from the night before fostered the beginnings of a bond that Raima's previous reassurances hadn't been able to do. A small satisfaction started inside Raima that maybe she could help Kim after all. She returned Kim's smile, the action feeling unfamiliar on her lips.

She sat on her bed, waiting for Terry to come and let them out of their room. "You remember what I said?" Raima asked.

"Be obedient," Kim answered, and then, as Raima nodded with approval, she added, "Why are you here?"

Raima's lips quivered. "I'm here because I'm lucky."

The door opened with a whoosh of air that sent Raima's heart thumping for a moment as Terry strolled in. He was smiling, but the expression didn't reach his eyes at all. "Ready for this sol's shot, Kimberly?" he asked.

Raima watched Kim, noticing the way the other girl's pink lips twitched with the start of a frown, but then went slack, abandoning the expression. Her gaze slid to Raima for a moment as she said, "Yeah, I'm ready."

Terry escorted Kim out of the room, leaving the door open for Raima to go to breakfast at her leisure. Alone, Raima leaned back against the wall and wrapped her arms around herself. Relief eroded the protective, numb shell that had sustained her for years. Kim would be obedient. She'd survive whether Raima was there safeguarding her or not.

SIX

On the last day of Kim's injections, a nurse intercepted Raima before she'd returned to her cell after breakfast and told her to start packing.

"You're being transferred by rover this morning. Take everything you want to keep. The rest will be thrown away," she said. "I'll be back in an hour to escort you to the rover."

Inside her cell, Raima gathered her things from the small bookshelf, loading them into her brown carrying bag. She'd arrived with it, a gift from the hospital staff that had spent so many long months treating her HIV. During her time at the Genoquip facility Raima hadn't accumulated much else to add to it. There were the picture books of India and Earth, gifts from Qi, but otherwise nothing else.

Raima had no pictures of her mother or other family members. When she first arrived on Mars with her mother they carried all their belongings in four tightly packed bags. Everything else was left behind, put into storage on Earth, sold, or thrown away. One of the things they kept was an electronic picture frame that held thousands of images, sorted into albums by year, event, or person. Raima remembered looking at the frame, scrolling through pictures of her grandparents, her deceased father, aunts and uncles, and a few close cousins. Her memories of those people and their faces blurred over time, obscured by her horror, fear, and pain after being trapped in the brothel for so long.

Ferde took their bags and kept or sold everything inside, even the picture frame. Of all the things Raima lost, she missed the frame the most. She longed to see an image of her mother again, smiling happily in some other life where she was a confident, smart, and courageous Indian feminist. Raima's parents never married to legitimize their relationship and their beloved daughter, a fact that had horrified both sets of grandparents. Raima barely recalled her father at all. She was very young when he'd been struck by a reckless driver on a busy city street.

Raima held her bag on her lap and waited patiently, turning her thoughts to Kim. When Kim returned to their cell after breakfast a few days previously she'd been ecstatic, telling Raima that Kaiden was alive. She finally saw him in the cafeteria, weak and ashen with illness, but alive. Since then, during their mealtimes Kim left Raima to sit with him. It hurt Raima, surprisingly, that Kim no longer sat with her, but she was pleased that Kim was happy and had found her brother. She hadn't realized how lonely she'd been since Qi left, how colorless her life was without a friend, without human contact that didn't involve tests, needles, and one-way mirrors.

The door opened suddenly, startling Raima and setting her heart pounding. Relief swept through her a fraction of a second later as she realized it was only Kim. She'd have a chance to say goodbye. She smiled wanly, seeing the grin on Kim's face. "You saw Kaiden."

"I did." Kim hurried to her cot and sat on it, leaning forward with her elbows on her knees. "He says GQ is doing the same experiment with the boys. He says he can already hear things talk to him, like you said he would. He's an Intuiter."

Raima smiled but said nothing.

"What's going on?" Kim asked, pulling back with a frown. She noticed Raima's unusual posture and the brown bag that read *Elysia City Community Hospital*.

Raima stroked the bag on her lap like a cat. "I'm leaving. They're transferring me today."

"Today?" Kim asked. "This sol?"

Raima nodded and fought to keep the smile on her face from wavering. "It's a good thing. I'll pay down my debts twice as fast over there."

"If they're paying that much more then you know it's going to be twice as bad," Kim muttered. "You should refuse to go. They can't make you, right?"

"They can," Raima said, sighing. "I signed some paperwork." She let the smile die on her lips and looked at the door, unable to hold Kim's gaze. "I have a lot of debts I need to pay down."

She shrugged, forcing a small, mirthless laugh from her lips. "Besides, I wouldn't know what to do with myself if I wasn't in a place like this. I've never had to manage money, I've never lived on my own." She found with a jolt that her eyes burned with unshed tears and her voice had started shaking. "No one would hire me. I don't have any skills or talents. I can't even cook." She stopped herself before she said anymore and broke down completely.

"You'd learn," Kim said. "Just like I would. Just like anyone here would."

"No," Raima said, glaring now at her roommate. "Half of them would end up back here, or selling drugs, working in brothels. Dead." She saw Kim tense, opening her mouth to disagree and Raima waved her hand in a motion for silence. "Never mind. Forget I said anything."

Kim was silent for a few moments, staring at Raima with close concentration and narrowed eyes. Raima waited, knowing she couldn't avoid whatever questions her words stirred in Kim, but she *did* know she wouldn't answer it properly.

"You can't know that," Kim said finally. "Why would you even say it? Do you *want* to be here? Do you *want* to be their slave?"

"The only thing I want is to survive," Raima replied coolly. "As for everything else—I don't have a choice. Neither do you."

Kim thumped her shoulders against the wall behind her. "God, you're depressing. What did you do to have so much debt?"

Raima shook her head. "It doesn't matter. I don't want to say goodbye to you like this, talking about depressing things." She pulled the bag higher in her lap, holding it close and cradling it. "I'm glad you've found your brother."

Kim laughed. "What am I supposed to do without you, huh? You know so much more than I do."

"You'll learn," Raima told her. "When you get out of here, you'll have a big paycheck waiting for you."

"I guess that makes me a paid slave," Kim grumbled. "Are you sure you have to go?"

"Yes," Raima replied and shrugged. The cold comfort of

numbness closed around her. Before she could speak again a mechanical sigh from their cell door announced the arrival of her escort and the end of her time at CF-Gen.

The nurse who told Raima to pack earlier stood just outside their room, waiting with a professional smile. "Time to head out, Raima," she said. "Have you got everything?"

"Yes." Raima stood, stiff and tense with unnamed emotions. They were foreign, unwelcome—and useless. Kim's anguish distracted Raima from the constant pain of her own buried past, but it also allowed self-pity and bitterness to creep in. Just like Kati, Kim made Raima stronger, but more vulnerable at the same time.

She felt Kim's eyes on her as she walked to the door. A few more steps and she'd be cut off once more from caring about what happened to another human being. She anticipated the relief with each step.

Kim shot to her feet behind her and cried out, "Wait!"

Before Raima could speak, Kim threw her arms around Raima's waist. The motion made Raima gasp with surprise at the unexpected contact. Raima didn't return the hug. She couldn't. She thought of Kati, bruised and bleeding, pleading for her help. She thought of her mother, holding her in the dark, stroking her hair. Now Kim, clinging to her as she left.

"We have to go," the nurse called.

As they broke the embrace Raima stepped back, putting distance between them. But she hesitated. It would have been so easy to spin on her heels and march out of the room, pushing Kim and her resemblance to Kati—and all the memories that dredged up—away. Instead, she opened her brown bag and dug through it. She found the stained teddy bear and held it out to Kim. "I—I want you to keep this."

Kim accepted the gift, a sad little smile on her downcast face.

"It belonged to someone I cared about," Raima said.

"Thanks," Kim said, turning the bear over in her hands. "Thank you for everything."

Raima shifted on her feet, feeling awkward and uncomfortable at Kim's gratitude.

"Raima," the nurse called again. "We need to go. The rover driver's waiting. TC-Gen has a schedule to keep."

Raima finally moved for the exit, refusing to look back as the nurse closed the door behind her and locked it. The nurse escorted her to a series of stairs that led up to a large airlock. Inside it, the nurse helped Raima into a spacesuit and then checked each individual seal on the joints before putting the helmet on and starting the flow of internal air.

The suit was bulky and heavy, the fingers inflexible. The nurse helped Raima pick up her small brown tote bag, then checked the seals a final time. She used hand signals to communicate, thumbs up for a good seal, a sideways slash of the hand to indicate uncertainty. To speak to Raima the nurse pressed her head close to the helmet and shouted questions or instructions.

"The rover's right outside and ready to go," she said. "I'm going to turn on the airlock. When the light changes to red you'll be in a vacuum. I want you to wait for thirty seconds to see if your suit is functioning properly, got that?"

Raima motioned with her hand, thumbs up. *Yes.*

"If your suit says there's something wrong, signal me or press the abort button over there." She pointed behind Raima to a large, flat, red button. It was labeled *ABORT* in English and Mandarin. The Mandarin characters stirred up a heavy feeling inside Raima, recalling Qi. She wondered how the word sounded in Mandarin.

The nurse yelled again, pulling her back to the present. "That will cycle oxygen back into the airlock. Do you understand?"

Raima again offered the thumbs up signal.

"If you have a problem outside of the airlock, use your suit's radio to call the driver. He's got his suit on and will come help you as fast as he can. Do you have any questions?"

Raima almost mistakenly gave the nurse thumbs up, but before she could finish the gesture she unclenched her hand, flattening it, and made the sideways slash. *No.*

"Good!" the nurse said, shouting, and withdrew quickly through the airlock, back into the Genoquip facility.

A moment later the room filled with a harsh sucking sound as the air emptied, leaving Raima alone in the soundlessness of vacuum. She had only walked in a spacesuit a handful of times in her life and it frightened her. While the airlock was pressurized she could still hear sounds—air filters and a faint electric hum—

through the suit's thick insulation. But once the air cycled out, leaving her in total vacuum, all noise ceased. Only her breathing and her heartbeat could be heard. She saw the nurse on the other side of the airlock staring at her through a glass porthole in the door. The nurse's face reminded her to check her suit for leaks or any other problems in functionality.

There were displays on the forearms, bright and touch-responsive. Raima reviewed them, flicking through screens, searching for anything amiss. The suit had been made in the United States, so its displays were in English with Spanish subtitles that popped up beneath most of the options. Nothing flashed red or showed any cause for alarm. The counter that visibly measured how much usable air she had left said three hours' worth. That seemed more than enough to make it to the rover.

Without looking at the nurse again, Raima hobbled to the airlock in the bulky suit. She lifted her head at the exit door, looking through the porthole. Outside Raima saw the bare, red-brown dirt of Mars. The same color as dried blood. A few lights glowed on a wall a few meters away, lighting a space that reminded her of a garage, except that no one bothered to put down a layer of concrete to cover the dirt. She pressed a large button, slapping it with her palm, and the door lifted.

At once a small measure of sound returned. Mars wasn't a vacuum and although its atmosphere was far too thin to keep humans from dying without the protection of a suit, it wasn't as frightening as the soundlessness. She could hear the wind whistling and howling, just as it would during a storm on Earth. Dust motes glowed in the lights above her.

She set her bag down on the ground outside the building and grabbed the doorway with both hands before taking her first step away from CF-Gen. Her boot sank into the dirt and pebbles a few centimeters. The sound of her rapid breath competed with noise from the wind. She expected to feel the cold force of the wind buffeting her even through the protection of her suit, but nothing changed as she left the airlock's shelter. Another step forward stretched her arms to their limit, forcing her to let go of the airlock. She glanced right and saw the rover. Light poured from it, duller than she'd expected.

"You there, kid?" a man's voice squawked in her ear, startling Raima as it filled her helmet with sound.

She turned back to her bag and picked it up, clutching it close with one hand as she looked down at her forearm displays and tried activating the radio. Her suit was set to channel three, but Raima didn't know if that was the right one. She tried it anyway, clearing her throat and calling, "Yes. Can you hear me?"

"Loud and clear, kid. Shovel on the coal. We got a schedule to keep."

Moving faster now, Raima headed for the rover. She walked alongside it until she reached a narrow, round hatch outlined in bright, reflective red paint. It was another airlock.

She hesitated. "Is it safe to open it?" she asked into her radio. The only other time she'd been in a rover was when MIHO brought her to CF-Gen.

"Yeah," the driver replied. "Just turn the latch. That section of the rover is an auto-airlock. It's been watching you the whole time." He chuckled, a low rumble from his chest that reverberated in Raima's ears, making her cringe. Too many johns had laughed like that. For all Raima knew, this man had been one of them.

She turned the latch, opening the rover's airlock. There was a brief whistle as air rushed into the airlock, but no alarms sounded. Raima ducked, slipping through the narrow, round hole of the airlock. Crawling awkwardly in the oversized suit, she managed to get inside without too much trouble. Lights flickered on. Raima found herself staring at a large screen with bright red lettering. It was instructions, in English, telling her how to close the airlock and cycle in a new, breathable atmosphere. Raima followed the orders, turning and kneeling to pull the hatch closed. The computer did the rest of the work, making the hatch jump in her hands as it tightened automatically.

When Raima looked at the screen again it asked, *"Is the hatch closed? Yes? No?"* Below the text another message flashed, telling Raima to touch the answer. She reached out and tapped the *yes* option.

A second later the small cabin roared with air. It ended just as suddenly as it came on. The computer screen displayed a green checkmark and assured her the atmosphere was safe and breathable.

Raima opened the hatch leading to the passenger compartment, ducking carefully through it. She almost forgot to close the hatch behind her as she went, dimly recalling safety regulations that her mother drilled into her before they came to Mars, and then again by her MIHO agent, who'd been appalled at her lack of knowledge. In the brothel Raima didn't need to know the safety protocols with spacesuits, hatches, airlocks, or even the difference between vacuum and Martian atmosphere. She thought, with the uncomplicated, uneducated simplicity of a child, that she could survive for a short time in vacuum by holding her breath. Mars taught her quickly how wrong she'd been. Airlessness didn't kill you in vacuum or low atmosphere, the lack of pressure did. Mars ripped air from the lungs and boiled away blood.

Inside the passenger compartment she saw a small camera monitoring her. There were several seats, each with its own black harness to secure a passenger in place. The seats reclined, becoming places to sleep—a necessity on a rover trip because the journeys were often excruciatingly long. Above the seats were portholes, large and oval.

She sat and fastened the harness, then removed her helmet. She let out a long sigh. The rover had a sharp scent, a mixture of clean, new plastic and the metallic ozone of Martian dust. The helmet buzzed and chirped in her lap as the driver said something, but Raima blocked him out, closing her eyes.

She leaned her head back against the seat and let the rush of tears start. It had welled up inside for years, like magma in an underground chamber, ready to explode and destroy the pristine, tranquil world above. She didn't know what awaited her at TC-Gen, but she hoped—and would've prayed if she'd been able to convince herself it would do any good—that Qi was still alive. The anxious anticipation that formed in her stomach at the thought reminded her of the promise of food at the end of a shift in the brothel. For years that was her sole reward, the only thing she thought of more than escape and revenge. Now her toes squirmed in the confines of the suit, wondering whether Qi would really be at TC-Gen. Perhaps the technician lied to lure Raima into a more dangerous experiment. Would she be able to survive this one?

She tried to slip back into numbness and apathy, but her subconscious was an uncooperative storm of confused, stifled emotions.

The rover trundled over the dusty, frozen, desolate Martian landscape. The sun climbed to its peak while Raima stared out the portholes of the rover, trying to keep her mind as empty and barren as Mars itself.

SEVEN
TRACTUS CATENA:
GENOQUIP MEDICAL RESEARCH FACILITY (TC-GEN)

The TC-Gen facility was smaller than the other Genoquip outpost, but more care had gone into its décor, making it feel friendlier. Hallways and rooms, painted in blues and greens, sometimes had stenciled motifs running along the tops and bottoms of the walls. Yet, despite this homey touch, Raima noted thick-bodied guards patrolling some corridors. The nightsticks strapped to their thighs, secured in black holsters attached to their waists, made Raima's heart thump and her spine stiffen.

She followed a nurse who reeked of stale coffee. Her nametag read *Victoria*. She listed rules as she led Raima through the facility, showing her the location of bathrooms, the cafeteria, study hall, and a nurse's station. Boys and girls were separated most of the time, just as in Genoquip's CF-Gen facility. Victoria took Raima past the boys' bathrooms and the boys' hallway, which led to their bunkroom, where all of TC-Gen's male participants slept.

"At night the doors to both bunkrooms are locked," Victoria said and laughed. "We wouldn't want any nighttime lover boys trying to peep at the girls."

Raima tried to copy Victoria, laughing as if she found the idea innocent and unlikely. Instead she tensed, on the verge of shaking with the reminder of sex. She fought the impulse to ask the nurse how secure the locks on the bunkrooms were and instead asked, "How many other subjects are here?"

Victoria sniffed and gave a dry, rough cough. Her lips pinched together as she considered Raima's question. "We can handle up to fifty subjects," she replied. "But there's less than half that here right now. Mostly girls." She eyed Raima. "Girls respond to the treatment more completely than the boys do."

Raima sensed more to the nurse's explanation, something deeper and darker that longed to break free from Victoria. Perhaps it had something to do with the death rate of this facility. Did fewer girls die here? Or was it more? At CF-Gen the male-female ratio had been about equal. What was different about TC-Gen's experiment?

Before Victoria led her away, back down the girls' hallway toward their bunkroom, Raima paused a moment, staring down the boys' hall. It was painted a cheery yellow, with a white trim at the bottom and decorative suns stenciled at the top. It was childish and innocent. Raima never thought of boys and men that way. She turned her back on the colored walls, disturbed by them, and quickly returned to her place following Victoria.

The girls' hall was a dark blue with waves at the top trim and an occasional fish painted with bright colors along the middle or the bottom of the wall. It was late at TC-Gen, an hour past her normal bedtime. Victoria was careful as she swiped a keycard in the slot on the door. She opened it slowly, minimizing the noise. Turning to Raima she motioned her closer, and whispered, blowing coffee-scented breath at her with each word. "Go inside and take any empty bunk you want. Try not to wake the girls. There's a bathroom inside with a small nightlight next to it. Go."

She pushed Raima through the doorway and closed it behind her. Raima heard her swipe the keycard again, locking it with a faint clatter of metal gears. Inside the room Raima heard the slow breathing of other girls, whistling and snuffled, low and high. She picked out the scent of harsh chemical cleaners, disinfectants, and something frail and foul beneath it: the smell of human sickness and suffering. In the darkness she could see very little, but gradually the nightlight that the nurse mentioned stood out. It was a bright, beautiful blue, making Raima think of jewels or still water reflecting Earth's sky.

Other details of the bunkroom emerged as she adjusted to the dark. Raima stood between two bunks. More extended in front of her, arranged in rows. Raima moved gingerly to the end of the room, toward the bathroom and the nightlight marking it. The walls were dark, probably decorated the same way as the hall outside the bunkroom. Raima paused beside one of the beds closest to the bathroom and knelt, feeling over the mattress and covers with one hand.

The bed was unoccupied—but flashes of emotions and memory-images left by its previous owner made Raima gasp and drop her tote bag with a loud clatter. Doused in a fearful sweat, Raima heard the groan of someone waking in one of the beds closer to the exit. She touched the sheets again with a jerky motion, but the intense sensations of seconds ago were muted. Frantic now, needing answers, Raima used both hands, fingers open and spread wide, palms making full contact with the mattress, the sheets—and then the pillow. . . .

The girl who slept in the bed before Raima's arrival was named Jia-li. Raima could see the girl's face reflected in mirrors, in snapshots of her over her lifetime. Jia-li was fourteen when she was rescued from a brothel in the Chinese settlement of Zui-Chu after being beaten so badly that she lost most of her teeth. Raima experienced the girl's memory of the blood, tasting it, feeling the intense pain in her jaw and gums, her face. She saw teeth in the girl's hands and shared her horror. Jia-li came into MIHO's care to pay down her debt to the hospital in Zui-Chu that nursed her back to health. Raima glimpsed the doctors and nurses, heard their chatter in Mandarin and felt Jia-li's melancholy and confusion, the familiar sadness of a survivor.

Then came Jia-li's memories of the facility. Her fear of needles, the screaming and tantrums she threw that brought out the TC-Gen nurses' anger. Raima felt the security guards' hands grip Jia-li, holding her down for each injection. First the shots went in the arm or the leg, or any muscle group, just like CF-Gen's injections. Then they became more horrific and bizarre.

The injections went into the neck for a few days and then there were exams where women held her down while a male doctor probed between Jia-li's legs. The man used a needle to dig deep into her flesh until Raima felt the tiny prick of the needle piercing her insides. She heard Jia-li's screams and knew they would soon be her own. Finally the injections went into the back of the head.

Hands held her down, pushing her head into a chilled metallic medical gurney as the needle drove into her skull.

Illness followed: intense fevers, exhaustion, confusion, and vomiting. Monstrous hallucinations sent Jia-li into constant panic attacks. People transformed, becoming beasts that growled and snarled instead of speaking. Reality slipped away, and her sanity soon followed. Memories and sensations dissolved into nothingness.

Raima pulled back from the bed, crying out. Her legs wobbled and gave way. She collapsed to the floor, breathing hard and fast. She groped within herself, seeking the protective coldness that sustained her through captivity, through adversity and the constant threat of pain, suffering, and death. Yet all she could find were Jia-li's hallucinations, her sensations as the needles buried themselves in her flesh, the base of her skull.

A warm touch landed on Raima's cheek and neck, sending a jolt of shock through her. She twisted around, searching the darkness, and saw nothing and no one, but the gentle touch of another person's hand hadn't left her skin. Raima reached up and brushed her fingers over her cheek and jaw line, trying to understand the strange feeling. The warmth of human contact changed then, fading *into* her head, into her mind.

A voice spoke, cutting through the silence. "Who are you?"

"I'm—I'm Raima," she answered in a hoarse voice. "I didn't mean to wake you."

"Don't talk," the voice said. "Just think. Not everyone's awake, but they will be if you keep making so much noise."

Raima frowned, baffled. "What do you mean don't talk? You're—"

"Shut up!" the voice scolded. "I'm not talking."

For a second Raima gawped at the air, unable to understand the speaker's meaning. She thought, *She's insane. She's like Jia-li.* Then she realized that there was something strange about the voice. Quiet and clear, crisp and fast, it lacked the natural throatiness of a sleeper's voice. It was as if Raima had imagined the voice and not physically heard it at all.

The voice came again and astounded Raima still more. "I'm not insane. And I'm not like Jia-li. She's dead."

"Who—what are you doing?" Raima asked, rising to her feet. She turned in a circle to pinpoint the source of the sound. That was another peculiarity. This voice wasn't directional, it couldn't be isolated because it was internal, originating right inside Raima's own head. *But that makes no sense. . . .*

"No," the voice said. "It makes perfect sense. You're right. Not as dumb as I thought you were, Indian girl."

Irritation flickered through Raima's mind, but she pushed it aside as finally she located a bunk in a far corner where a girl sat upright and motionless. It was too dark to tell if the girl was looking at Raima, but it seemed likely. Leaving her tote bag behind, Raima moved through the rows of bunk beds, taking each step in a slow, exploratory way, fording the darkness. Most of the girls still slept, their breath coming in little whistles and snores.

"That's close enough," the speaker said as Raima rounded the foot of the bunk at the end of the last row of beds along the wall. "That bed you're touching there hasn't been used in a long time. Maybe it won't bother you so much."

"How do you know that?" Raima asked in a harsh whisper.

"Shut up! Stop talking that way. I can hear you when you think. Just think what you want to say to me."

"How is that possible?" Raima asked. The idea of a mind reader wasn't foreign to her, but it belonged in the realm of fantasy and fiction, places within the human imagination that Raima hadn't spent much time discovering before her life became strictly about survival. Raima's mother scoffed at fortunetellers and magicians, embracing cold, logical science. Mind reading wasn't science, it wasn't reality. *"Everyone who claims to read minds, talk to the dead, or see the future is full of lies,"* Raima's mother said.

"I can't talk to ghosts, and I can't see the future," the girl said. Beneath her words Raima heard laughter. Impossible, but Raima heard both the words and the laughter at the same time. "But I've been reading people's minds for a long time now. You can read *things*," the girl went on. "I read *people.*"

Raima recalled the technician's description of the TC-Gen facility's experiment. He'd said it was a social project, Raima would be trained to read people the way she could currently read objects. Did that really mean reading minds?

"It's called *telepathy*," the girl corrected her.

Nausea bloomed inside her and she lurched on her feet, catching the mattress of the upper bunk next to her. "Stay out of my mind," she muttered.

"You'd better get used to it," the girl said, her voice heavy with scorn. "Until you can block us someone will always be inside your head, whether you know it or not. The techs want us to poke around inside your head too. But never let them know you're reading *their* minds!"

Raima stumbled backward, stunned. "I—I need to get some sleep."

"*Shhh!*" The girl hissed inside Raima's mind. "*Think what you want to say, don't actually say it!*"

Raima hurried across the bunkroom toward the nightlight and the bathroom. Once inside, she shut the door and flipped on the light. The bathroom was small but clean. The toilet lid was covered in fuzzy blue padding and the tub had a shower curtain decorated with a coral reef at the bottom, fish in the middle, and dolphins around the top. Raima set her bag down at her feet and turned on the cold water, letting it run into the sink. The gurgle from the drain filled the tiny space, but it stilled Raima's mind, calming her.

She lifted her head and gazed into a cheap mirror with scratches around the edges where the reflective surface had flaked off. Her face was ashen with tones of gray and yellow. She drew deep breaths, struggling to dispel the shock of sensing Jia-li's terror and illness, as well as the stunning revelation that Genoquip was making mind readers—*telepaths*—at TC-Gen. They planned to turn Raima into one—if the experiment worked and *if* Raima survived it.

I will survive this place, she thought as her hands gripped the edges of the sink. She'd face thousands of needles and dozens of frightening experiments if it kept her belly full and ensured no one beat her or used her for sex. Did it matter what Genoquip did to her in those experiments? Staring into her own eyes in the mirror, Raima tried to convince herself that this experiment didn't scare her. She envisioned real eggs and bacon, the rich taste of milk that didn't come from powder. There'd be suffering ahead of her, but there'd be rewards too.

Her hands relaxed their grip on the sink, then she cupped them beneath the chilled water from the tap and took a sip. The cold weight slid down her throat. She shut off the water and the bathroom light, then picked up her bag again and ventured back into the bunkroom.

This time she walked with a slow, stiff stride, determined not to attract anyone's attention no matter what horrors she Inuited from the beds. She knelt beside the closest bed and felt over its surface. Distant memories reached out to her, but they were too vague to be clear. Raima pulled up the covers and touched the sheets and the pillow. Both were dead to her fingers, lacking any memories. She set her bag down beside the bed and slipped between the sheets and the covers, sighing as she closed her eyes.

Morning came long before Raima was ready to get up. Her body was heavy with fatigue when she hauled herself out of bed. She ignored the brief flickers of memory from the covers, stifling them so that they couldn't push out her true thoughts.

"Raima," a voice cried, croaking and hoarse with sleep.

She looked over, blinking, trying to clear her head. Closer to the door leading to the rest of the facility a girl climbed out of her bunk. For a moment Raima saw nothing familiar about her. The girl was rail-thin and had the stretched, lengthy body and limbs of the Martian physique. Her hair was short, unrestrained, and dark black.

Suddenly, Raima recognized Qi.

Raima left her bunk and went to greet her first roommate with a smile, but as Qi drew closer, alarm cleared the expression from her lips. The last time she'd seen Qi the girl was plump, not gaunt and skeletal. "Qi?" she asked, hiding her reaction to avoid offending the other girl. "What happened to you?"

Qi shrugged and Raima saw the bony protrusion of her collarbones and shoulders exposed by the motion. Like all the girls in the bunkroom, including Raima, Qi wore gray scrubs, the same color and type as at CF-Gen, but now the ugly, bland outfit hung around Qi like a tent. "The experiment disagreed with me," she said.

But her lips didn't move enough and didn't correlate with the words that Raima heard.

Raima scowled, blinking with concentration. Something was wrong. "I'm sorry, what did you say?"

Qi grinned. The gauntness of her face, once so round, now held deep hollows. Raima wanted to look away but restrained the urge. Qi spoke again and this time her lips and mouth matched the words Raima heard. "What they do here made me feel bad."

Then Raima heard Qi speak again, but this time her lips didn't move at all. *"I'm sorry to see you here. It's tough. I'll help you through it."*

Raima took a step backward and bumped into the bunk behind her. She shook her head, dizzied by the impossible mental barrage. "You . . . you can do it too? You can read my mind?"

Qi said a few words in Mandarin, incomprehensible to Raima, but a moment later a voiceless translation flowed into her head. *"Damn! I wanted to be the first one to tell you what this place does. You know at CF-Gen they made us into Intuiters?"*

Struggling to control her reaction, Raima nodded, meeting Qi's dark black-brown eyes.

Qi's thought-voice went on, speaking directly into Raima's brain with perfect pronunciation and impeccable grammar. The voice was Qi's, but it spoke as the girl could not, fluently, without a Mandarin accent. In fact, the more the voice spoke, the more it transformed, adopting an *Indian* accent, becoming an imitation of Raima's own thoughts, her own voice, yet maintaining Qi's distinctiveness.

"This place makes us into something new—if it doesn't kill you. Everyone who survives can read minds. Marie and Manon call it telepathy. They were the first ones. Everyone who can read minds has part of the twins inside them. That makes us all sisters. You understand?"

Raima shook her head. "I don't know anyone here, except you."

"You will. In time." Qi's smile fell while she projected her thoughts, but now it spread wide again. "Breakfast now," Qi said aloud in her Mandarin-accented English. She grabbed Raima's hand in her own and tugged her toward the door. "I show you everyone."

Qi pulled Raima down the row of bunk beds. The other girls had assembled in a sloppy formation in front of the door, waiting for it to be opened so they could begin their day. Raima took in their lean shapes, the exhaustion and weakness in their stances, the defeat in some of their stares. One girl appeared deathly ill. Lying in the bunk bed closest to the door and to the left, she was barely breathing and her skin was gray. One hand lay on the sheets, exposed where Raima could see it. Every bone and tendon in the girl's hand was visible, with only thin, brittle skin stretched over it, covering the skeleton beneath. To the side of the girl's bed, an IV stood, dripping fluids into her.

Raima wrenched her eyes away from the gruesome image of suffering as Qi gestured at the girls in line, introducing them. "This is Limei." She pointed to an Asian girl, clearly raised on Mars. Tall and pretty, when Limei smiled she revealed a mouth full of clean but crooked teeth. Limei wasn't as thin as Qi, but she possessed the same telepathic ability. Before Raima could greet the other girl, Limei spoke inside her mind. *"Hello Raima."*

"Yes, yes," Qi said, waving at Limei, dismissing her. "You talk more later." She tugged on Raima's arm, turning her slightly to see three other girls standing closer to the door. All three turned together, as if Qi had called out to them. They examined Raima with expressions varying between curiosity and distrust.

"Izzy," Qi said and a girl with a round, babyish face nodded in response. She was olive-skinned with astonishingly bright green eyes. She was Earth-raised, shorter than Raima, Qi, and Limei, dwarfed by many of the girls around her. Raima guessed Izzy was about fifteen.

Qi pointed next to a dark-skinned girl who had her black, frizzy hair in elaborate braids. "Tiana," she said. Tiana was nearly as tall as Limei, but when she smiled Raima saw that some of her upper front teeth were missing, only partway erupted from the gums. She might be the youngest of all the girls, perhaps not even a teen yet.

"Ella," Qi said, indicating the last girl in the threesome beside the door. The redheaded Ella's face was covered in freckles. Her eyes were a very pale blue.

"We've been here the longest," Ella said, gesturing between herself, Tiana, and Izzy.

"No," Tiana objected. "Marie and Manon have been here the longest."

Raima listened to them, overwhelmed by so many new names and faces. She looked between the four girls she'd just met and decided that none of them had been the one talking to her the night before. These four by the door were all in better health than Qi.

"That's Abby," Qi said telepathically and at the same time an image of the bedridden girl flashed through Raima's mind. She saw Abby awake and healthy, plump and energetic. She was pale

with curly black hair and deep brown eyes. But in a kaleidoscope of memory-images, Qi showed Raima the way Abby deteriorated, growing weaker and thinner, convulsing with seizures and tremors, and then becoming too sick to leave her bed. *"She came here three weeks ago,"* Qi explained. *"She'll probably be dead by tonight."*

Raima sensed Qi's feeling of inevitability, of muted sadness and horror. Then the mental presence left Raima alone. Somehow, Raima felt colder and frailer without Qi's mind. The more these girls touched her mind, the more Raima accepted and adjusted to it. They were friendly, not loud and invasive like the voice the previous night.

Qi pointed again, this time away from the door toward the right. In the gloomier corner, Raima saw more girls sitting on their bunks against the wall. "Marie and Manon," Qi said and then with a serious undertone added, "The twins."

Two girls sat together on the same lower bunk. As Qi had indicated, they appeared identical to one another and seemed unconcerned with Raima and Qi. One of the twins was braiding the other's straight brown hair, weaving the strands with competence and care. Though there was no evidence, she was certain that one of the twins was the first to touch her mind. She remembered the coldness of the thoughts and she read the same attitude in the twins now.

Next Qi pointed to a blonde lounging on the bed to the right of where the twins sat. "Aine," Qi said. The blonde whipped her head around to glare at them when she heard her name spoken. Raima saw the dark, recessed circles around Aine's eyes. In her mind she heard Qi say, *"She barely survived. She's been here about four weeks."*

"Sarai," Qi said, pointing to the bathroom where an Asian girl preened in front of the mirror, poking at her cheeks and running her fingers through her hair. *"She's lucky,"* Qi spoke with her thought-voice. *"She doesn't have much talent, but she barely got sick at all. And the doctor just did a pap smear on her when he examined her, not the needle through her . . ."* She broke off, reddening with embarrassment.

Raima remembered the memories she'd read from Jia-li's bed. Genoquip always had a reason for the painful things it did. What was their goal this time? She whispered, "Why would they do that to you?"

Qi frowned. She spoke in Mandarin aloud, but Raima barely heard the indecipherable words over the projected translation that sounded off in her brain. *"Marie and Manon said they read the answer out of someone's head, but it didn't make sense to any of us. It sounds like something from a textbook, something you'd learn in school if you were becoming a doctor. They did it because of the* Weismann barrier *and something about germs."*

Raima shook her head. "It doesn't make any sense to me either."

"They stopped it," Qi said aloud. "The needle exams." She shrugged. "Just paps now. You lucky you here now, not before."

"Maybe," Raima agreed, but she recalled the technician at CF-Gen, the man who'd called her lucky. *I've never been lucky before*, she thought and knew Qi had heard her when her old roommate grinned.

At the front of the room the door opened with a clacking sound as the lock disengaged. A new nurse, different from the one who'd led Raima around the night before, stood in the doorway and ushered the girls out. "Come on now, girls," she called. "Breakfast is served."

83

EIGHT

erde was in the hallway, talking in a low, calming voice. Raima rose from her bed, curious despite her throbbing head and body, and the oppressive smell of the mold growing on the walls of her cell. She leaned against her door, concentrating on the sound until she was sure he was far enough away that he wouldn't notice her peeking. She opened the door just enough to peer out into the dim hallway.

She saw Ferde's broad, squat back, wearing his usual black leather jacket. He'd stooped in a nonaggressive posture, lowering himself to be on someone else's level. The brothel had many girls of varying heights, but Ferde himself was short even for an Earth-raised man. Only one girl could be that short: Kati.

Fear swept over Raima. Would Kati expose her? Raima had helped the other girl, swindling johns and working harder than ever before to share her income with the little blonde. Kati only bedded a john when he took special interest in her and forced her back to one of the private rooms. Raima both resented the other girl and admired her for such stubbornness. Yet as much as it was brave, it was also stupid. Raima's patience and endurance weren't infinite. Selfishness and survival were linked inside the brothel. Their captors didn't want to see the girls work together or get along. Selfishness was key, anything else would be punished.

"Do you like it?" Ferde asked.

"Please," the girl whimpered. Raima recognized Kati's voice, confirming the worst. She held her breath, straining to hear the conversation better. "I don't want this. I want to go home. Please, let me . . ."

"Shhh . . ." Ferde shushed her in a tone Raima imagined fathers would use on frightened children who'd woken crying from nightmares. But in Raima and Kati's reality, waking was the nightmare.

"Please," Kati begged again and let out a little sob.

"Why you want to go home?" Ferde asked her. "You are doing so well here. Two hundred munits tonight. You're so pretty." He extended an arm, apparently touching Kati, but Raima couldn't see how or where his hands went on the young teen's body. "You would never lie to me, right, little pretty one?"

Kati made a tiny noise of terror. "No. Please don't . . ."

"The other putas, they tell me you make no money at all. Nada." His tone had changed from gentle father to breathy killer in an eye blink. "So, who gives you the money?"

"No," Kati cried. "No one. Please don't hurt me. Please . . ."

Ferde's arms moved rapidly. Raima heard the sharp slap of his hand on the girl's skin. She shrieked and cried, squirming so that Ferde's body jostled as he wrestled with her, keeping the girl contained in his grip.

Raima's hands were sweating where they held the door. She swallowed and ignored the panic spreading through her.

"I won't hurt you," Ferde promised with the soothing lies of a monster delighting in prolonging the torture of its prey. "I won't hurt you if you tell the truth. Who gives you money?"

"No one!" Kati screamed, desperate to convince him.

Ferde smacked her, harder this time. Kati didn't cry out like before, instead the blow seemed to have stunned her. Raima flinched when a white shape fell and rolled over the uneven earthen floor of the hallway, stopping a meter from her door. For a moment Raima was dumbfounded, unable to recognize the harmless shape. As Kati let out terrified cries, Raima realized the white thing was a teddy bear.

Ferde had given Kati a teddy bear, trying to buy her loyalty, enticing her to betray whoever shared money with her. Soft and pure with its bright white color, the teddy bear mocked life in the brothel where nothing was soft, comforting, or clean and pure.

"Who gives you money, puta?" Ferde demanded, shouting now. "Tell me or I kill you!"

"An angel from God," Kati yelled, her voice quavering and almost indecipherable with hysteria. "An angel! God's angel!"

Ferde laughed. "Raima gives it to you."

"Raima?" Kati asked, gulping the name.

Ferde twisted his head, looking over his shoulder at Raima's door. His dark eyes found her, and his lips spread in a malicious, triumphant snarl. He shoved the girl away from him with a jerk of his arms and lunged for Raima's door.

As Raima sprang backwards, already aware there was no escape from what was coming, she saw Ferde's foot crush the teddy bear, pressing it into the dirt. Before she could try pleading for mercy, his fist hit her in the side of the head.

Raima shot upright in her bed, screaming and swinging at the air with her arms, kicking the covers with her feet. Sweat doused her body, her head swam with dizziness. When her scalp prickled she let out another cry of surprise, swatting at the darkness until her hand smashed into the support beam of her bunk bed. She gasped and held it close to her, breathing through the sudden, sharp pain.

"Enough already," a voice called from the darkness. Raima recognized Sarai's accent in the two words and knew it was verbal, not mental speech.

"Sorry," Raima said. Her heart beat out a frantic pace and each inhalation was harsh and loud. Weakness crept into her limbs as the adrenaline released by the dream faded. Chills passed through her and she shivered, clenching her teeth to keep them from chattering.

"Fever," Qi's voice and mental touch came in her head. "Nightmares. Ignore Sarai. She had it so easy." There was a pause and Raima moaned as her stomach flip-flopped. After only a week at the TC-Gen facility she understood why the girls were all so thin. The shots caused constant queasiness that made eating unpleasant at best. When Raima did eat, the meal usually came right back up.

"Do you need me?" Qi asked.

Qi had asked this the previous night when Raima woke from another nightmare about the brothel. She turned down the offer, confused and embarrassed by the concern, aware that all the girls were walking through her mind, peering into her memories. They never mentioned the brothel, never asked about her past, but when she saw the looks they gave her, mixtures of wariness, revulsion, and pity, she realized they all knew. Everyone except Sarai, maybe.

What do you mean? Raima asked, thinking the question. She never needed anyone except her mother. She'd heard johns say they *needed* sex, and the association disgusted her.

Qi's laughter rang out inside Raima's mind. *"Not like that,"* she said. *"I should have explained. Sorry. We ask that when someone is suffering. Sometimes you need to feel someone next to you just to get back to sleep, just to survive. The twins have each other, that was how they survived."*

Marie and Manon were almost worshipped by the girls at TC-Gen. The boys didn't care or know the history of the facility the way the girls did because of the twins. On her first day Raima received the lecture telepathically from Qi. Marie and Manon were the first survivors of a long line of failed genetic experiments that eventually produced telepathy. As unwanted children, they'd been given up by their mother at birth and didn't even know their surname. The one thing their mother gave them was their names. MIHO turned them over to Genoquip when the girls were eight years old. They endured countless experiments, many of which were centered on the fact that they were twins. They were often separated for days or weeks at a time. Researchers would electrically shock one of them throughout the day, and sometimes at night too, while they interviewed the other twin to see if she knew what her sibling was going through. If the girl being interviewed could correctly identify what was happening to her sister and when, the test would stop, and the girls would be reunited.

To survive those tests the twins devised a secret language to encourage each other without the technicians and scientists understanding what they were saying. Eventually this secret language became the scientists' focus of interest. The girls were asked to translate their language, to develop it further, but they resisted, making up fake words to satisfy the scientists.

By the time they turned thirteen the tests became genetic. Both girls came close to dying from the illness the experiments caused, but their love for one another sustained them. When they were fourteen the tests succeeded. Both girls developed telepathy. After that the twins became guinea pigs in a very new and different way, as repositories for the telepathic gene. Everyone who survived the experiment at TC-Gen carried the same new genetic material.

Now, only a year later, Marie and Manon had witnessed countless deaths, especially in the beginning as the scientists struggled to find the right way to pass the telepathic gene to each new subject. The twins didn't hide what they knew from the girls who joined the experiment at TC-Gen, and the truth was terrifying. As many as one in three died before developing telepathy.

The bedridden girl named Abby died two days after Raima's arrival. The injections ended her life in a little over three weeks. Now Raima was going to be the subject of the same experiment, but she was determined to survive, and hoped her body was willing.

Qi's question about needing comfort hung in the darkness. Raima didn't answer. She wanted the contact but dreaded it too.

A moment later Raima heard bare feet padding through the dark. A faint shadow moved alongside her bunk and then a warm, bony body scooted beside her in the narrow bed and pulled her close. Qi pushed peaceful, sleepy sensations at Raima's mind.

"You'll feel better, I promise. Limei did the same thing for me when I went through this. Do you remember CF-Gen? Do you remember when I helped you in the shower? This is the same. There's no shame in it. Please, I want to help you."

"I don't want it," Raima muttered. Her voice was hoarse and dry.

"I know you don't," Qi said. The peaceful emotion continued flowing from her, inundating Raima's tension and melting it away. "But you need it. I saw some of your dream. You didn't deserve any of what happened to you."

Stay out of my head, Raima thought at her, frowning in the dark and trying to glare at Qi, but the other girl's face was indistinguishable.

"You want to suffer alone? Why? You think you'll feel better that way? We have no secrets here. We're all sisters now. You don't have to be alone."

Raima gave in. Fighting sapped strength she didn't have. Qi pressed tightly against her until the other girl's body heat stopped her chills. The narrow bed was awkward and uncomfortable, but the closeness of another human being who wanted to help rather than harm her, or use her, offered a reassuring calm that guided Raima into a deep, peaceful sleep.

From her first full day at TC-Gen Raima participated in the facility's tests. Between meals a nurse came to escort Raima and Sarai from the classroom where all the facility's subjects—including the boys—studied together. The testing room was small with a round table and four chairs. Unlike the other halls and rooms of the TC-Gen facility, the test space was unadorned and unpainted. The walls were porous concrete, gray and rough to the touch. There wasn't a one-way mirror in the room, but Raima noticed several cameras mounted in the corners.

Sarai sat in one of the chairs and Raima followed her example. The nurse, a woman with a strange name, Vieve, sat across from them with a tablet clutched between her wrinkled hands. She looked at Raima when she spoke. "I'm going to ask you some questions. Don't say the answers aloud, just think about them. Sarai will provide the answers if she can by reading your mind."

Raima clasped her hands together in her lap and nodded, biting her lip to keep herself from protesting the experiment. Beside her Sarai picked at her fingernails, not even bothering to feign interest. It didn't bother Sarai that she was sitting close enough that Raima felt the other girl's body heat. The idea of a stranger exploring Raima's thoughts and memories paralyzed her, but she knew she had no choice.

"What's your favorite color?" Vieve asked.

Images of greenery from Earth leapt into Raima's mind. Beside her Sarai answered without glancing up from her fingernails. "It's green."

Raima's hands squeezed together hard, making the muscles and tendons hurt. Her heart thumped in her ears as she stared straight ahead, unseeing. The next question came. She tried to keep her mind still, but it was impossible.

"What sort of music do you like?"

Snippets of pop songs in Chinese popped out of her memory. Sarai raised her head, finally looking at Raima with a grin. "Chinese pop," she said.

Heat flushed Raima's face. She drew in a deep breath, making an effort to control her reaction. This was a new type of humiliation, an invasion of the mind rather than the body. It would take time for her to accept the change. The rest of the interview played out in the same way, embarrassing Raima as Sarai took answers from her mind without any effort or consideration at all. Vieve stopped the experiment a few times to give Raima a break, but the minutes still felt like hours until finally the nurse brought them both back to the classroom.

The next day the same test began again, only this time Raima's partner was Aine, the aloof blonde. After that Vieve paired her with a curly, brown-haired boy named Dominic. He was younger than Raima and scrawny with illness but sitting beside him made the little testing room feel even more cramped. Raima broke into a sweat with every question, certain she could feel Dominic's mind touching her like the grubby, greedy hands of johns at the brothel. The boy gazed at her periodically, but he never touched her. His voice was timid when he answered Vieve's questions. After enduring the interview with Dominic Raima was paired with Bryson, an older boy with a Martian physique who leered at her throughout the interview. Others followed, a new person every day until Raima went through the test with every subject healthy enough to get out of bed.

Before the end of her first week at the facility, Raima realized Genoquip was using her to test the talents of the other subjects. She was a *tool* for the experiment, not one of its true subjects yet.

As far as Raima could tell the goal of the test was to see how effective each subject was at reading Raima's mind. Nurse Vieve praised Raima for her compliance and obedience, especially as Raima sickened under the facility's regimen of shots. Sometimes Raima's illness interrupted the tests while she vomited into a garbage can, but both the nurse and the subjects were patient with her.

On Raima's second week at the facility the tests changed. Vieve took Raima and a Chinese boy named Fai back to the interview room as expected, but then she explained that now Raima had to answer for the telepathic subject. After enduring hours of testing with the old procedure Raima was somewhat accustomed to it. She anticipated the worst as Vieve began the interview.

"What's your favorite color, Fai?"

The boy shifted in his chair, inching closer to Raima as he turned his gaze on her. In the same instant Raima heard a voice speak in her mind, youthful and with the same accent as Qi.

"*Gold*," he replied.

Raima flinched at the sound, then flushed with embarrassment. She'd adjusted to hearing the girls' telepathic voices in her head, but the boy's intrusion was new. She cleared her throat and her hands fidgeted in her lap while she struggled to find her voice. "He says it's gold," she murmured.

"Excellent job Fai—and you too, Raima," Vieve praised. She went on with many more questions that day and for the rest of the week, again pairing Raima with someone new each day.

The results of this test were different from the first. All the subjects could read answers from Raima, but Sarai and Ella of the girls, and Bryson, Baojia, Jayden, and Junren of the boys couldn't project answers to Raima.

Nurse Victoria said that girls had the best response to this experiment. Raima saw how true this was. There were only six boys at TC-Gen and *over half* of them couldn't project their thoughts into another's mind. Of the nine telepathic girls at the facility only two of them failed the projection test. The correlation was clear, even to a newcomer like Raima. Girls were the winners in this experiment.

Despite the constant nausea and vomiting, Raima endured her injections and the resulting illness without complaint. It left her exhausted, weak-limbed, and lightheaded, but every morning she got up for breakfast with the other girls. Qi stayed at her side, holding her up when she could hardly walk or keep her balance, pulling her hair back when she heaved into a toilet or garbage can or even a sink. She slept fitfully, waking often from nightmares, delirious and confused with fever and sweats.

At the end of Raima's second week at TC-Gen a new subject arrived, a girl of about fourteen named Jenny. Thin-limbed and tall, stretched to the limits by her Martian physique, Jenny already looked gaunt before the treatments. The girls, with Marie and Manon as their ringleaders, offered Jenny a guarded welcome and astounded her with their talent while Raima and Qi sat on a bunk together overlooking the scene from a distance.

"You were born on Mars," Marie said. "On Mina 27, Sol Veneris."

Jenny snorted, unimpressed with Marie's attempt to back up

her claims that she and the other girls could read her mind. "Quit playing. That's easy stuff. I don't buy it for a sec."

With a cold stare Manon said, "You were sent here because you stole from a clothing store and your parents didn't have the money to defend you in court. You're from Glacier City, Hellas Basin." The glint of amusement in her eyes made Raima turn away. She'd seen similar enjoyment from girls in the brothel, delighting in the humiliation of another.

Jenny's mouth hung open, her face flushed. "How do you know that . . . ?"

"They already told you," Izzy said, her voice brimming with exasperation. "We're telepaths. You'd better get used to it."

Qi blew a raspberry between her lips. Raima tensed at the noise but relaxed as she identified Qi as the source. "What is it?" she asked.

Qi gazed at her out of the corner of one eye. *"Jenny,"* she said telepathically then spoke the rest aloud. "Too weak."

Raima, shivering with her own weakness, tried and failed to smother the dark thought that passed through her mind, unwilling to let Qi hear it. *Is that what you said about me when I came?* She expected that Qi would react to her thought, but the other girl was watching the twins embarrass Jenny and seemed oblivious. Surprised by Qi's lapse, Raima tried again, imagining herself shouting at the other girl. *Qi!*

Blinking with a frown, Qi turned her head, flinging her short black hair about. "Raima?" she asked. "Did you . . . ?"

Raima felt Qi's mind now whenever the other girl probed her. Over her time at TC-Gen Raima learned to distinguish each girl's telepathic touch. Marie and Manon aloof and proud, Aine cold and quiet, Tiana exuberant and loud, Ella gentle and warm, and Izzy bright and sharp with a strong projected voice that rang like the melodic tone of a bell. Sarai and Limei were both friendly and simple, but Sarai was self-absorbed while Limei was outgoing and selfless. Of all the girls, however, Qi was the one Raima was most familiar with. The Chinese girl had a clever mind, always busy and exploring, and constantly supportive.

Now, Qi gazed at Raima with raw surprise, poking into her mind the way a nosy nurse would prod with stethoscopes, needles, and blood pressure cuffs. Raima scowled. She physically shied away from Qi, breaking eye contact and moving aside, but that didn't stop the disconcerting movement in her mind. She imagined pushing Qi from her head, closing the door on her—and Qi's touch faded, almost cut off completely.

Qi let out a small yelp and babbled in Mandarin, then in her accented English. "You block me. Raima—your mind works!"

Blocking Qi took enormous effort. Raima gave up, her head throbbing in time with her heartbeat. She gripped her temples and massaged the scalp through her thick black hair. She let out a moan, unable to share in Qi's joy, too weak to relish it as the triumph it was. Qi and many of the other girls said that developing the trait meant she'd survive the shots and would live to see the end of the experiment—whenever and *whatever* that was. No one ever left the facility after developing the talent. Marie and Manon were certain that Genoquip kept them for some other purpose, like a hidden treasure, a secret they'd unveil at the right time.

Qi embraced Raima, keeping her from sagging. She shouted to the other girls, announcing Raima's success. At once Raima felt the other girls' minds swamp her, pressing in on all sides. She clenched her teeth and yelled, "Stop it! Leave me alone!"

"*Sorry,*" Limei said. A multitude of other apologies echoed after her and Raima sensed their warm pride, welcoming her wordlessly into a strange new family of sisters united by survival and a freakish talent.

The new girl, Jenny, stared at the girls in the bunkroom around her, taking in their gauntness. The entire group probably struck her as insane. Just like Raima once did, Jenny must be thinking to herself: *I'm looking at my own future. . . .*

The next morning Raima walked with Jenny and both nurses to see Bailey, the technician who administered the shots. The medical aid station where Bailey worked was a room with a flimsy curtain stretched over the entrance that hid equipment and the small fridges where TC-Gen stored its injections. Two seats were arranged along one wall where Raima and Jenny sat. Bailey chatted with them while prepping and injecting the shot. The nurses who'd accompanied Jenny and Raima lingered nearby, tapping at their tablets or contributing to the conversation while they waited for Bailey to finish.

This morning marked the start of Raima's third week at TC-Gen and when they stepped inside the medical station she wasn't surprised to see the staff's tight expressions. She knew something unpleasant was about to happen. Fear seized her, making it impossible to move. She remained standing as Bailey knelt near the fridge, pulling out only one shot. Jenny took a seat, dragging her feet with exhaustion, unaware that something was wrong.

"Today we're going to take Raima to the doctor's office," Nurse Victoria said. She smiled, but it was pinched.

Raima nodded, ignoring the cold dread spreading through her limbs. The nurses led Raima out of the medical aid station. Bailey drew the curtain over the entrance with a rattle from its plastic rings. Raima refused to look back. The nurses took her only a few meters away to a room with a closed door that Raima had never paid any attention to before. Nurse Vieve unlocked it with a keycard and ushered Raima inside.

Though the nurses called the tiny room the doctor's office, Raima hadn't seen anyone other than nurses, techs, and security guards at TC-Gen. Except for a metal gurney the room was empty. Seeing its icy glimmer under the fluorescent lights made Raima's heart race. She wanted to flee but kept her mouth shut, her teeth clenched. The door closed behind her. Raima whipped around to stare at it like an animal realizing it was caught. Both nurses were in the room with her. Victoria stood near the door, like a guard, while Vieve did the talking.

"All right," Vieve said. "As soon as Bailey's finished with Jenny he's going to give you your shot, but it has to go into the back of your head now." She raised her hands, as if preparing to fend off blows or protests from Raima. "I know that's scary, but it's absolutely necessary. The medicine in the shots can't work properly otherwise."

"It'll only be like this for a few days," Victoria added.

Their demeanors made it clear that they expected Raima to resist, despite her continuous obedience with all the previous injections. Raima wrapped her arms around her thin waist, feeling the sharp protrusion of her ribs. She inhaled several times, calming her heart. "I understand."

"You are such a dear," Vieve said with a tender, apologetic tone. "It'll be over quickly—but we need to restrain you."

"I won't resist," Raima said. Her fingers gripped her scrubs, bunching them in her hand. The horror of Jia-li's memories swam through her mind again, along with flashbacks to the brothel, the way so many men had held her down.

"We know," Victoria said. "But it's standard procedure."

The door opened with a metallic click and Raima's heart leapt in her chest. She swallowed hard as Bailey stepped into the room. The injection was at his side, tucked just behind his leg and out of Raima's view. He smiled at the group, but there was no warmth in his eyes.

"Are we ready to do this, kiddo?" he asked. "The sooner we start, the sooner it's over."

Bailey had a Martian physique that made him look weak, but the thought of his hands pressing her down almost sent Raima into a panic attack. She looked to Vieve, sensing that she was the gentlest of these medical caretakers, the one most likely to sympathize with her. When she spoke, it sounded strangled. "Can you be the one to hold me down?"

"It will be me and Vicky," Vieve said. "Bailey needs you to be absolutely still."

Hot tears prickled Raima's eyes and she blinked, fighting them. "Okay."

The nurses took her arms and helped her onto the gurney. The cold touch of its metal intensified Raima's fear. She closed her eyes as the nurses pressed on her head and shoulders. Bailey's clothing swished slightly as he stepped forward.

The needle pierced her skin, then drove deeper in. Just before she cried out with the excrutiating pain Raima heard the dull crunch of the needle scratching against bone. She strained against the nurses, pleading with them to stop—and they released her. She shot upright, rocking the gurney, then swayed with dizziness. Hands touched her, murmuring encouragement, but Raima batted them away. The pain faded, but her terror remained.

For the next shot the nurses asked Raima to bite down on a gag, encouraging silence. Raima accepted it, but she didn't meet their eyes. The same hate she'd felt toward Ferde broiled in her gut. They'd described the opaque substance inside the shots as *medicine* in their explanation, but Raima knew it was poison.

After the second injection, Raima was too dizzy to walk and saw double. While the other subjects, even Jenny, went to lunch, Raima stayed in the bunkroom, trying not to move which only intensified the agony in her mind and body. Time passed strangely. She felt as though hours passed when only seconds ticked by, but after the lessons in the classroom, when the girls returned to the bunkroom, Raima found gaps in her consciousness as conversations leapt, changing topic jerkily. The lapses were terrifying but Raima was helpless, incapable of stopping them. The other girls touched her mind periodically, brushing against her the way her mother's fingertips caressed her when she was sick as a child, but they didn't interfere and didn't speak to her.

The nurses came and turned off the lights, locking the door to the girls' bunkroom behind them. Before leaving, Victoria knelt beside Raima's bunk and checked her vital signs. Raima's mind slipped in and out of awareness during the brief exam. She heard Victoria's questions, curt and professional, and heard herself answering them, but didn't understand what she was saying. Apparently, Victoria didn't either because she repeated the questions a second and third time before leaving. Just before the nurse left her bedside, Raima hallucinated her mother's presence, firm and real, as solid as Raima herself. Emotions overwhelmed her, and she moaned, reaching for her mother, eager to speak to her, but it was Victoria, asking her the same questions again. Angry and disturbed by her mother's disappearance, Raima slapped at the nurse and felt relief when Victoria left.

Sleep washed over her, but Raima shivered and sweated, chilled as if she slept bare-skinned on the surface of Mars itself. When she clutched at her covers and sheets, Raima saw they were filled with snow and ice. She heard and felt Qi's thought touch. *"Fever."* Then Raima entered a different dream world and terror swallowed her whole.

"If you talk to her more," Ferde said through clenched teeth, "I kill her. Understand?"

"Yes!" Raima shrieked, ready to say anything if it would send him away. Her body was afire with pain. Every muscle shook, quivering

with shock and fear. She swallowed the blood in her mouth, certain that Ferde knocked a few teeth loose in this beating. Blood stained her bed in streaks and splatters where she'd bled on it or gripped it with blood-soiled hands.

"Be good and I won't have to hurt you," Ferde said, shaking his head and rubbing at his knuckles, as if he was the one in great pain and anguish after beating her. "Be good and I buy you new clothes."

"Yes," Raima whimpered. "Yes, please." She hugged herself, hoping she wouldn't fall over or pass out. Her head throbbed. Concentrating was difficult. She cried, unable to stop the tears from flowing, but the draining moisture burned in her bleeding, inflamed nose. "I love you. I'm so sorry I made you do this. You're right." The words were hollow, nothing more than a conditioned response that the girls gave after a beating, but it sounded genuine, even on Raima's lips. Terror made all of Ferde's slaves into brilliant actresses.

"Don't you worry," Ferde told her, sweetness dripping from his voice. "Be good and I won't have to hurt you. You know how I hate doing it."

"I know," Raima replied. She swallowed and grimaced at the clotted blood and phlegm that slid down her throat. "I love you."

"I love you too," Ferde said. He reached into his leather jacket and produced a wad of tissues. He strode toward her and gently wiped at the blood running down her face from her nose and mouth. Raima accepted the tissues and began sopping up the blood as well. New tears swelled in her eyes, sprung from a confused mixture of gratitude and hate.

"You know better than to trust stupid putas," Ferde said. "They always get you in trouble."

"You're right," Raima agreed.

"Good. You get cleaned up for tonight. If someone ask what happen to you, what do you say?" he asked, narrowing his eyes. If she answered incorrectly it would earn her another slap or punch until she got it right.

Raima supplied the right response as fast and as loud as she could. "I fell down the stairs." Some patrons wouldn't like knowing that their chosen whore for the night was beaten only hours beforehand. Most of them preferred to believe Raima and the other girls worked at the brothel willingly.

"Good," Ferde repeated and finally left Raima, shutting the door behind him.

When Raima saw Kati in the showroom later she obeyed Ferde's *order and ignored the girl, refusing to even look at her. She felt Kati's eyes on her throughout the evening, pleading for Raima to acknowledge her. At the end of the night, as Raima moved through the private rooms, changing bedding and restocking supplies, Kati found her.*

Seeing the younger girl's face, unblemished though pale with stress, Raima wanted to hit her. Ferde was true to his word and hadn't hurt Kati, but perhaps he'd expended all his effort on punishing Raima, knocking two teeth from her mouth and loosening another in the brutal attack. Usually he restrained his fury, unwilling to damage his chattel for fear of scaring away his clients and their money with them.

"What are you doing here?" Raima demanded. "Get out." The new gaps in her teeth whistled and ached. Anger pulsed through her blood like poison. She turned back to the bed and ripped the sheets off it with a furious grunt. Most of the girls still had their teeth. Losing teeth marked Raima as one of the lowest prostitutes in the brothel. Men could beat her as they pleased without fear of repercussions from the brothel owners because Raima was tainted from the outset, already broken.

Kati closed the door to the private room behind her and rushed toward Raima. Tears fell from her pretty blue eyes. "Please don't be mad at me," she begged, falling down at Raima's feet. "I didn't tell him—"

Raima ripped her leg out of Kati's grasp, sneering down at her. "You did enough. He almost killed me!"

"Please don't be mad," Kati cried, sobbing. "You're my only friend here."

"No one has friends here," Raima snapped. "We're not friends."

"God sent you," Kati insisted. "You're an angel."

"Screw your God," Raima snarled and moved around the head of the bed for the pillows. She brought one up and sniffed it to determine if it needed washing, but her nose was too clogged with clotted blood to smell anything.

Kati's eyes widened with horror and disbelief. "Don't say that!"

Enraged and disgusted with the little blonde, Raima threw the pillow at Kati even though the motion caused a brief burst of agony. "Smell that and tell me if it's clean. I can't tell through this." She gestured at her swollen, distorted face and screamed inwardly at Kati: You did this to me.

"I'm—I'm sorry," Kati whimpered. "I just wanted to thank you for being my friend. For helping me."

99

"I can't help you anymore," Raima growled, slurring the words through both her accent and her useless nose. "You have to help yourself."

"I won't," Kati said, suddenly whispering. "I mean, I can't. I can't live in this place. I won't live like this."

Raima wanted to laugh aloud with the bitterness that boiled inside but she knew it would be too painful, not worth the suffering. Kati was new to the brothel, having only been there a few weeks. She was a slow learner. Raima decided she'd educate the naïve Earthling. "You think you can run away?" she asked. "You're an idiot. A moron. Do you know how long I've wanted to get out of here?" She strode back around the bed and dropped down onto her knees, shaking with the pain. She glared at Kati, breathing through her mouth. "I've been here for more than three years," she whispered, rasping. "You can't get away. If you try, Ferde will kill you. Do you want to die, or do you want to live?"

Kati had stopped crying. Her blue eyes were bright and alert as Raima had never seen them before. "Die," she said.

Raima froze, stunned. Long seconds passed before she grabbed Kati and shook her, asking, "Die?"

"I want to die," Kati repeated. "God is waiting for me. Jesus has saved me. If I die, I'll be in Heaven with them." Her voice was firm and strong though her chin wrinkled, trembling.

Anger made Raima cold. Confusion clouded her reaction, slowing it while she read Kati's expression. Speechless and dumbfounded, Raima shoved the other girl away from her and got to her feet. On the floor Kati gazed up at her, blinking away fresh tears.

"You stupid puta," Raima said, channeling Ferde. "Stupid whore. This is your life now. Stop dreaming nonsense about Heaven. You're never going to be anything but what you are now. Do what you want but I'm not going to help you anymore." She touched her face and added, "I'm not going to let this happen again—not for you, not for anyone."

Kati let out a choked sob.

"Cry all you want," Raima snapped. "It won't help you. No one cares about you. No one cares about any of us." She pointed in a violent gesture toward the private room's closed door. "Get out before you get me into trouble again. Get out!"

Kati jumped up, able-bodied and unhurt compared to Raima. She bolted for the door and opened it, then ran out into the showroom.

With bitter satisfaction Raima thought that the blonde looked like a rat scurrying away from a cat.

She probed her missing teeth with her tongue and remembered that if she died without punishing Ferde her life would be meaningless and wasted. The idea gave her strength and stilled her mind, letting the numbness close over her, fueling her with the strength to ignore the agony in her body and the growing self-loathing in her soul. And then, as Raima slipped the last silken case off the private room's pillow, an alarm blared overhead. Dread bloomed inside her, gaping wide as she knew with some impossible sixth sense that Kati had just found a way to end her life.

"No!" Raima shouted and dropped the pillow and its case on the floor. She ran for the door, hobbling with pain.

The door opened for Raima in the dream-memory, but in the showroom on the other side she saw the girls of the TC-Gen facility standing about, staring at her. She reeled back from them, baffled as past and present battled inside her brain. She touched her tongue to the spaces in her mouth that had been raw, empty, and oozing blood in the dream, but now her tongue met with teeth, smooth and hard and whole. Faint memories returned of sitting with her mouth propped open, an IV in her arm, dentists' faces with white masks over their mouths.

In front of Raima in the showroom Qi said, "You had replacement teeth surgically inserted, remember?"

"You have a perfect smile," Limei reminded her and smiled wide, showing her own teeth, which were crooked in her jaw. "Makes me jealous."

Raima started, coming partly awake. The showroom faded. She became aware of the other girls' minds deep within her own, filling the metaphysical space with chatter and emotion.

"Get out of here," Raima shouted at them. Lying in her bunk in the darkness of the TC-Gen facility, she heard herself moan loudly.

In the dreamscape Marie stepped forward, closing the metaphysical distance between them until she was less than a meter away, staring into Raima's eyes. "You have to let us help you or you'll end up just like your friend."

"You mean Kati?" Raima asked incredulously. "This is a dream," she said. "What's going on? Are you doing this?"

Marie cocked her head to one side. Behind her, among the other girls, Manon copied her twin sister. "You didn't kill her," Marie said, ignoring Raima's questions.

"I did kill her," Raima insisted. "What I said to her—I made her do it."

"You tried to help her," Izzy said in a quiet voice. "Ferde would have probably killed her if you hadn't shared your money with her."

"That doesn't matter," Raima said, shaking her head. "What I said after that—"

"You didn't mean it," Limei whispered. "You were scared and angry that she'd throw her life away after you suffered so much to help her."

"It's no excuse," Raima muttered, holding back the sobs that nearly escaped.

"No," Manon said and stepped closer to Raima, stopping beside her sister. The twins regarded Raima with identical expressions over their pretty faces, intense and stern. "You blame yourself for everything that's happened to you when none of it—*nothing*—is your fault." She motioned to Marie and added, "When Genoquip tortured us in their experiments we thought we didn't deserve anything better either. We didn't know that most girls our age don't live like this. But when they brought in Izzy, Ella, Tiana, and all the other girls who didn't make it through the shots, we read their minds and their memories."

Marie nodded and picked up where her sister left off. "You're just like us. You think you killed your friend Kati and caused your mother's death. You feel you deserved to die for everything you've done. You go back to it over and over. We see it in your mind every sol. We know it haunts you and you know what happened to you was wrong, but you haven't stopped hating yourself for it. You have to forgive yourself—"

"—and accept that you are blameless," Manon interrupted, seamlessly finishing Marie's sentence. "You have nothing to be sorry for and no one to hate except the people who imprisoned you."

"And the people who *still* imprison you," Marie whispered. "Who imprison all of us."

Raima recoiled, frowning with confusion. "We're not imprisoned. They pay us. I'm paying down my debts here."

"Have you ever seen a single coin of that?" Izzy demanded. "A single *munit*? Has anyone ever told you how much money you owe MIHO? How much do you earn here? How much did you earn before?"

"I don't know," Raima stammered.

Qi said, "My father used to get statements every month about his gambling debts. They told him how much farther he had to go, and how much he was making in community service. It was so little that he *sold* me to them, along with his debts."

"The world isn't supposed to work like that," Aine added.

Raima looked to the tall, lean girl with her blond hair and arresting blue eyes. "There's nothing we can do about it."

"That's what you tell yourself. That's what they want you to believe," Marie said.

Manon nodded. "Just like the brothel."

"This isn't the brothel!" Raima shouted back at them.

"No, it's not," Qi said, almost whispering. Raima shouldn't have heard the other girl; she was too far away. Yet Qi's voice was so clear that it was as if she spoke right in her ear, so close that Qi's lips might brush her skin. "This is not the brothel and you're not alone anymore. No one will hurt you for talking to one of us, or all of us. We'll be with you." She paused and then spoke with more force, "I will be with you."

Marie and Manon shifted, drawing Raima's attention abruptly to them. They stood in the showroom only a few meters away. Raima knew the scene wasn't real—her body was in bed; this scene was inside her mind, but she took a step back anyway. They spoke simultaneously, as one girl and one consciousness, divided into two separate bodies yet fused into a single mind. "But someday soon Genoquip will kill us. When the experiment is finished, and they've learned everything they can from us, they'll kill us."

"You can't know that," Raima said, appalled and horrified. The twins had just destroyed all her strategies for survival.

The twins shared a knowing glance with one another, exchanging some secret message or signal, and then Manon said, "We can read their minds. All of the girls here have read Dr. Yoon's mind just enough to know Genoquip doesn't want us to get out so that Earth knows about us. We're useless byproducts of the research. When they've got the right results, they'll kill us."

Overwhelmed and weak, Raima covered her face with her hands and felt the chill of tears on them. She longed to run from this confrontation and wake in Qi's real, physical embrace. If she could only shelter there in Qi's protection a little longer she might find the courage to face this next challenge. She'd be safe.

"How are we supposed to fight any of this?" she asked, unable to stop the sense of despair brimming within.

"Once you can read others' minds completely," Izzy said, "you must hide how much you know and what you can do. Pretend weakness. Pretend not to have figured out what they'll do with us. Follow Marie and Manon's orders and we'll survive this together."

"How can we survive if they're planning to kill us?" Raima asked.

Qi grinned. "We escape. The twins have a plan."

"Where will we go?" Raima asked. "And how?"

"We do have a plan," Manon said, and Marie nodded, backing her up silently. "When the time's right we'll tell you everything."

As Raima turned her gaze away from the twins and toward Qi instead. Izzy spoke up, startling her. "We'll tell you our plan when you've proved yourself and not any sooner than that." She turned her head, glaring across the dream space of Raima's memories in Qi's direction. Raima sensed the flow of complex emotions between them but couldn't make any sense of it.

The other girls' minds fell away, winking out like lights, until only Qi remained, lingering. The brothel's showroom, already shadowy and unclear, faded into blackness. She heard Qi's voice, felt her regret—and something else, darker and dangerous. Was it fear?

"I have to go," she said. "They don't want me talking to you yet. I promise I'll come back. You're not alone. Not anymore."

"Don't go," she cried and floundered, struggling to find Qi's consciousness within her own, but the girl had vanished, taking Raima's lucidity with her. Nightmares loomed, monsters roaming the labyrinth of her memories, and without Qi or the other girls to focus on, like lights on a dark path, Raima slipped back into the mire and quickly lost herself.

NINE

The shriveled sun had been up for an hour when Ferde finally retrieved Kati's body. Raima stood with the other girls, aching and exhausted after another long night. They watched and whispered as the airlock leading outside chirped, cycling the pressure to admit Ferde inside. The brothel had two airlocks. One served as the front door, admitting johns in from Elysia City. The other, located at the back of the brothel's showroom, exited the shelter of the domed city onto the airless surface of Mars. The second airlock was only used for removing garbage and other refuse that was too big to fit through the small, automated garbage airlock-chute. That was the airlock Ferde was in now, carrying Kati's corpse.

"She went down the garbage chute," one of the girls said, muttering somewhere behind Raima. "Stupid blonde."

Raima closed her eyes, no longer feeling the pain in her body or the throbbing places in her jaw where Ferde had knocked out her teeth. I did this, she thought and swallowed, feeling the bile rise in her throat. I drove her to do this.

As the airlock opened with a whoosh, Ferde stepped into view at the end of the hall, beyond all the private rooms. He wore a bulky, dark gray suit that'd been streaked rust red by the Martian dust. But then the girl to Raima's right gasped and stepped backward, a look of horror and repulsion twisting her features. Raima looked again at Ferde and realized the red streaks weren't dust.

It was blood. Kati's blood.

The bulky black bag in his arms, also streaked with freeze-dried blood, didn't jostle as he stepped forward the way Raima expected it would. Kati's body was inside, but it didn't move the way a body should. It reminded her of a baguette, only larger and in a black bag. Kati was frozen solid.

Raima pushed backward, bumping into the girls behind her. They grumbled and cursed under their breaths, but they let her go. A few others peeled away, looking pale and sickly. The rest stared with morbid curiosity, unable or unwilling to miss catching a glimpse of the horrible way Mars killed its victims.

Around the corner, out of view, Raima tried to keep herself from hyperventilating. Her heart hurt, aching the way her nose and her jaw did, but no tears came. The image of Kati's tear-streaked face, with the garish mascara running down from her eyes in black rivulets, stayed fixed in her mind. She heard Kati begging her again and resisted the impulsive desire to clasp her palms over her ears, to drown out the sound—though she knew it was in her head, not from outside.

"Sick," one of the girls said, her voice trembling.

Raima heard Ferde's heavy footsteps as he entered the showroom. A few of the other men who worked as bouncers or bartenders scurried behind him with a rapid tread. When Raima turned to watch she saw the other men lay down a large plastic tarp. It crinkled as Ferde stepped onto it and bent with a grunt to deposit the body bag.

As soon as he stood upright again, Ferde removed his helmet, breaking the seal with a hiss. He dropped it to the tarp beside his feet and said, "Stupid puta crawled three meters before she died."

A somber silence filled the room, like the tension before a thunderstorm. Everyone waited, not knowing what to do next. Raima sat on the nearest couch and covered her face with her hands, wishing she could be invisible. The pain in her chest refused to subside, the pressure building with no release. She couldn't cry, couldn't think, couldn't leave.

The sound of a zipper tore the silence apart and most of the girls gasped, losing their nerve. Raima heard their footsteps as they scattered, suddenly timid. Though Raima had her hands over her face she closed her eyes anyway, as if the added layer of protection would change the horror unfolding just a few meters across the room.

Meters, she thought, remembering what Ferde said. Kati had crawled away from the garbage pile outside. She'd suffered, awake and conscious, long enough to drag herself over the freezing, barren Martian dirt.

Committing suicide using the garbage airlock was nothing short of brilliant. It wasn't designed to handle humans, only garbage bags and other waste that Elysia City sanitation workers came by once a week to collect in a massive rover. All the workers wore thick, heavy suits to protect themselves from the cold and deadly effects of depressurization. The refuse airlock was only a small chute that led directly outside. None of the brothel's men could fit through it naked, let alone while wearing a bulky spacesuit. Kati barely passed through it. In fact, she was big enough that the alarm sounded, announcing a jam.

"Take a good look, putas," Ferde said in his snarling voice. "This is what I do to you if you try and run away." He hawked and spat, but Raima didn't see if he'd aimed it at Kati's body. The sound made her flinch. Her throat convulsed, and she swallowed involuntarily, making a tiny hiccupping noise.

"Where's Raima?" Ferde said. "Where is that little whore?"

Raima froze, her body going cold.

"She's over here on the couch," another girl said, betraying her without any hesitation.

Ferde's feet thumped over the showroom carpet, like an executioner's drumbeat, coming closer. Raima began begging before he'd even arrived, but she knew better than to uncover her face or her head. "I'm sorry— I'm so sorry. Please—I love you, I won't do it again. . . ."

Ferde's hard, rough hands grabbed her bicep, wrenching her up off the couch He glared into her face, his lips curling in a sneer. "Don't you want to see your friend?" he asked through gritted teeth. "You want to see what you did to her?"

She shook her head, cringing away from him. The tears came now, fear forcing the reaction that grief couldn't. "No, please, I didn't mean to—"

He pulled her with him, jerking her across the showroom by the arm, heading toward the tarp. Raima went limp in his hands, only moving her feet to keep them from dragging on the carpet. With each frenzied breath she thought she smelled the salty, iron musk of blood. The scent of death would drown her, sucking the life from her the way Mars had boiled away Kati's blood.

Ferde pushed her in front of him and held her by the shoulders over the body. "Look at this," he said, growling out the words. "Look what you did."

Raima stared at the body, her mouth clamped shut, willing herself to stop breathing. Kati's body was a vision of what Hell did to those desperate enough to escape it. The mass of disfigured, bloated, twisted flesh that sat in the body bag was unrecognizable as being human, and yet an hour ago this had been Kati, beautiful and vulnerable. Her clothing had burst in some spots, broken open by her expanding tissue. In other areas the clothing proved tougher than her flesh, squeezing so tightly that the skin, muscles, and fat burst out around it rather than be contained. Kati's body was stained with vital fluids of almost every color. The blood was frothy and thickened, sometimes even crusted as if it had dried over hours or days, not mere minutes.

Ferde's gloved hands left cold, brown-red smears on Raima's arms and shoulders. When he relaxed his grip Raima started to pull away, but he caught her by the hair, yanking her back. He turned her head around until he could growl into her ear, his breath hot and rank. "You see her, Raima?" He gave a swift jerk on Raima's long black hair. "You did it to her. You did it. You treat her like a baby. You made her too soft. You killed her."

His gloved hand moved to her throat, the cold, sticky moisture of Kati's blood making Raima cringe with horror. "Next time," he whispered in her ear, "this is you."

When he released her for good Raima fled, racing for the stairs, the burning ache in her chest changed into a broiling hate. Seeing Kati's body displayed as a cautionary tale sparked something inside her, burning away hope and humanity. Maybe Kati was right all along. Death was the only way out, the only solution. In the end everyone in the brothel was just meat, blood, and bones.

That included Ferde. A plan started to form in her mind, filling her with a purpose more grandiose than simple survival and escape.

She would kill Ferde to avenge Kati, her mother, and herself. It might cost her her life, but she'd find a way to punish him.

Raima snapped out of the dream when she felt Qi's body and her mind, her fingers playing tenderly along her jaw line and then down her collarbone and shoulder, tickling. "Don't worry," she said and Raima heard the Indian accent in the Chinese girl's words and knew that meant something, but she couldn't remember what. *Not really talking,* she thought but couldn't fathom it.

"I'm not really talking," Qi repeated. "Yes. You're not at the brothel. You're with me. You're with your sisters."

"My sisters?" Raima asked but frowned as she realized she hadn't spoken aloud. She could hear the words, loud and perfect, with a touch of a British accent. As a girl she'd always thought British accents were the prettiest ways to speak the otherwise ugly English language. Yet she'd never mastered it the way she wanted. Hindi always snuck into her pronunciations even though she'd been speaking English since childhood.

"We're watching over you," Qi whispered.

Raima felt the trueness of this. She sensed the other girls around her, caressing her, embracing her. Knowledge flowed into her from them, like sweet aromas from her old life on Earth, like water in deep riverbeds lined with greenery.

"Stay with us," Qi begged. "We need you. Don't get lost in your memories. You might never make it back out again."

Raima moaned with pain. Her head felt as if it would explode. Her lips moved with real sound, not the auditory hallucinations of before. "Please—make it stop. . . ."

"Fight," Qi pleaded. "Fight for me. Fight for all of us."

Raima began to slip back into the nightmare-reality of the brothel, but just as she saw Ferde leaning over her, his lips parted in a savage grin, the scene faded and changed. Now she saw metal walls around her in a narrow room. Books and clothes were scattered about the messy room. Signs and posters hung on the walls with magnets. They were unreadable to Raima because they were covered in Chinese characters.

"Where am I?" she asked, spinning around to take in the unfamiliar surroundings.

"This was my first boyfriend's room back in Zui-Chu. I was only fourteen when we had sex. It was fun, Raima. He didn't hurt me or make me do it. I wanted to do it. That's the way it's supposed to be," Qi said gently.

There was a bed in one corner of the narrow room and Raima saw two figures snuggled together beneath a thin duvet. She moved away from the bed, driven back with repulsion until she hit the opposite wall. "Qi," she called. "What are you doing?"

"Let me show you. Please, your nightmares will drive you toward death, just like Jia-li's did."

Then Raima was on the bed beside Qi, and in the dream, unable to move away from the other girl. In the dream she saw Qi's face in the dim light, younger and plumper. The Chinese girl kissed her lips and Raima tasted the spices of her last meal, felt the moist warmth of her mouth and lips, the softness of her breath. She sensed the tenderness of the other girl, not the demanding, expectant need of all the men she'd been forced to bed.

If she'd been healthy and conscious, Raima might have pushed Qi away, rejecting her, unable to consider anything sexual in a positive or tolerable way. But the fever made her delirious and vulnerable and though she was afraid, she felt instantly that this was different from all her other experiences. When Qi touched her body, caressing her with gentle fingers, Raima could feel and hear the other girl's thoughts. A man's touch would've been rough, enthralled by her anatomy because it was so different from his own. When Qi touched Raima she did it not to explore new and exciting anatomy, but to offer pleasure and comfort in a way a man never could.

Shaking with fever, confusion, and uncertainty, Raima whimpered as shudders of pleasure passed through her, small but powerful. She had never felt such sensations in the brothel, only pain and disgust. Qi surrounded her, embracing her physical body along with her mind. "Please don't be frightened. I only wanted to let you feel something good. I'm sorry. Don't be angry with me."

Raima wasn't angry. A thick lassitude suffused her limbs, dulling her consciousness. She relaxed into Qi's embrace, too weak to focus her mind on a reply. As sleep tugged on her, heavy and irresistible, Raima heard Qi and the other girls talking without words, telepathically conversing around her.

"*You'll scare her away from us,*" Manon scolded.

"*I'm sorry,*" Qi shot back. "*She's so terrified and so weak. I had to do something to help her.*"

"*Sarai needs more help than Raima,*" Limei said.

"*Sarai's already dead,*" Marie snapped. "*We all knew it was just a matter of time before they killed her. She's too weak telepathically.*"

"*She's not already dead!*" Limei protested.

"*How do you know Raima will help us? How do you even know she won't be too weak, just like Sarai?*" asked a new voice, one Raima had heard only a few times before. It was Aine.

"*She's already as strong as Sarai was and her treatment isn't quite done yet,*" Qi replied. "*She's going to make it.*"

"*But will she help us?*" Aine asked again. "*We'll need everyone's help if we're going to kill the—*"

"*She'll help,*" Qi shot back. "*Now shut up, she can hear us.*" As the girls went silent Raima's mind slipped away at last into a dreamless sleep.

TEN

aima remained aware of the other girls in the bunkroom, but their voices and minds were distant, far removed from her private delirium. The sickness disrupted her sense of time. Lights came on and then went off, the girls came and went. Whenever a nurse knelt at her bedside, probing her neck or wrist, pulling on her eyelid and shining a light Raima guessed another day had passed. She lacked the strength to pull away or moan when the nurse rolled her over during each visit and injected her in the back of the skull again. Her nightmares came and went as shadows of her violent past reclaimed her for hours at a time before one of the girls, usually Qi, drew her out of the terror. She didn't remember eating or drinking but woke once to see an IV hanging at her bedside and remembered Abby, the girl who'd died, with horror.

Then, though Raima didn't realize it, the injections ceased. She went a day without feeling the excruciating prick of the needle drilling into her skull, then two. Throughout it all her mind changed, gradually. During her delirium and fever, Raima didn't notice. Even so, she *used* her mind by accident. It was as easy as breathing, as effortless as thinking. She knew whenever a girl came and went from the bunkroom. She recognized each girl by her emotions and moods. The nurses became familiar too. Raima knew who they were the moment they entered the bunkroom to check on her or Jenny. She knew who they'd just seen in the boys' bunkroom. She knew which subject each nurse thought would live or die.

On the morning that Raima woke finally feeling lucid again Qi was squeezed into the bed beside her. Raima's body was grimy with sweat but she felt refreshed, stronger than she'd been since arriving at the facility. The room was dark but the girls in the bunkroom stirred, sniffling and shuffling about. Raima knew without words that it wasn't night. It was morning before the call for breakfast. The lights hadn't yet switched on to begin the day.

Ella was hungry, anxious to get to breakfast. Tiana was with her, sharing in her hunger, wondering if there was any sausage or bacon left so late in the week. Aine hadn't slept well and now lingered in her bunk, unwilling to leave and start the new day. Raima knew all of it without opening her eyes or hearing any of the girls speak aloud.

Raima slowly realized she knew these details because she could *hear* or *feel* the knowledge from the other girls. This was a sixth sense, as natural for her now as her own breathing and as expected as the sun rising and setting. She felt Qi beside her and knew the Chinese girl celebrated Raima's success and survival without words.

"Now your life starts," she whispered in her thick accent. *"Now the real lessons start,"* she added in her flawless English with the soundless voice of her mind.

For the first time, Raima projected her thoughts at Qi, focusing them as she stared at the other girl's face in her blurry vision. *"Thank you,"* she said, needing to offer her gratitude to Qi before new trials emerged that might make her forget the kindness she'd received. *"You kept me going."*

Qi smiled. Raima felt warm affection. She saw Qi's face and realized that the other girl was much prettier than she'd thought. Raima hadn't meant for Qi to overhear that, but she did anyway and wrinkled her nose with mock anger. *"I'm not pretty,"* she said. *"Not on the outside anyway. But outside doesn't matter anymore."* She raised her hand in the tiny space between their bodies on the narrow bed and put two fingers to Raima's chest, indicating her heart. *"This is what matters."*

"This is what matters," Raima repeated. How could she ever repay Qi's kindness? How could anything Raima did compare in the slightest? She wanted to be like Qi, but she didn't think it was

possible. She was tainted by her past, cold and calloused, like a scar over an old wound that had lost all sensation.

Qi's mood shifted suddenly and Raima met her gaze through the dark, seeing the glint of moisture. She swallowed as her heart fluttered with fear, wondering if Qi overheard her thoughts. "*What?*" she asked.

"*Some hard things are going to happen. Marie and Manon are going to talk to you about it. I wanted to be first though. I knew you'd trust me more than them right now.*" Qi's eyes closed, and she tucked her chin down, moving her forehead to rest against Raima's eyebrows and nose.

Before Raima could object or question her, Qi flooded her with images, emotions, and information. She saw Limei, Aine, and Ella's memories, felt their tears and their terror as men—strangers and family alike—betrayed them. She saw the shadow-shape of a man cornering Limei when she was only a little girl, and then heard a fourteen-year-old Ella fighting with a pushy boyfriend, repeating the same word over and over: *No, no, no.* She didn't need Qi to show her how it ended. Then there was Aine's experience at sixteen, her horror as she stared down at a positive pregnancy test, knowing that the father was her older brother and that she could no longer hide the truth from her mother.

"*This is what happens to girls like us even outside a brothel,*" Qi said. Raima felt the other girl's despair and anger and couldn't tell which emotions belonged to her and which were Qi's.

"*Why are you showing me this?*" Raima asked, shaking with fury that any of this had happened and that no one could do anything to change it.

"*You'll see soon,*" Qi told her.

"No," Raima shot back and pulled away from Qi physically to speak aloud. "Tell me now."

"*You won't understand now,*" Qi said. "*After today you'll see why.*"

In the bunkroom the lights switched on and an alarm buzzed, signaling breakfast time. Qi moved out of Raima's bunk, careful not to pull on any of the tubing, IV lines, and sensors the nurses had used to watch over Raima from a distance. Raima sat up in alarm, blinking against the light, cringing with pain. "Qi?" she called aloud.

"The nurse will be coming to unhook you," Qi told her. *"Stay in bed."*

Disgruntled but obedient nonetheless, Raima laid back down, exploring the spot on her arm where the IV was. She felt the curious mental touches of the other girls, probing her, then emoting happiness and warmth as they registered her strength and wakefulness. Two minds were absent, however. Raima saw the new arrival, Jenny, in a bunk along the far wall of the room. An IV was mounted beside her bed. Jenny mirrored the way Abby had looked the last time Raima saw her. Raima knew it would only be a few hours or another day before Jenny died too.

But where was Sarai? While Raima drifted in and out of consciousness something had happened in the bunkroom around her. When she'd first become ill and bedridden, there'd been eleven girls at TC-Gen, counting Raima herself. Now the number had dropped by one. Sarai was missing entirely. Though Raima hadn't known Sarai well, the absence alarmed her.

Two nurses arrived at the girls' bunkroom. Nurse Vieve led the girls to the small cafeteria where they ate. Nurse Victoria came to Raima's bedside. Her smile lit up her eyes when she saw Raima awake. Raima heard the nurse's thoughts tick by. *Heart rate slightly tachycardic at ninety bpm. Ninety-eight percent saturation on room air. Respiration at eighteen a minute—high normal. BP one-oh-five over sixty-three. Temperature ninety-eight point nine.* She checked the IV and other sensors, then began removing them. "Can you walk?" she asked.

"I think so," Raima murmured and coughed, clearing the phlegm of disuse from her voice.

Even before Raima was out of bed and on her feet, the nurse mentally moved on to Jenny, thinking how sad this latest death was going to be. Raima held onto the bunks as her knees wobbled, breathing hard with effort as she decided to use her new talent to discover what happened to Sarai. She reached out, probing at the nurse's brain. She found it was like looking into a precipice, dizzying and vast, filled with an ocean of memories, thoughts, concerns, and all the other various activities of the mind. She was lost in it, drowning in this other person's identity. She saw medical terms, names with Latin parts that muddled and confused her. She saw numbers that represented the woman's paycheck and felt emotions connected with it. She wasn't being paid enough to administer to so many dying boys and girls, innocents . . .

The nurse grunted and rubbed her eyes, swaying slightly on her feet. "Whoa," she said and chuckled. Then her mind jumped with alarm and she looked toward Raima with narrowed, suspicious eyes. "What are you doing?" she demanded.

Raima recalled the girls' warning: *don't let them know how much you can do.* She gripped the bunk again and made no effort to disguise her weakness. "I'm catching my breath. How long has it been since I was out of bed?"

The nurse's eyes didn't lose their suspicious gleam. Raima knew the answer to her own question several microseconds before Nurse Victoria spoke it aloud. "About four days."

"Wow," Raima mumbled. "No wonder I feel so terrible."

The suspicion softened, easing as the nurse saw a patient who hadn't died, who was going to live—for now. *Marie and Manon are right*, she realized and felt abruptly weaker, stumbling. Nurse Victoria reached out and steadied her. "You're one tough girl," the nurse reassured her and smiled. "Can you make it to the cafeteria on your own? Do you remember the way?"

"Yeah," Raima said. Her skin crawled where the nurse touched her. She was frantic to escape the room and return to the girls.

Although she remembered the way to the cafeteria, she could have found her way with her eyes closed thanks to her new talent.

The cafeteria was abuzz with voices and emotions, many of them soundless, unheard by the nurses, guards, and technicians of TC-Gen. As Raima entered the room Qi rushed to help her take a seat. Tiana brought a tray with dry cereal, juice, and some bread. For the first time in what seemed like months, Raima was ravenous at the sight of food. She ate everything quickly and slurped her drink while Tiana grinned at her.

"Getting better is the only good part," she said and laughed. Other girls concurred, some using their real voices and others with their minds, without even looking.

The boys, across the room at a different table, were also interested in Raima's recovery. Their minds brushed against hers, invading her most personal space. Her body and mind clenched at their foreign presence. Because she knew she could now, Raima tried pushing them out of her mind. Most of the boys fell away, accepting her refusal. Some were just incapable of challenging her blocking, but Bryson responded by probing deeper.

"*You think you're too good to talk to me?*" he demanded. His mind was like sandpaper against hers. "*I know all about you already. I read your mind back on your first day. You're a whore! A filthy, slutty whore.*"

Raima cringed, lifting her head to scan the other table where the boys sat. The last time Raima saw the boys there'd been seven of them, but now there were eight. She saw Bryson, who'd turned to glare at her with a sneer. He was one of the biggest boys—in fact, in his late teens, Raima couldn't really think of him as a *boy* any longer. In the brothel she'd seen younger johns than Bryson more than once.

Other minds jostled around Raima and working together they pushed Bryson away with the same effort as one might use to scare off a fly. "*He's an asshole,*" Izzy said in Raima's mind. "*You'll learn to ignore him. He isn't as strong as most of us, but he's tenacious.*"

"*I thought he couldn't project,*" Raima said, recalling the tests she'd done before becoming a telepath herself. Each subject at TC-Gen was rated according to their ability to read another's mind and project their thoughts to communicate.

"*He can't project,*" Ella explained. "*Not to a non-telepath anyway. But between telepaths projecting thoughts is easy.*" She grinned when Raima looked her way with astonishment. Like Bryson and most of the boys, Ella failed the projection test. Sarai had too. Raima had never heard Ella's telepathic voice before, the sweetness of her unsaid words.

Marie and Manon pressed into her mind next, making Raima cringe again for a moment. "*Before breakfast is over you must know a few code words,*" Marie said. "*Manon will prevent the boys from overhearing these words. They don't know our secret language. We don't trust them because of Bryson.*"

Raima turned her head and stared down the length of the girls' table where Marie and Manon sat across from one another. They watched their food trays, seemingly absorbed in them while the other girls conversed. Raima scooped more cereal into her mouth and chewed to maintain a semblance of normalcy.

"*Manon and I made up this language as children, so we could talk without anyone else understanding it. Don't speak it aloud. The scientists can't know anyone uses it but me and Manon,"* Marie explained. *"If they know all the girls are using it they'll get suspicious. Do you understand?"*

Raima restrained the urge to nod while she chewed and instead thought, *"Yes."*

"Good. This sol you'll only get a few words. They'll do the mind reading test on you again, but this time they'll make you read answers from the new boy." Before, Raima had been the one being read, now she would be one of the readers. *"Then they'll take you to an exam room and drug you before they ask questions. They think the drug makes you unable to read their minds. In the boys it works, in us it usually doesn't, but no matter what they ask or what they say, don't even reach for their minds. If you do, they'll know, and they'll find a drug that really does work. Don't fail us. If you trick them and know you can still read minds even with the drug, touch our minds after the test and say this word: ve. It means 'yes' in our secret language."*

"Ve," Raima thought back at Marie, focusing hard on the word. She brought another spoonful of cereal up to her mouth.

"In the next few sols they'll let a doctor examine you," Marie said. *"We don't know when that will happen. They'll drug you for it but unless they put sensors on you, don't bother pretending the drug works. Be cautious but read everything from him that you can. You'll see from the doctor what they're planning."*

Raima frowned and then covered the expression by shoveling more cereal into her mouth, though she hadn't yet swallowed the last spoonful. *"What other words do I need to know for today?"*

"Ve is enough," Marie said, *"but I'll share some others because you'll start overhearing the language a lot. This will help you learn more of it."* She passed on several more words, enunciating them with great care. *Ge* meant *no*, *kiten* meant *doctor*, and *mezenae* was the term the girls used to identify themselves as sisters, united by their captivity and their talent.

Just as Marie promised, after breakfast Nurse Vieve arrived and separated Raima and one of the boys from the rest of the group. As the nurse escorted them out of the cafeteria and away from the bunkrooms, Raima snuck quick glances at the boy accompanying her. His skinny arms and legs made him appear much older than he was. This boy's chest and shoulders were narrow, making her suspect he wasn't even a teenager yet. She didn't recognize him. He must have arrived while she was sick in bed. She knew that if she probed his mind she could discover anything she wanted about him—but the idea of touching his mind was as unappealing to her as holding his hand or catching a whiff of his morning breath.

Nurse Vieve brought them to the little interrogation room where Raima participated in tests before becoming a telepath. The boy took a seat without hesitation beside Raima at one end of the table, but he gazed at a distant corner behind the nurse as the interview began.

Smiling at them, Nurse Vieve started out with introductions. "Raima, I don't think you've met Levi yet. Raima, this is Levi. Levi, meet Raima." She motioned to them both, as if expecting them to shake hands or hug.

Because the nurse expected acknowledgement of some kind, Raima cleared her throat and gave the boy a sideways glance. "Nice to meet you," she said.

Levi shrugged and let out a little noise in his throat to reply. Waves of distress and discomfort rolled off him, as powerful as body odor to Raima's new sixth sense. She recoiled, scooting as far away in her chair as she could.

The nurse seemed oblivious to it all as she explained the rules, the same ones Raima heard when she was in Levi's position. "I'm going to ask you a question, Levi, and I want you to think the answer, don't say it aloud. Raima, your job is to tell me the answer if you can. Are you ready?"

Raima nodded, steeling herself for this new unnerving experience—invading a male mind. Levi gave no indication that he'd heard Nurse Vieve, but that didn't stop her from asking her first question. "How old are you, Levi?"

Silence swelled, filling the room as Raima tried forcing her mind forward without looking at Levi, but she couldn't focus her talent and only picked up scattered fragments of thoughts and emotions from both Vieve and Levi. She turned to stare at Levi's hairline. A word reverberated through the air, loud and clear.

"He's twelve," Raima said.

"Very good," the nurse said. "Levi, when were you born?"

Levi's lips compressed, biting back the answer with a frown. In his mind Raima felt a flutter of fear clouding his thoughts, but it didn't stop her from picking up the answer.

"Capricornus third," she said. "2187."

"Where was he born?" the nurse asked, focusing on Raima now instead of Levi.

The boy sat back in his chair, crossing his arms and dropping his gaze to the table, struggling to keep his mind empty. Raima recalled doing the same thing when she'd been in his place, overwhelmed by the other subjects' frightening talents. Pity stirred in her, but she didn't care enough about his discomfort to stop seeking the answers to the nurse's questions. She didn't have to wade into the vast ocean of his memories and knowledge. It was like picking exposed shells and conchs from the shore without ever getting her feet wet.

After the interview Nurse Victoria took Levi away and Vieve guided Raima to another small room with a padded chair and medical machinery. As the nurse closed the door Raima noted the security camera overlooking the little space and took a short, quick breath. She moved to the chair, anticipating the nurse's next command without even trying to read her.

"Make yourself comfortable there," Nurse Vieve said as she strode to the left side of the chair where a tiny metal tray rested atop some other machinery. The setup reminded Raima of a dentist's office. Her body tensed with the memory of the agonizing hours she'd spent with her jaw agape as a man with a tool that sounded like a drill buzzed against her teeth. When the nurse lifted a small hypodermic needle from the metal tray Raima averted her eyes.

"Stick out your arm for me," the nurse ordered. Raima obeyed. She tapped at the skin on the inside of Raima's elbow, trying to expose a vein. "Little poke here," she said. "Just stay relaxed. You're doing great."

Is this what the twins said would happen? She wondered as the needle bit into her and a chill flowed out from her elbow. She winced, unable to restrain a shudder.

"All done," Nurse Vieve said and pressed a wad of gauze tight to Raima's arm, making the injection site sting. "You hold that there and I'll get the cap on you." She scurried around the chair to the other side and deposited the syringe and needle she'd just used into a sharps bin mounted on the wall.

"What was in the shot?" Raima asked in a quiet voice.

"It's a sedative," she replied. "It'll make you sleepy but that's all." She smiled as she stepped back in front of Raima, holding a white plastic cap with both hands. It was covered in small metallic bumps.

Raima stared into the nurse's eyes, reaching for the woman's mind before she slipped the cap over her head. As she'd suspected, Nurse Vieve knew that the cap would monitor Raima's brain activity, recording it digitally so that it could be deciphered later. Excitement charged the nurse's mind—she wondered if Raima would be the first girl to confirm their suspicions that the sedative didn't interfere with telepathy. Raima, obedient and demure, always eager to please the researchers, Vieve knew she'd tell the truth now.

The cap was pulled over Raima's head, but the nurse hadn't turned it on yet. Raima searched deeper, trying to puzzle out what Nurse Vieve knew about Genoquip's plans for her and the other subjects. How foolish were these researchers to think about their plans like this? Didn't they realize the danger? But, how could they? TC-Gen had stumbled upon telepathy in the twins, then spread it to more subjects—but they didn't understand it. Raima saw conclusions from longwinded reports inside Vieve's memory. Everyone at TC-Gen knew their subjects could pick out surface thoughts and some of them could converse telepathically, but everything else was guesswork. They needed to find out how powerful telepathy could be as a weapon and how to control it or protect themselves; so far, they'd been disappointed.

Nurse Vieve circled around Raima's chair, to a seat by a bulky piece of equipment just out of sight. Moving as little as possible, to avoid rousing the nurse's suspicion, Raima twisted her head around, watching the woman, still searching her mind. In the brief seconds before the nurse powered on the monitoring equipment, Raima caught an image of Sarai inside Nurse Vieve's mind—a recent memory. The girl was battered, left with swelling in her face and blood streaming from her nose. Her scrubs were torn at the waist. Vieve's hands pressed on Sarai's shoulders, holding her down and speaking in a calming voice. *"You're okay, sweetie, everything's fine. . . ."* But Nurse Victoria was there too—and she held a syringe with a needle in her gloved hands.

The nurse flicked on the machine behind her and as it started up with a high-pitched whine, Raima withdrew her mind. She squeezed the armrests on her chair in frustration and watched the nurse come to stand in front of her. For the first time she began feeling the effects of the sedative and blinked, clearing her bleary eyes.

"Are you all right?" the nurse asked.

"Yes," Raima said.

"Good, we'll start now. I'm going to ask you a series of questions and just do your best to answer them. What's your favorite color?"

"Green," she answered and let her eyes drift closed to keep from frowning. She didn't want to see the nurse's friendly face. The image of Sarai stayed imprinted on her consciousness.

"What's my favorite color?" she asked.

Raima gave a weak shake of her head. "I don't know."

"Can't you read my mind?" The nurse's voice was sour with disappointment.

"No," Raima lied, hoping the cap wouldn't be able to tell.

"That's a real shame," she said. "Are you sure? Are you really trying?"

"Please forgive me," Raima said, sighing. "I'm really tired. I'm sorry."

"That's okay," Nurse Vieve said, but her tone indicated otherwise. "Just answer what you can. What's five plus five?"

When she returned to the bunkroom for the evening, Raima noted that Jenny's bed was empty. The sheets were gone and the metal stand that held the IV and other medical equipment was absent. A stab of regret and loss passed through Raima, but the other girl's death couldn't dim her own triumph at surviving. Her belly was full after eating dinner in the cafeteria where a protective shield of fellow female survivors surrounded her, both physically and psychologically. The mental touching that at first so alarmed her now seemed as delightful and nourishing as a hearty meal. Even aloof girls like Marie, Manon, and Aine were comforting presences, strong and resolute, but supportive. But there was still one mind missing—Sarai—and Raima was determined to find out what'd happened to her.

Marie called Raima to the bunks in the corner closest to the door where she and her twin slept each night. Manon, who was

123

already sitting on her bunk, asked, *"How did it go?"*

"Ve," Raima replied, projecting the word into Manon's mind.

Manon nodded and called to several of the other girls. *"It's time for speech therapy,"* she said, using her thoughts and grinning with some dark humor that Raima didn't understand.

They began a strange lesson with Marie, Manon, Tiana, and Izzy, inundating Raima with the words of their secret language by speaking aloud in English, but then supplying an immediate translation. Though Raima suspected the exercise was for her benefit, she knew the rest of the girls in the bunkroom participated in it as well, listening and translating on their own. Qi was on a bunk across the room, talking with Limei, Aine, and Ella about something else in a high, jovial voice, seemingly paying no attention whatsoever to Marie and Manon's language lesson. However, Raima, who constantly watched and listened to Qi with a strange new intensity, could feel Qi and the minds of the other girls with her all repeating the same translations in the secret language.

"Tell us what you remember about Earth," Marie ordered Izzy in English. "Everything you can." Marie's translation of these words echoed half a second later: *"Ensha-livetainbocho choum auzaifen-lo pebau-Guhaumai. Auchae auzaifen-lo."*

Izzy inhaled, long and deep, and closed her eyes. Raima imagined her reaching far inside, digging out the memories from a locked vault of treasures, things she never wanted to lose. In fact, she *felt* Izzy doing it. She sensed the effort and the solemn, beautiful aura around the memories that Izzy's mind brushed against and sorted through as she put the images to words that conveyed the appropriate awe and gravity.

"I was thirteen when I made the journey," she said. *"Sosae-bo chau-ti zomet oiveten-bo."*

As the tales progressed, outwardly appearing to be nothing more than girls reminiscing about their pasts on a world of green that let them walk under a strong sun, Raima realized that Marie and Manon chose the speakers for their experience and expertise with the secret language. Tiana and Izzy, not to mention Marie and Manon, were the most familiar and comfortable with the secret language because they'd been at

TC-Gen longer than anyone else. These four were the teachers, weaving the telepathic girls together, uniting them into a single culture and family.

When Tiana, who was especially gifted with the language and had even created more words for it, finished the story of her own Earth memories, Marie called on Raima. "What do you remember about Earth?" Telepathically she supplied the translation, *"Choum lizan-lo auzaifensa pebau-Guhaumai?"*

Raima was silent for a time, scowling with concentration. She knew all the girls in the room were listening to her, with their minds as well as their ears. Across the room Qi and her companions fell into silence.

Facing *all* the girls made Raima remember that one of them was missing. She cleared her throat and decided to transform the lesson. "I was eleven when I made the journey," she said, mimicking Izzy's phrasing so she'd be able to anticipate the translation, but instead of broadcasting the sentence in the secret language, she asked, *"What happened to Sarai? Why isn't she here?"*

Marie, Manon, Izzy, Tiana, and Aine across the room parroted Raima's English sentence into the secret language but frowned at her silent questions. *"Sosae-bo be-ti zomet oiveten-bo."* Even before they completed the translation they glanced at each other, waiting for Marie or Manon's permission to break the lesson.

"Don't be shy," Manon said and sent a short jab of impatience at Raima's mind, much like a prodding finger. "Tell us more."

"Before I came to Mars I lived in India," Raima continued, but her voice darkened with determination. *"What happened to Sarai?"* she asked, stronger now so that even the weakest telepath in the bunkroom—Ella—would pick it up.

This time only Marie translated Raima's words. *"Poini sobenen-bo um-Aisuraidaum sonikoivan-bo olo-Indiya."*

"The scientists killed her," Qi replied. *"While you were delirious."*

Manon's expression soured with distaste. Out loud she asked, "What was India like?"

Taking her twin sister's lead, Marie tried to interject into the telepathic conversation, ending it. *"We're not going to talk about that yet. Manon and I warned you not to get attached to anyone. Only the strong and the lucky survive here."*

Limei stood up on the other side of the room. Her movement made the bunk she was sitting on squeak and thump once on the hard floor, catching everyone's attention. Raima twisted around and peered from beneath the shadow of the bunk above her head. Limei's tall, thin figure belied the fierce expression on her face and the hard, powerful touch of her mind. She had always been a small presence, softhearted and gentle-spoken, but now she was a lioness or an angry bee, provoked into boldness and rage.

"No," she said with her thick accent. "We tell."

"Shh," Izzy hissed before Marie or Manon could scold Limei. *"They watch and listen to us. You know that. Watch yourself. You'll get us all killed if you reveal too much."*

"You want to talk about Earth too?" Marie asked, shouting over to the other girls.

The dizzying game these girls played, the proverbial cat and mouse, confused and angered Raima. She took several deep breaths, trying to keep the multiple conversations straight. The researchers would be watching them, listening. The girls had to disguise their activities or risk exposing them. Surrounded as they were with suffering, strangeness, and death, they could be as emotionally stiff and stunted as the girls of Ferde's brothel. Their survival took a harsh toll on their hearts, minds, and souls.

"Sure," Qi said. She stood up and feigned a grin. Her black-brown eyes flew to Raima and her mental touch pressed in, whispering so that none of the others would overhear the thought, *"Don't ask about Sarai again. I will come to you after the lights are out and tell you everything you want to know. For now, just let the twins run the show."*

Raima made no reply except to brush against Qi's consciousness with affection and trust. Words weren't needed. Qi had shared her body heat to break Raima's fevers, and while Marie and Manon used Raima's nightmares to ask her to join their cause, Qi had tried to dispel them and replace memories of evil with something tender and holy.

Limei, Qi, Aine, and Ella walked to the bunks surrounding Marie and Manon, each taking a spot. Aine, always distant and quiet, took a top bunk farthest away from the twins, while Ella moved to share a spot on the same bed as Tiana. The smile that passed between redheaded, shy Ella and the dark-skinned, confident Tiana hinted at a deep friendship. Raima's tension dissipated, flowing away like rainwater falling from the leaves of trees. This wasn't the brothel, where girls were pitted against each other, ready to betray and abandon any of their sisters. The bunk beside her moved, sinking as Qi and Limei sat next to her.

Manon said, "Raima, tell us about India."

Several seconds passed, but no translation followed those words. Apparently, the language lesson was over. Raima started again, saying, "I was eleven when I left Earth. I lived in Chandigarh, that's a city in India. . . ."

She paused as she heard Marie's telepathic voice addressing the group: *"Sarai was killed with an injection. Sarai didn't know what was coming. She didn't fight it. She didn't work with us as a team. If she had, we could have protected her."*

"Go on," Manon prompted, speaking aloud to Raima. "I know it's hard to remember."

Raima swallowed to wet her dry throat, meeting Manon's brown eyes and nodding. "India is green everywhere. I remember parks with fountains. The sound of the water, the way the sun was so bright on the surface of it. I remember the way it used to smell right before it started raining. We had so much rain in India." She stopped as she heard Marie begin again in her head and realized with embarrassment that she'd started crying. She wiped at the tears, almost missing Marie's ongoing explanation.

"Sarai was only a little weaker than Ella, we think. We don't know exactly why they kill some of us and not others. But if they come for Ella, we won't let them do it," Marie said. *"We won't fight with our bodies. We'll use our minds. If we fought with our bodies they'd see it and they'd know. They'd just hold us down and do whatever they want anyway. Remember that."*

Manon's gaze narrowed on Raima. She motioned with impatience, trying to get her to keep talking.

Sniffling, Raima went on in a thick voice. "There were so many colors. I—I can't believe I took it for granted. I had clothing that was so bright and comfortable. I could run and feel the wind in my hair. I used to have spicy food—and fresh fruit. . . ."

"We can't teach you to use your mind," Marie said. She sent out waves of regret and fear. *"If Manon or I stood around and showed each*

of you how and where to fiddle inside a nurse's head, someone would notice. We'd never be able to keep it secret. The nurse would realize too. You must learn as much as you can by yourselves—and very carefully. Don't let them know what we're doing. Don't even give them a reason to be suspicious."

"I used to go see movies at the cinema," Raima murmured, struggling to continue the conversation aloud in a convincing way. She had already tried some of what Marie described by fumbling about inside Nurse Victoria's mind that morning. It was clumsy, and the nurse was obviously suspicious of her.

Marie hadn't stopped speaking and her thought-words were too compelling for Raima to speak over. Before she could cast about for more memories to say aloud, Qi rescued her. "I was born here," she admitted in the stilted, imperfect English that marred her audible voice. "This planet. *Huo xing*, we name it, is the only place I know. But I wish I saw the pretty places you talk about. I see only in pictures. Make me very sad." She leaned forward on the bunk to look around Limei at Raima. "I wish I grew up with you, in Chandigarh."

"Me, Manon, Tiana, and Izzy will protect everyone who works with us and follows the rules. We know just enough that if we wanted to, we could control someone." Marie glanced at Ella and smiled slightly. *"Ella's not clueless either. But most of you don't know how to do anything."*

"Start practicing," Manon finished, still watching Raima with a mixture of wariness and warning. *"But be careful and do as we say, or you'll end up like Sarai."*

"We think they kill the ones that are weak and the ones they think are fussing around too much in their heads," Marie elaborated. *"But we're not sure."*

Raima nodded, absorbing the information on the surface, but inwardly she erected a wall to shield her thoughts from the others around her. It wasn't dissimilar to what she'd done while in the brothel, protecting herself from the hateful, threatening culture there. When Ferde said, *No one cares about any of you, you're all worthless*, Raima listened with one ear and preserved her own core self, imagining her mother's voice whispering in the other ear. *You are not worthless.*

Now, though she didn't want to believe it, her instincts recognized a threat in the twins that made her tense. It was too reminiscent of the brothel. Like Genoquip, the twins dealt in veiled threats and dangers. The rules were still as clear as spring water: *be obedient.* But the dangers lurked like lightning, ready to strike without warning and with deadly consequences. *Do as we say,* Manon had said, *or you'll end up like Sarai.* If Ferde spoke those words, Raima would've known he'd killed Sarai. Was it possible that Marie and Manon somehow had a hand in who lived and who died at TC-Gen? Or were they only offering the warning about Genoquip, as Raima and the rest of the girls wanted—and might be *meant*—to believe?

The verbal conversation lagged again. Limei took it up, lamenting that she'd been born on Mars too. No one listened to her, instead all the girls were solemn as they contemplated their situation, how close they could be to death. How many more of them would end up like Sarai before they made their move to take freedom for themselves, once and for all?

There's more than one way to touch someone's mind, she realized. Non-telepaths were numb to the touch, but pushing beyond a certain point, from feather-light to a full grabbing pressure, made them aware of another's presence. Traversing the mind and remaining undetected required finesse.

As Raima headed back to her bed after Nurse Vieve finished her inspections, she brushed Jenny's bunk with her fingers. She wasn't surprised when she felt nothing at all except the creak of the bedsprings. What had happened to her talent as an Intuiter? Since waking that morning Raima hadn't felt anything from objects. Not even a whispered impression from a tool, so she suspected the ability was gone, vanished. But how, and why?

In her bed, Raima stilled her mind, closing it off, sheltering her thoughts and emotions from the rest of the subjects. She prepared her questions, anxious for Qi to answer them and eager to feel her closeness.

The lights went out. Nurse Vieve's keycard lanyard clicked as it slid in and out of the lock. Her footsteps receded down the hallway with its painted blue ocean and bright yellow, pink, and orange fish. In the dark Raima sensed the whispered thoughts of her companions. Some of them moved, leaving their beds to use the bathroom, or headed to other girls' bunks. Though Marie and Manon described the girls as *sisters*, all part of one family unit, there were cliques, splintering their group. Tiana, Ella, and Izzy made up the most distinct clique, but Limei once had spent her time close to Sarai, chatting with her and laughing. Of course, hearing Marie and Manon denounce Sarai as *too weak* to survive at TC-Gen would hurt her. True sisters in an actual family would never dismiss her death as inevitable.

Raima heard Qi's footsteps and scooted as far over on her narrow bed as she could. She flung back her covers and Qi crawled in beside her. Even before their skin touched, both girls caressed the other's mind. Qi set up invisible, psychic walls inside her mind. Raima copied them, learning through mimicry. They settled on the bed, facing each other, embracing to share the limited space. Qi's breath, flowing in and out, comforted Raima, as did the feel of Qi's chest rising and falling.

At first Raima didn't want to break the peace and contentment of their silence and camaraderie, but Qi's mind was sharp with urgency. She started with her most recent question. *"Why can't I read objects like I could before? Can you still do it?"*

Qi sent the telepathic image of herself shaking her head. *"I can't read objects anymore either. Not everyone here could read objects before they arrived, but if they could, like us, they lose it. I don't know why. I'm sorry."*

Raima smiled. *"Don't be sorry."* She could see the glint of Qi's open eyes in the dark, a faint sparkle like a star. There was something gloomy and obscure within Qi's mind that she kept tucked back, out of Raima's view. The thoughts and emotions were like shadows against a sheet or a wall. Raima saw fragments and hints, enough to know that they were there, and that she wouldn't like them. *"What's wrong?"* she asked.

"Limei watched Sarai die. It's been hard for her. She thinks Marie and Manon let Sarai die because they didn't like her or thought she'd be a liability in our escape."

Determined not to disturb her, Raima stifled her own complex emotions and suspicions, hiding them as Qi had. *"We've all seen too much death,"* she agreed.

"Marie and Manon haven't ever been outside of facilities like this," Qi explained. *"They've never known any love except what they feel for each other. They have such a narrow view. It's made them cold. Most of the time I know they're right. I know they'll save us, but the things they want to do . . ."*

Shame flooded Raima's mind, rushing in from Qi. Raima flinched from the intensity of it. *"Qi?"* she reached for the other girl's mind, stroking her arm.

"This morning, when I showed you Aine, Ella, and Limei's suffering," Qi said, *"I did it because Marie and Manon wanted you to know, wanted you to see."*

"Why?" Raima asked, unable to keep herself from feeling enraged by the topic. She didn't want to hear of the others' similar experiences because it reminded her too much of her own. The idea of their weakness and vulnerability as women, constantly abused by men everywhere, brought on a vicious, boiling rage inside Raima, dangerously close to spilling over. Hiding behind a wall of denial and avoidance, pretending that she was normal now and

always had been, was so much easier. And safer.

"Because so many girls come here with memories like theirs, and like yours. Many of the girls who've died were raped or abused too. Abby—do you remember her? She was raped by her father for years. Jia-li came from a brothel in Zui Chu, like you. There were girls before you came that died while I was going through the treatments. They'd been raped as well."

Raima pushed a burst of irritation at Qi, trying to silence her. *"Why remind me? Do they think I didn't already know?"* She blinked and felt bitter tears well in her eyes. Gritting her teeth in a hard grin-like grimace, Raima wiped the tears away, quelling the rest. *"What's wrong with them anyway?"* she asked, meaning the twins.

Qi's mind was wide as she listened, soft with sympathy and affection. At Raima's question she narrowed her focus, speaking again. *"Don't wonder why Marie and Manon sent me,"* she said. *"Ask why men do what they do to us. I know you have an answer for that. The twins wanted you to remember that answer during our escape."*

"There is no answer! Men are selfish and they like seeing us in pain. They—"

"Isn't that the definition of evil?" Qi interrupted, interjecting the thought with a powerful thrust of mental effort. *"You heard Bryson today. Today was nothing. If he was as strong as us telepathically he'd have already hurt someone. He taunts us all the time because he knows the researchers can't hear and wouldn't stop him anyway."*

"They would stop him," Raima objected. *"Of course, they would stop him!"*

"Maybe in the cafeteria," Qi countered. *"But Marie and Manon think Genoquip picked Bryson for this place specifically because he's violent. When he first came here three months ago they read his mind. He's a juvenile sex offender."* Raima felt anger building in Qi. *"Sometimes the researchers leave one of us in a test room alone with Bryson. They say they'll be back and then don't return for a long time, but they leave the sensors on our heads, watching our brains."*

Already Raima understood where the story was headed. She muttered aloud in a quiet voice, trying to drown out Qi's telepathic voice. "No, no, no—they wouldn't do that to us. They're paying us. . . ."

"At first Bryson taunted us mostly when we were left alone with him, but about a week ago, while you were sick in bed, they did the test

with Sarai. Bryson finally got bored of just sitting there." Qi swallowed audibly. *"He attacked her. There's a one-way mirror in that room. They sit behind it and watch. They knew what he was trying to do to her. No one came to help her. She tried to fight him with her mind, but she was the weakest of us all—"*

"Stop!" Raima whimpered. "Please, just stop." The story took her back to the brothel, to her first days on Mars deep belowground where Ferde broke in his girls. She remembered the leering smile on his face, the roughness of his calloused hands on her thighs, and his strength as he held her down. It wasn't difficult to imagine Bryson instead of Ferde. In the moment of silence that followed, Raima composed herself, locking away the memories. When she was ready she used her mind to speak. *"Why would they do this?"*

Qi shrugged, moving the covers with her shoulders. Although the motion was dismissive and flippant considering the gruesomeness of their subject, her mind was heavy with grief. *"The twins think they want to test telepathy as a weapon. They wanted to see what Sarai would do to Bryson to defend herself. But they took the weakest of us. When they saw she couldn't stop it from happening, they killed her, like ripping out a bad stitch on a seam."*

"Sarai was a dead-end road," Raima hazarded. "A bad investment." She thought of Kati and closed her eyes.

"They're going to keep testing," Qi added. *"Now that Bryson has gotten away with it once, he'll probably keep doing it. He knows like we do that the real test is how we act when we are alone, with him."* The hate that colored Qi's mind and mental voice were familiar. Raima felt the same way toward Ferde, her captors, and the johns.

"The twins don't think the experiment will go on much longer," Qi said. *"They think as soon as one of us is able to stop Bryson with telepathy, we'll all be slaughtered."*

"When did they give Sarai the injection that killed her?" Raima asked.

"As soon as they came in. They pretended to be shocked by what Bryson did to her. The nurse injected her with something and sent her back to the bunkroom. She was barely conscious when she got here. We only found out what happened to her when Limei went digging into her mind before she was too far gone even for that."

"When do we escape?" Raima asked, her mind brimming with urgent energy. Her heart pummeled her ribs, as if trying to break out. *"What do they want us to do?"*

"We don't know just yet," Qi admitted and sighed. She laid a hand on Raima's face, touching her cheek and her ear, then brushing at her hair. *"The twins think they want one more girl. There's only nine of us right now. Ten seems like the endpoint."* She paused and then said, *"If they find out we can stop Bryson with our minds—"* She broke off, uncertain. *"We just don't know."*

Though Qi hadn't said it, she sensed that Marie and Manon wanted to demand that none of the girls fight Bryson with their minds, to hide what they could do from the researchers. That meant tolerating Bryson's attack. Raima had done that for *years*. The thought of doing it again made her tremble with fury and revulsion.

Sensing Raima's emotions and thoughts, Qi made a verbal shushing noise. "Shh," she said and clucked her tongue like a mother scolding a child. "No worry," she said. "Sleep."

The Chinese girl pressed forward and gave Raima a kiss on her nose. She shifted, intending to return to her own bed, but Raima caught her hand and pulled on it. If Qi left Raima would have nothing to distract her from her dark thoughts and suspicions. *"Please, stay with me?"*

Qi obliged and settled back down under the covers, tucked close alongside Raima. *"We'll make it through,"* she said. *"I promise."*

ELEVEN

After breakfast the following morning, Nurse Vieve broke the girls' usual routine by shepherding them back to the bunkroom instead of to the co-ed classroom or for testing. Raima knew through the thoughts of the other girls that this change in procedure heralded the coming of a new subject. Jenny had arrived a little later in the day and ate lunch with them before her first injection—the beginning of her demise.

Although the girls suspected that they were about to meet a new subject, they remained tense. Sarai's death had shaken them, driving home TC-Gen's barely concealed deadliness. Raima walked with Qi behind her, a solid and comforting presence both physically and psychically. *"Ten subjects,"* Qi's remark cycled through her thoughts from their discussion the previous night. *"To round off the experiment."*

"But there aren't ten boys," Raima said, pushing against Qi's mind.

"Close enough," Qi shot back.

They moved down the painted, playful hall and Qi came forward, walking at Raima's side. It was a tight squeeze, making the two girls brush shoulders to avoid bumping against the walls. *"Do you see the paintings?"* Qi asked.

"Of course," Raima replied.

"Marie and Manon painted them years ago."

"Did they paint the boys' hall too?" Raima asked.

Instead of using her thoughts to answer, Qi nodded. The girls stopped in a tight group while Nurse Vieve opened the door to the bunkroom. At the front of the line, closest to the door and the nurse, Manon peeked through the heads and shoulders of the other girls. Manon's mind tugged on Raima's, violent and strong, catching her full attention. When their eyes locked through the crowd of their peers, Manon forced a hard, cold thought into Raima's mind.

"*If the nurse tries to give any of us a shot, will you help Marie and me kill her?*"

Raima couldn't stop the frown from spreading over her lips. "*You said we can only fight with our minds.*"

"*If they've decided to kill all of us we'll have to fight with both—will you help?*" Manon demanded.

Raima nodded, but she knew her mind would feel tight to Manon, restricted. She tried to hide her memories and emotions, reaching inside for the numbness that once protected and sustained her. But it was small and far away. In its place Raima could only think of her powerlessness, of the impending danger and doom awaiting these subjects, her peers—*her friends*. No, they were something more than that. For all their flaws, for all their outward differences in appearance, nationality, and background, they were indeed *family* as Marie and Manon claimed. The thought of losing them—particularly Qi—made Raima sick.

When she'd killed Ferde she'd done it with the expectation that she would die afterwards. She didn't care what happened to the other girls enslaved alongside her. Now she wanted to live and see to it that the girls around her escaped with their lives as well. Shared suffering and the intimacy of their telepathy bound her to them. Though she felt frail and vulnerable with these unfamiliar emotions, Raima knew she would be able to strike out in defense of her strange new family, her sisters.

Nurse Vieve opened the door and Raima felt the mood change in the girls from tension to relief. It spread outward from Marie and Manon, the first girls inside the bunkroom after the nurse. An image jumped from the twins' minds, directed back to the others still in the hallway. It was a view of Nurse Victoria with a small, frail-looking blonde just inside the door. As Raima caught the projected image her body flooded with the cold shock of recognition. The little blonde, with the shortened frame of an

Earther, held a stained teddy bear.

Qi, nearby and halfway imbedded in Raima's consciousness, took in Raima's reaction and asked, *"Is that Kim . . . ?"*

Raima pressed forward without acknowledging Qi's question. She passed through the door to the bunkroom and saw the scene for herself. Nurse Victoria readied the first injection, tapping the syringe with its wicked needle. The fluid inside was an opaque white-gray that made Raima think of semen with a shudder of revulsion.

"Raima . . . ?" Kim asked. Her brows knitted together, forming a hard crease over her nose. She clutched the teddy bear not in her hands but pinned by her long-sleeved arm against her body. It was a deliberate strategy, preventing the teddy bear from touching her bare skin. She was an Intuiter. For her the bear was tainted with the gruesome memories from Raima's life in the brothel.

"What are you doing here, Kati?" Raima asked and blinked as she heard her own real voice aloud. It was raspy with disuse. How long had it been since she'd spoken a full sentence aloud? Her mental voice was far more efficient. She'd almost forgotten that her lips and mouth could speak as well as eat and breathe.

"I'm not Kati," she snapped with sudden vehemence. "I'm *Kim Waller*. Kim. I'm not from your past." Kim's face wrinkled with anger. Her blue eyes were still the same shade as Kati's.

"What are you doing here?" Raima repeated, quieter this time. Her face was hot, burning with embarrassment.

"What do you think?" Kim asked. "They transferred me here." She looked to the nurse and scowled, cringing as Victoria rolled up her sleeve, prepping the injection site. "They took Kaiden and I begged to go with him." She paused for a moment and then said, "I knew you'd be here too. That's why I brought this." She shifted the teddy bear with her free arm in a slow, careful way, trying not to touch it. Then, losing patience, she grabbed the stained bear and tossed it at Raima.

Raima caught it on instinct. She stared down into its shiny, black marble eyes, remembering the deep despair and loss from her life in the brothel again. She'd known the teddy bear would show Kim her past, but she'd never expected to meet Kim again, never thought she'd see the other girl's reaction, and hadn't considered what it would be. Perhaps the Raima that left CF-Gen wouldn't have cared about Kim's reaction.

No, that wasn't true. She'd left the bear because it was the coward's way of sharing her story. Tired of being alone and numb, of wondering why she was still alive, Raima wanted to reach out and connect with Kim, but the fear of rejection held her back. She was too scared to face Kim and expose her past, so instead she'd violated Kim's mind with the bear, Kati's bear, forcing not just words, but the actual memories on the other girl. *Of course*, Kim would be angry. The bear, left as a gift, was a psychic landmine.

"Relax," Nurse Victoria ordered Kim. "It'll sting less if your muscles are relaxed."

"I know," Kim muttered. She let out a loud, short breath and her shoulders sank. Nurse Victoria took that as her signal that Kim was ready and plunged the needle in.

"I'm sorry," Raima said, unable to find any other words.

Qi nudged Raima's side then and pushed into her mind. *"Don't listen to her. She's not Kati. She's nobody."*

Raima frowned and glared at Qi. *"She's not a nobody."*

Stubborn and steadfast, Qi stayed where she was. *"She is if she's hurting you."* The Chinese girl ignored Raima's glare and instead turned one of her own on Kim. "You," she scolded aloud, "rude girl. Shut your mouth or I hit you."

"None of that," Nurse Victoria snapped. She pulled back from Kim and began packing up her medical supplies. "You girls play nice. Testing begins in about a half an hour." She pointed an authoritative finger, threatening Kim. "That means you, kiddo. Your first sol here is one of the biggest."

Kim nodded, her face releasing some of its hostility, but Raima sensed the mental effort it took for her to do it.

Qi grabbed Raima's arm and hauled her away. At first Raima resisted, trying to pull clear of Qi's firm grip, but she gave in as she felt the curious touch of the other girls' minds in the bunkroom. Uncomfortable and embarrassed by their scrutiny, Raima shied away from them, clinging closer to Qi. She shut the others out, muting them.

In a row of bunks on the far side of the room, Qi pulled Raima down to sit beside her on one of the beds. *"Your roommate after I left?"* she asked, forcing the thought past Raima's mental block.

Cringing at the intrusion, Raima relaxed the barrier and reached her mind out for Qi's with a tentative grasp. The familiarity of it brought instant comfort. She picked up Qi's irritation toward Kim, her worry over Raima's reaction, and her determination to correct the situation. Slowly, Raima raised her chin and looked from Qi's hand, holding her own, to the other girl's face. Though Qi wasn't as pretty as Aine or Limei, her teeth were straight, and her blackish eyes couldn't conceal her intelligence and the passionate soul she possessed, just beneath her skin.

"*Yes,*" she said. "*I helped her like you helped me.*"

Qi shook her head. "*No, I've seen your memories. You helped her, but it wasn't like how I helped you.*" She paused, staring at Raima, searching.

"*Qi?*" Raima asked.

"*I helped you because I liked you,*" Qi admitted. Her cheeks darkened with an embarrassed blush. "*And because it was obvious you needed help.*"

For several moments Raima didn't understand Qi's meaning, and without the gift of telepathy she might've missed the other's girl's true feelings entirely. *I helped you because I liked you,* she'd said, but what her mind conveyed was something familiar and yet foreign, wonderful and terrifying at once. If the words had been merely spoken, Raima would have smiled and replied with something similar, safe and bland. *I like you too. It's good to have a friend. I haven't had one in a long time.*

Friendship wasn't what was in Qi's mind. Along with the words came sentiments and memories that were impossible to share without the directness of their telepathic connection. Qi recalled their closeness, sharing the same bed, pressed against one another, relishing the radiant warmth. Raima found herself remembering her fever-dreams, the terrors of the brothel, but then Qi had inserted a very different feeling, a moment of pleasure and peace.

Qi's lips curled in a wide smile. "*You remember,*" she said.

Raima frowned. She couldn't stop trembling. "*I remember.*"

"*Please don't be angry,*" Qi begged. Her eyes were moist and soft. Anxiousness swirled about the edges of her mind, though she tried hiding it.

"*When you helped me shower at CF-Gen—did you see my past then? Did you know back then?*" Raima asked. Though she hadn't spoken aloud her throat convulsed anyway, catching her breath in a small gasp.

Qi gave a nod of her head. *"Yes,"* she admitted. *"But I would've helped you anyway."* She reached for the stained teddy bear that Raima still held in one hand. *"I hated seeing you suffer so much. I had to stop it, but it's more than that too. I—I think you're beautiful. Inside and out. From the first time I saw you."*

For a few seconds Qi blurred in front of Raima as the Chinese girl's memories filtered into her. She saw herself, pallid and thin, with deep brown eyes and a face made too long by constant suffering. There were heavy black circles beneath her eyes. When the memory-Raima looked out at the world it was clear she was haunted and empty, desolated by tragedy. Her body still lived, but her soul buried itself inside unfeeling walls of flesh, waiting to die.

Unnerved and pained by the image, Raima pulled away. She dropped the teddy bear, letting it stay in Qi's hands, and got to her feet. She shook her head, stumbling as she walked away from Qi, trying to clear her vision and her mind. "No, no, no," she muttered.

Over the rows of bunks Raima saw Kim sitting on the bed closest to the door, rubbing her arm where Nurse Victoria administered the injection. The frail girl lifted her head and gazed at Raima with a sour set to her lips, but then her expression warped, becoming a sad, scared smile. None of the other subjects greeted her and the knowledge filled Raima with pity.

It was always easier focusing outward rather than inward, evading the turmoil within herself. She didn't consider Qi while she evaluated Kim's situation. While she worried about Kim's well-being she didn't have to ask herself how she felt about Qi's admission. She didn't have to explore the frightening affection between them. If she could delay long enough one of the nurses would come and take them away to the classroom for testing. The quavering weakness inside settled. Raima's next breath was soothing rather than panicked and tight.

She heard the bed Qi was sitting on squeak as the metal springs uncoiled, releasing their tension when the girl stood. Qi joined Raima in staring out over the bunkroom at Kim. Her mind pressed with gentle insistence around the edges of Raima's. *"I scared you."*

The psychic words carried a crushing weight. *"I'm sorry; I didn't mean to do that."*

Qi's hand brushed over Raima's back, caressing between her shoulder blades. Raima quickly inhaled as both her mind and body reacted with a mixture of panic and longing. Pleasurable contact with another human being was still so new and foreign it overwhelmed her, but she craved more. Qi's hands made her remember her mother, but there was a breathless need and desire that complicated that basic emotion. Raima didn't know what it was, but it both terrified and intrigued her.

"You want to go talk to her," Qi said. It was phrased as a question, but not meant to be taken as such. Qi already knew the answer, but these words offered a release, a sort of permission.

She knew that Qi could see, feel, and read the tumultuous mass of emotion within her, but she didn't force Raima to dig into it or unravel it. The gratitude that swelled within Raima made her sigh. *"I have to apologize to her for leaving the bear. I have to tell her what happens here."*

Qi squeezed Raima's arm and looked at her, offering a warning. *"Don't get too attached to her, and don't tell her too much. In fact, don't do anything without asking the twins first."*

Bristling, Raima frowned. "Always the twins," she muttered aloud, thinking of Marie and Manon's cold expressions.

"Always," Qi repeated, nodding with her jaw clenched. "No forgetting, Raima."

Qi turned and moved back to the stained bear, which had fallen on the floor when she rose from the bunk bed. She stooped, snatching it up, and tossed it to the bed. "Go," she told Raima, without looking over her shoulder. "Go help her."

Raima started across the bunkroom with slow steps until she found herself standing in front of Kim. Kim sat on the bunk with her arms wrapped around her body, brooding.

"I'm sorry," Raima said, ignoring the throaty rasping of her voice. "I was afraid to tell you about what happened to me."

She could feel Kim's mind working—the worry, the anxiety, and the discomfort of a new place, a new testing facility. A new regimen of dangerous shots. The impulsive need to see Kim's reaction to the bear overcame Raima. She pushed her way into Kim's mind without difficulty and watched as the little blonde blinked, mildly aware of the invasion. Kim's brain was as vast as the nurse's. It stretched out like an ocean, alien and without any recognizable landmarks. Raima stood at its shore, feeling the surf on her toes, hearing the echoes of its waves.

She thought at it: *What did you see when you touched the teddy bear?*

The ocean rippled, rose up, broiling with a sudden storm.

Kim cringed. Raima asked out loud, "Did you hear me?"

"You said you were sorry," Kim muttered. She reached up and rubbed her temples. Gnashing her teeth together, she grumbled, "My head hurts."

Raima saw their old room at CF-Gen with her cot cold and empty, except for the stolid, dirty teddy bear. She watched Kim cross to the cot and sit on it, regarding the bear and contemplating the words of the technician who tested her every sol. *The talent must be awakened, usually by a foreign object.* Kim's hands closed over the teddy bear and her eyes sprang open wide as the memories crashed into her. Ferde's boot smashing the teddy bear into the red Martian soil; Kati's body, bloated and covered in blood; the knife Raima used to slit Ferde's throat and stab him, extinguishing his hateful life at last. Then came scenes from the hospital in Elysia City, Raima's crushing despair, and the doctor's voice telling her that she'd contracted HIV and needed an expensive complete bone marrow transplant from a genetically immune donor.

She changed the depth at which she touched Kim's mind, pulling back from the memories and bringing herself back to the present. She aimed her thoughts at the surface of Kim's mind, imagining that they rang out like words. *"Come with me,"* she said. *"I have to show you to the twins."*

Kim stared at her, confounded by the inconsistencies that her senses were experiencing. Raima spoke audibly, but her lips didn't move. Kim looked around the room. One hand stayed at her temple frozen mid-motion in the act of rubbing her head as shock took over. "Raima . . . ?" she asked.

"Come with me," Raima repeated, this time using her actual voice.

They walked around the line of bunks toward the bathroom where Marie and Manon were leaning against the wall. Aine, Ella, Tiana, and Izzy were with them. Although they appeared bored on the surface, Raima felt their interest electrifying the room. She knew they'd been waiting for her to bring Kim over. Now they received the new girl with a cold casualness that irritated Raima.

Perhaps they already pegged Kim as likely to die. Or maybe Marie and Manon decided they would orchestrate Kim's death to prevent the end of the experiment. Raima banished the idea with a flash of horrified rage. *No*, she thought. *We are family here.*

"Kim," Raima said as they reached the group of girls. "These are the twins, Marie and Manon." The twins, identical except for their heights—with Marie being slightly taller than Manon—nodded in time with the introductions, but they didn't smile. Kim lingered several steps behind, her eyes darting from one girl to the next.

Raima motioned to the other girls beside the twins. "Tiana, Izzy, Ella, and Aine," she said. "Marie and Manon have been here the longest, but Tiana, Izzy, and Ella arrived not much later. Aine's newer."

"Does she know?" Manon asked Raima in a small, hard voice.

"Do I know what?" Kim snapped, glaring.

"Does she know we're telepaths?" Marie clarified.

Raima shook her head. "Qi said I should bring her to you two."

Manon smiled with smug satisfaction that made Raima grimace with disapproval. It reminded her of the way girls in the brothel would smirk with a sick, twisted triumph after Ferde praised or rewarded them. It was the self-satisfied look of someone who'd jockeyed for power and won.

Worse than the reminder of the brothel's depraved female hierarchy was the sudden knowledge that sprang up inside Raima that Kim would resist the twins' rules. She'd been rebellious at CF-Gen, caring about nothing except her brother, Kaiden. It was the need to be with Kaiden that brought her now to TC-Gen and Raima doubted Kim had changed. Disobedience would be punished by everyone.

Kim and Kati. Raima's mind spun around the two girls, different people but both unable and unwilling to adapt to a system that demanded conformity. Twice now Raima tried inserting herself into the equation to save them. She thought she had some success with Kim at CF-Gen. That had partly made up for betraying Kati. Yet Kim had followed Raima and Kaiden into a new type of fire, a new trial. Raima couldn't avoid seeing the symmetry, the circular pattern.

Gooseflesh broke out over her arms and a chill raced down her spine as a thought that felt like premonition touched her: *Kim will die.*

"Who's Qi?" Kim asked. "What's going on here?"

Raima sensed the intercommunication between the twins, Ella, Tiana, Izzy, and Aine as they decided who would speak next. Finally, Izzy pushed off the wall she'd been leaning on and spoke to Kim for the first time. "This facility's experiment makes telepaths." At Kim's skeptical stare she added, "Mind-readers."

"You mean psychics?" Kim asked, raising an eyebrow.

"Pick a number. Pick an image. Ask me a question only you know the answer to. All of us will be able to answer it," Tiana said, grinning.

Kim threw Raima a sideways glance. She crossed her arms over her chest and shifted on her feet. "There's no such thing as psychics. It's impossible."

Ella, the weakest of the remaining girls, unable to project her thoughts into non-telepathic minds, said, "You were born in San Francisco, California on February 8, 2183. You're sixteen years old, but you were thirteen when you made the crossing."

Izzy started up where Ella left off. "You lived in Galle crater, at a settlement called Smiley. Your brother's name is Kaiden. Your parents' names were—"

"Shut up!" Kim shouted. Her shock and fury hit Raima like a hot wind. "What did you do? Steal my report with MIHO? Did the nurses tell you about me? You think this is funny?"

Marie and Manon watched Kim with a mixture of disgust and amusement, greeting her bafflement and disbelief the way they always did. They were like Ferde and the other men in the brothel, relishing the terror of new victims, basking in the magnitude and magnificence of their own power over the newcomer. This was a game for them. Raima was spared it because she arrived at an unusual hour and realized they were telepathic by using her senses. Most new subjects received an introduction like Kim's. The telepathic girls would demonstrate their startling, frightening power. They showed Kim they could steal her secret knowledge, forcing her to accept the fact and join them, or reject them and remain an outsider.

Sarai had been an outsider and she was killed. The injections were dangerous enough, but Raima couldn't dispel the grim certainty that this family of sisters was a hierarchy as well. The family might survive the coming rebellion and escape, but the outliers and outsiders would find themselves tossed aside like garbage.

In that moment, behind the protective shield she'd erected inside her mind to hide her thoughts from the twins, Raima saw herself as one of the outliers. Marie and Manon wanted her to join their cause and help with the escape, but that didn't mean she'd ever earn a place within their narrow circle of trusted, beloved sisters. Many times, during her weeks with them, Raima noticed the twins' wariness of her, their distrust. They were reluctant to open up to her the way they seemed to easily connect with Aine, Tiana, Ella, and Izzy. What held them back? Their distance could only mean one thing—they had something to hide.

Almost without thinking, Raima began interrupting the power display and the ritualistic humiliation of the new girl, spoiling Marie and Manon's pleasure in it. She heard herself say, "They didn't steal any files. They know what they know because they can read your mind. I thought it was impossible too when I first came here. It's hard to accept, especially now with us poking into your mind without you being able to feel it or control it, but it's true." She tossed a brief glare at the twins and then at Aine, Ella, Izzy, and Tiana. "We shouldn't do it like this—it's mean."

"I'm not scared," Kim replied, but her body language and the wideness of her blue eyes contradicted that.

Marie and Manon's faces blanked, but Raima knew they resented the interruption. The other five girls, Ella, Tiana, Aine, Limei, and Izzy all appeared startled by the change of routine.

Angry with them for their mindless support of the hazing, Raima said, "We're better than this. We should act like it." Looking to Marie and Manon, Raima broadcasted her next thoughts so that even Kim would hear them. *"We shouldn't be wasting our time like this. We have to think about getting out of here. Kim can help us with that."*

Manon hissed and stabbed psychically at Raima with a powerful burst of alarm. *"Shut up! We don't tell new girls about our plans until they survive the shots."* Her words were aimed at Raima, hiding them from Kim.

"This changes now," Raima said aloud. The scientists watched them through the cameras, observing them as if they were animals in a cage.

"You don't decide that," Manon shot back.

"We decide that," Marie put in, completing her sister's sentence.

Raima focused on Marie for a moment, sensing a wavering spirit. "Why should you be the one to decide it?" she asked, keeping her voice calm and gentle. "Because you were first?"

"Yes," Manon snapped. She jerked her chin upward in a motion that shouted a challenge, drawing Raima's attention back to her, away from Marie.

The instinct rose inside Raima again: *Marie is the weaker one.* She ignored Manon and stayed centered on Marie. "How would you feel if you were in Kim's position?"

"Stop talking about me like I'm not here," Kim muttered halfheartedly. She was clever enough to know something dangerous and beyond her comprehension was going on. She understood that saying as little as possible was the wisest thing she could do in the moment.

Raima addressed the group telepathically, including Kim. *"We're wasting time playing these stupid games with each other. We must think about surviving, about getting out of here. Marie, Manon, you told us that you want us to practice fighting with our minds. But learning on the nurses and technicians is dangerous. Why are you teasing Kim when you could be asking for her help? For the first week she won't have any power. We can test ourselves using her mind."*

"What?" Kim blurted, alarmed. She backed away from the other girls and Raima, holding her hands up in a defensive posture, as if ready to physically fight them off. "What the hell are you people talking about? Use my mind to t—"

Before Kim could finish the sentence, Raima reached out to silence her, but there was no need. Kim broke off and closed her mouth. Her eyes, which were wide and round with fear, fluttered as if she was about to lose consciousness and fall to the floor. She tottered for a second and might've fallen, but Raima steadied her small frame, supporting her.

"Are you all right?" she asked.

Kim flinched away. "Don't touch me," she growled. "Don't talk to me." She pulled free of Raima's hands and staggered back several feet, moving toward the door. She lay down on one of the beds closest to the exit of the bunkroom and covered her eyes with her hands, as if trying to sleep.

"You say *we're* the ones scaring the new girl?" Manon demanded in a snide tone.

Raima looked back at the twins and the four other girls, their closest allies. She saw a varied landscape in their faces: anger and outrage, confusion and wariness. All of them scrambled into their own minds, cutting themselves off. It was like they were retreating into soundproof rooms and slamming the doors shut behind them. But who were they protecting themselves from? Was it Raima, or the twins?

Then the truth hit her. Marie and Manon had possessed the power of telepathy the longest and already confessed that they knew how to make others do as they wanted. Kim hadn't cut herself off midsentence; Marie and Manon had silenced her.

Every new girl that came in, whether they lived or died, the twins learned from them. Every time. For a moment Raima was frightened, wondering when and how Marie and Manon manipulated *her*. Why couldn't she remember it? Which of her actions hadn't been her own? Did the others—Aine, Tiana, Izzy, and Ella—know? Did Qi and Limei know?

But Marie and Manon couldn't manipulate Raima or any of the other telepathic girls anymore. They could feel the mental touch now, no matter how light and delicate, and with effort they could block it out.

"I'm sorry," Raima said to fill the silence with sound, but she was glaring at the twins. *"I know what you did."*

"You should be sorry," Marie scolded her. "Look how upset she is."

"You made her that way," Raima retorted. Aloud she repeated her apology, "I'm sorry."

Manon replied to her telepathic words, shouting out so that her psychic voice filled the whole bunkroom. *"Thanks, Raima. You might've just killed us all by exposing our plan to an idiot who doesn't know any better than to talk out loud. You should be thanking us for stopping her from blabbing it. If the scientists knew we were plotting against them they'd just kill us and start over."*

"I'll talk to her once she's calmed down," Raima said, maintaining the illusion of the audible conversation. To Manon she said, *"You're no better than they are."*

"Are you stupid enough to really think that?" Manon demanded.

She pushed off the wall near the bathroom, leaving Marie alone with the other four girls. She approached Raima in a tall, tense strut, like some of the posturing men Raima had seen fighting over their favorite girl in the brothel.

Raima was taller than Manon by no more than a fingerbreadth. The difference was so minimal that it was unnoticeable, but Raima felt it nonetheless. After the uncountable men who'd beaten her, who'd pulled her hair, slapped her face, violated her body, and insulted her in every way possible, Manon wasn't a physical threat at all. Perhaps Manon sensed this or considered how she'd look to the scientists she always claimed were watching and listening to their every movement and sound. Whatever her reasoning was, she deflated rather than strike out at Raima. Instead Manon stood in front of her and said, *"You'll just have to wait and see how wrong you are."*

She smiled and then turned back to Marie and the other girls. "I'm done with this."

Ella exclaimed suddenly, startling everyone nearby. "I know! Let's do song poetry!" Her freckled face was smiling but it was a false cheer. She was a peacemaker, gentle and patient. Her pale blue eyes slid between the twins and Raima with obvious anxiousness. Song poetry was another name for language lessons. They recited song lyrics aloud to one another in a game that disguised what was happening on a telepathic level as they translated the words and sentences into the twins' secret language.

"I'm up for that," Izzy chimed in.

"Oh!" Tiana squealed with unfeigned joy, "I remember a really good one. . . ."

Safely ignored, Raima left the group to lie down on her bunk. She could sense Limei and Qi a short distance away, chatting about food, masking their private telepathic conversation. In the bed by the door, Kim was silent and exuding misery.

Foreboding closed in around Raima's mind, constricting her skull. It was the same feeling that accompanied every small rebellion in the brothel—the certainty that she would be punished by someone, somehow. She had broken the rules, making the mistake of assuming she could change them. In the brothel it would have meant starvation, beating, or rape. It was a relief to know what punishments were coming.

Not knowing was terrifying.

She closed her eyes and thought of Qi's warm, comforting presence, and her constant support and affection. She was almost asleep when Nurse Victoria came to escort them for their standard class and testing time.

TWELVE

During the evening meal, Raima sat with Qi across the table from her and tried to find her appetite. Their supper consisted of hot dogs, crinkle-cut French fries, and pudding cups.

Qi broke bits of her hot dog off and popped them into her mouth, barely chewing before swallowing. "They like American food here," she said, butchering the pronunciation with her accent and by speaking through her full mouth, but she projected her meaning straight to Raima, ensuring she understood. "So boring."

With a nod, Raima bit into her own hot dog, but the food was lumpy and tasteless on her tongue. She scanned the small cafeteria and saw Kim enter with her own tray. Their eyes locked for a moment and then the other girl turned away and marched for the unused middle lunch table.

Raima leaned to one side to see Kim around Qi and reached for the girl's mind, exploring her memory of the moment the twins manipulated her. Kim's perception of the conversation was completely changed. All mention of an escape plot was gone. Instead Kim remembered the event as traumatic because it was her first glimpse of telepathy. Yet that was altered too. Raima felt the lingering shock of the discovery, and then Kim's unthinking acceptance. The twins forced Kim to overcome her initial reaction with unnatural speed.

The sound of Qi tearing open her pudding cup startled Raima, bringing her mind back into her physical body with a jolt. She watched as Qi dipped her spoon into the black goop—it was chocolate flavored—and brought a mouthful back up to her lips. In her head she heard Qi say, *"She doesn't know what they did to her. She couldn't feel it."* Qi's black-brown eyes met Raima's and narrowed. *"Does it make you wonder what the twins did to you before you became one of us?"*

"Yes," Raima whispered aloud.

While she licked the back of her spoon, Qi flicked her eyes down the length of their table, indicating the other girls. *"Do you think Izzy, Tiana, and Aine ever wonder what the twins did to them?"*

Raima nodded but her gaze drifted away when she saw Kaiden enter the cafeteria and immediately move to join his sister. Kim greeted him with a smile, comfortable with her surroundings despite the strangeness. Kaiden's body language, meanwhile, displayed his unease. He sat hunched over, as if trying to hide his mind and body from the invasive telepathic touch of everyone around him.

"They haven't gotten to him yet," Qi told her. She slurped on pudding.

"Do they manipulate the boys too?" Raima asked. She hadn't considered that.

Qi scowled, as if unhappy with her food. *"I don't know—but they have a reason for everything they do."* She glanced away from her pudding, meeting Raima's eye. *"But they did the right thing this time. It was too early to let Kim know our plans."*

"If the twins even have a plan," Raima shot back.

As both the boys and girls finished their meals and headed back to their respective bunkrooms, Raima saw Nurse Victoria motion to Kim, drawing her away. The two walked back toward the testing and medical areas of the facility. Raima's heart pounded in her chest as a technician led them down the girls' hallway to their bunkroom. Once inside Raima went to her cot and lay down, trying to stay calm, and waited. An hour later Kim still hadn't returned. Manon reached out and grabbed Raima's mind while they waited, ordering her to welcome Kim back whenever she arrived and debrief her.

"Ask her what they did to her, what they said, everything. Then tell me or Marie. Will you do it?" Manon's dark, stubborn anger and resentment lingered. *This is your fault for questioning our authority.*

Raima, on her bed, struggling to relax, felt her face flush with impotent rage. She restrained it, knowing that if Manon caught the emotion she'd needle her more, feeling triumphant that she'd troubled Raima as much as she had. *"What are you worried about?"* she taunted Manon. *"You erased her memory and twisted her feelings. You abused your talent. She has nothing to tell them, nothing to reveal. Or are you just trying to shame me? The twins always know best, right?"*

"Just do what I tell you," Manon shot back.

When Kim came back, escorted by Nurse Vieve, she was rubbing her arm. Raima picked up her thoughts: the image of the needle with its sickly opaque solution, the sting as it pricked her and forced its toxic components into her body. While Kim sat on a bunk, pale with fatigue, Raima walked over to speak to her.

The hard concrete of the bunkroom was cold through Raima's thin gray scrubs as she sat down, but the chill in Kim's gaze was far worse. "What are you doing here?" she asked.

"I wanted to see how you're doing and to apologize for scaring you," Raima began in a soft, gentle voice. "Starting with the teddy bear."

The hostility in Kim's face quavered and gave way, revealing hurt. "Why didn't you tell me what happened to you?" she asked.

"I wanted to," Raima murmured, averting her eyes. "But I was sure if I told you it would have disgusted you." She paused and then asked, "What exactly did you see?"

"I don't want to say," Kim whispered. Her blue eyes flew around the room, taking in the other eight girls, all unknown to her.

"They already know everything about me," Raima told her with a small, mirthless smile. "While I was sick here in my first few weeks, I dreamt constantly about my past. All the girls here overheard it or dreamed along with me."

Kim's face reflected a mixture of horror and revulsion—but also sympathy. Raima heard her thoughts: *That would be so awful.* And then, her concerns changed, flicking swiftly to the shots. She leaned closer to Raima and asked, "Do these shots make you feel as bad as the others at CF-Gen did? Everyone here looks so . . . gaunt."

"It's worse," Raima admitted. She bit her lips, stopping herself from adding, *A lot more people die.*

A wave of dread spread through Kim and hit Raima like a wall. She flinched. Kim asked, "How many people die here?"

"Two have died since I arrived," Raima said. "There was a new boy—Levi—he came before you and he's still sick, but the twins think he'll live and they're usually right."

Kim's lips pinched tight. Raima didn't need to read her mind to know it was helplessness. She heard Kim's thoughts again: *I wonder what they say about me.*

"I'm sorry I was so mean when I saw you again. I guess I was just mad that you wouldn't trust me enough to tell me in person." She hesitated and Raima saw flashes of her memory from the bear, intolerable and familiar because they were from her own past. The taste of blood in her mouth after a beating, the gnawing sensation in her stomach from constant fear and hunger, the revulsion she endured each time a john touched her.

The Raima of those memories was a numb, desperate girl, tormented and deadened. The present Raima was transformed. Now she'd fight and kill for those living around her, not to escape and seek her own death, but to live on. A frightened thought passed through her before she could stop it—what if the twins changed her, manipulating her before she could feel it? Had she come to care for the other girls naturally, or had Marie and Manon forced her to do it? She flushed hot at the idea and then cold anger set in. She struggled to put the thoughts aside, knowing she'd never know for sure.

She turned her focus toward Manon's line of questioning and telepathically asked, *"I don't mean to alarm you, but I have to ask what the scientists were doing with you all this time. What tests did they run? What did they ask? Don't answer me aloud, just think what you want to say, and I'll hear it."*

Kim's eyes widened as she registered Raima's mental touch and voice. She thought, *This is so weird. Can you hear me?*

"I can," Raima replied immediately and smiled to encourage her. *"Lights-out is coming so we have to be quick, but you should know this—always watch what you say out loud. We're observed in here and everywhere. It's worse than CF-Gen. So be careful all the time what you say."*

Kim's expression went from surprised as Raima first began

speaking inside her mind to outright horror. Her lips parted slightly as she stared with mounting shock and fear. "I'll be careful," she murmured aloud.

"*Shh!*" Raima scolded. "*Think it, remember?*"

Kim nodded soberly. *Yeah.*

"*We're going to have two conversations so that we look normal, okay?*" Raima asked and then said aloud, "How's your brother?"

"He's good," Kim replied. "I'll get to see him more often here, I think."

"*What did they say to you today?*" Raima asked. "I'm glad for you. I was an only child."

"I'd be lonely without Kaiden," Kim murmured. She smiled and then concentrated, focusing her thoughts to continue the true conversation. *They asked me about what happened after I arrived. They did a lot of tests where they asked me a question and one of you or one of the boys answered.*

"*That's a normal test,*" Raima said. "*Tell me about their other questions with just you alone and how you answered.*" She cleared her throat and tossed her long black hair over her shoulder. "It wasn't that lonely. I had my mother. I loved her so much." She closed her eyes, restraining intense emotions from surfacing as she said the words.

"I miss my mom too," Kim said and suddenly her shoulders shook. She covered her mouth and blinked, trying to banish the tears. *They kept asking me about you and those twins, about what you wanted to use my mind for. I didn't understand what they were talking about. It was— it scared me. Like they wanted to dissect my brain or something.*

Luckily, the twins had purged the incriminating information from Kim's mind. The interrogators from Genoquip were probing Kim, hoping to find a crack in the twins' wall of secrecy. Raima knew she'd miscalculated with Kim. In protecting her from Marie and Manon she'd jeopardized all the girls. As much as she despised the twins' manipulative use of their telepathic power to change Kim's memory, it was necessary in this case.

She breathed out, long and hard. She hadn't known she was holding her breath while she waited for Kim's answer, but the dizziness in her head provided firm evidence.

"*Don't worry about that,*" Raima reassured Kim. "*You're safe. We'll protect you. I'll make sure of it.*"

The sound and vibrations of footsteps reached them. Nurse Victoria opened the door, announcing lights-out. Raima left Kim and headed back to her own bunk while the nurse began her rounds, checking all the girls' basic vital signs. As Nurse Victoria stopped beside the twins— Marie first and then Manon—Raima observed them out of the corner of her eye. Just as she had been hyperaware of Ferde's whereabouts and activities while in the brothel, she had become vigilant and suspicious of Marie and Manon. In the brothel she'd watched Ferde and her other captors with the intensity of prey staring down a hunting predator, but now she felt a different energy. She was biding her time, learning and waiting.

Tonight the nurse took longer with Marie and Manon. She hovered beside their bunks for a minute more than anyone else's. Although it seemed the nurse was following the standard nighttime procedure—listening to Marie's heartbeat or taking Manon's blood pressure—Raima sensed underlying activity. If the twins had the power to completely alter a memory or even remove it entirely, what other things could they do inside the defenseless minds of non-telepaths?

Raima let her mind float free of her body, open and listening. As Nurse Victoria left the twins, she invaded the woman's surface thoughts. Light and unobtrusive, Raima sought out any telltale signs that Marie and Manon might've left behind inside the nurse's mind. She found lingering clouds of confusion hovering over the psychic landscape. Unnatural eddies were stirring inside the vast, unfathomable ocean of the brain. Raima sampled them, dipping into the disturbances.

She saw fake and hazy memories of Kim yelling, fighting against shots, cursing at the nurse, refusing to cooperate. An idea spun inside the nurse's mind, alien and nonsensical—*Kim is a bad candidate for the experiment. She must be eliminated.* Then, in a related thought, Raima saw and felt concerns about herself within the nurse's mind. *Raima is too dangerous to be kept alive. She is the leader of the girls' unrest.*

Clenching her jaw, stifling her rage for the moment, Raima waited for Nurse Victoria to come to her bedside. The nurse's eyes were cold as she ordered Raima about and noted all her vital signs in her handheld medical e-chart. Just as the twins did, Raima made the nurse hesitate while she listened to her heartbeat or took her blood pressure. In the extra time, mere seconds, Raima dug through the nurse's mind, scooping out the irregularities, smoothing the disturbed surface thoughts.

She could've turned Marie and Manon's own manipulations back on them but decided against it. It was a despicable move, a dangerous and unnecessary power game where the loser might be killed. Raima refused to play that game, to engage the twins—and the other girls—in a useless, distracting struggle that divided and intimidated rather than empowered and encouraged. She hoped that Aine, Ella, Tiana, and Izzy would change sides, abandoning the twins and removing their power base. Then the group would be free of the twins' fear-based control and could unite with trust, mutual survival, and the need to escape.

The nurse's mind was an adaptive, fluid environment. While Raima deleted the twins' incongruous additions, the sea of Victoria's mind flowed seamlessly into the holes. The first tampering by the twins set the nurse on edge, making her tense. Raima's quick thought-surgery soothed the reaction and Victoria sighed heavily as she tapped into her e-chart, relaxing.

She finished the exam and walked to the door. "All right, kiddies," she said in her dry voice. "Lights-out. Go to sleep."

Raima kept her mind hovering near the nurse as she switched off the lights and shut the door. There was no sign of further brain-meddling by the twins, no mental energy buzzing in the air. She let her mind settle back into her own skull, like a bird returning to its nest to roost. She fussed with her thin sheets, putting on a convincing performance while she considered her next course of action.

This attempt by the twins to sabotage her had failed, but there'd be others. Raima had to dethrone the twins. Though Raima had dealt with female power struggles in the brothel her usual strategy was avoiding fights, not starting them. In the brothel she'd been docile, even if it meant she suffered as a result. But she wasn't the same girl any longer. She knew that backing down and submitting to the twins would only get her and Kim—even Qi—killed.

As soon as she heard the nurse lock the door, Raima sat up in bed, abandoning any pretense of sleep. She felt the other girls brushing against her psychically. Some with blank curiosity, but others exuded hostile vigilance. Raima kept them all out, imagining her mind as a hard shell, impenetrable and cold. She reached Qi's bed and hesitated, waiting as the other girl reached out with her mental touch, questioning.

She projected her thoughts into Qi's consciousness, saying, "I need to talk to you."

Qi shifted in the bed, moving aside to make room for Raima. A strange tension, distinct and different from her concerns about the twins' behavior, made Raima's back and chest taut as she joined Qi in the narrow bed. The emotions within her were impossible to ignore. She'd experienced many negative anxieties in her short lifetime: the fear of a beating or a rape; of failing to meet her quota with the johns and going hungry as a result; the childish crush of doom that came with her mother's disappointment or disapproval. This anxiety was unlike any of those things. It was something new.

Qi was the first to speak after Raima was under the covers. "I'm sorry about earlier. I scared you. I didn't mean to—I never wanted to do that."

"I'm not scared," Raima replied, evading that topic for as long as she could. Qi knew she was lying. Their telepathic minds were even closer than their bodies on the bed, not merely touching, but intermingling, ingrained inside one another. Qi's emotions passed through Raima's mind and tangled with her own in a confusing mass. Was she anxious about the threat posed by the twins, or was she afraid that she'd exposed herself too much and too fast? Was she worried about Kim's survival at the facility, or *jealous* of her?

The simultaneous gift and curse of telepathy was its potential to breakdown the self, dissolving the barriers between two or more people, opening their secrets to one another so thoroughly that there could be no denial and no misunderstandings. Raima grappled with that strain now, separating herself from Qi to take stock of her emotions, needs, and reactions. She'd resisted Qi's confession earlier, running from it. She was doing the same thing now, but only for a moment. Even considering it made her stomach flutter as if it was trying to take flight. She didn't want to explore it further, but she could already feel Qi's clever mind sorting out the cluttered emotions, uncovering the truth.

"I need to talk about—" Raima started to say, but Qi interrupted her with a burst of sudden, wild energy.

"You need to talk about the twins," she said. *"I know. You're right. There's something you should know—Limei and Ella, even Tiana, they're fed up with the twins."*

"But Ella and Tiana are always with them," Raima protested, baffled at the new information. *"Limei is with you, but I thought that was because you both speak Mandarin."*

"Ella is afraid the twins will let her die if she stirs up any trouble at all. And Tiana is Ella's best friend. She won't do anything to endanger Ella." Qi sighed, and her frustration hit Raima. *"Limei and Sarai were close. Limei nursed Sarai back to health when she was sick after first coming here. They talked a lot. Sarai never liked the twins. She didn't want to learn their secret language. She didn't want to escape. Even after she met the doctor she wasn't convinced."*

Raima saw images of an Asian man, plump around the midsection. His short stature revealed a background on Earth. The man was the doctor in charge of the TC-Gen facility as seen through Qi's eyes. Raima saw and felt the doctor's cold stethoscope, the roughness of his hands as he scraped her skin and cut her hair close to the scalp for various samples. And then there was the awkwardness of a pelvic exam, Qi's discomfort and tenseness as the doctor poked at her intimate parts, collecting yet another sample from her body.

"How could Sarai not believe if she'd read the doctor's mind?" Raima asked.

Qi blinked in the darkness. Raima was so close to the other girl that she heard the small, wet sound of Qi's eyelids opening and closing. *"She wasn't very good at reading minds. Or maybe she just couldn't handle it."* Qi shrugged. *"Either way, the twins don't have much patience for that sort of thing."* Her head shifted on the pillow and Raima felt her skin flush as she anticipated what Qi would say next. *"You're on their hate list now."*

"I know—so is Kim. Qi, I need your help. I don't know what to do." The admission came with surprising ease, but with it was an unexpected surge of weakness and neediness that Raima despised. She tried hiding the emotions, burying them so deep within herself that Qi wouldn't be able to find them, but it was too late.

The weakness was as slippery as an eel and seemed to have a mind of its own. It went swimming straight for Qi as if lured in.

Qi let out a long, slow sigh. She wrapped one arm around Raima's waist and leaned in, touching their foreheads together. *"You don't have to be afraid to care about me. And you can ask anything of me. If I can give it to you or do it for you, I will. Before you got here I was alone except for Limei. The twins were cruel to me because they thought I'd die. When I lived anyway, they still didn't care. I've never liked them, but I've always done whatever they wanted because Limei warned me that bad things happen to the girls the twins don't trust."* She squeezed Raima's arm, gentle but firm. *"But with you, I feel like we'll survive this place and not hate ourselves for what happened here."*

"We'll be able to look into a mirror without shame," Raima said, remembering Kati with a sting of pain.

"We'll know we didn't let Sarai die. We'll know we only did what we had to do to get out of here." She stopped for a moment and Raima sensed something brewing, rising until it was ready to spill out. Finally, Qi said, *"Raima, Marie and Manon haven't told you yet, but Ella, Limei, and Aine have all agreed that when we escape, we're going to kill the boys."*

Raima jerked physically with shock. *"What?"* she demanded, incredulous.

"You remember," Qi rushed to explain, *"when I showed you how Ella, Limei, and Aine had all been raped?"*

Stunned Raima answered in a whisper. "Yes, of course I remember that."

"Hush!" Qi scolded. *"The twins were going to tell you about this but then Kim showed up and now Limei came to warn me that the twins don't want me telling you anything else."*

The risk that Qi was taking became suddenly clear to Raima. The turmoil in her mind quieted as a rush of gratitude as admiration pushed aside everything else. She said nothing and didn't try to share the emotions with Qi because she could already feel Qi absorbing her reaction.

Qi gave a quiet little scoff aloud as well as inside her mind. *"Screw the twins,"* she cursed. *"I'm with you, no matter what anyone else has to say about it."*

"Thank you," Raima said, scarcely daring to breathe.

"Don't thank me," Qi shot back with a minor flash of irritation that transformed into self-deprecating humor. *"You're lying there thinking I'm brave, but I'm not. I'm not as good as you are. I just can't stop myself when it comes to you."*

Embarrassed by Qi's kindness—what Raima thought was flattery—she pressed on with the previous topic, determined to learn more. *"Why would Ella and Limei agree to do something like that? Why would the twins want to kill the boys? I can understand killing the nurses and the technicians if they try to stop us, but the boys are victims like we are. . . ."*

"Even Bryson?" Qi asked. *"The rapist? Would you call Ferde a victim if he was one of the boys?"*

Raima bit her lip and closed her eyes against the faint gleam of Qi's gaze, piercing even through the blackness. *"Ferde is dead."* Hearing his name in Qi's mental voice raised a sick sensation in her stomach.

"You wouldn't call him a victim," Qi answered for her.

"No," Raima snapped. *"He created victims. He tortured girls. He—"* She cut herself off, drawing in a deep breath to calm the furious pounding of her heart. *"This isn't the brothel,"* she said, repeating her mantra. *"Bryson isn't my problem and the other boys really are victims like us. Kim's brother is one of them. Why would the twins be so bloodthirsty, so stupid and cruel to—"*

Qi gave Raima a small but forceful shake. *"Those boys aren't all like Bryson, you're right. But the twins have this idea in their heads that if the boys escape when we do—if they live—then they'll use their telepathy to hurt other people, probably girls like us. The twins think they'll all turn into versions of Bryson."*

For a moment Raima envisioned all the boys at TC-Gen as she saw them each day during meals, class times, and the occasional test with the nurses and technicians. Several of the boys were frail, as awkward and pathetic as birds with broken wings. They were quiet, and laughter was rare. Bryson bullied them all as the oldest. They were pitiable, not the threatening monsters that Marie and Manon dreamed up for their own dramatic and cruel entertainment.

Qi caught Raima's mental image of the boys and snorted aloud before pulling her arm away from Raima and covering her mouth, silencing the laugh that nearly burst out. *"I know. It's dumb."*

"How could they get Ella and Limei to go along with that? And what about Tiana and Izzy? Could they really believe that nonsense?"

"They say something else too, something I don't understand about genetics," Qi went on. *"The twins have been here so long that they've read more minds than anyone else and actually understand some of what the scientists are trying to do here. They say that all of us will have telepathic kids someday. So even if none of the boys right now have a strong ability to read or control minds, their kids might inherit it. They might be like Bryson."*

"They're lying," Raima said with a burst of confidence sparking in her mind. *"They're scaring everyone here to control them."* She pushed some of her own knowledge toward Qi, explaining her lack of fear at the idea.

On Earth any genetic manipulation or experimentation that could spread through the population via inheritance was restricted or outlawed. It was common knowledge that standard, legal gene alterations could not physically be passed on to the next generation. Raima learned this during her hospital stay in Elysia City Hospital. Her doctor there had taken the time to explain the procedure that would cure her HIV infection, saying it involved replacing her natural immune system and using a bone marrow transplant from a donor who was genetically unable to contract the HIV virus. But the new immune system could not be inherited by any children she might have, which was in accordance with Earth-based laws governing the moral and ethical use of gene therapy.

"That's what I want to believe too," Qi replied. *"But Marie and Manon really do know more about this place and what it's doing. I mean, do you think what they're doing here is legal? If they can do an experiment that kills this many people, maybe the twins are right."*

Raima's body shook with nervous energy, certain she was right. *"No, I don't believe them. I don't trust them."*

"Me neither," Qi agreed. *"Don't let on that I told you if you can help it."* She hesitated and then said, *"And don't tell Kim."*

"But her brother . . ."

"Don't tell her. We won't let it happen, so why bother telling her, right?" Qi asked. *"Besides, she'd probably blab it to the twins and then everyone would know they can't trust me anymore. I'd be cut off."*

Raima agreed voicelessly. Sleep tugged at her, drawing her in. She fought it off, determined to forge escape plans of her own with Qi. *"Do you know anything else about how the twins planned to escape, or when? The sooner we do it, the better."* She yearned to be away from the constant threat of the facility and of ending the danger posed by the twins. She imagined a garden, a place of greenery and flowing water where she could take Qi's hand and walk with her under Earth's blue sky.

She could never go back to Earth, but for the first time in her life freedom was a real possibility.

"No," Qi admitted with a touch of sadness coloring her mind. She glimpsed Raima's mental imagery and shared the same longing. *"Sometimes I think the twins are scared of escaping and are just trying to trap us here with them."*

Fear of the unknown was a powerful obstacle. Even for Raima, who'd seen some of the worst that society had to offer, questions and uncertainties weighed heavily if she let them. Where would she live after escaping Genoquip? Where would she work? How could she survive with such enormous debts crushing her? For the twins, who'd never had to worry about any of these things, the glimpses they got of the outside world from the other subjects' minds must be a confusing mixture of paradise and hell.

"We've all got an advantage over the twins," Qi pointed out. *"We've lived outside. We know how the world works. We know what to expect and the twins don't. But now we don't have to play by anyone else's rules. You're not thinking right,"* Qi said and pressed closer until their foreheads touched again. *"What we can do with our minds—as long as there's a person to talk with—we can fool anyone. We can get new identities. We can take whatever we want."*

"But it's wrong. It's why the twins wanted to kill the boys." Raima frowned in the darkness, caught between the shock that what Qi said could be true and the realization that it might even be the *only* way she could survive away from Genoquip. With her enormous debts and lack of an education, where would she be able to work? She was trapped, as were most of the other subjects of the TC-Gen facility. Unable to live in an acceptable way that served society outside of Genoquip and MIHO, how could they do anything except use their telepathic talents?

The realization made Raima's mind spin with confusion and self-doubt. She'd just argued that the boys were victims and couldn't be exterminated like cockroaches or rabid dogs. But if the boys escaped too, they'd face the same societal challenges and restrictions. They'd use their talents, no matter how weak they were, taking what they wanted—which would be *everything*. And what would they do when they felt they needed sex? Would they seduce women and girls against their wills and then leave them to do it all over again with some new victim? Would they be able to resist the temptation to explore the full depths of their capabilities? Would telepathy, over time, naturally transform all of them into abusive, heartless men like Bryson and Ferde?

Raima shuddered, horrified and sickened by her own thoughts.

Qi closed the tiny gap between them in the dark and kissed Raima, gently pressing their lips together. The warm, moist sensation sent heat through Raima's body and shivers down her back. Thoughts about the boys' future vanished. The tension and anxiety she'd felt before about caring for Qi dissolved, replaced with a new and intense hunger.

She gripped Qi tighter, closer to her. Qi's excitement and joy spilled over into Raima's mind, mirroring the sudden burst of her own emotions. She stroked her hands down Qi's back, the long curving dip of her waist, and each rounded bump where the girl's ribs pressed out against the smoothness of her skin. Gooseflesh erupted, dimpling the skin at her touch and Raima sensed Qi's pleasure through the joining of their minds.

Qi broke their long kiss, brushing her lips over Raima's neck. The shivering delight that passed through Raima became a warm and delicious ache between her legs. She'd never felt pleasure in all her time at the brothel. It had always been pain, the ache of abuse. Now her body was alive in places that she normally dreaded any sensation at all.

Qi felt it and Raima heard the other girl laugh within her mind. *"This is what it's supposed to be like,"* she said. *"And this is just the beginning."*

All Raima's other concerns seemed faraway, too distant and small to care about. Only escape loomed with its promise of freedom. Raima kissed Qi again, relishing the softness of her lips, the glow of warmth and affection radiating through Qi's mind.

"Whatever happens," Raima said, mirroring Qi's earlier words, *"I'm with you."*

THIRTEEN

aima came awake with a rush of alarm. Breathing fast, she tried to sit up, but Qi's body was too intertwined with her own. Over the startled pounding of her heart, Raima heard the sound that had woken her: retching noises emanating from the bathroom.

Without using her mind to check, Raima could guess who was sick. Kim was the only girl undergoing the injections.

Raima extricated herself from Qi and walked to the bathroom. She leaned her head in, squinting in the bluish gleam of the nightlight beside the bathroom. In the deep gloom she saw Kim slumped near the toilet bowl, shivering.

"Are you finished" Raima asked softly. "I'll help you back to bed."

Kim let out a wet sob and countered Raima's question with one of her own. "Am I going to die?" Her voice shook along with her body. "This is just the start, isn't it? I'm already so weak. . . ."

"You'll be fine," Raima reassured her. "You're strong."

Kim sniffled. "Not as strong as you."

Raima scoffed at the compliment. "I'm just lucky." *I've never been lucky before*, she thought, recalling the conversation she had with the testing technician at CF-Gen. She didn't feel strong or smart, but Qi and Kim and even the twins all saw something in her that drew their admiration and fascination—or their fear. It was ridiculous to Raima. She'd been a mediocre child, one of billions in India. On Mars she'd been an orphan and a sex slave. It didn't seem like a recipe for a leader, a lover, a friend, or anything worthy of admiration. It certainly wasn't lucky. The only thing Raima could believe about herself was that she was a survivor.

"No," Kim said, wrenching more strength from her voice. "I lost my parents and my freedom, and I wanted to die at CF-Gen. I *wanted* to die. But what I went through—it was *nothing* compared to what you went through." She paused, struggling to breathe without hiccupping. "I'm not strong enough to—"

"Hush," Raima interrupted her. "Don't worry about it." She strode forward and knelt. "I'll get you back to bed. The only thing you can do is rest and get better."

Kim grunted with effort as Raima hauled her up and they began the walk back to her bunk. "If something happens to me," she said, ignoring Raima's encouragement, "I want you to look after Kaiden for me."

"Nothing is going to happen to you," Raima shot back in a quiet but forceful voice.

"But if it did . . ."

"You don't even have to ask," Raima replied.

She supported Kim as the girl crawled back into her bunk and pulled the covers over her body like a shield, as if that could protect her from the illness inside her. Raima considered climbing into the bunk with her but couldn't stop the selfish desire to rejoin Qi. This was only the beginning of Kim's illness. It would be a lot worse before the end.

Raima didn't allow herself to think about the consequences of Kim's death—or the fact that Kaiden was being transformed into one of "the boys." He would come out of the injections with the twins' telepathic gene and some measure of talent, or he'd die. Would letting him and the other boys survive be a grave mistake?

She returned to Qi's bunk, refusing to think about it. Under the covers she snuggled close to the one part of her life that was lucky.

When the nurses came to escort them to breakfast, classes, and the usual testing, Raima paid close attention to the twins and the nurses. Kim was too ill to leave her bed. Nurse Vieve left Kim with a large bucket for her to vomit into whenever necessary. She also promised to bring food if Kim could stomach it. Raima already knew an IV would appear at some point during the illness to rehydrate Kim and pump nutrients into her. For now, while the injections were just starting, Kim would have to muddle through.

Although nothing was obviously amiss, Raima's stomach stayed in a tight knot throughout breakfast. The twins behaved normally. They smiled and laughed and ate. They chatted with Aine, Tiana, and Izzy, their favorite companions. They even looked at Raima without malice, but Raima could still feel their dislike behind their deceitful smiles. Limei, Ella, Qi, and Raima sat together, slightly apart. Ella and Tiana sat between the two groups, chatting and interacting with the twins.

With the dynamics of the girls' group to distract her, Raima didn't notice Kaiden until halfway through her meal. Pale with sickness, the tall, lanky boy watched Raima from his spot at the edge of the boys' table. Unlike the girls, who at least appeared to be one solid unit of socialization, the boys were fractured. Bryson ruled them as a bully. The other boys clung together, but they splintered as soon as Bryson applied any kind of pressure. They had little to say to one another and were naturally wary of a newcomer like Kaiden—especially because Kaiden had family at TC-Gen and no one else, aside from the twins, had a sibling undergoing the same suffering.

When Kaiden took his tray to the girls' table and stood in front of Raima, everyone noticed. Raima felt the mental energy of both the boys and the girls focusing on Kaiden and herself. She slumped, trying to hide from the attention that pressed on her from all sides.

"Can I sit here?" Kaiden asked. His voice was weak and hoarse. He seemed unaware of the disturbance he'd caused as conversations faltered, and telepathic words buzzed just beneath the surface.

There was no official reason why boys and girls stayed segregated during class and mealtimes, but it happened without fail. Though the boys and girls were in the same room while eating, learning, or testing, they rarely interacted and never sat together. The twins disapproved of such fraternizing and the girls' unified front intimidated the boys. But Kaiden was new and he'd been eating with Kim at the unused third table.

Feeling the focus of the entire cafeteria on her, Raima hesitated.

Kaiden stared at her, his hazel-brown eyes imploring her to accept him. There was a clear family resemblance between the siblings in the smooth, refined curve of his nose, and the waviness of his brown-blond hair. She heard Kim's voice in her head, the memory of it shaking with weakness and emotion as she asked Raima to care for this boy.

"Go ahead," she told him and forced a smile. Further down the long, rectangular table, Raima could already feel the twins' outrage. Raima couldn't be certain whether their reaction was to Kaiden seeking her permission to sit among them, her allowing him to sit with them, or if it was just the breech of tradition.

Kaiden sat down, forcing Qi to scoot closer to Limei until their shoulders touched. One of the lines separating the twins' group from Raima's blurred and disappeared. The division was only an extra inch of space between Limei and Izzy, but now it was entirely emotional as the physical divide on one side of the table dissolved.

"Sorry," he said to Qi, smiling with nervousness.

"You are Kim's brother," Qi said.

Qi's thick Manadarin accent gave Kaiden pause. "Yeah," he finally replied. "My name's Kaiden Waller." He looked over his shoulder, gazing back at the boys' table as if regretting his decision.

Raima could already overhear his thoughts and guessed without telepathy why he'd crossed the unspoken chasm between male and female. He was worried about Kim. Though he didn't look all that healthy himself, he was still strong enough to have ventured to the cafeteria, so he could eat something between bouts of retching.

"Your sister's fine," Raima said. "She's sick, but she'll be fine."

Kaiden's head whipped back to face Raima. "You're sure?" he asked, failing to mask the pleading tone of the question.

The boy's eyes were ringed with dark circles and his long body, already stretched thin by the lighter Martian gravity, seemed puny. Even the few zits dotting his forehead were pale and washed out.

"Don't worry about Kim," she reassured him. "I'm taking care of her." She leveled a gaze at him that she hoped was confident rather than condescending. "You have to worry about yourself. I can't take care of you both. If you don't feel strong enough to come out here, then don't. Kim wouldn't want you to ki—" She cut the sentence off, seizing up her throat to do so. She tried again, this time omitting the word *kill*. "Kim wouldn't want you to hurt yourself for her."

"She followed me here," Kaiden said. His head drooped with despair. "She begged for them to transfer us together. I can't believe they listened." He brushed his hands through his hair and blinked, keeping the tears away. "Now I wish they hadn't." He continued in a quieter voice, "That bastard Bryson likes to tell everyone how many people die here and that I'm next."

Raima clenched her jaw, despising Bryson's cruelty. At least the twins wouldn't forecast a new girl's death straight to her face.

"It's not as bad as he makes it out to be," Raima lied to give him courage.

"I hope you're right," Kaiden said, nodding. He smiled. "I mean—I haven't seen anyone die here yet." He chuckled with dark humor. "Everyone *looks* like death warmed over, but that doesn't mean . . ."

"No," Raima agreed with him. "It doesn't mean anything."

"How did you get through it? Why are there more girls here than boys?" Kaiden asked and his gaze swept over the girls at the table, appraising the situation. Raima heard his thoughts spinning with worried suspicions. Did girls survive the injections and tests here better than the boys? Was it true that the facility developed *telepathy* and that the girls were always stronger?

Raima spoke before he could ask more on that topic and frighten himself. "They bring in more girls, that's all." She smiled, passing this off as truth.

"Oh," Kaiden murmured. His anxiety and tenseness dropped a little. He sighed and Raima grimaced as she caught a whiff of his breath, still tinged with bile from vomiting. His tray was almost untouched where it sat in front of him with a half-glass of milk made from powder and a bowl of brown, flaky cereal.

"Eat," Raima ordered him. The stiffness in her voice surprised her and she made an effort to soften it. "If you can."

He nodded, and his large hands groped for the plastic spoon. He had the hands of an adult already, though Raima knew he was only thirteen. Young, innocent, and weak, Raima tried to imagine the boy in front of her with a telepathic mind that he would use against others, robbing them, hurting them, erasing memories, and invading their privacy. If she watched his face while he choked down his cereal and scowled with distaste at his food and milk, she couldn't imagine it at all. But if she focused only on his hands, dexterous despite shaking with weakness, she could feel herself slipping back into memories of the brothel where men with large hands like Kaiden's held her down and beat her.

She turned her attention to her own tray, but found it was as unappealing as the sight of Ferde's clenched fists, as repulsive as his hairy body crushing her beneath him.

The afternoon testing and class time began as it usually did. Kim was absent due to her illness. Kaiden returned to the boys' bunkroom after breakfast. Raima picked out the lingering uncertainty from the girls, particularly the twins, about Kaiden's unexpected visit to their table, but no one expressed anything, whether it was verbal or telepathic.

Early into the class time a technician appeared and summoned Raima away from the larger group. The typical procedure for testing involved more than one subject, so when Raima saw that the technician hadn't called anyone else, her stomach tightened with apprehension. The tech took her to a small office equipped with many of the same machines she'd seen used to monitor their brainwaves. A camera watched her from the corner above the doorway. As the technician, a short man of Asian descent who clearly grew up on Earth, strapped a blood pressure cuff onto her arm, Raima eyed the camera and the equipment, trying to decide if she was in imminent danger. She turned her mind to the technician and probed him to discover what sort of test this was and quickly found the answer.

The time had come for her interview with the doctor, the man running TC-Gen. The name inside the technician's brain was *Dr. Yoon*. Tension built inside her as the technician continued recording mundane vital signs. The twins had warned her about this meeting some time ago, but in the recent chaos and emotional trauma of her life at TC-Gen, Raima couldn't remember what they'd advised. Even if she remembered it exactly, how could she know it was reliable and not merely another way for the twins to control her?

Then the technician pulled out a syringe that was loaded with clear fluid. He tapped at the tube, preparing to inject it into her. Raima's throat constricted. She opened her mouth to speak, torn between questioning him about the shot and refusing it outright. She remembered Sarai's face, pretty and plump despiteenduring the illness, and then saw it in a brief snippet of memory from Qi— cold, gray with death, the girl's dark brown eyes staring out, dry and lifeless. Was this a kill shot? She lashed out at the technician's mind, grabbing it and taking control, as if squeezing it inside her fist.

The little man froze in his place. His jaw went slack. His hands convulsed slightly, the muscles tightening as his neurons fired in random bursts, confused by the bizarre impulses from his brain. The syringe squirted fluid out the needle. An acrid smell entered the air, stinging Raima's nostrils, but she barely noticed what happened in her own body as she poured her consciousness into the technician.

The ocean of his brain parted for her, wide and yawning—but also inviting. She realized she could do almost *anything* to him and he'd be powerless to escape it. The parts of his brain identified themselves at her touch, surrendering their information. There was the portion that regulated memory, another that brought him into sleep, and still others that controlled movement, perception, speech, reading, writing—and deep at the very bottom of this mental sea was the stem that kept him breathing and prompted his heart to beat.

She knew she could jerk on that basal part of the brain and knock him unconscious. She could stop his heart for a moment. She'd thought rewriting a memory would be difficult, but now she saw that it was ridiculously easy. The technician's brain had become her own. It was defenseless.

She asked his brain, "*What's in the shot?*" He answered with a drug name that meant nothing to Raima. "*What does it do?*" she asked. The technician believed the drug sedated the telepathic talent of the subjects. Raima had received the drug before and followed the twins' instructions about pretending it worked. She let out a short sigh of relief and blinked, returning to reality.

The technician staggered as she released him. He puffed hard, as if he'd been exerting himself. His eyes were wide and terrified, reminding Raima of a chicken she'd seen being slaughtered back in India. His back faced the security camera and Raima quickly took hold of his mind again, with more finesse this time, preventing him from calling for help or revealing what happened to the invisible audience.

The man tensed but didn't have the same jerks in his hands, arms, and fingers. She searched out his most recent memories and scrambled them. Then she decided that removing the strange memories completely in case he ever regained them was the best decision. She imagined scooping them out of the sea entirely. Doing that left an erroneous blank inside his mind. The twins managed to rewrite and warp Kim's memories. Could Raima figure out how to do the same within the technician's mind?

"What did you expect would happen?" she asked his brain and found herself inundated with past injections he'd done, all simple and routine. She snatched one up and placed herself and their current location into it, conjuring an image within her own mind and then projecting it into his memories. His brain grasped her falsified images, eager to piece together something that filled the holes in its information. The technician's own brain completed most of her work for her. In a matter of seconds his mind went from a place of turmoil and unease to calmness and peace.

There was only one other problem to fix. Raima focused on the technician's hands, prompting him to act out his memory. He smiled at her, but his eyes were dull and unseeing. His hands moved forward with the injection. The needle gleamed. Raima glanced at the security camera, checking to be certain that its view of the injection and her arm were both blocked by the technician's body. Then she paused his memory and made him stop completely as she pried the syringe from his hands with the arm that his body obscured from the camera. She turned the syringe back toward the technician, touching the needle to his white lab coat, then emptied the tube into the fabric.

The sharp smell of the chemical and the faint streak of moisture on the man's white lab coat were the only signs that Raima wasn't injected with the telepathic sedative. She closed the man's hands around the syringe again and probed his mind to be sure nothing was amiss and that he had no memory of her taking and emptying the syringe. Then she let the technician free with the impression that he had finished his duties with her.

As he smiled at her and turned to leave, Raima's heart hammered inside her. Had she gotten away with such a blunt, easy trick? She wouldn't know for a few hours at least, long enough for the staff to investigate with the technician and look at the surveillance footage.

The doctor entered the room a few minutes later. He was a tiny man, much like the technician. His nose was large, almost bulbous, and his eyebrows were big and bushy. "Hello," he said as he closed the door to the small office behind him. "I am Doctor Yoon. You are Raima Kothari?"

His accent was much lighter than Limei, Qi, or Sarai's, hinting at a lifetime of multilingualism and his frequent—probably constant—use of English. When he looked over her with a calculating gaze, appraising her like property, Raima shuddered, suppressing her nervousness. "Yes," she replied.

Dr. Yoon held an electronic writing tablet. He tapped at the screen and tipped his head up and down, trying to see above or beneath his large, thick glasses. Raima picked up his concentration on the handheld screen and knew without trying that he was navigating subject folders, seeking her information.

Wary of the camera overhead, Raima gently touched his mind, exploring it with caution. The doctor's concentration slowed on the computer. It took him longer to find her information than it should have while she diverted his brain power, distracting him though he didn't know it. She saw memory streams of his time researching, ordering tests, discussing results with other medical people and then with men and women in business suits. She felt the pressure riding on him, his deep fatigue and frustration with what he'd been convinced was a brilliant project that *should* have had more results by now.

"Ah," he said. "Miss Raima. I've been excited, waiting to meet you."

"You have?" Raima asked, surprised by the admission.

"Yes," Dr. Yoon said and nodded. He tucked the tablet into a large pocket in his lab coat and pushed his glasses further up on the bridge of his nose. "CF-Gen said you were very good. Obedient." He smiled and chuckled. "We need that here."

Raima waited for him to go on, but the doctor stayed silent as he moved closer to her and pried open her eyelid to shine a light into her eye. Wincing at his touch and at the light, Raima's hands clenched into fists in her lap. She held onto his mind as he worked and when the doctor's brain churned with alarm she seized the emotion with a panic of her own. Dr. Yoon expected to see her pupils react in an abnormal way because of the sedative. When he didn't see it, he realized she hadn't received the injection at all.

Aware of the camera, Raima cut out the new perceptions and the alarm Dr. Yoon felt. Then she called out one of his many memories involving the other girls and fabricated the new experience just as she'd done with the technician. Dr. Yoon began going through the motions of the exam at a slower pace, flashing the light into her eyes. He didn't see Raima's pupils at all, but instead relived the false memory.

"All normal," he said after a moment. He pocketed his flashlight and took out his tablet instead. "All good," he added as he recorded his false impressions of normality into the tablet.

When he'd finished he said, "I like to meet all the subjects after their treatments have been completed. I wish I could see you all more often, but I travel so much." He gestured at the light above them to indicate the sky on the other side of the thick concrete and thousands of pounds of rock that kept the cruel cold and airlessness of Mars outside.

Raima was inside his mind, following his thoughts as they became words. She saw his memories of spaceflight, the grueling journey between planets, and of his traveling just between different outposts on Mars. Meetings and conferences, machines and charts, computers, images, names, drugs, and diagrams. His mind was filled with complexities. Raima struggled to keep breathing as the sensation of drowning in this other person's identity and lifetime threatened to choke her.

"This sol I am here to take a few samples of cells in your body, if that's all right." He looked at her in silent question, as if she really did have the authority to deny him access to her body. Raima had never had that right, but she longed to say, *No, you can't touch me.*

Instead she nodded and watched as Dr. Yoon pulled on some latex gloves and moved to the small desk in the exam room and unlocked a drawer. He produced a sealed plastic bag filled with syringes, needles, tubes, and cotton swabs. Then he pulled out the speculum. It thumped on the desk and gleamed in the light from overhead.

"Speculum?" Raima asked with confusion.

"Ah, yes," Dr. Yoon said. "One sample is to be taken from the cervix for testing." As the doctor opened the bag and began prepping the syringes and other samples for collection, Raima dug through his mind with as much precision and caution as she could. The doctor was thinking about how much easier it'd be if his most promising subjects were male instead of female. Curious, Raima prodded his mind in that direction and let him feed her the answers she sought.

Boys provided samples of their sex cells effortlessly. There was always some embarrassment as Dr. Yoon asked them to masturbate to fill a small sample cup, but the boys could experience pleasure while supplying the doctor what he needed while the girls had to endure discomfort and the anxiety of having their privacy invaded. Dr. Yoon pitied them and regretted the need for such samples, but cervix cells were far easier and less traumatic to gather than actual egg cells. In the past he'd ordered his nurses and technicians to extract actual eggs, but the procedure was frightening for the girls and took too much time and money. It made little difference whether he checked the genetic code on eggs or cervix cells; the altered genes were always present. The vector was too thorough, despite the changes he'd made to it over time. It infected somewhere between 50-75% of all cells in each subject's body.

Raima remembered Jia-li, the Chinese girl who'd left behind the imprint of her suffering on one of the facility's bunks. Raima had intuited the other girl's trauma from the mattress, particularly her fear of needles and the madness brought on by the injections that TC-Gen gave to its subjects. Dr. Yoon had been in charge of that and Raima would now have the chance to learn *why*.

Dr. Yoon approached Raima's seat in the middle of the little medical office and said, "Open your mouth for me, please." He held a small cotton swab mounted on a short, flat stick. "This will scratch some, but not hurt," he said and gripped her chin with one hand, thrusting the swab into her mouth and rubbing along the inside of her cheek.

Raima ignored his work with her body and continued exploring his mind. She scrolled through his memories, careful to stay at a level in his consciousness that would slow his physical work but not stop it. Dr. Yoon was concerned about something called the *Weismann barrier*, and that his *vector* had broken it. Raima didn't understand what either term meant. She pushed his mind for the definitions.

The doctor's brain responded to her with a flood of information. He was proud of his vector, whatever it was. It consumed much of his life's work. During his time in medical school, Dr. Yoon was part of a research team designing and investigating the medical uses of nanites, or nanotechnology. Most of his teammates only had an interest in nanites that extended to standard medical practices—like repairing a heart or clearing a blocked artery, or even fixing brain and nerve cells. Yoon had less traditional ideas he wanted to try. He wanted to use nanites to carry small gene sequences into the cells of the human body, infecting them with the new DNA, much like a virus.

The *vector* was the microscopic tool of genetic engineering, Raima realized, and Yoon used nanites in TC-Gen's experiment. Every shot that Raima had received carried millions, perhaps even billions of nanites, each loaded with the twins' genes for telepathy. It was more than just TC-Gen, however. CF-Gen used nanites as well, and on a much larger scale. Yoon was trying to prove the worth of his method for genetic engineering, but there was a problem.

Earth regulations forbade genetic engineering that could be inherited. The *Weismann barrier* was the term to describe the fact that genetic changes to a person's cells over a lifetime—or through most legal gene therapies using limited vectors—couldn't be inherited. A man could get cancer because of mutations that accumulated in the genes of his cells over a lifetime, but that change couldn't be inherited by his children because his offspring received all their genes through his *sex cells*, not his body's cells. Unless his sex cells already had a genetic predisposition to certain cancers, his children would have no increased risk.

The Earth genetic laws were based on an idea that the human genome was pure and should be left alone. Yoon disagreed with this wholeheartedly, feeling that the next stage of human evolution involved engineering the genome, artificially creating a better humanity—free from disease, death by old age, and possessing a new and enhanced intelligence. It was the grand idea that drove his life's work and eventually brought him to Mars where he could escape the tight restrictions that Earth's "genetic purists" and fear mongers placed on the burgeoning exploration of genetic engineering.

Dr. Yoon withdrew the swabbing stick from Raima's mouth and inserted it into a tube with a label on it. "There," he said as he screwed on the lid to Raima's cheek swab sample. "Now we do the skin scraping."

Raima pushed deeper, irritated by Yoon's self-righteous obsession. He was so enmeshed with his goal that he ignored what he had to do to get anywhere near his dream. The multitude of deaths, all young and otherwise healthy teens, were little more than names inside virtual folders on his computer. They meant nothing to him. In fact, he'd probably never even seen their faces in life or death, but their bones lined the path to his lofty goal.

His mind was filled with dense, unfathomable medical jargon. Raima waded through it, digging until she could find something understandable and simple. Yoon was breaking the law by using his nanites as a vector at TC-Gen and possibly even with CF-Gen, but Raima could have guessed that the high death rate of the experiments made them illegal already. Though she didn't know exactly why, she felt her heart and chest tighten, sensing that she was on the verge of learning something that would change her future, reshape her reality.

Nanites were indiscriminate vectors, and this was what made them illegal in the eyes of Earth's genetic purists. They infected all the body's cells, inserting their genetic payload into a certain place inside the DNA of each individual cell. Most vectors used in standard gene therapy were specialized, based off altered viruses that targeted only specific cell types. If a doctor like Yoon wanted to treat a fatal or debilitating disease that caused illness in a specific organ, he'd have to find and alter a virus that infected that type of tissue. But to change a person's entire body to make them into a telepath or an Intuiter took a vector that could target any and *all* the cells inside a person's body—including the sex cells.

The doctor cleared his throat and Raima blinked, seeing that he was ready for the next sample and was waiting for her compliance with his orders. She hadn't heard him say anything, but his mind was wide open to her and obliged her instantly. He repeated himself in a patient voice and even smiled. "Could I see your arm, please? I will scrape it with this." He held aloft a metallic object that Raima recognized as a razor. "I will collect surface skin cells and hair with it. No pain," he promised.

Raima lifted her arm and pulled back the sleeve of her gray scrubs. Dr. Yoon took her arm and scraped at her skin. Then he pressed some sticky, translucent tape to her arm, collecting the hairs and skin cells.

Raima slipped back into his brain. In only the last few minutes working with her talent in this way, Raima had learned how to mark another's mind, tagging areas of interest almost like a bookmark that she could come back to investigate when she was ready. She dove into Yoon's deep, thick medical knowledge, absorbing it with a rapidness that even a computer couldn't compete with.

Yoon's nanite vector infected sperm and eggs in his subjects, meaning that the altered genes would be passed on. Any children that Raima, Qi, Kim, Kaiden, or any of the other subjects had in the future would be born with the genes for telepathy. Their children, the grandchildren of TC-Gen's subjects, would inherit the altered genes too. It would be unstoppable, like a wildfire through a forest that had gone too long without rain. Unseen, it would plague civilization as children and parents and entire families found that they had the power to take whatever they wanted, do anything to anyone who didn't share the same talent. . . .

The regulations on Earth hadn't made much sense to Raima before. She hadn't cared one way or another while she was sick with HIV in Elysia City whether her bone marrow transplant broke any of Earth's laws regarding genetic engineering. Now she saw the purpose behind such rules. She felt Yoon's fear of losing control of the altered genes once his subjects reentered society.

That was why the subjects were terminated at the end of the experiment. Even Yoon could see the danger of telepathy. He hadn't wanted to investigate Intuiters or telepathy; he'd wanted to engineer better intellects, stronger bodies, and greater biological tolerances. But those changes were even more complex and involved multiple genes that worked together to make a living, breathing, functional human. Intuiters and telepaths required only a few genes in one location on the genome for the changes to take effect. It was cheaper to start with that and sell the results to Earth-based governments. From there it could be used to turn spies into telepaths. Those men and women who agreed to it would be sterilized for the cause.

"I need a blood sample, now," Dr. Yoon said.

Raima didn't bother faking a smile as she extended her arm again and let the doctor slap her flesh, trying to expose a vein. The empty syringe with its sickening needle pierced her skin. Raima bit her lip as a mixture of rage and despair crashed into her. Dr. Yoon, all the nurses and technicians, MIHO, and Genoquip viewed her and all the other subjects as soulless heaps of muscle, sinew, bones, and flesh. They would profit from using their bodies and then toss them aside as waste when they'd drained everything and anything of value from them. In that way they were no different from the brothel at all.

There was only one other question Raima knew the doctor could answer. She pushed her mind once more into his as he drew her red blood out of her vein for his own greedy purposes—like a vampire living off her life force, an ugly, fattened parasite. Only a few hours ago Raima might have struggled with guilt for slicing through his brain with her talent, invading his privacy so deeply. Now she had nothing but disdain for him and for Genoquip and all the hypocritical, bitter human society that enslaved her since her arrival on Mars.

The twins were right. As much as she hated admitting that, she realized most of the twins' practices were essential. By hiding the true power they possessed they'd allowed Raima this chance to discover the full truth. They'd laid a groundwork that would make escaping much easier. But were their fears about the boys of TC-Gen overblown? Dr. Yoon feared the genes for telepathy escaping from TC-Gen in both boys and girls, but could the boys ever rival the girls in mental strength? Why were the girls stronger telepaths?

Yoon's mind supplied that information readily. His personal theory on the girls' increased chances of displaying a strong telepathic talent was that they were better wired, with both halves and all the different sections of the brain communicating better. The girls' minds weren't compartmentalized the way boys' minds were, allowing telepathy to come through more strongly. However, Yoon believed the boys would be just as capable as the girls were if they were born with the talent instead of developing it so late in life. He hoped someday to test this theory by using newborn infants, but even on Earth most babies found adoptive parents and never came under the control of government programs for orphans until they were older—possibly too old for Yoon's test.

It was a great blow to Genoquip financially because most of the investors interested in buying telepathy would want to use it on men to create spies. Women were too weak, too vulnerable—despite the telepathy. He'd hoped to see better results between Bryson and—

Raima recoiled physically, jolting back in her seat.

The doctor sealed the blood sample he'd taken from her. Raima blinked with surprise as she saw he'd drawn not one vial of her blood—but *three*. He looked at her with a faint note of concern. "Are you all right?"

"I'm—I'm fine." She closed her eyes and felt the soreness in her arm from the needle. There was a bandage over the inside of her elbow. "How much more?" she asked and swallowed the thick saliva in her mouth, trying to get rid of the wavering quality to her voice.

"Just cervix cells," Dr. Yoon said in a tone that was supposed to be reassuring.

Raima wrapped her arms around her waist, hugging herself. She longed to hold Qi, to feel the comforting solidity of the other girl's body. "Time to get it over with, I guess," she said, already feeling her body recoiling at the prospect of the physical invasion.

"Very good," Dr. Yoon said. "Now, undress from your waist down." He smiled. "No pain, I promise."

FOURTEEN

The technician escorted Raima back to the classroom as soon as her time with the doctor finished. Raima busied herself with digging through his brain as they walked. It was the same Asian man who'd tried and failed to give her the sedative injection before her interview and exam with the doctor. His name was Zhu Liu and his mind was disjointed and fractured. It was like looking over a stormy sea toward a horizon layered with thick, heavy clouds. Externally the technician revealed nothing, but Raima knew he was miserable. His head ached at the temples and he was irritable.

Raima spent as much time as she could inside his mind, probing him for knowledge about the facility. When did rovers arrive with new subjects, medical supplies, and food shipments? Where were the facility's records and genetic samples kept? She quickly learned that rovers arrived at TC-Gen once a week, in the afternoon or evening of Sol Mercurii. Supplies and food were unloaded on the same sol by the technicians and the security guards employed by the facility. Samples and records gathered over the previous week were then loaded onto the rover the following morning. The rover driver, who the technician knew simply as Mike, was the same man that had driven Raima to TC-Gen. Mike spent one night at TC-Gen each week, resting while his rover was prepped for departure.

Where do the samples and records go after that? Raima queried Zhu's mind. The rover returned to CF-Gen, but beyond that the technician didn't know. Some samples would be destroyed, lost in tests where genes were extracted and examined. But others would be stored somewhere for safekeeping. Zhu Liu didn't know where and didn't care.

The classroom came into view. Raima could see the doorway over Zhu Liu's head as they approached the end of the hall. While the technician slid his keycard through a scanner to unlock the door, Raima examined the security camera overhead and prayed that whoever watched on the other side didn't have the ability to lockdown the door. She focused again on Zhu's mind and took everything he knew about the facility's security personnel and procedures.

Zhu thought that TC-Gen was an unusually paranoid place, reminiscent of his Chinese homeland in some ways. There were more full-time security guards than nurses and technicians— twelve now, and more would be hired in coming weeks. Yoon arrived with the rover yestersol and would complicate Zhu's life for the next week before the doctor would finally leave TC-Gen again. Zhu's supervisor was a woman who Yoon hired to watch over the subjects and the facility in his stead. Her name was Eva Fuchs and she'd always been an anxious, busybody of a woman, but now her concerns for the facility crossed over into what Zhu considered a paranoid madness. But, in keeping with the hushed secrecy TC-Gen favored—and that again reminded Zhu of China—no one ever briefed the nurses or technicians about the cause of the internal, frenzied paranoia that warranted so many security guards. Enough laws were already broken, was it really necessary to turn TC-Gen into a prison with armed guards?

Where does Yoon usually stay? How are the facility's records stored? Raima prompted. Zhu's brain conjured up an image of a dim room brimming with computer servers, wires, flickering indicator lights on display panels, and dozens of small, flat-screen monitors. It was a control room as well as a server and records storage area, located on the far side of the compound near the airlock. Yoon and his head assistant were often in a small side office attached to the control room, reviewing video footage of various subjects. But otherwise the two could be anywhere: inside a lab, in an office, even in the break room pilfering a snack from the community candy bin. Zhu suspected that Yoon and Eva Fuchs were lovers and spent much of their time inside the little side office of the control room having sex.

And if you wanted to get back at them, how would you destroy their precious research, all the records? Raima asked. It was easy to trick his mind into immersing itself in this fantasy because Zhu was disgruntled and cranky. He felt unappreciated and overworked. Falling into the trap, he imagined himself sitting at a console in the server room, logging on, and then deleting files with a series of commands.

The door to the classroom clicked as it unlocked, opening with a faint hiss of air and a whir of electronics. Raima examined the hinges on the door carefully as she went by. They were thick and tucked into the doorframe to make it airtight. The door was an airlock, likely designed to seal itself shut to minimize deaths in the event of a breach in the outer walls of the facility and a resulting loss of atmosphere. Not all TC-Gen's doors were designed this way, but Raima was wary of them because she didn't know how they could be used during an escape attempt. Could they be shut and sealed without a breach or a severe air leak? Did people control them, or was it only a computer that reacted when it sensed a drop in atmospheric pressure?

Her head swirled with everything she'd learned from both Yoon and the technician as she moved to join the girls in the classroom. The nurses put on an educational film, but Raima barely managed to feign interest in it. Qi sat in a small desk close by, and Raima sensed the mental energy and alertness of the Chinese girl, watching her. The twins did a better job of hiding their reactions, though Raima felt the surreptitious movement of their minds, hovering in the room like vultures, watching and waiting for weakness or death.

The day passed with agonizing slowness. When the girls finally returned to their bunkroom, Raima found Qi at once. They sat together in a far corner of the room, positioned where the bunks obscured the lone security camera's view of their discussion. Huddling close to Qi, Raima made no effort to hide or dismiss the needy, hungry desire for affection that had grown within her. She clung to Qi, nestling into her shoulder, breathing in her scent. She was weak with the heaviness of the task ahead, filled with fear at the certainty that the escape would go awry. Qi waited for a long time, holding Raima, sharing emotions without words. Eventually Raima explained everything she'd learned, beginning with the rover and ending with the most horrifying revelations she'd picked out of the doctor's brain.

"The doctor created the tests with Bryson. The twins were right that Bryson was handpicked because he's violent. The twins were right about killing the boys too. If we get out and don't kill the boys, they'll have telepathic kids. Their sons won't be weak, like the boys are now. They'd be just as strong as any one of us, maybe stronger. The genes will get loose and spread. It'd be a disaster. The only way to stop that is to—"

"*—kill them,*" Qi said, finishing the thought for her. She sighed aloud and lifted one hand to stroke her fingers through Raima's hair, then traced her ear.

Raima closed her eyes as a wave of tranquility passed through her body.

"*But what about our kids, someday?*" Qi asked, intruding on Raima's peacefulness as gently as possible.

"*We'll have to take a vow together,*" Raima suggested. "*We stay together, like family, and we never have any children of our own.*"

Qi sighed again. "*I always wanted to be a mother, but I agree with you. The boys couldn't stay true to a vow like that.*"

"*They don't always know when they get someone pregnant,*" Raima agreed. "*And they usually don't care.*" She frowned as she thought of the countless johns who'd come to the brothel to spill their seed, unworried about the consequences.

Qi nudged Raima, both physically and telepathically, rousing her out of her dark memories. "*What do we do with the boys, then? What about Kaiden?*"

Raima sat up, pulling away from Qi. She stared at the other girl, searching for an answer, but there was nothing. The other boys were just meaningless names and faces, but Kaiden? Finally, Raima shook her head and said, "*He and Kim aren't done with the treatments. They aren't telepaths. They don't count.*"

Qi scowled, disagreeing at once. "No," she said aloud. She went on telepathically after a moment. "*If you touch their minds right now, only a few days in, you'll feel they already have some power. It was the same with you.*" She nodded at Raima, emphasizing her unspoken words with the gesture. "*Soon they'll be able to block others and overhear thoughts that aren't sent right into their brains.*"

"I don't know what to do," Raima admitted. She looked down into her lap where her hands clasped one another, useless. She brought up Kim's face in her mind, and then Kaiden's. Her chest felt tight as she imagined Kim's face in anguish.

"You shouldn't make this decision alone," Qi counseled. She reached out to grasp Raima's arm and squeezed it reassuringly. She sent images of the other girls: Ella with her frizzy red hair, beautiful blonde Aine, Tiana with her childish grin, little baby-faced Izzy, and Limei with her kind eyes and crooked teeth. *"You can't make a plan to escape and then start it without their help. You can't demand suddenly that they take a vow right at the moment of escape. It's not fair. They should get to have a say."*

"The twins would never let me—"

"No one supports the twins. The others will support you. I know they will."

"I don't even have a real plan yet," Raima said, protesting.

Qi's eyes, so dark in color that the irises were indistinguishable from the pupils, darted around the room quickly, taking in the positions of the others. *"Let them help you, like a real family. Like real sisters. The twins try to make everyone believe we're like family, but they don't want to share power with everyone. They scare everyone else into obedience, and I'm sure their escape plan is nothing but talk. If you show Izzy, Tiana, Aine, and Ella that you're different, the twins will lose all their support and be forced to go along with the group's plan."*

"The only thing I know for sure is that in six days the rover will be back and that's when I want to get out," Raima said. She frowned. *"It doesn't sound like much to me."*

Qi laughed aloud, tossing her head back so that her fine, short black hair flew out at every angle for a few seconds. Her teeth were white and even—possibly her best feature aside from her hair, which was as smooth as silk—but looking at the Chinese girl, Raima saw only beauty. When she'd first met Qi she'd despised her loud, joyous laughter, feared her carefree nature, the love of life that Raima couldn't fathom. Now she marveled that she ever disliked Qi and knew that what she'd really felt was envy and the desire to discover the strength to laugh, even when life was at its lowest.

"More than you think," Qi said, grinning. *"You have a date on it,* and real info to give the others. Can you imagine the twins saying that? Of course not!"

Raima smirked, withholding the laughter that wanted to erupt out of her. "No," she said aloud.

Qi leaned closer to her, as if she would whisper conspiratorially. Her lips moved, twitching as her smile softened. Instead of using her voice, Qi's thoughts did the whispering. *"We have six days—sols—until we get out of here. There's no time to waste. We have to start the conversation. We have to start talking."*

"You mean issue the challenge," Raima said. The twins would see anything she suggested as a challenge, a threat to their power and control. She was simultaneously eager and terrified of the simmering conflict that was building toward an explosion.

"You're scared," Qi said, touching on the mixture of tumultuous emotions inside Raima's mind.

"Aren't you?" Raima shot back. She probed at Qi's mind and found a different emotion that didn't quite equate. It was a tense, nervous excitement that drove Qi to energetically launch herself into the unknown outcome ahead of them.

"No," Qi replied without any consideration or hesitation. *"I'm excited. I want to be free. I want to stay with you and the others. It's not like I have anyone who's missing me out there. My father is probably so drunk right now he wouldn't recognize me, and he'd be broke from gambling."* She sighed, rolled her eyes. *"I'm sick of always being stuck inside four walls. I want to walk under the dome in Zui-Chu and see the sky."* She fell silent for a heartbeat and took Raima's hand in her own, holding it tight. *"And you'll be there with me."*

Now Raima did laugh, though the sound was quiet. She gave Qi's hand a returning squeeze. *"But I don't know any Chinese,"* she teased.

Qi let go of Raima and spoke aloud, motioning with her hands. Raima heard the foreign words of Qi's native language, Mandarin Chinese, in full, long sentences. But overlaid atop the unknown words was an English translation. *"Haven't you already figured out by now that you don't need to speak any language when you're a telepath? Besides, it's never too late to start learning something new. So, with that in mind, let's go teach Marie and Manon something new. How about it?"*

"Now?" Raima asked, sobering.

"Six days," Qi said. *"Not much time. But wait until lights-out."*

They stayed together, drawing comfort and confidence from each other until Nurse Vieve arrived and ordered them to their own separate bunks. Raima waited with growing anxiety as the nurse toured the room, checking the girls, lingering over Kim, who was unconscious. After the nurse finally departed, turning off the light and shutting the door, Raima left her bed and met up with Qi at the end of the row of bunks. They stood together near the bluish glow from the bathroom; the nightlight illuminated Qi with a surreal eeriness.

Taking in a long breath to steady herself, Raima searched the bunkroom, locating all the girls with both her eyes and her mind. *"Where do I start?"* she asked.

Qi grinned. "Let me." She clasped Raima's hand in hers and strode forward through the dimness. Uneasy but committed, Raima followed Qi away from the wall near the bathroom and toward Izzy's, Aine's, and Limei's bunks. The three girls were speaking inaudibly with telepathy, pretending to sleep for the benefit of the lone security camera.

Izzy was the first to notice Raima and Qi. Her mind jumped into place and she sat up in her bunk, staring at them. The undercurrent of invisible and intangible mental communication ceased as all three girls turned their attention to Qi and Raima.

"Can we talk?" Qi asked. Her next words she spoke aloud in a low voice. "Come with us?"

Wary reactions flew through their minds, but when Qi turned to go Limei rose from her bunk and followed. After a significant pause Aine and Izzy left their spot as well and trailed after them. The group crossed the length of the bunkroom, still led by Qi, to the area close by the exit door where Tiana and Ella were. Both got to their feet, standing close together as a united front before a conquering army.

"We want to talk," Qi said in a loud whisper. She gestured around the bunkroom to indicate everyone inside it. "We want to talk with all the girls . . ." she finished the sentence telepathically, tossing the final words into the air like brightly colored confetti *". . . about escaping this place."* They could all hear what she said— including the twins and the half-unconscious Kim.

Manon inhaled a hissing breath from the twins' corner, drawing all eyes toward her. "We don't want to talk. It's lights-out." Telepathically she boomed out an angry warning. *"Marie and I, we have the escape plan all figured out. We've been here the longest. We know everything there is to know about this place. We're the only ones who can get every one of us out of TC-Gen alive."* She fell silent for a moment as the bed she was on creaked. She stood up and peered over the tops of the bunks, glaring at the group through the near darkness. Then her gaze landed on Raima and narrowed with hate. *"You're going to get them all killed, Raima. You don't know what you're doing. The researchers could kill you tomorrow and you'd never see it coming. You're stupid to—"*

Before realizing that she was doing it at all, Raima took a step away from the group, coming closer to the bunk that separated her from Manon. She was bristling with outrage, her mind swirling with Ferde's constant insults. You stupid *puta*, he'd called her and all the brothel girls over and over again. And she'd believed it, right up until Kati's death when she'd snapped. Now the same fury that gave her the strength, cunning, and bloodthirsty determination to slaughter Ferde rose within her and she lashed out.

Raima reached for Manon's mind, but found that it rebuffed her. Driven by her rage, Raima tried again. She imagined her consciousness as a knife, stabbing its way into Manon's flesh, and this time the twin's mind gave way. Manon was broadcasting her thoughts to the group, but Raima cut her off, twisting about inside her mind, causing a blinding pain that made Manon cry out and grab at her head.

"We're going to talk," Raima said between clenched teeth. "You can join us, or you can mope in your corner. I don't care." She bit her tongue and withdrew from Manon's mind to communicate telepathically to the group, ignoring the twins in favor of winning the others over to her side.

"We are not stupid. I am not stupid. None of you have to listen to me, or to them," she said, feeling the frightened reactions from the girls assembled around her. *"They'll say anything, threaten anything, because they're scared. They've never seen the real world. Their whole lives they've been subjects. They're power mad. They just want to control you. I've seen that before—inside the brothel. I'm sick of hearing*

it, because it's wrong." Uncaring that the camera might see it even through the dark, Raima jabbed an accusatory finger toward the twins in their corner and said, *"Marie and Manon like to say if you don't do exactly what they tell you, you'll end up dead like Sarai. But the truth is they are the ones who try to decide who lives and who dies among us. I've caught them rewriting the nurses' thoughts, trying to get me into trouble, and trying to get Kim killed."*

"You bitch!" Marie cursed. *"You're lying!"*

"She attacked me," Manon said and whimpered for melodramatic effect. *"Izzy,"* she called. *"Come help me!"*

Izzy started walking away from Raima's group, but Qi shouted to her and the others telepathically. *"Izzy—why are you running to help her like a slave? She has Marie to help her if she really needs it."*

When Izzy halted Qi went on, driving home her point. *"The twins lied when they said it was hard to control minds. It's easy. It's so easy that they learned everything they know by playing around in your minds before you finished your treatments. Did they rewrite your thoughts and feelings, Izzy? Is that why you like them so much even though they're never really kind to you? What about you, Aine? Why are you with them so often? Is it by choice because the twins are so much fun to be around? Or is it because you're afraid and you don't really feel like you have a choice?"*

"We never hurt anyone," Marie objected. Her mind vibrated with varied emotions, including fear. At her side, Manon got up without anyone's help. She glared at Raima, seemingly willing the other girl to drop dead.

"Not physically, no," Raima admitted. *"But when I realized what you did to Kim right after she arrived, I knew you'd done it before. When I came here, did I live in nightmares for two weeks because of the injections, or did you and Manon force me to dream about the brothel? You like to call us family, like we're all your sisters, but you don't treat us like it. You humiliate and ignore every girl, you cover up and bury the deaths of others—like Sarai—and I can't help but wonder if that's because you set her up for it. Did you make the researchers pick Sarai for the next test with Bryson because you were afraid of what would happen when he tried to attack a stronger girl?"*

"It's true," Limei said, letting out a little sob. *"Sarai went through the test with Bryson three times. Marie and Manon never got picked."*

"What will happen when...?" Aine asked, stammering and then cutting herself off. She'd slipped up, accidentally voicing the question aloud. She swallowed, her throat making a wet sound as all eyes and minds landed on her. She tried it again, this time telepathically. *"What will happen when Bryson attacks a stronger girl? I know we can block him out of our minds, but...?"*

"You won't have to find out," Qi reassured her. *"Because in six days Raima will lead us out of TC-Gen."*

"Bullshit!" Manon retorted with rage. *"You're all going to get us killed!"*

"We're exposing ourselves." Marie reminded them.

"You're right," Raima said. *"I wanted to do this quietly, but you insisted on fighting us."* She motioned to them, inviting them to join. "Do you want to come and talk with us?"

"No," Manon said.

"Yes," Marie answered in unison with her sister's negative response. The siblings looked at one another, each questioning the other. They argued voicelessly for a few seconds and then came to an agreement.

Manon sneered at Raima as she said, "Yes, we'll talk with you."

"Let's talk about what we want to do in the future, when the experiment is over," Raima said.

The girls around her all conveyed the same wariness at her suggestion. Discussing such a topic aloud seemed dangerous, as if they were inviting the researchers to come and interrogate them. But the scientists didn't know for certain that their subjects had figured out that the end of the experiment entailed their deaths. There was no harm in the girls dreaming about the outside world and what awaited them in years to come. It was also useful to Raima because it would tell her about each girl's goals. How many of them planned to find families outside and would resist taking a vow of childlessness or staying together as a new family of sisters?

The girls sat in a wide circle, in full view of the security camera overhead. They were scattered about the dark room on bunks and on the floor, some leaning against a bed frame or standing. Occasionally their eyes caught the blue glint of the pale nightlight. Only Kim was excluded from the circle, sleeping some distance away in her cot, her mind spinning in dreams.

RACHAEL ROBIE

Qi, sitting on the cold floor within arm's length of Raima, began the topic aloud in a hushed but proud voice, boasting of her plans. "When I leave, I no want to live with my father." She punched at an imaginary image of her father that only she could see, as if beating the stupidity out of her sire. "Gamble, gamble, gamble. Play, play, play. I go to him, I go hungry. Bastard. Son of bitch." Her anger disrupted her English, making her harder to understand, but her emotion and her meaning were clear nonetheless. Her outburst was both serious and comical. The girls picked up on her humor and chuckled softly, relaxing and warming to the verbal discussion.

But the telepathic topic had yet to start. Raima watched the dark shapes of the twins out of the corner of her eye and wished they'd declined her offer to join the planning. Marie and Manon settled on a bunk as far away from Raima as they could manage. It was also the most removed position in the group, breaking the outline of the circle. Raima knew they hadn't agreed to join the discussion because they really wanted to help. Instead they were spying, undermining Raima's authority and arguing for their own plan, whatever it was.

Qi sent Raima a questioning probe before she began rambling again. She asked the silent question, *When are you going to start planning?* Then she continued the discussion. "Maybe I work for a mine outside. Good money, people say. Have to hide from my father. If he find me, he take all my money! Go throw it away. Gamble, gamble, gamble! Make me so mad!" Telepathically she broadcasted an image of her father's face, slack-jawed and dead-eyed as he gazed at a slot machine, pumping change into it.

The girls giggled, reacting to Qi's image. Raima let them finish, enjoying the group's lightheartedness as they connected with Qi's dilemma. She didn't want to begin the darker topic of escape, but it had to be done. As soon as the girls quieted, Raima sat forward and cleared her throat, preparing to speak both mentally and physically.

"Honestly, I haven't really thought about what I'll do in the future," Raima admitted with quiet sadness. "I was hoping to get some ideas from everyone else here. What I really want is to go back to Earth, to India. But I've heard that going back when you spent some of your growing years here . . ." She broke off and shook her head with resignation. "I've heard Earth's gravity will cripple me if I try to go back." Her throat convulsed, suddenly overwhelmed by a surge of painful emotion. Blinking with determination, she forced herself to broadcast the next words telepathically. *"We need to come up with a plan to get out of here, or the researchers will kill us. In six days the rover will return and stay overnight. We can take it and get out of here. But how?"*

Silence greeted Raima's words, both verbal and telepathic. Qi's presence beside her was encouraging, but most of the others lowered their eyes, staring into their laps, disheartened and depressed. Unable to stop herself, Raima turned her head and looked swiftly at the twins, sensing Marie and Manon watching her. It was easy to feel their resentment.

"What about the boys?" Limei asked, surprising everyone. All heads and every set of eyes jerked in her direction. Limei leaned against the wall beside the exit door. *"Marie and Manon said the boys will get out of here and abuse their power. They'll hurt people— girls like us. Their kids will be born as telepaths too, and they'll do the same thing. Is that true?"*

Raima thought of Kaiden and frowned. She twisted around, peering behind her where Kim was unconscious.

"It is true," Manon interjected, answering Limei's question. *"The boys will spread out everywhere. Some of them are young enough they might get back to Earth. They'll seduce women, reading their minds to lie and cheat and trick them. Then they'll just leave after they take what they want. And their sons will be as strong as we are."*

"Raima won't give you the truth because she doesn't know it," Marie added, baiting her.

Angrily, Raima glared back at the twins and refuted their challenge. *"I did know it. I even know how you two know it. You read it in Dr. Yoon's mind. That's where I read it too."*

"But you're weak," Marie shot back, sneering. *"You won't do what needs to be done to fix it because of her."* Marie tossed out the image of Kim to the entire group.

"Say it," Raima snapped. *"Say what you think needs to be done."*

"No problem," Manon replied with cold pride. *"We kill the boys, all of them. We kill the researchers. We kill the nurses. We kill the doctor. Everyone here has to die."*

Something in Manon's wording sent a shiver of repressed horror through Raima. Reacting on impulse, she asked, *"Everyone? Including us? Because our kids, our sons and daughters, will all be telepaths too. Just like the boys. We should all kill ourselves to keep the outside world safe, right? Is that what you want to happen? You're scared of getting out, so maybe you and Marie want to die. Is that it?"*

"Of course not," Marie muttered aloud.

"If that's not what you want, then you're hypocrites. You call me weak, but your logic is completely flawed. I agree with you," Raima admitted and sighed. *"I don't want the boys to get out of here alive, but any boys we have in the future would be just as dangerous."*

"We have a choice," Qi interrupted. *"We can all take a vow to stay childless. That way telepathy dies with us and no man will ever be able to abuse it. We can be like real sisters. We'll live and work together in the outside world. We'll take care of each other and be a true family."* She smiled as her dark eyes swept over the group, willing them to agree with her.

"But what about the boys?" Limei pressed again. *"Do we kill them like Marie and Manon want?"*

"I don't want to kill anyone," Tiana murmured, pushing a deep fear and sadness at the others to convey her moral objections.

"Maybe we don't kill them ourselves," Ella suggested. *"There are guards at the other end of the facility where the rover docks. We could control the guards and let the boys fight it out with them."*

"The guards have guns," Marie added with a burst of excitement. *"The boys wouldn't stand a chance."*

"No one kills Kaiden," Raima said suddenly. When she received looks and telepathic touches laced with confusion and disapproval, she elaborated on her decision. *"He's Kim's brother. She's one of us, even if she's too sick to talk about this. We can't just kill her brother. He's exempt from this."*

"But he's dangerous," Manon argued. *"Just like the other boys. In a few years he'll be like Bryson. Then you'll still be too weak with sympathy for your precious Kim to do the right thing, won't you?"*

"We've been silent too long," Izzy said. *"Someone say something out loud. They're watching. We'll never last six days if we keep acting like this."*

"So gloomy," Qi said at once. "So angry." She'd turned her head toward the twins, glaring at them as she spoke in subdued tones.

"Bad eggs are like bad thoughts. Throw them away, like garbage they are." To make sure that everyone understood her meaning, Qi sent out a quick thought explaining that *bad eggs* referred to people. In this case she meant the twins. She grinned with mischievous amusement as the twins sneered their disdain at her, but several of the others struggled to hide smirks of amusement.

"*Bitch,*" Manon cursed telepathically at Qi.

Limei laughed with a heavy mixture of animosity and enjoyment. "Bad eggs," she said aloud and snickered even more.

"*This isn't helping us,*" Izzy scolded them. She coughed into her hand and said, "I can go back to Earth once they're done with us. I came here too late to grow into a Martian physique. Earth's gravity won't break my bones if I go back." She looked to Raima. "Why would I want to stay here on Mars?"

Raima wanted to frown, but also to cry, though she didn't understand why. She envied Izzy, who had the short stature and thicker bones of an Earthling. Transitioning back to Earth would still be difficult for Izzy, but her body would adjust, building muscle, strengthening her joints and heart to withstand the two-thirds greater force bearing down on it. Izzy's reward would be the paradise of wind, water, rain, clouds, a bright, hot sun, and the endless presence of green. Even in the most populous cities, filled from horizon to horizon with cement, concrete, and skyscrapers that blocked out the sunlight, Izzy would be able to find weeds growing in cracks, flowers planted in pots, and decorative trees whispering in the wind. On Mars there was nothing but red and brown dirt, an ugly sky that made Raima think of a bruise, and the eerie moons Phobos and Deimos, misshapen and alien.

Raima forced herself to smile, though she wasn't sure Izzy would see it in the dark. "I'm sorry," she murmured. "I can't think of any reason that would make me stay here if I could go back."

"I can," Qi said, barely containing her irritation. Glancing between Izzy and Raima, she made a circle with her hands and fingers, projecting the image of it outward with her mind. "Family. The people you love." She dropped her hands down into her lap with an almost defeated demeanor. "You are orphaned," she said to Izzy. "Who you go back for? Who you have?"

Izzy stared at Qi, stricken speechless, frozen as she struggled to hold back an unknown, escalating emotion inside her.

"You have no one, right?" Qi persisted. "You would be on Earth if you had any person to pay."

"You're right, Qi," Izzy snapped back at her. "Are you happy, now? I haven't got anyone on Earth who gives a rat's ass about whether I live or die. That's why I'm here in this hellhole." She covered her face with her hands and tried to withdraw her mind deep inside, where no one would feel it but her. Breathy, muffled sobs erupted, filling the darkness.

Raima crawled over the floor across the circle of girls and scooted to a spot right beside Izzy. She hesitated then, uncertain about touching the other girl. She tried speaking to Izzy to calm her. *"I'd be a terrible person if I forced you or any of the others to stay here when you could return to Earth, but you understand why I'd ask it, right? Any boys we have someday will be telepaths. They'll be dangerous. I want you to stay with us because we're all telepaths. We're all sisters. We can be a new family. Sometimes members of a family travel, don't they? You could go back to Earth. I'd just ask that you send us lots of pictures and videos. I want to see the water and something green again, under a blue sky."*

As Izzy's crying softened, Raima embraced her, overcoming the nervous bubble inside herself to make the contact. Izzy's body was tight with tension when Raima first touched her, but as the seconds ticked by Izzy relaxed, accepting Raima's hug and her reassuring words, melting into her arms. Her crying reduced until she was only sniffling occasionally.

Steadfast and stubborn, Qi scanned the other girls while Raima watched from her place comforting Izzy. *"Who will agree to the vow? Anyone? You see the danger, right? Our kids will be telepaths. We have to stay together, like one family, and protect each other."*

"What about baby girls?" Limei asked.

Qi shrugged. *"I guess. It's a risk though, even with a girl. What if she didn't agree to follow our rules when she grew up?"*

Limei nodded in agreement. *"I'll take the vow. I've never had a family before."*

"Me too," Tiana piped up. *"This is the closest thing I've ever had to a family."* She let her feelings flow out, wired with unreserved joy and hope.

"I have family outside this place," Ella said, souring the mood. "When I get out, I want to rejoin my family."

"Lucky," Aine muttered, furthering the audible conversation for the sake of the camera. "My only family is my older brother—that sick bastard." Aine's voice was so soft and feminine, and heard so rarely, that everyone watched her in surprise. With all attention focused on her, Aine jutted out her chin with a cold, proud set to her mind. *"I'll take the vow. Only one thing I want in return."* She turned her gaze on Raima and then to Qi, seeking their approval—not the twins'. *"Once we're out, I want your help killing my brother. We'll go to his prison like we're going to visit with him, bring him treats or some shit. Then we'll kill him. Slow."*

"I'll help you," Raima replied and felt a surprising passion at the bargain. She knew that Aine's older brother was like Ferde, a man who had long deserved his death at the hands of a woman he'd harmed repeatedly. *"I'll even enjoy it."*

Aine grinned and the blue light from the bathroom gleamed in her eyes. She stared at Raima while a somber, dark triumph burned within her. *"I can't wait to get out of here!"* she gushed.

"I couldn't kill all of my enemies," Raima said, interjecting caution. *"There were too many of them."* She drew in a long, shaking breath, watching Aine. *"I envy you. I hope that killing your brother will set you free. Just one death. But when you kill him out here, in the physical world, make sure he dies in here as well."* Raima patted her chest with one hand and then knocked on her temple with the other. She sent the images telepathically to be certain that Aine understood.

"I'll help you when we get out," Aine promised. *"I'll be there to help you kill every last man who hurt you in that brothel."* There was a fiery passion building in her. Raima could feel it swelling inside Aine's mind too. The aloof, lackluster, and most silent member of the group was now a wrecking ball, a raging bull that could not be contained.

"Who else will take the vow?" Qi went on, pressing the others with her mind. Tiana, Aine, and Limei all exuded pride and triumph while the girls who hadn't agreed yet evaded Qi's probing mental touch and stared down into their laps.

"What will you do to us if we don't agree?" Marie asked. Aloud she said, "Manon and I have never had a family to go home to." The sadness in her words was unfeigned and heavy.

With a spurt of irritation directed at her sister, Manon whispered harshly, "We don't need any other family or any home. Wherever you go, Marie, I go, that's home. That's family."

Not for the first time, Raima realized the twins weren't as unified as they seemed. Marie was more personable, more likely to agree with someone other than Manon. Marie could see reason and agree with it, regardless of what her sister said, but Manon would deny something just because it came from someone other than herself or her sister. Now, in this discussion, Raima sensed Marie's temptation to take the vow, to join the group.

Qi looked to Raima, waiting for her answer to Marie's question. After a moment's hesitation Raima admitted a truth she was certain would make her weak in Manon's eyes, bolstering the twin's determination. *"Nothing. I can't stop someone from leaving us or having a baby in the future. I'm not going to threaten you or scare you into agreeing with me or staying with us against your will. I'm not a jailer. I want you to stay with us out of affection as well as personal obligation. We owe it to ourselves and to the world not to let our talents be born into men who will abuse the gift in the most heinous ways."*

"Absolute power corrupts absolutely," Aine put in.

Raima nodded her approval. *"Exactly. I know what I'm asking you to do is strange, but we were tossed together by Genoquip, experimented on, enslaved. We're a family, united by our suffering already. But they made a mistake when they gave us telepathy and decided to kill us. Now we have the power to escape, and our talent binds us together in ways we can't even comprehend yet."* She looked to Ella and said out loud, "I'm glad you have a family to return to."

Wariness erupted from Ella's mind, flashing like a signal fire to the telepathic group. She lifted her head and spoke. "I want to go back to them."

"I know," Raima murmured. *"But when you do, everything will be different. They're normal, but you're not. You'll read their minds, catch their emotions, all without meaning to. Telepathy will be like a curse then. It will be like a weight around your neck, choking you. I would never want to keep you from seeing the people you love from time to time, but please, think about what life will be like outside of this place."*

"You'll come back begging to take the vow," Qi predicted. *"You can't*

go back to a normal life anymore. You're not the same. You'll never be normal again."

"*I'll deal with it,*" Ella snapped, but her mind had darkened with a visceral fear. Tiana, as always sitting beside her, scooted closer and wrapped her arms around Ella in a clumsy embrace.

"*Please say you'll come and see us,*" she begged. "*Even if you don't take the vow. Raima will let you.*"

Ella's head swiveled in the dark, looking to Qi and then to Raima. Her wordless thoughts held the question. Raima answered it without hesitation. "*Even if you never take the vow, even if you have a baby, you can come back and see Tiana any time. Even if you don't want to think of us as family, we'll be calling you our sister.*"

Painful, conflicting emotions trickled out of Ella. She sniffled, fighting tears. "*I always wanted to have kids someday,*" she said and let out a weak sob. "*But I know you're right.*" She brushed at her tears with irritation and returned Tiana's embrace. "*I will take the vow too.*"

Izzy, who was still close to Raima, added her support. "*I will too.*"

Qi spoke to the twins now, the last holdouts in the whole group aside from the unconscious Kim. "What you plan to do with your future?" she asked. "*Will you take the vow?*"

Marie glanced to Manon, seeking her approval. The silence between them lasted only a few seconds before Manon answered for both. "*Why wouldn't we agree to this vow? It's the same thing we wanted from the beginning! Of course we agree!*"

"We don't know what we're going to do in the future," Marie said.

"No one ever knows their future for sure," Raima replied. "*Two years ago, I thought I would be killed the night I escaped the brothel. I had no plan, no hope, nothing. I might be killed when we escape in six days. Any one of us might be.*" She swept the group over with her eyes, letting her gaze land purposefully on each girl, each subject—each *Sister.* "*But this time I have hope, and I'll have a plan. And most important of all—*" she paused and glanced at Qi, smiling tenderly "*—I won't be alone like I was before. None of us will be alone. Never again.*"

"*We are Sisters,*" Qi said, envisioning the word with a heavy, powerful significance and a burgeoning new definition. "*Sisters in our gift. Sisters in life. Sisters in death.*"

"Sisters in suffering and joy," Raima added. "We are Sisters forever, bound as family by our talent." She felt the others rallying with her, all except the twins, who remained withdrawn while the rest of the girls smiled or grinned with nervous excitement. In six days they would take control of TC-Gen, and from there they'd be free to take whatever they wanted from all of Mars itself. They would carve out a future for themselves as one family unit, shaping something beautiful out of the ugly, blood red dust of this new world.

FIFTEEN

The nearest settlement is Rahe Crater," Qi said while she ate her oatmeal. "There are scientists and miners. It's north of Ceraunius Tholus." After she'd swallowed her mouthful of food she said, "Boys take last eggs today. Bah!"

The girls appeared sleepy and subdued, picking at their food and speaking only occasionally. Raima watched the nurses with her peripheral vision as she listened to the confusing mixture of voiceless and audible conversation from the girls. The two topics—one deadly, the other trivial—set her mind swirling. But she also worried—were the nurses looking at them more often? Did they suspect anything? She took a deep breath and sipped her milk as Tiana questioned Qi, "Are you sure about it being the closest? We can't afford to get it wrong."

Qi raised another spoonful of oatmeal to her lips, but she halted with it in front of her face and leaned forward to glance down the length of the table at Tiana. "Tharsis Quadrangle is Chinese territory. I learned about it in school." She pushed an image at the group of a crater shaped like a teardrop. "See? I even know what it looks like."

"I've heard about Rahe too," Limei said, adding her support. Then she asked, "Think we have eggs next sol?"

The Martian word made Raima bristle against her will. "Tomorrow, you mean," she said, trying to keep her voice light and cheery. Hearing the Martian slang reminded her that she couldn't go back to Earth. She might get away from Genoquip, but she'd never escape Mars.

"What about Sharon City?" Aine asked. This morning she'd chosen to sit beside Raima, abandoning her usual spot close to the twins. In fact, a noticeable divide had formed as the girls sat closer to Raima, leaving Marie and Manon at the far end of the table.

"Sharonov crater," Limei said and frowned down at her tray, as if disgusted by her food. "That's too far away."

"We should go wherever's closest, but we need to see a map before we make a real decision," Izzy said. She turned her head, tossing a glare toward the twins. "You both have nothing to contribute? Do you know anything about geography here?"

Manon didn't look at Izzy, but Marie did. Her expression was bitter as she said, "What do you think? We've been trapped here and tortured our whole lives. We haven't seen real sunlight in years."

Nurse Vieve walked toward their table, drawing Raima's attention. She reached out with her mind, touching it with a firm but light hold, and queried Vieve's brain like a computer. What do you know about the Tharsis Quadrangle? Where is the nearest settlement?

The nurse reached their table, but she hesitated, swaying a little on her feet before she said, "Time to dump your trays and head to the classroom."

Her brain pictured the same crater that Qi had imaged for the girls. Rahe crater. As she headed for the boys' table, Raima broadcasted her discovery to the others. "It's Rahe crater. Qi and Limei are right. I searched Vieve to find out."

The girls accepted the answer, though to be thorough they read Nurse Victoria's mind when they got to the classroom.

That night before lights-out they splintered into several groups, pretending to chitchat to disguise their continued planning.

"We need to make sure we take the driver with us when we escape," Ella said. "Qi and Limei might know a lot about this area, but I don't like the idea of them driving us." She sat across the room from Qi, with Tiana as usual. She didn't try to meet Qi's gaze, but she pushed bashful emotions out into the air, aiming them at her. "Sorry—I don't mean to doubt you or Limei. We just can't take any chances."

Limei, Raima, and Qi had made themselves comfortable on the chilled floor in their own group. Raima grinned when she saw Qi's expression darken with mock disapproval. "No respect," she said, lacing the words with humor so that everyone would know she wasn't serious. Aloud she continued their cover conversation, "Right now, my father gamble, for sure."

"I wouldn't want either of us to drive," Limei said. Raima kept up their verbal performance, asking, "Where does your father get all his money?"

Qi shrugged. "He beg for it on the street."

"Then it's agreed," Izzy put in. *"We take the driver with us and wipe his memory once he gets us to Rahe."*

From their gloomy corner Marie and Manon at last spoke up. *"We need to talk about revenge,"* Manon said. *"Who do we kill on the way out and how? I say we kill everybody—they're all evil. They've had it coming for a long, long time."*

A second later Marie chimed in as well. *"And we need talk about getting rid of the boys."*

"We can use the guards," Tiana said from her bunk near Ella. *"I like that idea."*

"Is that safe though?" Aine asked. *"What if a bullet goes wild and hits us?"*

"What if a bullet hits one of the windows on the other side of TC-Gen?" Limei asked. Her eyes opened wide, glinting with fear. She shared her memories of walking into TC-Gen for the first time, stepping out of the rover and craning her neck up to stare at the steep walls of Tractus Catena. Raima and the others fell silent both verbally and telepathically as they absorbed Limei's memory and knowledge. Limei's awe passed through them, making Raima shiver. Everyone else arrived during the daylight hours, disembarking the rover in time to see TC-Gen's entrance shadowed by those cliffs. Raima came in the dark and trudged to the door with her head down, watching the rocky ground. Now that she'd seen the entrance through Limei's eyes she couldn't stop herself from imagining the steep cliffs collapsing and burying them alive.

The other girls went on, considering the potential danger of a firefight inside the facility. TC-Gen was built mostly underground, but its front entrance peeked out of those sheer walls. In that area there were skylights and large, circular windows. Could it be bulletproof? The fear of depressurization made them cautious to accept the gunfight idea.

"Why risk it?" Manon asked. *"We can kill everyone ourselves."*

"I won't kill anyone," Tiana insisted.

"It's kill or be killed," Marie shot back. *"If you want to live, you'll do it."*

"We don't need to kill the nurses or the technicians. They don't understand everything that's going on here. They're just doing what they're told to do," Raima said, frustrated with the twins' rabid desire for violence—for revenge. *"We have to kill Yoon and his assistant and wipe out as much evidence as we can about the experiment."* She paused and looked over her shoulder to Marie and Manon. *"You guys can kill Yoon and his assistant and anyone else in charge. We can't let them have enough data to try this again on others."*

The twins were silent for a moment, communing together before Marie said, *"We'll do it."*

"Good," Raima said and glanced at Qi as her lips formed a tired smile. *"No surprise they agreed to that,"* she said, directing the words to Qi alone.

"Bad eggs," Qi muttered aloud, grinning. "My father is a bad egg. Rotten whole way."

"What about the nurses and technicians?" Limei asked. *"What do we do to stop them from stopping us?"*

Before anyone else could interject, Raima answered. *"We'll control them like puppets. There's no reason to kill people who can't stop us."* She shared her experience controlling the technician named Zhu Liu.

"We can wipe out their memories of us," Tiana suggested. *"And everything they know about the experiment. That lets us be safe and keeps them alive."*

They heard the steady thump of a nurse's footsteps approaching the bunkroom and disbanded, heading to their bunks for the night. Raima watched and turned her mind toward the twins as Nurse Victoria took their vital signs. There was no sign of a pause to indicate Marie and Manon manipulated her mind, but when the nurse approached her bed Raima checked her mind for signs of invasion anyway. She found nothing. Either the twins improved their workmanship, learning to hide it, or they hadn't meddled with the nurse at all.

The week carried on and with each new day the plan evolved further. Each evening they took advantage of the time before lights-out and discussed the escape. The biggest source of contention came whenever they considered the boys. All of them—except for Kim, who remained exempt from their plotting as her illness progressed into fever dreams and constant exhaustion—agreed that the boys must be killed. What they disagreed on was *how* they should do it, directly or indirectly? On the night of Sol Lunae—Monday—two days before the escape, they were still arguing about it before lights-out.

"*What if the security doors are programmed to go into lockdown at the sound of gunfire?*" Aine asked, fidgeting on her bunk. "*What if a bullet punches through a window and the doors seal? Some of us will suffocate to death while the rest of us will be trapped inside.*"

"*It's too risky,*" Manon agreed. "*We have to kill them without guns.*"

"*The glass will be stronger than that,*" Qi retorted. "*It'll hold.*" She sighed out her frustration, her eyes flickering over the other members of the group: Raima, Izzy, Ella, and Tiana—all the girls who supported using the guards to execute the boys. Aine and Limei had legitimate fears, but as far as Raima could tell the twins disagreed just to cause division.

"*This needs to end,*" Raima said, scolding everyone. "*We only have two days left.*" Out loud, while staring at Qi, she said, "Do you miss being an Intuiter?"

Qi gave a little snort. "No."

"What was that like?" Izzy asked. She'd never been to CF-Gen and had only been on Mars for two years.

"Eh," Qi replied, shrugging. "Same hold, same hold."

"Don't you mean same *old*?" Tiana asked, giggling.

"Aiya," Qi grumbled, waving one hand, dismissing the correction. "Who care how I say it? You know."

"*We should vote on what we're going to do about the boys,*" Ella said. "*We have to agree so we can move on to other issues.*"

"*If we vote you'll win,*" Marie complained. "*That's not fair.*"

"*Majority rules,*" Izzy shot back with irritation.

Raima longed to scream with exasperation but she bit it back. Her head felt swollen, full of unnatural pressure. The constant telepathic communication over the last few days wore her raw. The anxiety building inside her as they came closer to their last day didn't help either. With a burst of determination, she said, "*We vote and settle it for good. We can't put this off any longer."*

Ella nodded and broadcast her thoughts to the whole group. *"Everybody who thinks we take the facility, then use the guards to take care of the boys, say aye."*

Raima noted the careful way everyone—except Marie and Manon—described the plan, omitting words like *kill* and *execute.* But that was what they were discussing. How strange to realize that, when she looked at the situation that way, the twins were the only honest girls in their group.

"Aye," Qi said. Tiana, Ella, and Izzy all followed her. After a pause, feeling the others' eyes on her, Raima raised her telepathic voice to join them. *"Aye."*

"That's five of us," Ella said. She lifted her head, staring back toward the twins' corner. *"Everybody who thinks it's better to slaughter the boys with our bare hands first thing, say aye."*

"Shouldn't it be nay?" Aine asked.

"Who cares," Qi exploded, thumping her clenched fist into the open palm of her other hand. *"Just vote!"*

"Aye," Aine said and huffed aloud on her bunk. The twins echoed her from their corner.

A brief but tense silence stretched out as they waited for Limei. Finally, she said, *"I sit out."*

"One abstains," Ella said. *"Five to three in favor of using the guards. We win."* She grinned at Raima and then at Tiana. The real victory was Tiana's, Raima thought. She hadn't wanted to be involved in the killing, so using the guards and their guns to do it was the next best thing to sitting out entirely.

Except it wasn't. Using the guards to kill the boys didn't leave the girls' morally innocent. Raima had told Qi that they'd be able to leave TC-Gen with their heads held high, that they could escape and still look at their faces in the mirror. They wouldn't be ashamed of what they'd done to survive. Yet this wasn't like killing Ferde. Raima felt nothing toward most of the boys, excepting Bryson. Survivors never escaped unscathed, emotionally or physically.

She blinked away the tears before they came into her eyes, refusing to be weak now. The girls needed her—and so did Kaiden.

"We have to keep Kim's brother safe," she said, choosing their next topic. *"He escapes with us. Everyone agreed?"* She knew the twins

would fight her even before she spoke and, sure enough, Manon shifted in the corner with her sister and startled everyone when she spoke aloud.

"What?" she demanded in an incredulous tone.

"No one's talking to you," Izzy snapped. *"Remember they're watching,"* she said. *"Start talking, say anything. We have to hide what we're doing."*

"Did you ever see that movie *Star Wars*?" Ella asked.

"No," Raima replied, then picked up the telepathic conversation again. *"Kim and her brother, Kaiden, haven't finished their shots. He's not a threat."*

"How do you know he won't be in twenty years?" Marie asked.

"Not all men are bad," Izzy said.

"You hypocrite, Raima," Manon said, radiating with animosity. Raima could feel the emotion throwing heat like a flame onto her as Manon focused her hate. She'd positioned herself where she couldn't see the twins without turning around, but Manon found a new way to pester her nonetheless.

"What if Marie was a boy. Imagine that," Raima said. *"Would you be able to kill her if she was your brother, not your sister? Because that's what we're asking Kim to do."*

"We're identical twins," Manon snapped. *"So, Marie couldn't be my brother. Stupid question."*

"Can we really stand having a boy in our group?" Marie asked. *"It'll change everything."*

"Only if we let it," Raima retorted. The room was tight with an anxious energy, but Raima sensed the others' remaining doubts toward Marie and Manon overall. Manon's answer to Raima's question about killing her own sibling lingered. Manon claimed Raima was a hypocrite, but even she failed to pass her own standards at the thought of having to kill Marie.

She tried it again to drive her point home. *"Marie, your turn this time. If Manon was your brother, would you be able to kill her just because she was a boy undergoing the shots? I don't care that it's impossible because you're identical twins. Pretend. Could you do it?"*

The bunkroom stayed silent and tense, waiting for her answer. As the time stretched on Raima closed her eyes, sighing to calm her pounding heart. Sticky moisture coated the fine lines in her palms. She wiped them off on her scrubs and lifted her head in time to see Qi gazing at her with a tense expression. She felt Qi's touch inside her mind, sharing a thought that only she could hear. *"Manon won't let Marie answer with the truth. You know that right?"*

Raima forced herself not to nod and give away their silent communication. *"I know."*

"You know how Marie asked about if we could handle a boy in our family?" Qi asked, the sorrow in her black eyes dulling them. *"The real question we should be asking is if we can stand having the twins in our group. They're only family to each other."*

The unspoken insinuation that perhaps Marie and Manon should perish with the boys rang with terrifying loudness inside Raima's mind. Cold flushed her body while her face burned hot.

She shot Qi an angry thought, *"No."* As she looked away from Qi, Raima noticed that Izzy watched them, her face a pensive but unreadable mask. She felt the blood rush to her face, her ears, hoping she and Qi managed to keep their thoughts hidden from Izzy's sharp, strong talent.

Then Marie finally answered, saying *"Stupid question. You're wasting our time Raima."*

It may have been a stupid question, but Raima could see the way it affected the others. Some of them had siblings outside the facility, or cousins they could imagine were brothers or sisters. She was about to say that, but Ella beat her to it.

"Did I ever tell you guys about my two little brothers?" she asked aloud and then added to it voicelessly to support Raima's argument. *"I couldn't kill them just because of the shots. What's one boy with these genes? He might never have any kids at all. We don't know that."*

"You're lucky to have brothers you love and who love you back," Aine said, carrying on the topic Ella started. "Some of us don't." After those words she used her mind to speak, *"I always dreamed about having a good brother, or an older sister who'd protect me. I really hate Kim for having a good brother, but it's only because I'm jealous."* Aine's complex emotions rolled off her, invisible but powerful, like turbulent winds in Earth's thick, life-giving atmosphere.

"Kim hasn't taken the vow," Qi pointed out suddenly. *"She might not even be a telepath when she recovers after we get away."*

"She's still one of us," Raima countered. *"She's suffering just as we did, and the researchers will kill her the same way they plan to kill us eventually."*

"But the vow," Aine pressed. The girls' minds electrified the air around the room as all of them listened at once from their separate spots. *"She's so new; none of us really know her."*

"I know her," Raima snapped. *"She's an orphan. Her only family is her brother."*

"She could go back to Earth," Izzy said. *"And never come back to us, never talk to us again."*

"She can't do that," Raima replied. *"Kaiden has a Martian physique. He'd be crippled like most of us. She won't leave him."*

"Forever? For the rest of her life?" Manon asked, taunting her. She didn't bother hiding her resentment. In fact, she pushed the emotion at the whole group as if she could infect all of them with her sheer willpower alone. *"You're sure confident about that. How well did you know her at CF-Gen?"*

"What do you think about that, Qi?" Marie added. She laughed aloud from her bunk beside Manon in their dark corner. They whispered together in a childish chant, but the audible words were in the twins' secret language, not English.

"I think you're both idiots," Qi shot back. *"That's what I think."*

Raima tried to restrain the uncomfortable blush that spread over her cheeks but failed. She looked to Qi and shielded her next thoughts to keep them private, between herself and Qi. *"You know how I feel about Kim. I—"*

"You can't keep her straight from Kati," Qi said, smiling without humor. *"You liked Kati. You wanted to help her, but you couldn't. You're trying to make up for that with Kim, but they're not the same person."*

"I know that," Raima blustered.

Qi took hold of Raima's hand next to her and squeezed it to reassure her. *"Go see if you can get Kim to wake up enough to take the vow. It'll suck all the wind out of the twins' sails."*

Raima gave Qi's hand a quick squeeze. She moved across the bunkroom to where Kim lay motionless on her cot with her eyes half-closed and unseeing. Raima sat down on the floor beside Kim's bed and fumbled under the covers, seeking the bare skin of the other girl's hand. She could feel the others' interest, all watching her, but distracted by continued discussion as they vented concerns and ensured that everyone remembered exactly what to do on Sol Mercurii. Raima blocked them out, focusing entirely on finding Kim's mind where it was hiding, somewhere deep inside.

She took Kim's hand in a light grip and stared at the girl's ashen face, reaching inside her mind. The bed in front of her blurred as Raima fell deeper into Kim's consciousness.

"Kim?" she called and nudged at her both telepathically and physically with a little jerk. *"Kim? Are you there?"*

She saw a scene opening for her and felt herself slipping into Kim's feverish reality. The world was gray around her, thick and impenetrable. Raima looked down at the imaginary floor and saw that her bare feet were moving over a dense matting of green grass. It was cool and moist, prickling her toes. Raima's own memory inserted the scent of wet grass, freshly cut. Distant thunder rumbled in the heavy, clammy air.

"Kim!" Raima called again.

This time the air rippled and the mist gave way, admitting an exhausted, shaking Kim. The fragile blonde, short but built with strong Earther's bones, looked at Raima with a mixture of confusion and fear. Her blue eyes swam with tears. She spoke with her dream lips, not her thoughts. "Why didn't you come sooner?" she asked. "I can't find Kaiden."

"I'm sorry," Raima said. *"I should've come sooner."* Kim's delirium had ensnared her, making her believe everything she dreamt was real. Raima wondered what would have happened if she'd stood back and watched the dreams unfold rather than calling for Kim. Could she direct the dreams or control them? Had the twins done that to Raima?

"Do you know where Kaiden is?" Kim asked. "Have you seen him?"

"He's fine," Raima said, hoping to comfort her. *"I've seen him. He's safe."*

"Where is he? Can you take me to him?"

Raima shook her head. *"You're sleeping, Kim. You're dreaming. I need to talk to you."*

"*Dreaming?*" Kim asked, incredulous. She turned, taking in her surroundings.

"Important things are about to happen," Raima went on.

"Dangerous things. I'm going to keep Kaiden safe, but to do that I need you to promise me something."

"What?" Kim asked, but Raima knew from the activity in her mind that Kim hadn't meant: *What do you need me to promise?* Instead she was just confused by the exchange. *"Take me to Kaiden,"* Kim pleaded.

Raima could feel the deliriousness of Kim's mind growing, swelling beyond control. Trying to talk to her or extract the vow from her would be as pointless and impossible as arguing with a typhoon. Raima withdrew, pulling her mind and her hand back from Kim. She blinked, staring at Kim as the other girl moaned and rolled over in her bed, troubled by the darkening mood of her dreams.

"What did she say?" Limei asked into the silence of Raima's mind.

"I couldn't get her to believe anything I said," she replied with irritation. *"She's delirious. It's pointless to try making her take the vow now, before she's sane again and recovering."*

"It was good of you to try anyway," Qi said and pushed a comforting warmth and tenderness at her.

Raima accepted the emotions, absorbing them, letting the frustration dissolve away. She turned and looked over her shoulder toward where Qi sat, leaning against the wall. The Chinese girl smiled, showing her mouth filled with perfect white teeth. Raima smiled back. *"Tomorrow is Sol Martius—Tuesday—and the day after we'll make our escape. By Thursday we'll be at the Rahe crater."*

Qi finished her thoughts with jubilation. *"We'll be free!"*

Sol Martius was the same as every other day. Nurse Vieve escorted the girls to the cafeteria and then lingered about the large rectangular room chatting with Nurse Victoria while the subjects ate. The girls ate together and shielded their thoughts from the boys. Raima quickly took note that Kaiden wasn't with the boys again, but there was nothing alarming about that because he was ill with the shots, just like Kim.

The breakfast that morning was exceptional in its blandness, as it always was on Tuesdays and Wednesdays. Raima now understood why. The rover brought in fresh food and supplies once a week, and by this time the raw ingredients for better food—eggs and meat primarily—were eaten or had gone bad. That left them with frozen waffles, pancakes, and dry cereal topped with milk made from powder.

Late in their breakfast time, after Raima already finished her own sparse and boring meal, Limei grabbed at her mind with an alarmed, frantic need. Raima blinked with surprise and looked to where Limei sat only a few meters away, beside Qi. *"What is it?"* she asked.

Limei's dark brown eyes were crinkled with the effort of restraining her distress. "Bad food today," she said in a loud voice, trying to maintain a nonchalant appearance. To Raima she said, *"I overheard the nurses talking about a rover that arrived late last night. I read their minds when I was returning my tray to the kitchen."*

Qi and many of the other girls caught Limei's words as well. Varying degrees of panic spread through their minds and colored their faces. Izzy and Tiana looked to Raima with hope, as if she was their sole commander and must have foreseen this new development. The twins were also eyeing Raima with some silent expectation, but they were waiting for her to fail and fall apart under new pressure.

"Quit the whining," Qi snapped aloud. "Bad food, bad food. You lucky. My father let me go hungry to take food money to casinos." She mimed a man playing slot machines. A few of the girls managed to chuckle at her antics, despite the undercurrent of growing terror among them.

"Is there anything else?" Raima asked.

Limei brushed at some crumbs left on the table by her toast as she answered. *"The nurses thought it would be food or supplies, but it was security guards. Six of them."* She looked up at Raima and her eyes were bright with unshed tears that she blinked away. Despair and panic weighed down her thoughts. *"They know what we're planning. They're going to stop us. They're going to kill us for it."*

"*They can't know anything for sure,*" Raima said hurrying to fill the fearful, silent void. The old horror, the certainty that she—they—were doomed spun inside her skull.

"Unless someone told them," Izzy put in. She looked toward the twins with a raw, visceral rage.

Marie scowled and opened her mouth to refute the unsaid

charges aloud—but she caught herself in time and said, "I can't wait until Sol Jovis when we have real eggs again!"

Manon spoke telepathically to the group. *"Why would we tell them anything? We want to escape as much as you do!"*

"Nothing has been out of the ordinary," Raima said, trying to defuse the situation. Though she suspected the twins as well—it was impossible not to,—it didn't make any sense. *"If they knew what we were planning, we'd all be dead by now."*

"They know we're doing something," Aine added. *"They watch us all the time. They have to have figured out that something is happening."*

"There's a rover here now," Qi said with sudden excitement. *"Yoon could leave on it. We can't let that happen. We have to act now, before the rover can leave today."*

"Escape now?" Ella asked. The blue in her eyes stood out stark against her pale face as she stared in shock.

Qi jerked her head in Ella's direction. Her gaze was fiery, lit from within. *"If Yoon gets away he'll start another experiment when we're gone. New people. New telepaths. More deaths and suffering. He has to die."*

"This is even better than the other plan," Tiana agreed. She grinned with anxious energy, trying to reassure Ella. *"This way we can escape before the normal rover gets here. All the nurses and techs and cooks and janitors who we leave trapped here, but alive—"*

"—they'll be able to leave on the incoming rover," Raima finished for her, seeing the wisdom in the changed plan.

"But six more guards with guns," Izzy said and shook her head. *"We're all going to get shot. How many people can we control at once? We don't even know. Can we control more than one at a time?"*

"I miss cinnamon rolls," Aine said and picked up a bit of uneaten toast on her tray and dropped it into her half-empty, fake orange juice. "I'd give away a kidney if someone could give me a lifetime supply of cinnamon rolls." On the surface she gave a convincing performance, feigning extreme boredom. But her eyes were as fiery as Qi's had been. Telepathically she said, *"I want to get the hell out of here. Now sounds good to me. And we'll never find out how many bastards we can control without taking a risk."*

"I miss cinnamon rolls too," Ella said. *"I'm ready."*

"Everyone's agreed then?" Raima asked, leaning forward as if

whispering. *"We escape today, now?"* She looked to Marie and Manon, who'd been silent during the discussion. "How about you guys? Do you two miss cinnamon rolls?"

"Yeah," Manon muttered.

"We agree," Marie answered. *"We escape now."*

"When the nurses lead us into the classroom, we start the plan." Qi said, glancing toward the two women. *"The boys get to lead the way and take on the guards. Watch their progress but stay safe. Let them get guns, but make sure you get one of your own. Take control of anyone who gets in your way, but don't linger. The only way it works is if we move too fast for them to be ready for us. Keep an eye out for the rover driver. If you find him, keep him alive and with you."*

"Destroy the cameras every chance you get," Raima added.

"I'll clear out the bunkrooms and get Kim and Kaiden on their feet," Aine volunteered.

"Good," Raima said. She scanned over the other girls. *"Aine needs someone to back her up if she can't control all the kitchen workers at once."*

"I'll go," Tiana offered.

"We'll go into the offices to find Yoon," Manon said, motioning at Marie. *"Then we'll kill him and his head assistant Eva Fuchs."* She grinned in a hard, bitter triumph.

Raima nodded at them and smiled with grim approval. *"Good."*

SIXTEEN

Nurse Victoria shouted in her dry voice, interrupting the girls' planning, "Time to head over to the classroom. Dump your trays, kiddies."

All the subjects began to move, standing up from their tables. Some went towards the kitchen, depositing their trays for the workers to clean and restack for use at lunchtime. Others, who'd already disposed of their trays, moved at an unhurried pace to join Nurse Vieve, who would escort them through the door to the classroom.

As Raima left her tray, she acknowledged Qi with a quick glance and a small smile, but telepathically she embraced the spunky Chinese girl, exchanging wordless and nameless emotions. There was no certainty that either of them would live through what was to come.

"Thank you," Raima told her.

Qi cocked her head in silent question. *"For what?"*

"For saving my life," she said and smiled again.

Qi rolled her eyes. *"I never saved your life."*

"I've been dead since I came to Mars," Raima said and then abandoned telepathy to speak out loud. "You taught me how to live again. So, you did save my life. See?"

"You scared?" Qi asked, also giving up the silent communication. Her eyes flicked to the nurses and the door. "You want me to start?"

Raima shook her head. "I'll do it."

Clenching her fists, Raima let her mind flow out and take hold of Nurse Vieve. She stood near the door to the hallway with Nurse Victoria at her side. The keycards to the medical area were attached to a lanyard around her neck. They flopped against her rounded, plump stomach when she walked, making a plastic clanking that was somehow less satisfying than the metallic tinkling of keys. The nurse's mind was vast and calm, but it churned the moment Raima poked around inside it.

Give me the keycard lanyards, Raima ordered Nurse Vieve. She met resistance as the nurse's mind thickened and slowed. Nurse Vieve looked toward Raima with a baffled expression. *Give me the lanyards*, Raima repeated and pushed the command with more force, embedding it into the nurse's consciousness as a compulsive imperative.

Nurse Vieve pulled at the cord around her neck. The keycards clunked dully, jostled by the motion. She pulled the lanyard up and over her graying hair, then clutched the unsteady bunch of plastic keycards in her fist. Her eyes never left Raima. The nurse crossed the short distance between them. Raima extended her hand and Nurse Vieve gave her the lanyard.

At the other end of the cafeteria Nurse Victoria froze in place, silent. Then the nurse slowly removed her own lanyard, which held the keycards to the bunkrooms, and walked toward Tiana. In less than half a minute both lanyards had come into the girls' possession. The plan had begun.

Qi jumped out of her spot at the table. *"Tiana, can you control them both?"*

Raima sensed Tiana stretching out, reaching with effort into Nurse Vieve's mind. The two girls brushed against one another's consciousness while inside the brain of a third person. It was a dizzying, disorienting experience. Raima withdrew gradually and watched Nurse Vieve's reaction as Tiana held both nurses under her power.

"I got them," Tiana said out loud.

"Don't talk," Marie scolded. *"Think."*

"Can't do that and do this," Tiana shot back. She rose from her seat and began walking toward the hallway that led to the girls' bunkroom. Aine got up and followed her at a fast-paced jog. Tiana passed the lanyard to Aine. Both nurses followed Tiana and Aine to the bunkroom.

Raima noticed the boys' reaction immediately. She felt the tightness of their shock, the tingling charge of their excitement. They were clever enough to understand what was happening, but they were also too downtrodden to embrace it without question. Bryson spoke up first, as the girls guessed he would.

"What the hell's going on?" he shouted, pounding on a nearby lunch table with one thick fist.

Qi snapped at him, "Small brain. Too bad."

Izzy explained telepathically. *"We're escaping. We need your help. There are lots of armed guards at the far end of TC-Gen. We need to get to them, take their guns, and get out of here."*

"How the hell did you make the nurses give you the keys?" Bryson demanded.

"We're stronger than you are," Qi told him, making sure that all the subjects, male and female alike, could hear her.

Raima ran to the medical area door and quickly searched through the keycards. Without looking up she said, *"Someone knock out the camera."*

One of the boys sprang into action. He snatched up trays, plates, and silverware from the boys' lunch table and began chucking all of it at the security camera mounted on the back wall, overlooking the whole cafeteria. Raima snuck quick looks at him, checking his progress. Regret flickered in her. The boy was of Asian ancestry, tall and lanky with a Martian physique, but he was still very young—not even Kaiden's age yet. His black hair was shiny in the dull fluorescent lights overhead. His eyes were alert and intelligent as he searched for more things to throw.

One of the boys called out encouragement, "Go, Fai!"

Bryson joined the effort, shouldering Fai back. "Never let a chink boy do a real man's job," he said and guffawed. He was taller than Fai and thick-bodied. Instead of trying to destroy the camera by tossing things at it, Bryson chose a more direct approach. He pushed the whole lunch table closer to the wall and stepped up onto it. The boost in height was more than enough to let him reach the camera; he stooped slightly to keep his head from bumping on the ceiling. Bryson grabbed the camera, tugging on it with a guttural grunt.

Satisfied with the boys' work, Raima slid the keycard through the slot along the wall next to the door and opened it. The hall beyond was painted a calming blue-gray with a trim of stenciled clouds and rainbows in a childish design. Considering the amount of suffering these hallways had seen, Raima thought the stenciled decorations mocked everyone who'd died at TC-Gen.

"*Limei!*" she called. When the girl rushed to the door, Raima said, "*Go and get Kim and Kaiden. They're weak, you'll have to help Aine and Tiana with them.*"

As Limei retreated, Marie and Manon came to the doorway. "*Yoon?*" Manon asked even before she'd gotten into the hall. Her eyes roved the area, taking it in with a grim expectation.

"*No sign of him yet,*" Raima told her. "*He could be anywhere. Go ahead of us and look around quickly.*"

"*What about the techs?*" Marie asked with concern.

"*Trick them. Convince them to stay inside their offices. Close the door. Make them believe nothing's wrong. Put them to sleep—I don't care. Just go!*"

Marie and Manon were rushing ahead before Raima finished her sentence. They moved like robots, identical to one another in determination and speed. They opened doors and peeked inside offices. A few yelps came as they surprised some technicians inside, but the twins silenced the reactions and shut the doors again. Raima watched them and felt the energy of their minds working rapidly, like wind churning the air, as they reworked three different minds. *Three technicians,* she thought. There were less than a dozen throughout the whole facility.

Inside the cafeteria Izzy coached the boys, promising that everyone would survive with the girls' help. A brief stab of guilt and regret coursed through Raima again, but she dismissed the feelings when she saw the security camera mounted over the next doorway. On the wall ahead, there was a small portable fire extinguisher, painted bright red like blood. Raima snatched it with both hands.

At the far end of the hall Marie and Manon waited beside a locked door. Their faces were tight with anxiousness and impatience. "*The key!*" Manon called.

Raima ran the rest of the way to reach them. She grabbed the lanyard and pulled it up and over her head. "Here," she said and handed it off to Manon. "Go."

"The boys," Marie said. "They're too slow."

"I'll motivate them," Raima replied and motioned at them to go on. *"We can't miss Yoon and he has it coming from you both. Only you."*

With a somber look Marie nodded while Manon was already tampering with the keycards. Raima hoped she'd seen respect in the other girl's gaze but couldn't help but doubt it. As soon as the door clicked, unlocking and admitting them through, Raima shoved the fire extinguisher into it, propping it open. Marie and Manon rushed into the next hall and a woman yelped with alarm.

"What is this? What are you doing here?"

Behind Raima, at the door to the cafeteria, the boys entered the hallway, hurrying to join her. "Get a chair or a desk or something," Raima shouted at them. "From one of the offices!"

Many of the boys were Asian, the third or fourth generation of the very first people to walk the surface of Mars two hundred years ago. They chattered together in Mandarin, pointing at the open office doors. When they reemerged a few seconds later their arms were laden with any office equipment they could carry or push. They were like a river, energetic after being dammed up for so long, ready now to wash away everything that stood in their intended path.

Raima took a large chair from one of them and pushed it into the doorway, then reclaimed her fire extinguisher. She let Fai pile a large boxy machine onto the chair to further ensure the door would stay open and then urged the boys through.

After they'd gone, Raima hefted the fire extinguisher up and swung it overhead, bashing the security camera. A shower of sparks exploded around her for a moment and she cringed, backing away from it. As the light of the little fireworks show faded, Raima saw that she'd succeeded. The camera dangled from a few electrical cords, useless. She swung at it one last time and knocked it to the floor.

"Watch where you're swinging that thing, bitch," Bryson said from behind her.

Raima restrained the desire to look in his direction. This was one person who deserved the death that had been planned for him. "Go on ahead. The boys need your help."

"No shit," Bryson said, raising his voice as he came closer. He closed in on her. He was breathing through his parted lips and his eyes glimmered with a malicious excitement. Raima grimaced at the stink of his breath and that was enough to make Bryson pounce.

His hands moved like snakes, one wrapping itself around her throat in a paralyzing grip and the other jerked on the fire extinguisher. "I think I want this. You're going to give it to me."

Old fears and instincts battled with new determination and pride. She could give in and he might move on without any further trouble, or she could resist and earn punishment. She remembered Qi smiling and laughing with her, the touch of the other girl's forehead against her own, warm and comforting.

You're not thinking right. We can take whatever we want.

Raima reached for his mind and simultaneously spat into his face. Bryson reared back, roaring. At first, he wiped at his cheeks and eyes, distracted by her spittle, but a heartbeat later he grabbed his head and moaned with pain. Raima lifted the fire extinguisher up, ready to smash him with it.

"Get going through that door and help the other boys," she ordered him in a deep voice. "Or I will rip your brain out of your skull with my mind. Do you understand me?"

"Yeah," Bryson replied.

"Get moving," Raima shouted at him.

Bryson glared through his mask of pain, but he moved for the door. More boys came down the hall after Bryson, and Raima realized that they'd seen some of her exchange with the older boy, their ringleader and bully. Their body language and mental energy lingered about them, heavy with caution and nervousness. Yet their eyes, when they glanced at her in brief glimpses were filled with awe.

Qi, Izzy, and Tiana entered the hallway, jogging. Izzy called out to her telepathically. *"Kim and Kaiden are in the cafeteria with Limei, Aine, and Ella."*

Raima let out a long breath as the instinctive fear from her encounter with Bryson left her, only to be replaced with the ongoing concern over the progress of the escape and the gnawing certainty that it would not go according to plan. *"Limei knows what to do?"*

"Yes," Tiana said. *"The twins and the boys go first, then us. Limei, Aine, and Ella will help Kim and Kaiden to the airlock. They'll be just behind us."*

"Guards soon," Qi said aloud in her thick accent. "Guns. Death soon."

Raima nodded. She set aside the fire extinguisher, knowing it would slow her down. "Let's move—the twins will need our help."

They entered the next set of offices and labs. The first thing Raima saw was a woman lying in the middle of the hallway, face down in a puddle of blood. The hair was brownish, similar to the twins', and for a moment Raima's stomach lurched with horror. Then she saw the streaks of gray in the fallen woman's hair and noted the short legs that marked her as an Earthling.

The hall stretched out ahead of them, much longer than the previous one and with several branching intersections. Distant cries rang out, then a choked, wet scream. Chills rippled through Raima's body. Though she'd seen blood and carnage before, coming upon it when she hadn't expected it made her woozy with shock. She leaned against the wall to steady herself as more cries echoed deeper in the facility. *This wasn't how it was supposed to be*, she thought.

Izzy knelt beside the body and, with trembling hands, took hold of her shoulder, turning her over. Raima inhaled as the woman's face came into view. It was obscured by blood and gore, but the cause of death was clear. Her throat had been cut in a ragged slash, uneven and sloppy. Qi chattered in Mandarin to herself at the sight of the wound.

"I've never seen this technician before," Tiana observed in a weak voice.

"She probably never saw us," Raima muttered. "Just ran samples or worked on the computer."

"Her body is still warm," Izzy whispered. When she looked up her face was ashen. She rose, swaying on her unsteady feet and hugged herself as if cold.

"Come on." Qi nudged them psychically.

They came to the first intersection in the hall and saw more bodies, blood, and carnage. All the doors had been opened, some with force, as the shattered doorknobs, locks, and hinges revealed. Computers were tossed about, sometimes into the hallway, further cluttering it. Blood arced over the walls in arterial sprays around many of the bodies. The blue-gray walls with their cheery stenciled trims—this time in the shape of bright yellow suns—had become epigraphs of a vicious rampage.

The four girls separated at an intersection, checking through the halls and offices that split off the main passageway. Most of the rooms were empty, though they showed signs of a search and much of the equipment had been knocked over in a hasty attempt to destroy it. Raima saw no further bodies and when she met up with Qi, Tiana, and Izzy again, she learned that they'd seen only two other dead. That left the count at five bodies.

"Were any of them Yoon?" she asked.

All three shook their heads in the negative.

"Did the boys do this?" Izzy asked. *"Or was it . . . ?"*

"We have to catch up with them," Raima said, ignoring Izzy's questions and the implications.

They moved with less caution through the halls now, not bothering to investigate side rooms or intersections. They followed the path that was marked for them in blood.

They passed the body of a man who'd slumped over with his back against the wall. His chin was pressed to his chest and blood flowed from his neck like a waterfall onto the floor. The man was on his knees, as if he'd knelt to be within easy, comfortable reach of his executioners. None of the boys had guns. Only the twins could have commanded that level of submission from a powerful, tall man whose large biceps and thick legs hinted at the likelihood that he only recently came to Mars and would've overpowered any of the Martian subjects.

Footprints littered the floor around the body. The twins and the boys tracked thick, crimson blood around on their slippers. Raima, Izzy, Qi, and Tiana took care avoiding the pools of blood around this slain man and all the other dead technicians. As they rounded the corner another dead body came into view. Tiana let out a little cry, recognizing this tech. "It's Bailey!"

"Keep moving," Raima said. She didn't look at his face as they passed. She added his death to the growing count inside her head.

In the next section of labs and offices someone had brushed their blood-soaked hands along the blue-gray wall, streaking it red-brown. Tiana made a small gagging sound, a little restrained retch. Raima could feel the younger girl's emotional trauma building in the air around them—but it wasn't just Tiana. Izzy, Qi, and even Raima herself were rigid with anxiety or shaking in shock at the carnage around them.

There were voices ahead, getting louder. Raima rounded a corner and found herself staring down a bland, unpainted hallway where the bluish paint and stenciling on the trim had been ripped off or omitted, leaving only the cold grayness of hard plastic coating the inside of the facility's walls. A large, sturdy doorway stood at the end of the passageway where three boys scurried about, trying to prop it open with machinery. Like some of the other doors, this one had once had a security camera mounted over it, but it'd been destroyed, leaving wires dangling.

Beside the door, slumped over on his side, was a man dressed in black, the first security guard they'd seen. He'd been killed with a jagged cut to the throat, like all the others. His nightstick was missing and Raima guessed that he'd had a gun, but it was gone too.

The boys, all grunted with effort as they propped open the door. The pant legs of their gray scrubs were soiled with blood that looked almost black.

"What's going on here?" Qi demanded, broadcasting the words to reach everyone. *"Who's been killing everyone?"*

The boys glanced at the girls and their work came to a standstill. One of them chattered to Qi in Mandarin. While he spoke, and Qi listened, Raima joined the other two boys, kneeling to add her own limited muscle power to their efforts. Izzy went with her and together they wedged open the door with small, heavy boxes to keep it from sealing.

Qi touched their minds, telling them what she'd learned from the boy as they worked. *"The twins did all this. They have some sort of pointy office tool. I think it's a stylus or even a pen. Baojia called it a chopstick."*

Baojia, Raima thought and remembered sitting through tests with the Chinese boy during her first days at TC-Gen. She watched as he clambered around the blocked doorway with the others, trying to catch up with the twins. He was taller and skinnier than Fai, the other Asian boy.

"Bryson and all the older boys went on ahead to be with the twins," Qi went on, appearing queasy. *"Baojia says Manon has the guard's gun. Bryson took the nightstick."*

"*At least now they won't have to slit people's throats,*" Izzy said. Bitter rage clouded her mind.

"*They were never* slitting *throats here,*" Raima pointed out with fury of her own. "*You can't cut anything with a pen, or a stylus. They're just ripping the flesh out after stabbing through their necks.*" She felt hot and cold in turns, as if she was about to vomit at the thought of it.

"No time," Qi said, scolding them all. She pointed at the door and started to say, "We go—" but the rapid, popping chatter of gunfire cut her off.

SEVENTEEN

They hurried for the door, pushing through it one at a time. Raima had expected to see bodies littering the corridor again, but the floors and walls were bare, unscathed by violence.

The passageway lasted only a few yards before it broadened, becoming a long rectangular room. Shelves ran along the walls, each laden with boxes of supplies. Some were familiar, like dried milk mixes, plastic silverware and napkins. But alongside those items were completely foreign things: glass pipettes, black rubber tubes, and hunks of metal and plastic—probably spare parts for the rover or some of the lab equipment.

On the other side of the storage room a door had been propped open with a large box. The girls ran to the door. The hallway beyond was wider than the others in the medical area and undecorated. The lighting and the walls were already depressing, but now more of the twins' victims lay strewn over the floor. Bullets had punched perfect circular holes and oblong gouges in many places around the room. The three men lying dead on the floor wore black uniforms, identical to the first guard's. They'd been killed with shots to the head. Bits of white skull stood out, stark against the gray floor. Many of the men were still bleeding out. As Raima stepped past the first body the edge of her foot touched the pool of blood draining from his head. The viscous liquid soaking through her thin slippers was so warm it was almost hot. She swallowed hardand didn't let herself look down at her bloody footprints.

The guard's guns were missing.

The sound of gunfire from somewhere ahead continued, driving Raima and the others onward past the bodies. She added them to her ongoing count of the dead. They'd planned to kill the guards from the start but talking about it was so different from seeing it. Raima had imagined fighting for her own life, not coming across the gruesome aftermath of the slaughter.

They passed through long hallways that functioned as dormitories for the guards. Beds were unmade, recently slept in.

Six more bodies cluttered the floor at intersections between the hall and various rooms. Like the previous men who were killed with guns rather than cut throats, these guards were shot in the head and face. Had they taken up defensive positions inside the doorways only to be driven out by the twins' telepathic power and shot to death? Bullet casings and additional punctures in the walls offered silent testimony to the brief and vicious firefight.

Blood was tracked far beyond the place where the guards died, defining the killers' path. Raima, Izzy, Tiana, and Qi could all see the streaked crimson that marked every deviation from the rest of the group as someone explored an office or storeroom. The marks were fresh, glistening wetly in the dull fluorescent lights, or oozing in drips down the walls.

At the end of that corridor they jogged through more storage spaces, half-empty rooms stocked with boxes, electronics, and other detritus, all of it meaningless to the girls. They caught up to the younger boys, including Baojia. The boys were working to find more gear they could use to further prop open the nearby door and going through the rooms, looting them. Raima and the other girls moved on.

Another door stood in their way, propped open like all the others with assorted, easily-grabbed junk. There were voices nearby, just beyond the doorway. Qi was the first to reach it.

"Be careful," Raima called to her telepathically. Her heart fluttered inside her chest. The suppressed fear that the escape would claim their lives resurfaced, making her breathless and jumpy, bracing herself for whatever horrors came next.

With one shoulder touching the door, Qi craned her neck around and gazed back at Raima. She didn't look frightened, but her mind held the same tension as Raima's. *"See you on the other side,"* she said and grinned, clenching her teeth together.

She pressed her weight into the door, scrambling around the boxes and into the room beyond. Raima went next, rushing for the door as it swung back and impacted the rubbish obstructing its path with a dull thump. Raima stepped into the room and she recognized it as the processing area where Nurse Victoria had brought her immediately after her arrival at TC-Gen. Natural, rust-tinged sunlight spilled into the space from a set of thick, domed windows along one wall and skylights set into the ceiling overhead.

This room was painted green and the floor was made of a hard plastic, molded to resemble real wood. A large, tall desk divided the room into halves. Office equipment and a large computer screen were set up neatly when Raima passed through this area the first time with Nurse Victoria. Now everything was scattered and broken. Bullets left holes in the desk and in the walls. A dead woman slouched in the chair behind the desk. Her head, mostly missing, was tossed back, curled over her seat. Her brains, bits of white skull fragments, and gray-brown chunks, were splattered on the floor and the walls.

There were two boys on the other side of the desk, standing as far away from the dead woman and gory spray as they could. Both were armed with handheld pistols. They held their guns with a false confidence, the bravado of their sex requiring that they be fearless and incautious, pretending to be comfortable handling such weapons.

One of the boys was Fai, the other was fair-skinned with curly brown hair. Raima recalled his name, as if remembering it from another lifetime—*Dominic.* They were talking in quiet voices before the girls barged in, but now, as Izzy and Tiana joined Raima and Qi, they only stared. Their eyes carried a strange, unreadable anxiety, as if both boys were seconds from breaking down and crying for their mothers, or just running away. Yet Raima recognized their mental energy. They exuded the same feverish, wild hope that fueled her own actions—the nearness of *freedom.*

"Where are the twins?" Raima asked.

"The control room," Dominic replied. "With Bryson, Wesley, and Jayden."

Qi started chattering in Mandarin. She hopped over the desk

and walked with a swaggering gait toward Fai and Dominic. Fai frowned at her and his companion gawked as Qi snatched the guns from their hands.

"Hey!" Dominic protested. "Wesley told me I could have that."

"If you want another, go and take it. Some of the guards still have guns," Izzy said.

"We need these," Qi added with a stern tone.

Raima crawled over the desk to join Qi. Izzy and Tiana followed. They avoided glancing at the dead woman or the gray mess of her brains, but Raima registered the others' repulsion. Qi handed Raima the handgun and then glanced to Izzy and Tiana. *Do either of you want this?*

"I'll take it, if you don't want it," Izzy answered. Qi passed the second handgun to her and Izzy examined it, then pointed it at the ground.

Something in Izzy's demeanor made Raima realize the other girl was more comfortable with guns than she had let on, but there was no time to ask about it before Qi began telepathically instructing them. *Through there—* she pointed, stabbing her finger toward a closed door behind the desk that had been splashed with the dead woman's blood and brains *—is the control room. The twins had the keycards, and no one propped it open.*

What about the other door? Tiana asked. There were three doors in the room. The first was the one that the girls passed through to enter, the second was the small door behind the desk that Qi claimed led to the control room. The third door was on the outside of the desk, and like the entrance it was large enough that two plump adults could walk side by side through it with space to spare.

Airlock, Fai answered, making all four girls and even Dominic look to him with surprise.

Raima nodded, agreeing with him. "That way is the airlock, I remember it." She searched the edges of Fai's mind. He was intelligent and Raima could sense his telepathic power budding, strengthening in this new, dangerous scenario. The boy at his side seemed comparatively dull, simultaneously less valuable and less threatening.

It's locked, Fai added.

The keycards didn't work on it? Tiana asked.

Fai shook his head. *"No one's tried it yet. But it won't open just by pressing the button."*

Qi cursed in Mandarin and Fai let out a childish chuckle, understanding the language. His voice was starting to change, breaking with the increasing influence of testosterone from puberty, but it hadn't yet lost its youthful tenor.

"What do we do?" Izzy asked with a note of despair. "No one blocked the door to the control room. It's locked now. We're stuck in here."

Raima glanced at the narrow door to the control room, guessing at its strength. "There are six of us. We can probably break it if we—"

An abrupt hiss of air from the doorway leading to the airlock caught everyone's attention. The door unsealed with a beep and a whir of electricity. In a moment it slid open, admitting four armed guards into the room. Male voices erupted, shouting with panic. They fired without hesitation.

Raima dropped to the floor, overwhelmed with the sudden shock of the attack, forgetting that she had two weapons to fight back with—her mind and her gun. Her heart pounded inside her chest, as loud as the gunshots that tore through the air. The men shouted on the other side of the desk, but their words were mangled and lost in the fray.

"Raima! *Raima!"* Qi called to her from somewhere nearby, also on the floor, with both her true voice and its telepathic counterpart. *"Did they get you?"*

"No," she replied at once, without bothering to check over her body for wounds. There was no pain, only the liquid, trembling of an adrenaline burst. Izzy's feet brushed Raima's left arm, and someone else was over her legs. The fake wood floor was sticky and wet with blood and brains from the dead woman.

"I got one," Fai announced. *"Get the others and shoot them!"*

For a moment Fai's words confused her, then she realized, with a flash of insight from Fai himself that the boy had snatched hold of a guard's mind and frozen the man in place. Dark admiration for Fai and his talent rushed through her, but Raima quashed it, refusing to be distracted.

Izzy, Tiana, and Qi all reached out with their minds, each focusing on one of the three remaining men. They seized each brain, locking it up, freezing the men in place.

"Raima," Izzy said. "You're going to have to shoot them. I can't hold them still and shoot."

Raima sat up on her knees as soon as the firing ceased and set her hands, holding the handgun, on the desk. Two of the guards had come within a few feet of the desk before the girls and Fai stopped them. A few more seconds and they would've been able to shoot over it.

She aimed for the men beside the airlock door first and squeezed the trigger. The weapon leapt in her hands and let out a deafening burst of sound as it fired. Raima cried out, startled against her will, but as she gritted her teeth together, recovering her courage, she saw the man she'd shot slumping to the floor. Blood welled up from his chest like a crimson fountain, bubbling. She tore her gaze away and aimed at the next man by the airlock, aiming again for his chest. This time she stayed quiet when the gun fired, recoiling in her hands. The second man went down and Raima shot next at the men closer to the desk, aiming for their heads.

The men near the desk died in a burst of gore as their heads ruptured, spilling their blood and brain matter to the floor a few seconds before their bodies collapsed to join the rest of the mess there. By the airlock the men shrieked, stumbling forward onto their hands and knees. Blood dripped and then poured from their wounds. The last of the men gave a wet, hacking cough and blood gushed from his mouth as he collapsed, drowning in his own blood.

Raima stood and let her arms fall to her sides, along with the handgun. She was shaking, overwhelmed with the mass of blood and death.

"Raima?" Qi asked. She touched Raima's arm, trying to offer comfort.

"Take their guns from them," Raima ordered, gradually regaining the cold, desperate hope that had fueled her this far. "I need someone to go back and find Aine, Limei, and Ella to make sure they're all right. We need to get Kim and Kaiden through the facility and to the airlock here."

Qi and Tiana hopped over the desk together. They took two

of the guards' guns from their unresisting hands and then went through the open door that led deeper into the compound.

"Can we take the other two guns?" Fai asked. He meant the weapons that the guards still held as they bled out onto the floor. Raima tried to block out the wet gurgling from one of them by imagining it was a man who'd hurt her, a john or one of Ferde's goons, but even that failed.

There was no logical reason to say no to Fai, except that the boys would be more dangerous with weapons of their own. She struggled to find something to say, any way to justify a negative answer, but before she could form a single word the door to the control room opened with a gentle click.

Raima and Izzy turned, facing the doorway and reaching out with their minds. A man screamed and stumbled through the opening, grabbing at his temples. He roared unintelligible curses as Raima and Izzy recognized his gray scrubs, the same color and style that all subjects wore, and withdrew their probing minds. Fai shouted, "Bryson!"

"Don't let the door close!" Izzy yelled and lunged for it. Bryson let out a crazed bellow and swung at her before Izzy could reach the door. He had a gun and as his fist impacted Izzy, striking her head, his finger squeezed the trigger.

Izzy slipped, falling to the floor with the power behind Bryson's blow. The unexpected gunshot was deafening. Dominic cried out somewhere behind Raima as the bullet hit him. Bryson's hand was unsteady, shaking. He fired again, and the blast of wind wafted against Raima's face.

Raima lifted her own gun and fired twice. The first shot missed, skimming off the door to the control room and striking the wall instead. The second bullet ripped through one of Bryson's arms just above the elbow. He shrieked with pain and recoiled, dropping his gun.

Izzy groaned on the floor, but she was moving, already sitting up, fumbling for her gun. Raima stayed with her weapon trained on Bryson. She heard her own rapid, harsh breathing and felt a powerful burst of surprise. Words spilled out of her, almost against her will. "What the hell is wrong with you?"

Bryson lifted his head. Sweat coated his skin, thick and beaded.

He'd faded to a gray color, somewhat reminiscent of the unpainted walls in some of TC-Gen's halls. "Bitch," he sneered, curling his quivering lips around the word.

"You shot Dominic!" Fai said, aiming the words at Bryson. His mind buzzed with panic. Fai crouched on the floor beside his friend.

"Shut up, you little shit," Bryson snapped, spitting. Sweat dripped from his nose. He trembled, gripping his ruined arm. "Those crazy twins," he went on, rasping. "They made the guards shoot us. Wesley and Jayden are dead. They killed them. . . ."

"How many guards did you kill in the control room?" Raima asked, calculating the death toll again. *Ten dead earlier, four dead here—that's fourteen accounted for. . . .*

Bryson glared at her with a mixture of incredulousness and exasperation. "What the hell are you asking about them for?"

From the floor Izzy raised her arms. Clutched in her bloodied hands was her handgun. Bryson let out a terrified gasp and tried to get out of her range, but he wasn't fast enough. Another gunshot shattered the air and Raima flinched. Bryson's leap became a sick, slow-motion fall. He crashed to the desk and flopped to the floor, limp and harmless. Moisture and other debris splattered Raima's head and shoulders. She cringed, and the sudden body-wide tensing made her pull the trigger on her gun, but the bullet flew into the wall near the door.

The door to the control room clicked as it opened again.

"Stop firing!" Marie yelled from the other side. "It's just us."

Shaking, drawing deep, ragged breaths, Raima lowered her gun and brushed her face. Her fingers were already smeared with the dead woman's drying blood and brains, but now new blood, bright and viscous, covered her hands. She swallowed bile.

"You shot him," Fai said to Izzy, booming the silent words in shock. It took Raima several seconds to realize that Fai had also been jabbering aloud in Mandarin before broadcasting a translation. Her ears rang, shocked by the loud sounds.

Marie stepped through the door. Like Bryson she carried a handgun, but it was lowered, pointing at the floor. She ignored Fai and everyone else in the room as she approached Bryson's body. She kicked it and scowled with disgust. "What a mess," she muttered.

Manon appeared just after her sister, taking in the scene with a cool, calm demeanor. She also had a gun. After she'd scanned the room Manon's attention fell on Raima. "Red isn't your color," she said and laughed.

Raima brushed her face again with her sleeve and spat on the floor with a grimace. The fabric of her long-sleeved scrubs darkened to black with gore and blood. The entire room smelled putrid with death. It was the salty iron stink of blood and raw—*human*—flesh. The twins were both coated in blood themselves, bathed in the arterial spray of the technicians they'd butchered.

The escape was a bloodbath. Raima closed her eyes for a moment, desperate to clear her head, to quiet the ringing in her ears left by the gunshots. *It wasn't supposed to be like this*, she thought. The only innocent people who were supposed to die in the escape were the boys and perhaps a few technicians in crossfires.

"Why?" Fai cried. "Why all shooting?"

Manon knelt and extended one hand down to Izzy, helping the shorter girl up. "Are you okay?" she asked Izzy with tenderness, transforming from a slick general assessing the battlefield into a maternal, loving friend in microseconds.

"I'm fine," Izzy snapped and pulled her hand away from Manon. She moved close to Raima and motioned at her gun. "You're empty," she said.

Raising the gun up, Raima noticed that it was open, letting her see down the length of muzzle. "You're right." Her voice was strained, the words choked.

"Let me give you some of mine," Izzy said. Her hands moved with confidence over the handgun, preparing to reload it.

"No," Raima said, shaking her head. "I don't need anymore. You keep yours." She placed her empty gun on the desk, grateful to be rid of it.

"*Raima,*" Marie said telepathically, hiding her thoughts from Fai. "*Izzy. It's time to kill the boys.*"

"*It was only right that Bryson be the first to die at our hands,*" Manon commented and grinned.

"*Dominic needs help,*" Fai said. "*He's bleeding a lot.*"

Manon's grin faded. She stepped past Izzy until she could see Fai and Dominic. The Chinese boy held Dominic, who'd been shot in the chest and bled with no sign of stopping. Raima guessed that blood loss would kill him no matter what they did. She tensed, steeling herself against the guilt and horror that would follow.

"I don't think he's going to make it," Manon said in a mocking tone and raised her gun.

Fai's face filled with horror. His lips and mind formed useless words. *"No, please don't—"*

Raima closed her eyes and turned away. Two shots rang out and it was over.

"It had to be done," Marie said in a gentle voice. "We all knew it did. We planned it."

Rage flared inside Raima and she whipped around to face Marie, almost slipping on the blood-soaked floor. "We agreed that the boys would be killed in firefights between the guards. We agreed that we'd spare most of the technicians too. Weren't you *listening?*"

Marie blinked with a blank expression in the fullness of Raima's fury and averted her gaze with what could have been shame. Izzy moved in a quick, furtive motion and grabbed Raima, embracing her. The stillness of the room swallowed Raima from the outside while guilt ate at her from within.

"They were all going to kill us," Manon said. "We just did it faster than they did."

"Your plan wouldn't have worked anyway," Marie muttered. "Yoon would have stopped us if we'd been any slower."

"He's dead then?" Izzy asked.

"Yeah," Manon replied, trading the position as speaker with her sister. She smiled and said, "We took our time with him and his head assistant."

"Fuchs," Marie supplied the assistant's name with a snigger that mirrored Manon's.

"Enough talking," Raima snapped. "Let's just finish doing what we have to do. Are there any guards left alive?"

"No," Manon replied. "It looks like you killed the last of them here."

"Were you able to delete the facility's records?" Raima asked.

"We were a little busy," Marie said, still smiling.

"Give me the keycard lanyard and I'll do it," Raima ordered, impatient to finish their plan and avoid further involvement with the boys' deaths. "Then Izzy will get the door to the airlock open.

Find the driver—if you haven't already killed him."

"Anything else, drill sergeant?" Manon quipped.

Before Raima could say anything, Izzy said, "Yeah, there is something else. Go help the others get here safely."

Manon hesitated for a moment with an uneasy expression. Was she unhappy at receiving orders from both Izzy and Raima, or was it more than that? The united front posed by both girls, one of whom had always been the twins' ally, must have troubled her.

She snorted then and motioned to Marie. "I'll catch up."

As Marie hurried to the door leading deeper into the facility, Manon pulled the lanyard up and over her head. The plastic keycards clunked against one another as she set them in Raima's hands. "We'll see you after we get rid of the other boys," she said and turned to hurry out the door at her sister's heels.

Raima unlocked the control room door and then passed the lanyard to Izzy. "Get the airlock ready." Izzy nodded and hopped over the desk.

Raima slipped into the control room. It was small, dark, and cluttered. After the brightness of sunlight just outside, Raima found herself blinded. She held her breath, listening to the whir and faint humming of electronics. The scent of raw flesh and blood lingered in the air, mixed with hot electronics and plastic, but Raima knew that some of the smell came from the gore on her own body.

Her eyes adjusted to the dimness. A light from the ceiling dangled by its wires, shattered by a blow and riddled with bullet holes. Bright points stood out as computer lights blinked or shone on despite the carnage. A white glow from the other side of the room revealed numerous bodies lying on the floor.

She stepped forward and felt the warm, sticky blood around her toes through her slippers. The bodies in this room were crammed together, having fallen on top of one another as they died. Raima stepped on several of them and flinched away with primeval revulsion as she felt the dead flesh.

The white glow came from several monitors that displayed security camera feeds from around TC-Gen. Some monitors showed only static and others had spider web cracks from where bullets had pierced them. There was a chair in front of the monitors and a desk littered with small illuminated buttons and switches—and a touch screen computer interface.

She touched the computer screen and it flickered, flaring with life, but Raima's fingertips left a thick smudge of crimson blood. She brushed her hands off on her scrubs, trying in vain to clean them, but no part of her was completely untouched by the twins' carnage.

Raima navigated the computer, accessing the facility's data management software that controlled how their records and other important onsite information were stored. She remembered Zhu Liu's information and entered it into the system to gain access to the low-level formatting tools and ran them. This would wipe the server clean, destroying the records. The computer showed a progress bar as it worked, building with maddening slowness. Raima didn't have the time to stand by it, safeguarding the deletion process. Any surviving technicians could stop the wipe, but they'd never be able to recover the data they'd already lost.

Raima turned to go, but as she took her first step toward the door her eyes fell on a strange shape in the blackness. She blinked, struggling to see, and knelt to get closer. Two small, straight objects, each one no larger or longer than a pencil, stuck out of one of the corpses. In the faint light from the monitors Raima recognized Yoon's face. He'd been stripped of his large reading glasses and each of his eyes stabbed with a tablet stylus—the same kind that the twins used to tear out the technicians' throats.

Raima pulled back and covered her mouth with one hand, but the stink of blood and death and gore on her palm overwhelmed her. She lunged for the door, exploding out of it and into the equally horrific room beyond. The natural light dazzled her eyes and she stumbled over Bryson's body, barely managing to catch herself on the desk.

Over the loudness of her breathing, Raima heard the quick *bang* of shots and screams deeper in the facility. Killing Ferde hadn't been like this. His death was a triumph, a deep and personal victory that bought Raima her freedom. She succeeded over impossible odds and the tremendous wall of her own self-doubt and terror. The escape from TC-Gen was a massacre.

She remembered Yoon's fear of losing control of telepathy, of unleashing it into human society. What had Aine said? *Absolute power corrupts absolutely.*

We had no choice, she thought. *It's almost done. The worst is over.* She wanted to cry but the tears wouldn't come.

239

EIGHTEEN

The door to the rest of the compound swung open. Raima looked up at the motion and sound, then felt her heart warm as Qi came through the doorway. She was silhouetted in the natural light from the window behind her and still had a gun clutched in one hand. Splattered as she was with blood, Qi shouldn't have been beautiful, but she was like an angel to Raima.

"We are free!" she shouted to Raima, grinning.

The brightness and power of Qi's presence rejuvenated Raima, giving her the courage to ignore the slaughter and butchery surrounding her. She clambered over the desk and hurried over the sticky floor to embrace Qi. The tears that horror and regret couldn't unleash from her now flowed at her joy. She could feel the pureness of the tears cutting through the half-dried gore on her face. *"We're free,"* she said, speaking both physically and telepathically.

Ella and Tiana appeared next and moved without stopping for the door to the airlock. Raima released Qi, slow with her reluctance, and called out to them, "Are the boys all—"

"Yes," Aine's voice interrupted, coming from the doorway. *"They should be dead by now."*

Raima and Qi turned to watch as Aine and Limei entered the room, one after the other. They walked with care, weighed down by their living burdens. Kaiden clung to Limei, able to use his legs to support himself and move with her, making her job a lot easier. Kim, meanwhile, was too weak for that. She appeared conscious with her eyes open, but Aine carried her cradled like an oversized infant in her arms.

"Where's Izzy?" Limei asked.

"I think she's already in the airlock," Raima explained. "What about Marie and Manon?"

"Just behind us," Aine replied and then telepathically added, *"Finishing off the boys."*

Kaiden looked around the room, absorbing the corpses, the carnage, the smattering of brains and skull amidst the buckets of blood. He started to speak in a raspy, throaty voice, "I'm going to—" but he broke off, heaving and gagging to one side, trying and failing to avoid splattering Limei with vomit.

"Again?" Aine complained. "Poor Limei."

"You can carry," Limei said in a voice thick with disgust, meaning Raima.

Raima ducked down to help Kaiden put his arm over her shoulder, but the boy struggled, fending her off. "I can walk," he said, groaning. "What—what happened here?"

He gazed at Raima and then to Qi, the desperation in his hazel-brown eyes arresting. Raima could sense his thoughts, swirling with the first ripple of telepathic ability. She felt his horror at the scene around them, the terrifying questions lingering. Who'd done all of this? Was it just the twins? Had Raima been part of it? Why were they killing the boys? Was he next? Why was he being saved?

"Don't worry about it," Qi said, pushing the words into his mind along with a heavy dose of reassurance and artificial tranquility. She was trying to force him to be calm, to accept what was happening without thinking about it, but Kaiden was already too far along in his genetic treatments to succumb to the method.

He cringed at the touch of her mind and the rush of foreign emotions, sucking at the air between his clenched teeth. "What are you doing?" he demanded with a flash of anger. His mind rebuffed Qi, pushing her influence out of his skull.

Raima thought of Fai, his strength as a telepath, his helpfulness in the escape, and his death. His corpse was just behind her, his young blood and brains intermingled with his friend Dominic's. Fai would have been a powerful telepath, perhaps approaching the level of some of the girls, and surpassing Ella with ease.

Kaiden had that same potential, even though his treatment stopped early and would never finish. His mind and body would grow around the talent, enhancing it as he learned how to use it. He would be dangerous someday, physically and mentally, if he chose such a path.

"Sorry," Qi said, quick to apologize and mask her surprise. *"Just trying to comfort you."*

The door behind them opened and the twins appeared. They'd added more blood to their already soaked scrubs, wet and black on the gray material. Marie ditched her weapon somewhere, but Manon wasn't empty-handed. She'd kept one of the handguns, though it was lowered.

Seeing the gun Raima wanted to demand that Manon put it down. All the guards were dead and gone. There was no one else to shoot. But Qi distracted her, taking her hand and squeezing it. "Let's go," she said and pointed to the airlock. "Freedom."

They passed through the large door leading to the airlock. A short hallway stretched beyond, lined on each side with lockers where EVA suits and other supplies were kept. Several of the lockers were open. They stood empty now, but Raima saw bloody handprints on the locker handles and knew that Izzy, Ella, or Tiana had done it.

As the full group piled into the changing station around the entrance to the airlock they saw Ella sitting on one of the plastic benches. She'd partly donned an EVA spacesuit over her soiled scrubs and offered the group a wan smile. "There are only eight spacesuits," she said. "We have to take it in turns."

"Did you find the driver?" Aine asked as she came forward with Kim and deposited her next to one of the closed lockers. Kaiden moved to be with his sister, kneeling at her side and speaking in a low, comforting tone.

"Yeah," Ella said. "He was in the rover. We got here just in time. It was prepping to leave."

"Only good luck we've had the whole time," Qi said to Raima, shielding the words so only she could hear them.

Feeling exhaustion and relief, Raima shook her head. *"No, we've been incredibly lucky. We're all alive. We're one last step from freedom. The easiest step."*

"Where's Izzy?" Manon asked.

"Out in the rover," Ella answered. "Tiana went out there to control the driver too."

"Who goes first?" Aine asked. There were ten girls—with Kaiden that brought the number to eleven. Izzy, Tiana, and Ella already claimed suits of their own, leaving the other eight people to divide the remaining five suits. Three people would need to stay behind until the first group could change out of the suits and send them back with someone.

"Kim and Kaiden should go with the first wave," Raima suggested. "They'll need a lot of help getting into the rover and into their suits."

"I have a better idea," Manon said with an icy authority that sent a sharp anticipatory terror through Raima's spine. Manon pressed deeper into the little locker room, one hand tilted slightly behind her, hiding it from view. Raima knew it was a gun and that Manon was going to execute Kaiden the same way she had with Fai.

Raima leapt from her place beside Qi, halfway stumbling over the bench that Ella was sitting on to reach Kim and Kaiden before Manon did. She stood in front of Kaiden, using her body to shield the boy. She shouted, "No!"

Most of the other girls stared with mixtures of shock and alarm. Ella scrambled up and away from the bench. Her red hair frizzed around her head, reminding Raima of the blood that had been sprayed over the walls as the twins cut the technicians' throats. All the death and bloodshed that shouldn't have happened.

Manon's lips curled in a condescending sneer. She looked back to the other girls and asked, "How many of you think any of the boys should escape here with their lives? How many of you are going to regret letting just one get out of here with us? How long before he leaves us with his stupid sister and goes around hurting people, just taking whatever he wants and whoever he wants . . . ?"

"What are you talking about?" Kaiden demanded.

"*Stay quiet,*" Raima shot at him telepathically.

"Aine," Marie shouted, supporting her sister as always. "This boy could be your brother! You know what we're saying is true."

"Don't listen to them," Raima snapped, glaring at Manon. "It doesn't have to be this way. Kaiden isn't Aine's brother. He's Kim's brother. He isn't dangerous."

"Maybe not now," Manon said, dismissing Raima's defense. "But why would he want to stay with us or play by our rules once he knows we would've killed him with all the others if it weren't for his sister?"

Raima could feel Kaiden's mounting horror and dread passing from him in waves. Kim's reaction was muted, weakened by her diminished physical state. But Raima heard Kaiden's little intake of air and felt a sting of shame. She tried to refute it, but Manon interrupted her. "That's not true—"

"It isn't? You agreed to kill all the other boys," she said. "And you might've killed them both if Kim didn't remind you so much of your precious Kati."

"You know we're right, Raima," Marie said in a gentler voice, trying to soothe rather than antagonize. "In a few years Kaiden will be like one of the men who hurt you in the brothel and you'll curse yourself for letting him live."

"No," Raima insisted, but she heard her own refusal weakening and she could feel some of the girls wavering. In desperation and growing fear, she searched around the room with her eyes, seeking some weapon. She sensed the dangerous bloodlust in Manon and suspected words alone wouldn't dissuade her from killing the last of TC-Gen's boys. "We agreed Kaiden would be spared."

On the bench closest to the airlock, several meters out of Raima's reach, there were two handguns, unnoticed and abandoned. Izzy and Tiana had left the weapons there while they changed into their spacesuits. If Raima moved to get either gun Manon would be able to shoot Kaiden. Raima stayed in her spot, her back rigid and her feet rooted to the floor.

"Only because of Kim," Manon pressed. Her hard, humorless smile spread wider. "Right?"

"No," Raima repeated a little stronger.

"You're too emotionally attached to do it," Manon said with a strange mixture of disdain and pity. She raised her hidden hand and arm, revealing the gun Raima already knew was there. "That's okay. Just step over and I'll do it for you. No blood on your hands. No guilt."

"Please," Kaiden said in a shrill voice. "Don't do this. I've never hurt anyone in my life. I just want to live with Kim and get out of here alive. I'll do whatever you say. . . ."

"Don't worry," Raima said to Kaiden. "Nothing's going to happen to you. Manon is just a little trigger happy." She glared at the other girl. "Isn't that right? Why don't you put that gun down before you hurt someone?"

A faint, croaking voice came then as Kim spoke up, defending Kaiden too. "Please," she begged. "He's the only family I have left. We'll do anything you want us to. *Please*, just don't hurt him. . . ."

Manon cocked her head to one side. She had an unobstructed view of Kim, but Raima still stood in front Kaiden, protecting him. "Let me make it easy for everyone," Manon said and without any further warning Manon's arm swiveled, moving the gun to point at Kim. She pulled the trigger.

Kim made no sound as the bullet pierced her body, but the rest of the room erupted in chaos. Ella screamed and Kaiden shouted his sister's name. Qi shrieked in an incoherent blend of English and Mandarin and rushed forward, but Marie stopped her, grabbing for the handgun that Qi still held.

The struggles in the rest of the room faded for Raima. When she realized Manon shot Kim—not her or Kaiden—she knelt to be with the siblings, trying to save the stricken girl. Kim was shot in the chest. Her blue eyes were wide and staring, stunned. Already pasty with illness, shock made her white like snow. She and Kaiden were some of the cleanest of the entire group, but no longer. Her own blood dotted her chin and red blood spilled from her wound, soaking into her gray scrubs, turning them black.

She looked to Raima and then to Kaiden. Her eyes clouded with tears and her throat moved as she tried to speak—but only blood emerged. Any words she'd wanted to say were choked as she gave a weak, wet cough. Blood dribbled down her chin.

"*Kim!*" Kaiden wailed. "*Kim!* Stay with me, it's all right." He pushed closer to his sister and covered her with his body, uncaring of the ongoing danger to his own life. "Kim, you're going to be okay—I'm here for you."

"See?" Manon said. "Now there's no reason to keep him alive."

Blood frothed at the corners of Kim's mouth as she struggled to breathe. Expressions of terror and despair crossed her wan face. She reached out for Kaiden. Her fingers streaked blood on his cheek and chin.

Raima saw Kati instead of Kim for one second, and then felt the crushing misery and ruthlessness of her old life bearing down on her. She remembered how Kim pleaded for Kaiden's life. *We'll do anything you want us to.* How many times had Raima used those words, trying to barter for her own life while someone as cruel and heartless and power-hungry as Manon bullied and threatened her? Raima tried to guide and save Kati, but she'd failed. She'd saved Kim at CF-Gen only to lead her into death at this moment.

The only important thing to Kim was Kaiden's survival. *If something happens to me I want you to look after Kaiden for me,* Kim had said. And Raima made the promise, expecting that she would never have to honor it because Kim would survive.

"Manon!" Marie shouted. The sound drew Raima out of her emotional stupor. She got to her feet and turned to face Manon just as the other girl was distracted, reacting to Marie's cry for help. Toward the back of the locker room Qi and Marie continued wrestling with each other, fighting over control of Qi's gun. The other girls pulled off to either side, too startled and afraid of gunfire to risk intervening. The path was clear for Manon to do whatever she wanted to defend her sister and Raima's heart lurched when she saw Manon raising the arm that held her gun.

Raima charged at Manon, colliding with her. She grabbed Manon's wrist and jerked it around. Manon yelped with surprise and she dropped the gun to the floor. Fueled by the same rage that drove her to escape the brothel and kept her alive through countless rapes, beatings, a traumatic bone marrow transplant, and two different genetic experiments, Raima rammed Manon against one of the lockers. She pressed her forearm to Manon's throat and into her airway, cutting it off. Manon's eyes bulged, and she made sick little gasping noises. She scratched Raima's arm and slapped at her body and face.

Another gun fired. The sound made Raima flinch, certain for a microsecond that the shot had hit her. Manon struggled against her and managed to knock Raima away enough that she could breathe again, sucking at the air.

Hands snatched hold of Raima, restraining her. Raima fought them, blinded by rage, uncaring who was trying to stop her or why. "Let go of me! Let go!"

Then Manon screamed, keening like a banshee. The room went still and Raima realized something new had happened, an unexpected twist. She stopped struggling and her gaze flew at once to where Qi stood at the far end of the little locker room. She held a gun in her quaking hands as she stared openmouthed at the floor in front of her. New blood splattered her scrubs. Bright crimson droplets dotted her face and even as Raima watched they began to pool and drip, rolling down her cheeks like tears.

Marie was on the floor, twitching and choking as she fought to breathe. Her neck was torn open by the blast of Qi's bullet while the two struggled in the seconds after Manon shot Kim. Manon shrieked, inconsolable with grief and ran for her sister first, then she lunged for Qi.

Aine and Limei intercepted Manon, pinning her with their combined strength. Manon lashed out with her mind next even while she was still screaming in her grief-stricken frenzy. Qi let out a little cry and backpedaled until she ran into the door of the locker room. She kept a death-grip on the handgun, refusing to drop it where someone else could use it to harm her.

"Stop it!" Aine shouted and shook Manon. "Stop it! This was an accident!"

"What Manon did to Kim wasn't an accident," Ella pointed out.

Raima stumbled back from the turmoil ahead and glanced behind her to Kim and Kaiden. Kaiden sobbed quietly over Kim's limp form. Raima's legs buckled beneath her. Raima covered her face with her hands, uncaring that they were coated with cracking, sticky dried blood. Stunned by the horror of their bungled escape, and her grief for Kati, Kim, Kaiden, and even Marie, despair swelled in her until she was certain it would split her open from the inside out.

The others were still talking, trying to calm Manon, to bring her back to sanity. When the airlock buzzed, and the doors opened, admitting Izzy into the locker room, no one really noticed. Raima saw Izzy enter and recognized the spacesuit in her arms, but she couldn't bring herself to care. Ella spoke to Izzy, explaining what had happened.

When Ella finished, Izzy stepped over the nearest bench and, after depositing the extra spacesuit she'd been carrying, she picked up one of the handguns that were abandoned there. Alarm colored Ella's voice as she asked, "What are you doing?"

It was the sound of Ella's distress that made Raima lift her head to see Izzy in action. In a burst of memory, Raima saw again the way Izzy handled the gun after receiving it, the knowledge and confidence. She checked the weapon to be certain it was loaded.

Ella asked again, "Izzy? What are you doing?"

Izzy ignored her and stepped over the second bench. She headed for where Limei and Aine held Manon, near Marie's body. Raima recalled how Izzy shot Bryson with the same cold expertise that the twins displayed when they executed Fai and all the other boys. And when Manon helped Izzy up off the blood-soaked floor, Izzy had jerked her hand away with disgust. Raima accused Marie and Manon of manipulating Izzy into being their servant, little more than the twins' puppet. It was enough that Izzy switched sides, joining Raima, but perhaps what Izzy felt wasn't mere dislike and distrust—but hatred.

Limei, Aine, and Manon remained distracted by Marie's death. Ella stared in mute shock as Izzy advanced on the other three. Raima opened her mouth to call out to Izzy, to try and dissuade her from what she was about to do—but then she remembered Kim's blue eyes as she'd looked up at Kaiden, seeing only him for the very last time. She looked back to them now and saw they hadn't changed. They remained locked together, the living and the dead, hopeless and helpless, tied together for eternity by the bonds of family and love.

She stayed silent.

Izzy reached Limei, Aine, and Manon. Her voice boomed out telepathically. *"Aine, Limei. Don't move."*

They turned their heads at the same moment that Izzy placed the muzzle of her gun to Manon's head. "Hey Manon," she shouted so she could be heard through her EVA suit's speaker. "I don't think Marie's going to make it."

She pulled the trigger and Manon's head exploded. Limei

screamed and recoiled, but Aine stayed in her place, holding Manon as her legs gave out. She died before she hit the ground. As Aine released Manon's body, letting her land atop Marie's corpse, Izzy lowered the gun to her side and said, "Bitch got what she deserved. Both of them did."

No one moved for several heartbeats. In the dense silence only Kaiden made any noise, continuing to cry for his sister.

Eventually Limei asked, *"Do we kill the boy now that Kim's gone?"*

"No," Raima said and stood up. "Marie and Manon did things without consulting the rest of us. They planned this. They ignored what we wanted and acted recklessly. Izzy's right. They got what they deserved. The real tragedy here is that they took Kim with them."

"We honor Kim," Ella said. "She gave her life for her brother. That should be our true vow." Her bright blue eyes had darkened with tears as she swept over the group, taking them all in. "We live for our Sisters, for the group. Anyone who doesn't do that has earned her death."

"Kaiden is one of us now," Raima said. "No one is to question that ever again. Kim shouldn't have had to die to make us see it." A pain started in her chest and suddenly Raima felt tears flowing down her cheeks. Kaiden was numb to their conversation, completely deaf and removed. Kim had become his entire world. Raima wanted to join him, but she knew she had no place mourning the frail little blonde. Failure was a bitter taste in her mouth, tangy like iron. Like blood.

Across the little room Qi dropped her handgun and rushed to Raima like a child seeking comfort, but when they embraced one another it was Raima who shed the tears and Qi who held her and stroked her back like a mother. *"We are free,"* she reassured Raima. *"It's over. It's finally, really over."*

Izzy, still wearing her EVA spacesuit, said, *"I'm going back to the rover. I suggest the rest of you do the same. I think there's enough suits now that it should only take one trip."* She began walking toward the airlock, unfazed by the remaining shock in the room.

Slowly, the girls began suiting up. Qi brought Raima two spacesuits and then retreated to fetch one for herself. She knew Raima wouldn't be walking with her to the rover. Qi worked with Limei, suiting up together and checking the seals on their suits, following all the safety procedures.

Raima made no move to do the same for several minutes. She watched Kaiden instead, hoping the boy would leave Kim voluntarily before all the other girls were gone but knowing that if she were in his place she never would. Eventually Raima knelt close to him. She carried both suits in her arms, clutched like children.

"Kaiden," she called to him.

He moved, lifting his head almost imperceptibly. Raima felt his mind nudging at hers. The grief in his consciousness was all-consuming, the kind that ate at the soul. Raima felt it when her mother died and then again when Kati committed suicide. What she felt for Kim's loss would never compare to Kaiden's grief.

She cleared her throat, finding it raw with emotion. "Kim made me promise to protect you," she said, "if anything ever happened to her. You know she would want you to leave with us, to live. If you stay here, you'll be captured. The researchers will kill you to cover up what they've done here."

Instead of making Kaiden draw away from Kim the words seemed to have the opposite effect. He held her tighter and rocked slightly in his spot, as if cuddling a sleeping infant. "She could have gone back to Earth," he said and his voice broke, dissolving into deep-throated sobs.

Raima waited a moment and then, feeling pressed for time, spoke over his grief. "I know you have no reason to trust us, but I never wanted this to happen. I wanted to keep you and Kim safe. I failed." She choked back her own sob at the admission and went on. "I won't fail again. You must come with us. The twins were the only ones who wanted to hurt you. They got what they deserved. Now, I'm sorry, but you have to come with us."

Kaiden pulled back a little from Kim. Her face had softened into a calm, peaceful expression as she died. The repose was beautiful after all the half-missing faces and other butchery Raima had seen in the escape. "Her body . . ." Kaiden started to say, taking a ragged breath.

"You can't take her with us," Raima said. "The vacuum . . ."

"I know," Kaiden cried. He laid Kim down on the floor and arranged her hands over the wound in her chest, covering it. He placed his hands over hers, staring into her face as more tears fell down his cheeks. "I don't have anything to remember her by," he said, and his shoulders shook as he repressed a sob.

"You are the memory," Raima encouraged him. She held the suit out, anxious to leave. This was a memory she knew no one wanted to carry, but it was the only thing Mars let them have. "We have to go. This is what she would have wanted."

He nodded and took the EVA suit from her hands.

A short time later they passed through the airlock and over the barren red dust of the Martian soil. The light from the sun was faint and pinkish overhead and Raima remembered that it was only morning or early afternoon, though she felt as though she'd lived several lives over the course of the escape. Raima helped support Kaiden as they boarded the rover. After the automatic airlock cycled a proper Earth-standard atmospheric pressure into the car, Raima guided Kaiden into the passenger cabin.

Qi was there and had already removed her helmet. She offered Raima a melancholy smile. *"Our new lives begin today,"* she said, broadcasting to the whole group, including Kaiden. *"Tiana has control of the driver and in a few hours, we'll be at Rahe crater."*

"Where do we go from there?" Aine asked.

Raima felt their eyes land on her, expecting an answer. She fumbled with her helmet, taking it off and holding it in her lap. Kaiden sat on the bench seat across from her, motionless and wrapped in his thick misery—but alive. The rover jerked as it started to move forward and some of the girls whooped with excitement and triumph.

Feeling the movement shook Raima's grief enough that she tried to find something to say, to rally the girls for their future, wherever and whatever it might be. She looked over the assemblage of faces, a wide blend of races and nationalities all united by their suffering and the gift—or curse—of telepathy. They were bloodstained and shell-shocked, but *alive* and *free*.

Qi smiled and Raima suddenly knew why she had the tenacity and courage to keep on living despite the many horrors of her short life.

"We go wherever we want," she said. "We do whatever we have to do to help each other because we're Sisters, and we always will be. No one can stop us now."

EPILOGUE
HELLAS CRATER: GLACIER CITY

The sun was bright, dazzling Raima's eyes. She raised one hand to shade them, squinting against the light as the world came into view. Greenery leaped out at her, as intense and startling as the sunlight. Trees rose up, straining their leaves toward the top of the dome where the weak Martian sunlight was enhanced and filtered to mimic the effect of Earth's atmosphere. The dome overhead was the same azure as Earth's sky, deep and clear blue, just as in Raima's memories. Rich soil had been laid down and lush grass planted that now created a vast, living carpet of green.

"Is it like Earth?" Qi asked at her side. *"Easy to see why it's called the Garden Dome."*

Raima wanted to speak, but her voice was hoarse with emotion. She nodded to share the overwhelming sensation that the beauty stirred in her.

Qi smiled. *"They planted the trees twenty-five years ago,"* she said. *"But because of the lower gravity they look like they've been growing for twice as long. They're going to have to close the place down for a while so they can make the dome taller."*

It was called the Garden Dome, a specially-designed Martian greenhouse, built as a tourist attraction in the prosperous, burgeoning Glacier City of Hellas Basin. From outside it, in Glacier City's red-brown streets, it looked like a colossal bubble—a dome within a dome. People flocked from all over the red planet to see this speck of green, defiant as it flourished so far away from the Eden of Earth. Every few years the Garden Dome's owners added onto the greenhouse or made some innovation to draw in more tourists. Some sections of the dome far above their heads were holographic screens, projecting more light down into the garden below. They occasionally displayed puffy white clouds, slowly forming and gliding over the artificial sky. Raima read that the screens overhead would eventually be programmed to simulate rainstorms. Sprinklers already built into the dome in case of fire would be reprogrammed to shower guests with artificial rain.

Raima watched a golden flicker as koi in a decorative pool splashed, making the water frothy. Tiana and Kaiden knelt beside it, reaching out to toss little brown nutrient pellets into the water. The fish swarmed together, fighting over the food.

Tiana squealed. "It bit me!"

"It doesn't have any teeth," Kaiden reminded her, laughing.

Qi smiled. *"Someday I'm sure they'll put a swimming pool here. They've found enough water in eastern Hellas to make a whole sea!"*

Raima had never seen an ocean, unless it was in pictures or from orbit. The idea thrilled her, but she didn't take it seriously. Plenty of people—artists, scientists, and ordinary citizens alike—dreamed of seeing Mars restored to the watery glory of its long ago past. Raima didn't believe it was possible, but the Garden Dome itself was more beautiful than she'd thought anything on Mars could ever be. The Garden Dome wouldn't be able to simulate a rainstorm for several months until its latest round of construction finished. Raima would have to wait until then to feel rain again. Even if her mind knew it was fake, it was real enough that her body and her heart rejoiced.

Ella, Aine, Limei, and Izzy lay on the grass a short distance from the koi pool, staring up at the artificial blue sky with its fake clouds. The air was warm and humid, fragrant with the scent of living things. Raima expected to smell the harsh, acrid stink of the Martian soil underlying the loam, but there was no trace of it. Every breath she took transported her heart back into her memories—back to Earth and her mother. Images from Earth could evoke a bittersweet longing, but they could never compare to the power of scent or the pleasant sensation of sunlight on her skin.

"I want to come here every day," she said, suddenly seized with bliss. "I can almost forget that we're still on Mars."

"Yeah," Qi agreed. Telepathically she added, *"Maybe we won't be trapped here forever. They're finding new planets all the time and space travel is getting faster and faster. The newest manned ships can go from Mars to the Saturn colonies in only a few days! One of those new planets they're finding in other solar systems is bound to be like Earth, and it might have low enough gravity that we could go."*

"Right now," Raima said quietly, smiling with tenderness, "This is enough."

A loud gasp from Tiana drew their attention then. They watched as she shook her hand, her body shuddering. She shouted telepathically to the whole group. *"I can feel the fish's mind! I can feel their minds!"*

Tiana's discovery with the fish shattered the illusion of the greenery, reminding Raima that her struggle—and the entire group's—was far from over. The Garden Dome could mimic Earth, but it couldn't transport Raima off Mars. It couldn't erase anyone's past; couldn't restore everything they'd lost—but it was comforting.

There were countless things to worry about: Genoquip's continued existence, the ongoing need for money, food, and a place to stay. Their talent aided them everywhere they went but it also set them apart from everyone else. That kept their group from splintering in the months since they'd escaped TC-Gen, though their makeshift family wasn't always a happy one.

"You worry too much," Qi scolded her. Raima felt the other girl's warm hand slip into hers and squeeze it. *"Be happy right now. Come on."* She stepped forward, walking over the grass, tugging Raima's hand to make her follow.

With a fresh smile on her face, Raima let Qi lead her toward the koi pond where Tiana and Kaiden once more began feeding the fish.

Tiana scooted over to give them room to sit at the edge of the koi pool. Kaiden retreated and Raima caught a flash of discomfort from his mind, a vague distrust. Though he was close with Tiana and Ella, Kaiden was shy and wary of Raima. His talent was strong enough that he could keep his mind closed to the others if he wished, but in this group of girls he was the oddball. If only Kim had survived. . . .

Qi yanked on Raima's mind, diverting her attention. *"You've got to try this,"* she said and guided Raima's hand to the water. As many as twenty koi squirmed in front of them, opening and closing their mouths, eager to suck in the food pellets. Raima let one fish gum her fingers, feeling its chilled, soft mouth. She sent her mind forward, tentatively making telepathic contact with one of the koi. The fish sucking on her fingers had a simple consciousness, tranquil and content. It lived only in this moment where all was well—there was food in its belly, the water was clean and pleasant, and it was content. Happy.

"Feel that?" Tiana asked, probing Raima's mind, sharing the experience.

Qi laughed. The sound was as beautiful as the water and the greenery. "I wish I was fish!"

Raima turned her head to look back at Tiana and the others, then returned her gaze to Qi. She smiled, and replied, *"I'm happy just being me. Just being here, with you."*

ACKNOWLEDGEMENTS

First and foremost I'd like to give a big shout of thanks to everyone on the ChiZine team for their time, passion, and hard work! A special thanks to Sandra Kasturi for giving me the chance to share this story and letting me join the ChiZine family. It has been a pleasure working with you all!

Last, but definitely not least, I'd like to thank my friends and family for their support. My husband, who wouldn't let me give up, no matter what. My dad, who reassured me I wouldn't starve getting an English Writing degree. My mom, who put up with me reading passages of *Lord of the Rings* aloud and just geeking out for years. Both my sisters, who inspire my writing and characters probably more than anyone else. To Jessica Holman, thank you for championing all books—especially those by us Yoopers! And all my coworkers, for their interest and enthusiasm when they learned about my writer alter-ego. To each and every one of you: Thank You!

ABOUT THE AUTHOR

Rachael Robie is a science fiction junkie who grew up watching '90s TV show *Babylon 5* and reading Ben Bova and Stephen Baxter novels. She has a small obsession with Mars and spent an embarrassing amount of time researching the Red Planet. She has a Master's degree in English Writing from Northern Michigan University. She now resides in Utah with her husband and their cats.